MW00911751

TALES FROM FADREAMA

Candace N. Coonan

BOOK 1

The Darkest Hour

Book Illustration
Kelly Crossfield

Design Concept
Gayle Pickett
Heather Pickett

Candace Coonan
2004

Printed in Victoria, Canada

Note for Librarians: a cataloguing record for this book that includes Dewey Classification and US Library of Congress numbers is available from the National Library of Canada. The complete cataloguing record can be obtained from the National Library's online database at: www.nlc-bnc.ca/amicus/index-e.html

ISBN 1-4120-1277-5

TRAFFORD

This book was published *on-demand* **in cooperation with Trafford Publishing.** On-demand publishing is a unique process and service of making a book available for retail sale to the public taking advantage of on-demand manufacturing and Internet marketing. **On-demand publishing** includes promotions, retail sales, manufacturing, order fulfilment, accounting and collecting royalties on behalf of the author.

Suite 6E, 2333 Government St., Victoria, B.C. V8T 4P4, CANADA

Phone	250-383-6864	Toll-free	1-888-232-4444 (Canada & US)
Fax	250-383-6804	E-mail	sales@trafford.com
Web site	www.trafford.com	TRAFFORD PUBLISHING IS A DIVISION OF TRAFFORD HOLDINGS LTD.	
Trafford Catalogue #03-1655		www.trafford.com/robots/03-1655.html	

10   9   8   7   6   5   4   3   2

CONTENTS

Part Four: The Thea Mountains and Devona

Appendices

For my parents, who always
saw my inner light.
And for anyone who has ever been told, "You're not strong enough."

Preface

The inspiration for this novel and series in general, cannot be traced back to one specific event. Rather, it is the accumulation of roughly 20 years of life experience, which, I must admit is not a great deal. Considering I wrote the first draft of this novel at age 14, I did not have much to work with besides my imagination. Thus, a great deal of revision has taken place over the years and the final product is now before you (though there may come a day when further revision may be required).

When I first wrote this book, it was not intended to be a series. The truth of the matter is that as the plot progressed, I began to feel as though I were merely an observer recording events, with little control over the fate of the characters. Some of the occurrences came as a surprise even to me and I was just as eager to see what would happen next as any reader of the tale. The writing of this novel was an adventure for me, as I sincerely hope it will be for my readers. My wish is that as one enters into the world of Fadreama, they will be able to grow and learn with the characters. Though the world is not ours, the emotions of the characters are quite real and resonate through the boundaries between realms.

So many people helped and supported me during the process of writing this novel. This is of course wonderful, but makes writing acknowledgements extremely difficult. I am about to put forth my best effort to thank all who should be, but even if someone is not explicitly mentioned and they assisted me, my thanks goes out to them. First off I must thank my parents, Lloyd and Sophie, for without them, none of this would have been possible. It has been their support, encouragement and faith that has kept me going with this project. If everyone in the world could be blessed with such a wonderful parents, no one would ever miss out on achieving their dreams. I must also thank my brothers, Terrence and Derek, who stumbled over my awkward early drafts and did not withhold any opinions. My sincere thanks are extended to all others who read and edited my early drafts, including the Hamptons and Jane Schaefer. Thank you so much to Gayle and Heather Pickett, as well as Kelly Crossfield, who helped me with the artwork. My gratitude also goes out to Marlene Isnor, who was kind enough to let me edit at work and arrange an interview for me. Thanks to Chad Anderson for my first interview! Also, thank you to my high school English teacher Larry Boyd, who not only read a draft, but also gave me such wonderful encouragement and support. Thanks to my Grandma Helen and Aunt Dianne, who read early drafts and to my friends, who never stopped believing in me, especially my Anam Cara, Brandy

Riske. My eternal gratitude goes out to the Lord, who bestowed upon me the ability to write and granted me the support system to make my dreams a reality. I am also forever grateful for, and to, Kristopher and Angela, you know who you are.

I truly hope you enjoy the first instalment of "Tales From Fadreama," and decide you want to continue the journey in the novels to come, including *Where Shadows Linger* and *The Break of Dawn*. There may even be more in the series than this, for who knows where the path will lead and what will come as the story progresses. Only time will tell how things will unfold and really, no tale has an ending, for life is continuous.

Candace Naomi Coonan
June 29, 2003

The Darkest Hour

The darkest hour is just before dawn,
When all seems lost and hope long gone.

As the sky turns its deepest hue,
And the light of the sun is far from view,
That is the time you must stand tall,
Never looking back, for that's how you fall.

Hold on to hope and banish your tears!
Now is the moment to conquer your fears!

When all seems lost,
And you've bowed to your knees,
Feel on your face,
The easterly breeze.

For in the sky,
The dawn is breaking,
And the very foundations of evil are shaking.
Rejoice and weep,
Celebrate while you may,
The night is banished,
For another day.

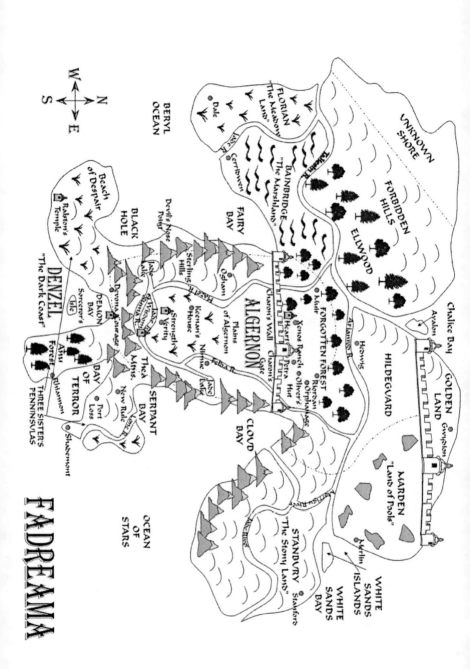

Part One

The Forgotten Forest

CHAPTER ONE

Strange Dream

S HE WAS SCREAMING *hysterically and racing about the cluttered
and disarrayed nursery. Her plump face was flushed from fear
and her eyes protruded painfully as they darted wildly around,
like those of a frightened bird.*

*"The heir! The heir!" was all the frightened woman could scream.
She tore at her grey hair, sending strands flying in all directions.*

*Four young girls, each with long brown hair and blue eyes (with the
exception of the smallest girl, who had brown eyes) watched the scene
before them with absolute horror. Their little hands where linked tightly
to one another, as large, silent tears rolled down their pudgy red cheeks.
In the frantic woman's hurry, she roughly knocked the girls onto the blue
mosaic floor, without seeming to notice. None of the girls uttered a sound
at this rude display, but merely shivered at the chaos around them.*

*Outside, the sounds of stones crumbling and people screaming seemed
to meld into one horrid droning hum that tore one's very soul. Vibrations
of impacts on lower levels of the castle shook the nursery, sending colourful paintings crashing to the floor, in a shower of wooden splinters. The
scent of smoke wafted in through the window and hung in the air, burning
the nostrils of all those present.*

*The smallest girl wiped her burning eyes with the back of her dirt
smeared hand, which tears paved black trails through. The little girl looked
to be no more than two years of age, while the others did not appear to be
much older. Another great tremor rocked the nursery and the tiny girl's
gaze swept across the room to a baby boy of about one year, who was
kneeling on the window seat, chubby hands covering his ears. The boy
scrunched up his face and began to wail pitifully, his cries mingling with
those of terror from the outside.*

*Suddenly, the smallest girl wretched her hand away from the other
girls and began to race towards the crying boy, whose clear blue eyes
were drowning in tears. The girl took the boy's tiny hand in her little one
and placed it on her cheek, as a mother would do to her upset baby. The
boy's sobbing subsided slightly, as he flung himself down into the girl's
arms. The two children clung to each other for a mere second, before the
great woman swept the boy up into her large arms.*

Immediately he commenced screaming once again and waved his arms

13

in the direction of the girl on the ground, who was nearly lost under the woman's bustling, but charred skirts.

"Lis! Lis!" the child screamed and kicked in the strong woman's arms, as she put a restraining hand on the black locks of his head.

"Ssssh!" she shushed him, none too gently. "Someone will hear! We must flee little one!" With that, the woman raced out the nursery door with as much speed as she had entered, leaving the four girls completely alone.

"Edric!" came the mournful cry of the little girl who had held him. She collapsed on the floor in a huddle of tears and was soon joined by the other three girls.

Suddenly there was a great commotion in the hall where the frightened woman had exited. The sounds of a multitude of footsteps, like that of an army resounded off the walls.

"Halt, in the name of the Dark One!" ordered a deep male voice.

"NO!" came the plump woman's horrified scream. "You can't have him! I promised the Queen I'd get him to safety!" Her tone was defiant, but a tinge of defeat laced its edge.

The sounds of a great struggle could then be heard, with the woman wailing relentlessly and the little boy screeching for 'Lis'. Suddenly a muffled thump resounded in the corridor, quickly followed by the retreating taps of a number of feet.

The four girls stood huddled in the nursery, whispering, "Mommy. Daddy."

Then without warning, the youngest girl once again broke ranks with the others and charged forth into the corridor through which the screaming boy had been taken. "Edric!" she called wildly in her high baby voice.

Without fully understanding, she ran towards the heap on the ground, which had once been her nurse. She shook the woman's hips with little avail and only succeeded in seeing a sight no child should ever have to witness. The girl's eyes went wide with terror and she shrieked the scream of a thousand deaths.

Then out of nowhere, a figure appeared from the shadows of the hall and with great agility, scooped up the petrified girl and bore her swiftly back to the nursery. The other three girls appeared to recognize the man for they went into his arms quite willingly. The man squeezed the four children tightly and said, "We must be patient. Now is not yet the time."

After this, things start to get cloudy and distorted, as they do when heat rises from the ground. Images begin to flash rapidly, one after another... strange, eerie images. A bearded man... a bright light... a strange tune... a jewelled crown... then darkness.

I awoke with a start and drenched in a cold sweat. I took a few deep breaths to try and calm my rapidly beating heart, which felt as though it might burst out of my chest any second. My body trembled violently, but I knew it wasn't from cold. I had dreamed this dream a hundred times before, but I was still not used to it. I always awoke just as terrified as when the dream had appeared to me for the first time, although now I no longer got sick physically.

This nighttime event had plagued me for nearly 13 years now, incidentally the only years of my life that I could actually remember. At first it had been only every few months and then every week. Now, the horrible nocturnal vision visited me nearly every night, although as of late, it seemed to be getting clearer and more detailed. Before, I hadn't been able to make out what the people were saying. Everything had more or less been in the form of faded images, appearing and disappearing like smoke curling above a flame. However, now I could follow everything quite easily, as though I were right there in the room as the events were unfolding.

I sighed deeply. How could that be true? It was only a dream... an awful, gruesome dream. Maybe something was wrong with my mind, for me to have so disgusting and realistic nightmares. Why did my imagination take me on such a terrible journey, rather than using it's creative powers to whisk me off to some fairy realm, where I could meet a fairy prince? It simply wasn't fair. My greatest desire was to forget the contents of the dream and to shrug it off. Yet somehow, deep down inside of me, I wasn't so certain it *was* just a dream.

I rubbed my weary eyes and glanced around the orphanage bedroom to see if anyone else was awake. I could see all three of my sisters lying in bed, still sound asleep. Emma, the oldest at age 18, had her covers thrown off and her bottom sticking slightly in the air. Clara, who was 17, had dropped her feather pillow on the floor and was snoring peacefully. Lily, who was just a year older than me at 16, had her left leg dangling over the bed so far, that I was surprised she hadn't fallen off yet. The other fifteen or so girls in the room appeared to still be in dreamland as well, hopefully seeing things far nicer than what I had seen.

I decided that there was no use in my staying in bed when I couldn't sleep and I didn't want to fall back asleep and risk dreaming again. So slowly I pushed back my thin patchwork blanket, which I had sewn myself. As I swung my legs over the side of my bed, the rusty old thing squeaked terribly. I drew in a sharp breath, so much for being quiet. However not one soul stirred, although I thought Emma's eyes twitched.

I made my way along the cold wooden floor to the window and pulled up a small stool. I breathed deeply as I swung the window shutters open.

Somehow the world always smelled fresher at dawn. The sun was just coming up through the trees to begin a new spring day. Outside, no snow remained, except perhaps in the deepest shadows where the sunlight never reached. The large trees that surrounded the glade, in which the orphanage was built, looked as though they were just about to burst open into new leaves.

Reluctantly, I reviewed the events of my awful dream, just as I had done so many times before. Surely it meant something of importance. Was my mind so creative as to conjure up such a detailed scene? Somehow I highly doubted that. For one thing, the emotions were far too intense. I could feel the burning sting of tears, the gut wrenching terror and heart breaking sensation of loneliness.

Leaning out the window for a better view of the rising sun, I heard a faint 'clank', on the windowsill. I absently glanced down at the rectangular golden pendant, which hung about my neck. Not wanting to make anymore noise, I scooped up the cool metal in my hands and stared at my reflection in the shiny gold. I saw a slender 15 year old girl, with deep brown eyes and straight brown hair, slightly mussed from a restless night. I wondered briefly if I would be considered pretty. I hadn't anything really to compare myself to, besides the other orphanage girls and my sisters. Still, I liked to think that my image wasn't all that displeasing.

I leaned further out the window, letting the cool morning breeze caress my face. Maybe my fairy prince was out this morning with his fairy court to celebrate the arrival of spring. I could fairly imagine the tiny figures dancing merrily in a ring of colourful mushrooms. I would often pretend that the handsome little fairy would see me gazing longingly out the window and upon setting eyes on me, would take me away with him to his mysterious realm. Such a lovely fantasy… I sighed. Perhaps I was capable of making up my strange dream.

Still, my life truly was full of mysteries and the golden pendant, which held my reflection, was one of them. It was a very strange piece of jewellery indeed. At the very top, my name, Alice, was engraved in flowing cursive writing. Below that, something was written in a language that was foreign to me. The words read, 'Oc Jykpea Yh Focohla'. I could read better than most of the other girls, but this writing wasn't in any language I had ever studied.

The exquisite pendant was strung upon an exceedingly long, but very sturdy and beautifully crafted chain. The entire piece was of such high quality, that I couldn't imagine why I had it. However, I was not the only one adorned with such an expensive pendant, for each of my three sisters had one, with their own names engraved upon them.

Perhaps the oddest aspect of the pendants was the fact that none of us had any idea where we had received them. For as long as I could recall, my sisters and I had always worn these precious items, despite our lack of knowledge about them. Only once had I ever questioned their origins and I had not received any answers for my efforts.

When I was about eight years old, still a bold and disrespectful young-ster, I had gathered all my courage and asked our strict headmistress, Ms Craddock, where the pendants had come from. She simply regarded me with the eyes of cold disapproval and stated, "They were on you when you arrived as a baby."

This was of course, not enough information for a child such as myself and I had unwisely continued to pester her all day. The only thing I got was extra chores and no supper. Since then, I've learned to respect my elders a little more... but only a little.

"Who am I?" I whispered out into the wind. The chirping of birds and the rustling of brush was my only answer. Why can't I remember any-thing? I suppose it could be because I had been only two when I had come to the orphanage, but you'd think some memory would remain... if only a fragment. Unfortunately, there was nothing. Even my older sisters drew blanks in regards to our history. "I wonder what my mother was like," I mused. "Surely I should be able to remember her hugs and kisses..." I closed my eyes tightly. Nothing. Not even one image. "It's not fair!" I shouted, forgetting myself momentarily.

"Alice!" came a voice from behind me.

I started and nearly fell out the window, but a firm arm grabbed my waist and dragged me back into the stuffy confines of the bedroom. "Emma!" I exclaimed in a breathless voice as she sat me firmly down into a chair, well away from the window.

"Just what were you doing? Look at your cheeks! They're so red from the damp morning air! You're going to catch your death!" Emma fussed and draped an itchy wool blanket about my shoulders.

"Oh Emma," I laughed, "I wouldn't have fallen... but your yell al-most made me," I teased.

Emma rolled her eyes. "Now don't try to shift the blame onto me." She paused and her gaze softened. "Alice, why were you up so early? Did you have that dream again?" She tenderly put her arm around my shoul-ders.

"There's no fooling you, is there?" I attempted a smile, feeling un-comfortable as the images were refreshed in my mind.

Emma tightened her grip on me. "Don't worry Alice. You're safe. I just don't understand why you have such nightmares."

"I can't help but wonder if it means something." I pulled my knees up to my chest. "It just feels so very real and it gets more real every time."

Emma smoothed my hair gently. "Now Alice, what could it possibly mean? Don't let that imagination of yours run so wild. It's bad enough you believe a fairy prince is going to whisk you away in the night."

"I don't know…" I mused thoughtfully, as a sudden thought struck me and I chided myself for not having thought it before. "Perhaps it's a memory."

Emma jumped slightly in surprise, her face registering shock and denial. She raised her eyebrows and asked cautiously, "Of what? Our past? If it's half as frightful as that dream of yours, then we should all be thankful not to remember."

Good practical Emma. I got up from the chair and tossed the blanket onto the floor, which my sister diligently picked up with a shake of her head. "I think we should ask Ms Craddock. She has always known something more. I can feel it," I suggested as I reached under the bed for my faded blue dress.

Emma approached me with a sad look in her eyes. "Alice," she began in an exasperated tone, "I honestly don't think she's going to tell you anything, besides sending you to bed without supper. We're abandoned children and it's time for you to accept that fact. You need to put these childish fantasies about our past away. It's not healthy to trick your mind like that you know." Tears seemed to be forming in the corners of her eyes. Wearily Emma dropped onto my bed.

"But Emma," I pleaded, "what about the pendants we wear? The strange language? Does this not strike you as odd? Why would four abandoned children have such fine jewellery? They're solid gold you realize." After a brief pause I pressed, "Emma, you're now 18 years old. Ms Craddock won't keep you here much longer. What then? Will you just go off and leave the rest of us? It's time to find out the truth."

Emma looked down and sighed. After a moment, she threw her hands up into the air. "I suppose you have a point, but I'm definitely not leaving you girls. I guess we should do something." Emma looked thoughtful. "Here's where the wisdom I've gained in my four extra years comes in. Tonight after supper, we'll question Ms Craddock… but, all of us will do it and we'll do it with tact. There's no need to get the old biddy upset. Besides, if we ask after supper, then she can't withhold it from us!"

"Oh, Emma!" I hugged her waist tightly. "Tonight we discover our past."

"Let's just hope we don't regret it," Emma warned, with a troubled look swimming in her blue eyes.

CHAPTER TWO

The Question is Raised

"THIS DAY is going so slowly," I murmured, as I slid a dusting cloth along the top of a rickety old bookshelf.

"It's not like you have anything better to be doing," commented the sarcastic redhead Liza, as she passed by the library door.

I stuck my tongue out at her. Liza never seemed to have an encouraging word for anyone. There were a few things I'd like to tell her, but Emma always stopped me from doing so.

"Just ignore her Alice," Emma told me, right on cue, as she brought in a clean bucket of water to rinse our dusting rags in. "You give her exactly the reaction she wants when you even acknowledge her."

"Emma, do you ever run out of words of wisdom?" my sister Clara giggled as she jumped down off the chair she had been standing on to dust above the doorway.

"Never," Emma smiled back.

"Liza doesn't mean anything by her comments," Lily put in quietly. "She just craves attention, as we all do."

"You don't crave attention," I told her with a laugh. "And you have too big of a heart to admit what terrible manners we all have when compared with you, sweet Lily." I made a sweeping bow at her feet, causing her delicately pale skin to flush a soft pink. Lily was the quietest of all four of us and she never seemed to have a harsh word for anyone, though I was certain sometimes she thought them, especially when we had a rough time.

The truth was, the four of us were loners at the orphanage. For one reason or another, the rest of the orphans ignored us most of the time. One would never guess that we'd been there for so long, for we had no friends outside of one another. It was a lonely existence, but then, we had each other and that was enough.

"So is everything still a go for tonight?" Clara asked suddenly, while wiping a bead of sweat from her forehead.

"Keep your voices low," Emma warned, putting a finger to her lips.

Clara mocked Emma, by putting her own fingers to her lips and then motioned us all into a huddle. "Do we even know what we are going to say?" Clara wondered, excitement shining from her eyes. How adventurous Clara loved intrigue! She fairly shook with anticipation when Emma and I had informed her of our plan to question Ms Craddock after supper. This was perhaps a good thing in case we lost our nerve, for Clara's immense strength of will would carry us through with the plan. There was no turning back once she set her mind to something.

"That's easy!" I laughed. "We simply ask her where she got us from."

"I'm afraid it won't be that easy Alice," Emma shook her head. "Ms Craddock is not the most open woman. I think she carries a great burden."

Lily nodded in agreement. "Yes. Despite her hard exterior, I feel she is very sad on the inside," then Lily smiled shyly, "though it's difficult to see that when she is ordering us to scrub the floors."

Clara stretched here arms in the air with a soft moan. "She has been good to us though. Think of all the years we've been here. We've never truly been hard done by. Food, clothing, a bed… what more could one ask for?"

"A fairy prince?" I piped up with a giggle, to which Clara promptly smacked me playfully with her dusting cloth.

"You and your fairy prince," she laughed and stood up. "Oh well, I guess we'll just say whatever comes to mind."

"But with tact," Emma reminded us all.

*   *   *

Although I was glad we didn't have to cook today, we did have to wash dishes and to me, that was worse. I absolutely hated washing dishes, mostly because the other girls would leave their things a complete mess just to make the job longer and harder. Emma tried to say it was giving me good life lessons, but it truly just seemed like a lot of work. Sometimes, when I would lie awake at night trying not to think of my dream, I'd wish to have even half the wisdom of Emma. She always reassured me that I'd gain wisdom as I grew older, but that seemed far off. I did however have enough brains to know that I was not wise in the ways of the world. We had never left the orphanage before, so I knew that I was ignorant of outside ways. It seemed to me that my sisters had taken all of the good traits. Clara was so bold and daring while Lily was so sweet and mild. The only thing I seemed to have was an imagination and mind full of dreams.

The kitchen was now void of all souls with the exception of my sisters and myself. Clara stood at the waterspout, pumping out water into the large sink while Emma and Lily scrubbed the plates. It was my duty to rinse and dry the dishes then put them back in the cupboard. Normally we could get this task done rather quickly between the four of us, but tonight we were moving extra slow in order to speak with Ms Craddock. Unfortunately, she had exited the room before supper and had not returned.

Silently, I went over in my head what we were going to say… what *I* was going to say. After all, this was my idea. I was slightly nervous though, for Ms Craddock's emotions were always very unbalanced. One minute she was as kind and gentle as a lamb, the next minute she was a fierce dog, barking out orders. No matter what the occasion, my encounters with her had always left me feeling a bit edgy.

I stole a quick glance out the side window as the last few rays of sun faded behind the tall trees. I was glad there were plenty of candles lit, for the darkness suffocated me.

"Taking our time with the dishes I see," came a sudden voice from behind.

I whirled around; there was Ms Craddock, standing in the doorway. Stiffly, she shuffled into the room with a stern look on her face and her hair pulled up into a tight bun that stretched her thin skin severely. Ms Craddock's hands were tightly clasped over a plain grey dress that suited her personality well.

Boldly, Clara was the first to step forward and speak up. "Actually ma'am, we'd like to ask you a few questions..." Ms Craddock's scowl made even Clara shrink slightly, "if we may," she added hastily.

"Questions?" Ms Craddock raised a thin eyebrow, causing numerous wrinkles to appear on her forehead. "What kind of questions? You girls must have idle time on your hands if you are thinking up questions."

Suddenly, it was as though a strange force took over my body and I ran forward. "Our past!" I blurted out urgently. "You know something about our past that you aren't telling us!" Immediately I clasped my hands over my mouth in horror. What had I done? The earth would shake now.

"Nice tact," Emma murmured back to me.

The tension which filled the room was stifling and I had a powerful urge to open the side window and if not jump out, at least let some air in. Then, without warning, Lily spoke in her soft voice, "Please Ms Craddock," she begged, "if there is something going on, we must know. We have spent far too much time wandering alone in the dark. If it is within your power, shed some light, if only one beam, into our darkness."

Ms Craddock stood still and emotionless, like a roughly hewn statue. I wiped my sweaty hands on my dress and whispered to Emma, "Be prepared to run if she loses her temper."

Emma looked apprehensive. "Why isn't she saying anything?"

Suddenly, Ms Craddock turned her back to us silently. I couldn't make out what she was doing, but none of us dared move. She didn't speak or shake an angry finger as she usually did when upset. All she did was stand there, hiding her face from our wide eyes.

Clara summoned up her strength and gently touched the stiff woman's shoulder. I held back a gasp… waiting for the reaction. None came. "Ms Craddock?" asked Clara. "Are you alright?"

It was then that I saw Ms Craddock's shaking shoulders and heard her muffled sobs. Ms Craddock, the unmovable mountain, was crying. My heart automatically went out to the woman whom I had feared for so many years. The stern face she had spent 13 years building up, melted away in seconds.

Still the silence continued on. The only sounds were the occasional creaking of the floorboards on the upper level, where the rest of the girls were sleeping, or at least they were supposed to be.

It was Lily though, who went to the window and opened it allowing a cool, but pleasant breeze to refresh the atmosphere. Still staring out the window she declared, "The truth is going to be painful, is it not? Do not worry Ms Craddock, for we may be young, but we are brave. Just relax and let destiny take its course."

I marvelled at how amazing Lily could be. Underneath her quiet demur, lay a very deep thinking and philosophical girl. I had heard of people who could sense the unseen and there was no doubt in my mind that if anyone could, it was Lily.

After a brief moment of silence, Ms Craddock spoke. "Yes, the truth will be painful… as much for me as for you. I regret that the information I have to reveal is limited. The larger picture of this issue was never made clear to me." A sudden glow of youthfulness came into her cheeks. "I shall tell you girls all I can and then I will send you on your way." She rubbed her red eyes and sniffed in a dignified manner.

"Larger issue? On our way?" I echoed and took a step back, only to bump roughly into a washbasin.

"Alice," Emma scolded, "don't raise your voice so loud. We don't want the girls upstairs to wake up." She then turned to Ms Craddock. "What Alice meant to say, was that we don't entirely understand what you mean ma'am."

Ms Craddock looked faintly amused. "Don't worry about the girls upstairs hearing you… it doesn't matter anymore." The headmistress then sighed deeply, as of one who is experiencing great inner pain and conflict. "I always knew this day would come. I tried to push the thought to the back of my mind, but it always came back to haunt my dreams. For 13 long years, I've prayed to the Power that perhaps a mistake had been made and that I wouldn't have to do this to you. One part of me always nurtured the hope that you would stay in the orphanage forever… then another part of me knew that no matter what, that could never be."

This speech shocked and frightened me right into the core of my heart. Lily left the window and linked her arm into Clara's, trembling slightly.

Emma was attempting to look dignified and unruffled, but I could see that her mind was awash with emotions. Where was Ms Craddock planning on sending us? Perhaps beyond the orphanage grounds... if we had ever been there before, no memory remained of it. I wondered what the rest of the world was like.

"Please," said Emma approaching Ms Craddock for the first time, "we need the truth now. Let's not waste anymore time with this small talk, for it shall surely drive me mad."

"Of course Emma, you're absolutely right," Ms Craddock agreed, forcing a smile and almost reaching out to touch her. "But we can't talk here! Oh no! We must go to where I can *show* you the past... at least what I know of it. I've had everything set up for years now. I can't believe the time has come to use it," she explained while motioning for us to follow her out of the kitchen.

Lily still clung tightly to Clara's arm, but there was a soft expression on her kind face. A wisp of brown hair straggled in her blue eyes, but she seemed not to notice. I had the sudden urge to grab Emma's hand, but I vowed to be strong and handle everything like a lady.

"What do you think is going on?" Lily asked with a shiver.

"I can't imagine," Clara murmured, trying to keep her voice down. "Alice, you're the one with the imagination, what do you think?"

I shrugged uncertainly. For once I was at a loss to even imagine what could possibly be going on. The fact was, I didn't *want* to imagine what was happening. I sensed that it might be fantastic enough without my adding to it. Something was about to occur though... a revelation that would change our lives forever.

"Keep your voices low," Emma reminded us in a strained voice.

Ms Craddock was walking so briskly that it was all we could do to keep up with her. She led us down many halls with tattered red carpets and carved wooden ceilings. These were the areas that had always been closed off to us as we had grown up. The orphanage was actually an enormous manor, but since there were so few of us, we didn't need most of the living space.

The further onward we went, the more Lily looked shaken up. I gently took her hand in mine and walked beside her so that she was between both Clara and I. Reassuringly, I squeezed her hand. She smiled gratefully and it suddenly struck me as odd, for here I was comforting my older sister who, for years, had comforted me. However, despite the fact that I was trying to help Lily feel better, it was also helping me feel more secure.

Clara appeared to be very busy examining the unique woodwork on the walls. I don't think anything would have surprised or disturbed her, for she lived for moments like these. Emma, on the other hand, did look distraught. It occurred to me that perhaps she felt a great responsibility for us. If anything happened, I suspected she would view it as her fault, being the oldest and nearly a full-grown lady. The thought crossed my mind that Emma would make a remarkable ruler, as she kept her emotions under such tight control. I knew she was afraid, for she was continually wringing her hands together and her mouth was set in a tight, pale line.

Ms Craddock halted abruptly. The hallway had ended suddenly and in front of us lay an enormous oak door. I looked and could see no door handle of any kind on it. How were we to enter? On the center of the otherwise plain door, was a golden circle, with four strange rectangular impressions on it.

Ms Craddock smiled mysteriously. "I trust you still have your golden pendants?" She indicated towards the golden circle with a bony finger and didn't wait for our reply. "To open this door and others like it, you must each insert your pendant into a hole on the circle." She looked expectantly at us.

Releasing Lily's hand, I pulled my pendant off and stared at it blankly for a moment. My uncertain image stared back at me. Slowly, I approached the ancient looking door. My sisters held back, probably waiting to see if anything terrible would happen. I gulped, and with a shaking hand, placed my pendant into one of the four impressions. I quickly closed my eyes, in case there was an explosion or something.

After a brief pause, I blinked in surprise, for nothing extraordinary had occurred. Clara, suddenly sensing that I had beaten her to it, stepped forward next and inserted her pendant. A hesitant Lily followed her closely. Just as Emma was about to place her pendant into the remaining hole, Ms Craddock grabbed her wrist forcefully, dim eyes sparking with purpose.

"You must realize that once you open this door and view its contents, there will be no turning back. You must accept what you are told without question, for by opening this door you are resigning yourself to fate. It's a bit like swearing an oath, though without words," Ms Craddock explained in a hauntingly musical voice, totally unlike what we were used to hearing from her.

Emma looked back at us uncertainly and her hand wavered. "Should we?" she asked.

Without speaking the agreement was made. It was hard to explain, but at that moment we all knew that there was no other choice. This was the way it was meant to be, come what may. So, silently and swiftly, Emma inserted the last golden pendant.

The strange circle turned around five times, all the while clicking methodically. After the fifth turn, the circle's outline sparked and shone with a brilliant blue light. Then violently our pendants clattered to the floor with a metallic echo and the enormous oak door swung open.

CHAPTER THREE

The Quest

MY EYES fluttered as I stared hard into the poorly lit room before me, which surprisingly enough had any light at all, considering no one had been in it for ages. The room looked nothing like I had expected. There were no grand pillars of black and white swirled marble or enormous sparkling lights crafted from diamonds.

It was a relatively small room, with only a few candles in plain iron holders mounted to the yellowing walls. The floor was covered with what once might have been a lovely burgundy floral carpet, but now was nothing more than a worn and faded piece of fabric, ripped open in some areas by mice. At the far end of the room, there were two doors mounted into the wall which I presumed was a closet. A dim, full-length mirror covered with dust, was leaning against the wall opposite the closet. Other than the mirror, the room was completely void of furniture. *This* would help us discover our past?

"What is this place?" asked Clara, squinting in an attempt to make out our new surroundings.

"This," began Ms Craddock, "is where your quest will begin and my half of the bargain comes to a close," she finished, while handing us back our pendants.

"Excuse me? Our quest?" I repeated, as a strange sensation formed in my chest.

"An adventure!" Clara fairly squealed with delight, while Lily looked increasingly uneasy.

"Whose quest exactly I wonder?" Lily murmured to herself quietly.

Ms Craddock headed towards the closet at the far end of the room. She strode with purpose and a new sense of determination, as though she had finally worked up the courage to do what she had to. Obediently we followed her, but drowning in a sea of confusion.

"What is this quest that you speak of?" asked Emma, slightly annoyed by Ms Craddock's suspenseful silence.

"Why, to restore the rightful monarch to the throne of course," she answered, as though the answer had been obvious. She folded her arms across her chest and stared down at our gaping mouths.

I could only gaze blankly ahead in disbelief. This was definitely unexpected! Of all the things she could have said, I don't think any of us could have seen that one coming. I hadn't even been aware that the ruler of our kingdom, Algernon, was not the rightful one. Come to think of it, who was our ruler? History had not been a subject Ms Craddock had taught us. We knew reading, writing and some mathematics, but not history. It had never struck me as odd until this moment and yet I had known history existed.

Ms Craddock had taught us a minute amount of geography... only enough to recognize Algernon on a map. Our kingdom occupied the interior of a peninsula in the land of Fadreama, which was comprised of several other kingdoms as well.

A sea faring nation called Denzel the Black or Dark Coast, surrounded Algernon on all three sides, as well as occupied the Three Sisters sub-peninsulas in the south. Just the name 'Black and Dark' was enough information for me. I was also aware there were two rather large bays surrounding Algernon, but the names were evading me at the moment.

As for the other kingdoms of Fadreama, or lands across the sea, I was completely ignorant and up until this moment, it hadn't seemed to matter. Now I found myself filled with a burning desire to learn more about my kingdom and my world, but all of that would have to wait.

"Algernon is under the rule of a tyrant, girls," Ms Craddock broke the silence. "The rest of the kingdom fares poorly and things grow worse by the day. We are somewhat protected up north in the Forgotten Forest, but *his* darkness will reach here soon."

Still we were silent. What could we say? I was at a loss for words, which was really quite rare. Even Clara, in all her boldness, had nothing to say. Ms Craddock's face seemed to fall and she shook her head sadly. "You really don't remember anything, do you?"

"I'm afraid not," Lily piped up, though almost in a whisper. She was fairly hiding behind Clara, though her eyes were not those of fear, but of deep contemplation.

Emma quickly added in earnest, "Please tell us exactly what we are suppose remember. Maybe something will come back to us."

"I doubt it," answered Ms Craddock. "You aren't supposed to recall the past. Everything was arranged so that none of you would have any memory of your lives before the orphanage. Perhaps you had better sit down," she added and motioned towards the floor as there wasn't a chair in sight. Ms Craddock leaned on the cracked wall and wiped the beaded sweat from her prematurely wrinkled forehead. Despite the grey hair, I guessed that she truly wasn't all *that* old. Looking after the orphanage seemed to have drained the life out of her.

As we seated ourselves crossed legged on the faded carpet, I couldn't help but notice that Lily was looking worse and worse. "Are you okay?" I asked her.

She forced a smile. "Of course Alice... it's just that... I feel a sense of impending doom. I know it sounds odd, but... oh never mind." I wanted to ask her to explain herself, but Ms Craddock had begun her tale.

"As I mentioned before, I don't know all of the information about your situation. Even what I do know, I'm only allowed to speak of certain parts. Anymore or any less will be breaking the agreement I made." She took a deep breath and paused for a brief second, eyes glistening in remembrance.

"I can scarcely wait to hear this!" Clara squirmed around excitedly.

"I know," I whispered back. "Finally the answers we seek."

"Or the answers that sought us," Lily added softly.

"Quiet girls!" Emma reprimanded us sharply. "This is important."

Ms Craddock seemed not to hear our exchange. At the rate she was going, we'd be in this stuffy old room all night. It was getting late, but Ms Craddock took no notice. With a graceful motion, she picked up the dusty mirror and held it before us. Leaning towards the dim glass, she whispered some inaudible words and it was as though she had polished its reflective surface, for the mirror sudden lit up brightly. An image began to form out of tendrils of fog, slowly becoming crisp and clear, deep within the realm of the mirror.

It was an image of a beautiful city, with rows of tall, gleaming buildings of various cheerful colours, complete with bright thatched roofs. Happy looking merchants lined the streets, selling a wide variety of wares. I could fairly smell the scent of fresh bread wafting out of the bakery. The city walls looked well kept, with its smooth grey stones, snugly fitted together. Friendly looking guards, suited in shining armour, stood watch upon the walls, though there didn't appear to be anything to watch for. As the mirror took us through the winding cobblestone streets, an enormous white castle came into view, overlooking the bustling city. There was a peaceful air about everything, from the pleasant faces, to the joyous flags fluttering in the breeze.

"Not so long ago," Ms Craddock began, "Algernon was a peaceful and prosperous kingdom. Oh we had our share of troubles to be sure, but it was mostly a pleasant existence. Everyone had enough food to eat and a decent home to live in. Starvation and poverty was never a concern, as far back as anyone could remember. The concept of war was virtually unknown. The Ages of Darkness our world had experienced were nothing more than ancient history. There was no army either... only a few guards as a formality. The idea of an attack was absurd and Algernon had enough land. There was no need for expansion."

Ms Craddock looked dreamy as she recalled better times. "All of this success was due to Algernon's consistently fine line of rulers, known as the Light Dynasty. An ancient family really, but they never failed to keep the kingdom in balance. The most recent ruler was the good King Alfred and his beautiful wife, Queen Rose-Mary." She bowed her head and brushed away a tear that had escaped from the corner of her eye.

We remained silent, seated on the cold tattered floor, looking and feeling ridiculously ignorant. None of us had ever heard of King Alfred or Queen Rose-Mary. In fact, this was the closest to a history lesson we had ever been.

Ms Craddock's grey eyes looked pain filled as she quickly passed her hand over the mirror, thus changing the scene dramatically. "About 13 years ago, in the cursed year of 4685, the most horrible event occurred... an event that would change the people of Algernon forever. I... I don't know what one would call them... demons I suppose. They came from over the mountains... from Denzel, The Dark Coast. They were savage tribes from the Three Sisters Peninsulas. I cannot and will not describe them to you, as not even the mirror will show you the Denzelian warriors."

As she spoke, a dark cloud moved over the image of the city. I could almost feel the frighteningly cold wind blowing through the streets, as terrified people ran screaming in agony. The beautiful buildings now went up in flames and the protective city wall crumbled in an instant.

"But the Denzelians were not working alone you see." Ms Craddock's face twisted angrily. "No, they could not have accomplished such destruction without their leader, one of a higher evil. His name was Ralston Radburn, heir to the throne of Denzel. His dynasty had long ago been overthrown, but somehow he clawed his way back into power with the use of black magic." She shivered at the thought. "It has been rumoured that once Ralston was a normal man... as normal as Denzelians can be, but in order to regain control, he sold his soul to the demons of the underworld, in exchange for their support in overthrowing the King of Algernon."

"But why did he want to overthrow the King?" I wondered out loud, unable to comprehend the situation fully.

"Did you not see how prosperous Algernon was?" Ms Craddock breathed heavily. "Regaining control of Denzel was not enough for Ralston. He'd had a taste of power and now he craved it for survival. For thousands of generations, Algernon had been the very model of success and happiness. Ralston loathed such things and found it within his power to destroy them. Needless to say, Algernon was unprepared for any attack, let alone one of black magic. Our kingdom fell swiftly to the Denzelians and what seemed like an everlasting night descended upon us."

The terror in the mirror was relentless. We watched as the King's few guards fell rapidly to the ground and what seemed to be a ghost-like mass advanced and blanketed the city. I tried to pick out where the vile Ralston was, but it was impossible to tell.

The mirror's image suddenly dissolved into what was obviously a throne room. King Alfred was unmistakable in his long red velvet robes. He was tall and broad shouldered, with a pleasant face and deep set blue eyes. His face was covered with a well-trimmed brown beard, which matched the shade of his shoulder length hair exactly. For some odd reason, there was no crown upon his head. A defeated look was written upon his face and he appeared exhausted.

Alfred's wife, Queen Rose-Mary, stood silently beside him, her face soaked with tears. She was indeed the most beautiful woman I could ever imagine. Her long raven hair fell loosely around her waist and there was a thin gold circlet upon her head. Bathed in tears were her large dark eyes that I imaged would sparkle when she was happy. However, Rose-Mary dressed in a royal blue gown, looked as though she were ready to die. I myself could scarcely choke back my tears at her mournful gaze.

Ms Craddock was not even trying to hold back her tears anymore, which freely slid down her cheeks. Licking her salty lips, she leaned forward slightly. "Finally, the inevitable occurred: Ralston broke into the castle. He forced his way into the throne room, taking out the last of the King's guard."

A loud noise sounded in the mirror. A look of fresh horror swept over the King and Queen's faces. We however, could not see what they were looking at. The mirror went dark once more. When the images returned, they revealed a dark ghostly city, less than a shadow of its former glory.

"Ralston murdered the King and Queen right there in the throne room," Ms Craddock finished with a sob, "along with many of the nobles and anyone else who happened to be in that room. Ralston was relentless and remorseless. It wasn't just murder… it was a slaughter. You do not want to know what happened to the bodies and I shan't tell you, not even if you wanted to know."

Emma by this time was trembling like a leaf in the autumn wind. Suddenly she burst out, "Why didn't the people do something? Anything! Surely they could have rebelled or… .or… .I don't know! It's simply not right! Something should have been done to stop that monster!"

Ms Craddock shook her head sadly. "The people tried to stop Ralston from entering the castle, but he was too powerful. Even after he took over Algernon there were those who rebelled valiantly against him. I'm afraid those souls paid the ultimate price. There have been no more rebellions. Most citizens simply submitted and gave up on the idea of Algernon ever being peaceful again. Each day, Ralston's reach stretches further and further north. He has been quiet for the past few years, but that was only to prepare his demon army. Soon Ralston will reach us in the Forgotten Forest and then he will move on to the rest of Fadreama... maybe even over the sea to other lands as well."

The mirror continued to flash images of the burned out shell of a city. "Those poor people," Lily whispered.

"That was once the great capital city, Devona," Ms Craddock sighed. "It is no longer."

"Can't we enlist help from the outside? I'm certain other kingdoms would be willing to help put down this threat," Clara reasoned.

"Oh Clara, if only it were as simple as that, but Ralston cast a very powerful spell over all of Algernon. No one can either leave or enter anymore." Ms Craddock clenched a fist by her side tightly.

At that moment, the scene changed once again in the mirror and instead of a place, it now showed a person. It was the little boy from my dream! I gasped and my head started to pound. Could my dream be connected to something after all?

Emma, unaware of my panic, inquired, "And where do we fit into all of this? It's tragic I know, but if all the people of Algernon could do nothing, what can four orphan girls do?"

"You make yourself sound too insignificant my dear Emma," Ms Craddock smiled gently. "You see, the King and Queen had a son by the name of Prince Edric. He was only one year old when the attack took place, but it has been said that he survived the pandemonium somehow. Unfortunately, no one knows what became of him after the siege on the castle. Ralston had guards search everywhere for him, but to no avail. The young prince, heir to the throne, had somehow vanished into thin air."

"How can someone just disappear?" I questioned. "Someone must have taken him," I speculated, thinking of the bustling woman in my dream.

"Oh no doubt," Ms Craddock agreed. "The question is, who? Rumours abound but they are only rumours. Some say that the Queen did not die immediately during the attack. It is said that she somehow ordered a nursemaid to find the boy and bear him away to safety. Of course there is no one alive to confirm that report."

"But why would Ralston trouble himself so much over a tiny baby? Certainly he was of no threat to such power," Clara commented as she shifted her position and stretched her stiff legs.

Images from my dream flashed through my mind. The nursemaid had been screaming about the heir. I could hear the little boy shrieking in panic and the menacing sounds in the hall. All of these noises echoed with lifelike clarity in my head. My mind briefly flitted over the images of the girls, but at the moment they seemed insignificant. I sat straight up and stated, "Ralston wanted to get rid of Prince Edric because he was the rightful heir to the throne and could pose a threat if he grew up."

Ms Craddock nodded approvingly at me. "Yes indeed Alice, you are quite correct. Ralston must have feared that Edric would somehow learn of his past and gather the people in a full-scale rebellion. Unlikely I suppose, but it is said that Ralston will never rest until he knows for sure that there is no one to stand in his way. And despite all of his black magic, he has not found the child, though he murdered many out of hatred and spite."

My stomach turned at this disgusting thought. "How terrible," I murmured, then stated mostly to myself, "Edric never showed up to save the day."

"No Alice, he didn't." Ms Craddock looked gently down on me. "But that is no reason to give up hope for Algernon, for Edric was a mere baby when all of this took place. He required time to grow and become strong. By now he must be about 14… not yet a grown man, but well on his way."

"And that is where we come in, is it not?" Lily asked in a subdued voice, as she pulled her knees up to her chest and held them there tightly.

"Clever girl!" Ms Craddock exclaimed mysteriously. "You four girls have been chosen to locate the heir Prince Edric and restore him to the throne which is rightfully his. This will subsequently free the kingdom of Algernon and all of its oppressed people," she finished neatly folding her hands.

Clara jumped to her feet. "An adventure!!" Her blue eyes shone with renewed brightness.

I stood up as well and reached down to help Lily, who seemed to be suppressing shivers. "But why us?" I questioned over my shoulder. "What makes us so special?"

"Indeed," Emma declared pensively as she brushed her skirt off briskly. "And you still have not informed us of how we came to be in this isolated orphanage, buried deep within the Forgotten Forest, the likes of which we haven't been permitted to leave." This statement was delivered quite plainly and although it was not meant to be so frank, that was precisely how it had come out. Emma was tactful, but I suspected that her patience and nerves were wearing thin, in light of the depressing information we had just received. Still, though Emma was tense, she maintained her lady like air and amazing dignity.

If Ms Craddock was offended by this demand, she did not show it. Instead, she slowly exhaled and replied in an even tone, "This is where things start to become difficult for me to relate. For one thing, I cannot tell you on what basis you were chosen for this mission. I swore a vow of secrecy on that detail." Purposefully she strode over to the large closet doors and spun around with unexpected bounce. Then, she did something rather astonishing. Ms Craddock reached up to the tight knot of hair atop her head, which stretched her face so severely and removed the numerous pins that held it there. Her grey hair fell gently down her back with a surprising amount of wave and body… certainly unlike the hair of an older woman. What was going on?

"Ms… Craddock?" I stepped forward.

Lily grabbed my shoulder lightly and pulled me back. Putting a finger to her lips she whispered, "Shhhh… let her have her moment." A comment like this from Emma would have elicited a rebellious response in me, but because it was Lily, I felt it imperative to obey.

Ms Craddock appeared to be deeply locked within an intense memory of her past, for her grey eyes stared blankly beyond our slender figures. "13 years ago, I was a beautiful and young woman in my prime. I know that is difficult to picture now, but there is more to me than meets the eye." She gently fingered her wavy dull locks of hair. Wistfully she continued, "My hair was jet black… no one had darker, glossier strands than I. And my eyes… how they used to sparkle! Such a vibrant shade of amber they were! Now… reduced to lifeless grey. Perhaps the only good physical aspect I've retained is my figure." Daintily she pressed her finger to the corner of one eye and sniffled. "Look at my complexion girls. What do you see? Hmmm?"

"What are we supposed to see?" Clara ventured uncertainly.

"You see wrinkles, correct? Old, tired skin, stretched thinly over sharp features. Guess my age. Go on, guess," Ms Craddock pressed, feigning a smile.

Without even considering very long, I suggested, "60?"

"My point is well made," Ms Craddock sighed. "I'm 32."

I covered my mouth, feeling very foolish and embarrassed. I needed to learn to think before I spoke.

"I was but 19 years old, when an old man named Nissim of Quinn approached me one day, deep within the forest near my home." She paused, then added, "You must realize that my family was faring poorly at that time because of Ralston's takeover. My father was a merchant and with our borders closed, we quickly fell into poverty. We were so desperate… mother had seven other children besides myself to feed. That is why I accepted the offer Nissim made me, despite its consequences."

"Consequences?" I repeated, only to receive a tight squeeze on my hand from Lily.

"I don't regret anything… not even now." Ms Craddock shook her head fiercely. "I saved the lives of my family. Nissim told me that he required a noble, trustworthy young lady to be headmistress at a girls' orphanage. I declared that it sounded like a wonderful job and with the money I earned I could keep my family alive. However," Ms Craddock narrowed her eyes, "I soon discovered that there was more to Nissim's story than he had first revealed. It would be no ordinary orphanage I was to be given charge of… but one under a powerful spell of protection. This spell would isolate all who dwelled within the orphanage from the rest of the world, thus keeping the occupants safe from the turmoil of Algernon. Still, my young mind believed this to be a good thing until… Nissim revealed the source of the power for the spell." Ms Craddock shut her eyes tightly. "The magic used to maintain the enchantment, would draw its strength out of my body, thus aging me prematurely."

Emma let loose a horrified gasp. "You mean it's been sucking the life out of you?"

"To put it quite bluntly yes," Ms Craddock sighed. "But I had no choice… my family needed help and Nissim was giving me the opportunity to provide it. I agreed to take the job, but Nissim was not through yet. He delivered four little girls into my care and declared it my duty to raise them. These girls had golden pendants with their names on them and they were never to take them off. Then, when the time was ripe, I was to explain all that I have done tonight."

"Why did you not tell us this before?" I demanded. "We had the right to know at least who brought us here. Are we this Nissim's children?"

"First off," Ms Craddock held up a finger, "I was warned that if I mentioned one word before the appropriate time, my family would suffer the consequences. Secondly, no, I don't believe you are Nissim's children. He was a very old man, but extremely agile and swift. I think he is a wizard of sorts. I can say no more on the matter." She looked pained. "Please understand why I did what I did. I raised you as best I could, teaching you lessons through good, honest work."

"Of course we understand," Lily spoke up, her voice trembling slightly. "You were entrusted to do the job in a certain way and you did."

"So what happened to Nissim?" Clara questioned. "Did he say that he was coming back?"

Ms Craddock looked surprised. "I've often wondered what became of that elf like man myself. The last time I saw him was when he presented you girls to me 13 years ago. He told me that one day all of you would save Algernon and that he would be awaiting that time. I'm terribly sorry, but I can tell you no more or else I risk breaking the contract." She spun about quickly and flung open the closet doors.

Inside on a smooth golden rack, there hung four different coloured dresses. In addition to that, there was a brass bound trunk tucked in the far corner of the closet. I marvelled at how strange everything was shaping up to be. We had come looking for answers and only found ourselves asking more questions.

"What's all of this for?" I inquired as Ms Craddock removed the dresses from their storage and draped them over her arm.

"Nissim instructed me to give these items to you before you began your quest. Now hurry and change." She tossed us each a garment. "We haven't a moment to lose, as Algernon grows darker by the minute."

I briefly inspected the simple dress which had been thrust in my direction. It had no doubt been made for traveling, for it was simple and well sewn. The bodice and long sleeves were a rich tawny colour, while the skirt was a soft rose.

"Alice, stop staring and put the dress on," Emma instructed, while giving me a nudge. I realized that she had already donned her own dress, which was a blood red and forest green. She looked quite regal, despite the simplicity of the garb.

As I nimbly began to undress, I glanced over at Lily and Clara, both of whom were nearly finished dressing. It was amazing, for the dresses fit us perfectly. Clara was easy to fit, as she was an average size, but Lily was so slender and yet the royal purple and beige dress fit her to the smallest detail.

Clara spun around, her navy blue and burgundy dress a flutter. "It's a plain dress to be sure, but I feel so luxurious in it!"

"I can assure you that luxury was not the intended purpose." Ms Craddock gave us a tight smile as she suddenly revealed four brown, woollen traveling cloaks. She passed them out to each of us and produced yet another surprise: leather walking shoes. As I donned these items as well, my stomach began to turn.

"Ms Craddock, are we going someplace?" I inquired as I nervously fastened the cloak about my neck.

"Have you forgotten your quest already?" Ms Craddock raised an eyebrow at me. "I hope you are not too young and are able to fully understand the gravity of this situation. Nonsense," she waved it off, "you're 15 and should be able to handle it." The worried look did not leave her face. Gravely she eyed us. "Girls, I want to be quite clear. Your task is this: seek out the true heir to the throne of Algernon, Prince Edric. Nissim suggested you start your search in the capital city Devona, since that was where the prince was last seen. It's a long journey, but I have faith in you."

"Aren't you coming with us?" Emma asked as she absently hooked a stray hair behind her ear.

Ms Craddock shook her head. "No, my job is done. I will return to my life as just plain Eve Craddock. My family is waiting... it's been so long... so many lost years." She looked earnestly as us. "Be courageous and strong girls. Listen to your heart for guidance and your mind for wisdom. They will never lead you astray. You must rely on each other for support and most importantly, never lose hope. Keep in mind that the darkest hour is just before dawn." She pulled the trunk out of the closet and motioned to us. "Use your pendants to open it."

Obediently we huddled down near the cedar-scented trunk. Then quite suddenly, I felt a cold wind and the lights seemed to dim. A sinking feeling and darkness seemed to enclose my heart. As I looked up, I had to stifle a shriek, for Ms Craddock and the orphanage had completely vanished, leaving us alone in the dark forest.

CHAPTER FOUR

Escape to the Forest

AS I STOOD COMPLETELY still in the silver light of the pale moon, a shiver overtook my being despite the warm cloak about me. "Ms Craddock?" I whispered in disbelief, hardly daring to move a muscle. The entire orphanage building was gone... and the other girls with it. But how could this be? I slumped to the pebbled ground against the large trunk, which was the only evidence of civilization.

Emma turned around in slow circles, a horrified expression playing across her dignified features. "I don't believe it," she murmured, placing a frantic hand to her forehead. "Everything, everyone... where did they go? People and buildings can't just vanish into thin air!" Level headed Emma was on the verge of hysteria.

"Good riddance," Clara muttered, seeming not to care, though I detected a hint of fear in her clear eyes. "At least we won't have to put up with annoyances like Liza anymore."

"I think Liza was the least of our worries," Lily commented quietly, as her slight frame trembled in the cool night wind. She sighed. "Don't you see? The orphanage was merely a cloak meant to hide us from something or someone. It was never meant to be permanent. Only Ms Craddock was real... and now that everything else has fulfilled its purpose, it has dissolved."

We stared wide eyed at Lily's calm figure, standing placidly in the darkness. At this moment there was not a doubt in my mind, nor my sisters', that Lily had some sort of gift... a sixth sense.

"But where did Ms Craddock go if she was real?" I inquired as I absently kneeled to inspect the trunk on which I leaned.

"She is with her family now," Lily replied quietly and drew her cloak about her arms tighter.

Somewhere off in the distance an owl hooted and I could hear the sound of swift wings flapping. "This is all too much to comprehend in one night," I was interrupted by an enormous yawn. "I'm so tired. Normally we would have been in bed long ago."

"Indeed, we must get some rest," Emma concurred, "but rest will not be found in this small clearing. We must find shelter elsewhere."

"We could sleep under the stars," Clara suggested, turning her gaze towards to the multitude of twinkling lights above.

"Stars are beautiful, but they are indifferent to what happens down here on the ground. They are cold and distant," Lily commented staring straight ahead.

"But the Power beyond the stars is good and kind," Emma reminded Lily with a smile. "Now let's get moving. Clara, open that trunk and see what supplies, if any, are in there." Emma appeared to be fighting her hysterics by taking charge and assuming the role of leader. I was so weary and stunned from the recent events that I was glad to have someone to follow.

"Emma," Clara began, "we are all needed to open the trunk. One of us cannot do it alone."

Rubbing her tired eyes, Emma stooped over the chest. "Whatever do you mean Clara?"

"Well, remember what Ms Craddock said? We need to use our pendants to open it." She indicated to the four slots arranged in the form of a circle on the trunk's lid. In one swift movement Clara had her pendant in one slot, while Emma and I followed wearily.

I glanced over my shoulder at Lily, who was staring off into the depths of the forest, seeming not to notice our efforts to open the chest. There was something in her eyes that frightened me, for they were distant and did not seem to be focused on reality, but to something further… beyond anyone else's reach. I touched her pale hand, which lay lifelessly at her side. It was like ice. "Lily," I whispered, "come use your pendant. Is something wrong?"

She suddenly turned her gaze towards me, as I sat huddled on the ground amongst my other sisters. With deathly pale lips she managed a smile. "Nothing's wrong dear Alice." She bent down and inserted her pendant in the slot, causing the chest's lid to pop open, nearly catching Clara in the chin.

"Oh my!" Emma exclaimed as she examined the contents of the chest. "There almost seems to be an unreal amount of supplies in here… I mean, too much to fit into a container of this size. I feel magic of some sort must be responsible."

"No doubt Nissim is the one who packed this," Clara observed, as she eagerly drove her hands down into the supplies and began tossing them out onto the ground. "Look! There are four large leather satchels! One for each of us!"

In addition to the satchels, there was a tightly rolled up parchment, presumably a map, some cooking pots, four water flasks, blankets, a bag of golden coins and candles, in addition to other various living supplies. "There's no food," I commented vaguely.

"I don't think Nissim would put food in a chest which was to sit idle for 13 years," Emma told me with a laugh, which died on her lips as she caught sight of Lily, who was once again staring off into the trees. However, this time her gaze was fixed solidly in reality and she seemed to be listening intently.

"Lily?" Emma took a step forward.

"Did you hear that?" Lily whispered, not taking her eyes off of the darkness which surrounded our four small figures.

Involuntarily my fingers dug into the coarse, winter-dried grass beneath my hands as I strained my ears. Then I heard it, the crunch of dry leaves in the distance... many feet were moving about cautiously. "Someone's out there," I whispered and grabbed Lily's hand tightly. "Do you know what it is?"

A lonely howl suddenly broke through the silence and was immediately answered by howls from all around. My stomach lurched as I realized what was going on. "Wolves," I breathed, feeling my body break out into a cold sweat.

"We're surrounded!" Clara anxiously jumped to her feet and began to shove items carelessly into her satchel.

"Hurry girls," Emma ordered, as she mimicked Clara by gathering up the supplies. "Grab all you can carry, we must get out of here!"

Lily still did not move, but continued to keep an eye on the forest's edge. I commenced filling not only my satchel, but hers as well. Still, I could not help but look into the foreboding darkness. I gasped as I saw a shadow dart between bushes. "I saw something!" I exclaimed, as I hitched the satchel to my shoulder and handed Lily hers.

"They're moving closer." Lily shook violently. "We have to leave now!"

Emma grabbed my arm roughly and pulled me towards her and Clara. Clara had in the meantime drawn Lily close. With our backs all facing each other, we had a fairly good view of the entire clearing. Still the howls grew louder and more urgent. The hair on the back of my neck stood up as I felt a tear roll down my cheek. Ashamed by my childishness I angrily wiped it away, lest one of my sisters should see it.

"Where do we run?" I suppressed a sob. My eye spied three more shadows move stealthily underneath a low hanging branch. My head began to feel light, for the wolves were closing in from all sides. We could see them clearly now, for they had advanced out of the shadows and into the silver moonlight. There was an entire pack of them hungrily eyeing us up, ranging from tiny pups, to full-grown adult wolves... and just one adult was larger than all four of us put together. Their eyes glowed yellow in the darkness and I caught a glimpse of snarling white fangs, barred in anger.

"There is a path somewhere around here," Lily announced slowly. "I think… it is that way," she raised her frail hand, "towards the west."

"Then that is the way we must go," Clara whispered tensely. "Somehow, we must get through there."

I stared hard in the direction Lily had indicated. Although it was difficult, I did observe the faint outline of the entrance to a path. I never would have noticed it though, had Lily not pointed it out.

"The wolves have left a small space in that direction," Emma observed. "It's not much, but perhaps if we run fast enough…"

"We must try something," Clara agreed. "It we stand here, we die, but at least if we die running, we died trying."

I wiped my sweaty palms on my dress. I was a fast enough runner, as were Emma and Clara… but Lily was most definitely not. How would she manage? This thought was shoved violently from my mind when I heard Emma speaking in a serious tone.

"On my count, we run straight for the path," Emma instructed. "Don't stop for anything and don't turn around. Just keep on running west… even if one of us falls."

"Just leave the person there?" I asked incredulously. "Emma, that's wrong."

Emma grabbed hold of my shoulders tightly and looked deeply into my dark eyes with her piercing blue ones. "Alice, sometimes you have to keep going and not look back in life. If you stop, you may fall as well and all will be lost. Always keep on moving ahead, no matter what happens. Do you understand what I'm saying?"

I nodded meekly and jumped as a snarl came frighteningly close. "There is no time left to plan!" Clara shouted. "The wolves are upon us! RUN!"

Although we must have whirled westward with great speed, everything seemed to be in slow motion. Even the wind felt as though it had slowed its gusts. I could see every detail of the giant wolves, but they appeared to be moving with a strained effort. Their steely eyes slowly blinked and the slobber dripped from their mouths with the speed of tree sap. However, they were indeed moving into position for a chase.

I aimed myself towards the dim path, lowered my head and used all the strength I could muster. My limbs were stiff from the night's chill, but fear had limbered them. I never glanced back, nor to the sides, but I knew my sisters were there, for I could feel their presence.

A sudden weariness began to overtake my body and fear clutched at my throat, as I realized my energy reserves were fading. It was late, I was hungry, cold and very frightened. I felt my legs starting to grow increasingly heavy and slow, despite my mind's orders for them to push onward. Ms Craddock's words echoed through my head... she had mentioned strength, courage, wisdom and heart.

MOVE! My mind continued to scream at my body. The world was becoming a hazy cloud. MOVE! DON'T GIVE UP! BY THE POWER BEYOND THE STARS MOVE! I realized fearfully that it was no longer my own voice that was urging me on... it was an unfamiliar one. It was ancient and powerful... as well as urgent.

The sound of the wolves started to close in behind me. I could almost feel their piercing teeth on the back of my legs. I was only vaguely aware of my surroundings when I reached the narrow path and even then, I couldn't stop running. I felt as though I was somehow detached from my body and merely observing my fearful flight. My legs continued to move even though my mind had long ago given up on calling out orders. The forest was covered in haze... I could not see the trees, path, or my sisters. All I could think, do and feel, was to run... to escape. For an eternity I went on through this blank cloud of nothingness, until I began to feel myself falling and there was nothing I could do to stop it.

I felt myself hit the ground and my body shook with a painful jolt, but it all still felt very unreal. Silently I apologized to Ms Craddock, Nissim (whoever he was), and my sisters for failing them all. The wolves would be coming soon and I would be no more.

However the sharp tearing teeth never came. I waited, numb and motionless, feeling myself slowly seeping back into painful consciousness. Though I had never actually lost consciousness, I still felt so detached and disembodied.

With a great effort, I opened my eyes which apparently I had tightly squeezed closed, for they were terribly hard to open. I thought that I could make out the shapes of my sisters lying in a great heap nearby, but I couldn't be sure. I could feel the hard cold ground beneath me and my mouth tasted like dirt. However, I could not muster the effort to raise my head. I felt so weary and an overpowering mossy scent filled my nostrils.

Suddenly, I heard faint footsteps on the uneven forest floor... the wolves? My heart began to beat faster and once again I tried to move unsuccessfully. No... wait... the noise didn't sound like wolves... it was human. Then, two feet appeared on the ground in front of my squinting eyes. Emma? Clara? Lily? No, they were much too large to be my sisters' delicate feet. A man? A boy? The boots were brown and made of weather beaten leather. They stopped their advancement only a short distance from my face. Who was this stranger and what did he plan to do? I tried desperately to speak, but only managed a cough and barely audible, "Who?" I attempted to speak once more when I felt a face hovering in front of mine. I couldn't make out the features though, for the numbing darkness was closing in once again and this time, I didn't fight it.

CHAPTER FIVE

The Hermit

I OPENED MY HEAVY eyelids slowly, only to be greeted by warm sunbeams shining upon my face. For a moment I lay in complete confusion. This did not feel like my bed... Where was I? Why hadn't Ms Craddock awakened us earlier? I put a hand to my head gently and felt a bruise, as the past night's memories came flooding back. Ms Craddock and the orphanage were gone. A wizard named Nissim had sent us on a quest to the capital city Devona. We were supposed to find the heir to the throne of Algernon, Prince Edric. My eyes opened wider as the images of wolves jumped into my mind. Where were the others? And where exactly was I?

Carefully I sat up and realized that I was lying on a rather firm bed with a faded blue, down filled quilt. To my relief, I discovered that all three of my sisters were nearby and sleeping peacefully. Lily in fact, was right beside me in the bed. Her face looked considerably less pale than it had the night before, but her eyebrows were upturned, as if she were witnessing something disturbing. Emma and Clara were sleeping together in a makeshift bed of straw upon the floor.

I ran my fingers through my tangled hair, still wavy from being in a braid. A memory flashed through my mind of my hair being swept free from the braid as I had fled for my life. "I wonder what happened last night?" I whispered to myself, while scanning our new surroundings.

The entire house, for that's what it was, appeared to be no larger than one room, divided in half by a grey curtain which hung limply from the ceiling on nails. The curtain was drawn back, allowing for a perfect view of the square dwelling. At the farthest end of the room, there was a stone hearth with a merry fire crackling and snapping strongly. A large black pot hung over the blaze and I could see thin wisps of steam rising out of a crack in the lid. The right wall had no windows, but instead was lined with many shelves filled with flasks and bowls of every colour imaginable. The left wall had one large window with a tattered yellow covering, roughly drawn aside, allowing the sun to warm the room. Under this solitary window, was an old round table, which was cracked and splintered from years of use. Two wooden chairs, bleached grey by the sun, sat at opposite ends of the table. Three other stumps of wood had been carefully arranged around the table, but were obviously not the usual furnishings.

"I imagine an old man must live here," I mused out loud, as I continued to take in our surroundings.

"Oh not so old," came a voice from the door. "I'm not as young as I used to be, that I'll admit, but I've still got a few good years left in me."

I felt my face grow hot, as a boy, no older than myself, entered the house with an armful of wood. "I'm so sorry," I stammered, pulling the blanket up to my neck, wishing I could dive beneath it and hide my burning face.

"No need to apologize." The boy grinned good naturedly. "I'm just glad to see you're awake. I was beginning to wonder if you had some wounds that I was unaware of." He dropped the wood into a box by the hearth and removed his patched coat, hanging it on a nail by the door.

Although I suspected the boy was aged 14 or 15, he was exceedingly tall, which seemed to add years to his appearance. However, he was boyish and skinny, with a kind of awkward uncertainty that made me smile. His black hair was unruly and fell over his blue eyes in a roguish fashion. I decided that I liked him immediately.

A stirring on the bed next to me, revealed that Lily had awakened and now was sitting up. The dark circles under her eyes made me shiver. A rustling of hay marked the awakening of Emma and Clara, who gazed about in disbelief, memories of the previous night flooding back.

"So you're all awake now!" The boy clapped his hands together briskly. "Wonderful! Oh I suppose I ought to introduce myself. My name is Oliver Renwick, hermit extraordinaire." He bowed with a graceful flourish. "And who might you young ladies be? I never have guests and then all of a sudden, I'm surrounded by beautiful young women! How lucky can a hermit get?"

His charming manner seemed to melt away the tension I had felt building in the room. "My name is Clara," came my sister's strong voice, as she stood up from the bed of straw and began to brush herself off.

"I am Emma," added my oldest sister, who was smoothing out the rumples in her skirt with the air of nobility. "That is Lily and Alice sitting on the bed," she continued briskly.

Oliver nodded his head vigorously. "I already knew your names from the pendants around your necks, but thanks for the introduction anyway," he laughed and moved over to one of the shelves where he produced a stack of plates, which appeared to be carved out of wood.

"You certainly don't act like a lonely old hermit," I pointed out as I jumped out of bed, eager to hear what he had to say.

"Honestly Alice, you are so very rude," Emma scolded me quietly.

Oliver smiled and cocked his head to the side as he set the table. "Actually, I'm not really a hermit by choice. I used to live with my uncle, a man named Arvad, but he died this past winter." A brief look of sadness crossed Oliver's face, but was gone in an instant. "Arvad was a good man, but he aged quickly. I haven't decided whether or not I'm going to continue living out here in the wilderness, or move to a nearby town."

"I'm sorry Oliver," came Lily's sudden soft voice. "I'm sorry about Arvad. It must have been tough on you."

Oliver looked gently at Lily and replied, "I get by." Then quickly he continued, "So what's your story?" He poured some hot water from a jug by the hearth into a basin. "You can wash up in this," he added. "What are four young girls doing out in the forest alone at night?"

As I waited for my turn at the washbasin, a memory of leather boots flashed before my eyes. "You saved us, didn't you?" I exclaimed suddenly. "You stopped the wolves from eating us alive!"

He began to spoon some gruel from the black pot onto the wooden plates. "You might say that, but I didn't do anything really impressive."

"What do you mean?" Clara questioned in a shocked tone. "You saved our lives! I'd call that impressive! Especially when it was just you against a whole pack of wolves!"

I patted my face dry with a cloth Oliver had provided and we all seated ourselves at the table. "How did you manage to scare off the wolves?" Emma inquired, eyeing the boy carefully.

Oliver looked down at his gruel and stirred it absently. "You might not believe me... and this may sound stupid... but I used magic." He squeezed his eyes shut as if waiting for laughter.

Lily touched his arm softly. "What kind of magic? White or black?"

Oliver's head shot up. "White of course!" he exclaimed. "But you believe me?"

"Indeed!" Clara laughed. "After what we've been through, I believe anything is possible, especially magic!"

"Well now, I really must hear your story!" Oliver appeared unembarrassed once again and was grinning broadly. "But first I will just add one more detail to my story, so you needn't wonder anymore." He spooned some gruel into his mouth and swallowed quickly. "You see, Arvad was a wizard of sorts." Our ears perked up at the mention of a wizard. "He taught me a little bit of magic, nothing really powerful... in fact nothing powerful at all, just basic survival techniques. He has a potion... It's more of a dust really, for protection in the wild. Last night while I was out hunting, I had some with me. When I witnessed you girls come racing by and collapse, I used the last of my dust to ward off the wolves. I brought you to my house and here we are!" He laughed. "Now, please, I'm dying of curiosity, what is your story? Are you from the north? Hildegard or

Ellwood perhaps? Stanbury? Bainbridge? Surely you're not from as far away as Marden or Florian!"

"No," I giggled, "we are from Algernon, same as yourself."

"My sister speaks the truth," Clara chimed in. "We are from the orphanage in the clearing, a short ways back in the direction we were running from last night."

Oliver scrunched up his face in a confused manner. "An orphanage in the clearing? Out here? No offence, but I know this area well and never have I come upon an orphanage. I believe I know of the clearing you referred to... but it has always been just that... a clearing. Surely if an orphanage had been there I would have seen..." he trailed off.

"What's wrong?" asked Emma, a concerned look on her motherly features.

"This may sound strange, but sometimes, when I passed through the clearing while hunting, I could have sworn I heard voices... female voices. Other times I smelled food and sensed a presence, but I always waved it off. There is magic at work here no doubt."

I shook my head, sending dark strands of hair flying. "Yes you're right! And that's not all! We're on a quest!"

Oliver's eyebrow's shot up. "Really? What kind of a quest?"

"Alice!" Emma shot me an angry glance. "You are not very good at keeping secrets are you?"

"Who said it was a secret?" Clara defended me. "He saved our lives Emma, the least we can do is tell him our tale, as fantastic as it may seem! Perhaps he can send us in the right direction."

Emma looked to Lily for support. "Lily?"

She smiled faintly and looked up. "You can trust him Emma, he means no harm."

Emma appeared to be reassured by Lily's soft answer. "Very well Oliver, we shall tell you our story, but I must warn you, it's terribly long."

"I think I can fit you into my busy life," Oliver chuckled.

*   *   *

An hour later, I stretched my arms above my head and sighed. In revealing our entire story to Oliver, it had renewed our urgency to move along. Fatigue, fear and disorientation had nearly wiped our memories clean, but in having to retell the tale, our quest came back with a vengeance.

"We must be on our way immediately," Emma declared abruptly standing up. "Please take no offence to our sudden departure Mr. Renwick," she pleaded. "However, much depends upon our mission and as much as I'd like to forget it... I know now that I can't." She paused thoughtfully.

"In the misty darkness of the night, such a tale can seem unreal, but here in the bright sunshine, the urgency of the situation has a greater impact."

Oliver rubbed his bare chin thoughtfully, his bright blue eyes twinkling. "I understand your reasons for wishing to depart," he sympathized, "and believe me, I take no offence. Your tale isn't as far off as it sounds. Arvad always told me that there are things in the world that we can't explain, but that everything has a purpose. Destiny, you might say," Oliver grinned. "We don't always understand why things happen the way they do, but we must continue to believe in the grand scheme."

"You believe we have a great destiny?" Clara exclaimed with excitement.

"Indeed," Oliver nodded. "I think this Nissim chose a fine lot of heroes or should I say heroines?"

"Which is why we must go," Emma declared, motioning for us to get up.

"Yes, we must leave right away," Oliver nodded. "Your satchels are right there by the door."

"Are you coming with us?" I asked Oliver excitedly. Somehow I personally would feel a lot better about traveling across the kingdom with this grinning companion.

"You? Come with us?" Emma looked taken aback. "We couldn't possibly have you do such a thing. You would be throwing your life away!"

"Would he?" It was Lily who spoke. Her face looked contorted with grief. "In the past day, I have come to believe that nothing happens by accident. I have always suspected it, but now I know. We were meant to meet up with Oliver... somehow his destiny is tied into ours. For a short time, all five of our destinies will follow the same path, before they each fork out into different directions."

I grabbed Lily's arm pleadingly. "Lily, our destinies are all one and the same. All of us... together." An unreasonable fear had gripped my being, causing a wave of nausea to sweep over me.

Lily gently touched my hand. "Of course Alice, you are right... .together."

Somewhat comforted, I turned my attention back to Emma, who was looking torn in her decision. Finally the tension left her young face. She swept a stray hair from her eyes and declared, "Very well Mr. Renwick, you may join us. But I must warn you, untold dangers lie ahead. You can quit at anytime, for this isn't your fight."

For the first time I saw a shade of anger cross Oliver's handsome features. "Not my fight?" he repeated. "This is everyone's fight Emma. Everyone in Algernon that is. I've heard of Ralston before... Arvad spoke of him often and I've grown to despise the man, if that's what he truly is.

Now I have a chance to help get rid of him!" He turned his head sideways. "I cannot in good conscience pass up the opportunity." He suddenly brightened and grinned... something I gathered was his trademark. "I'll pack a bag." He hurried away to the cupboard, leaving the four of us to gather up our own satchels.

"I'm so excited!" Clara fairly skipped about. "Our adventure truly begins!"

"I think there will be more to this adventure than any of us ever realized," Lily sighed. "This is not a game Clara." Lily was solemn. "This is real and in reality, bad things can happen." A cheerfully twittering bird outside lightened Lily's dismal prediction.

"Lighten up Lil," Clara smiled. "It shan't be all doom and gloom. Oh look, here's the map in my satchel." Carefully unrolling the thick paper, Clara studied the map of Algernon. "Our kingdom is much larger than I thought."

"Which way must we go?" I wondered, peering over Clara's shoulder.

"There looks to be a marked road straight through Algernon, which ends up in the capital Devona. We should take that route," Emma pointed out.

"It's getting to it that's the problem," Clara mused thoughtfully.

"Oliver!" I called out. He was just hitching a sack to his shoulder. He glanced up with a smile upon hearing my voice. "How do we get to the main road?"

He thought for a moment, furrowing his forehead. "I believe we can reach it from the village of Petra, which is just a ways beyond here. Yes... that's right. The main road runs straight through Petra. We can walk there in a few short hours." He turned and smiled fondly at the house. "So long!" He saluted the rafters.

Emma rolled her eyes as we headed out the door and into the bright sunshine. "Are you sad to be leaving this place?" I asked Oliver as I walked beside him.

He shrugged. "Not really. Without Arvad it means nothing to me."

I paused then asked uncomfortably, "What happened to your parents?"

He looked up towards the clear sky. "I don't recall much, but Arvad told me that my father was a woodcutter. He died in an accident when I was just a baby. My mother couldn't care for me herself, so she gave me to Arvad to train as an apprentice. I guess that idea failed," he laughed in spite of the sadness of the situation. "But that was long ago. I'd like to leave the forest and live someplace else... maybe farm or something."

"The forest looks so much more inviting than it did last night," Clara commented as she stood with her hands on her hips. "Just smell that fresh air!" It was true, for the sweet scent of spring was in the air and all around the birds warbled an encouraging tune.

"Which is the quickest way to Petra?" Emma inquired, glancing at Oliver. She still appeared to be uncertain about his accompanying us. "I know we must head west, but the map shows no road that way."

We followed Oliver to a small footbridge, which crossed a tiny trickling stream. On the other side of the bridge, there was a narrow pebbled trail. "This way," he indicated, but was drowned out by an enormous clap of thunder.

I jumped and felt my skin prickle… there wasn't a cloud in the sky! "What's going on!" I screamed just as the wind picked up, sending dust flying everywhere.

Coughing, Oliver cried, "Look up in the sky!"

I glanced up just in time to see a brilliant white light that shone and sparkled like an enormous diamond descending towards us. Lily grabbed onto the trunk of a tree to steady herself. She was so deathly pale that I feared she might faint. Emma simply looked concerned, while both Clara and Oliver had a slightly amused look on their faces. I fought the instinct to run and stood dumbly in the open as the light stopped just above our heads.

As lightning flashed and the wind grew stronger, I dropped to my knees. Out of the corner of my eye, I noticed that Oliver had run behind a tree…yet still peeked out curiously. It felt as though we were in the middle of a summer storm, but the sky above looked calm. The thunder was deafening and relentless. I started to fight the wind and crawl towards the shelter of the trees. It was too much! I had to get away from whatever was happening.

"STOP ALICE!" a booming voice commanded.

Fearfully I turned to face the light, which seemed to be clearing and forming something… It was a head! My breath caught in my throat as I stared at the wizened, yet alert looking old man's face and whispered hoarsely through the dusty air, "Nissim!"

CHAPTER SIX

A Long Road Ahead

*T*HE OLD MAN encircled by light, cracked a toothy grin and fixed his deep green eyes on my cowering figure, shivering on the ground. "You are most perceptive young Alice, but then, you always have been," Nissim of Quinn stated, never taking his eyes off of me.

"Y... y... yes sir," I replied in a weak and shaky voice. All I could think of was running away... not from the grey bearded face looming above me, but from the power I sensed he wielded. I could feel his magic, for it was indeed great. It pressed upon me from all sides, as though testing to see if I were real. I didn't want Nissim to see just how scared I was, but with his kind of power, I realized that there was no point in trying to hide anything, so I let my knees knock freely.

At last he blinked and shouted, "All of you, come out and stand before me!" When this wizard commanded, we felt there was no choice but to obey. Even Oliver came out from his hiding place and stood obediently under Nissim's hovering form.

Clara appeared to be in such awe, that all she could do was state the obvious, "You're a real wizard."

"I am indeed Clara," Nissim answered, nodding his head. "I am in fact a royal wizard," he revealed with a sort of pride, then a look of sadness swept over his features. "At least I *was* a royal wizard. Now that King Alfred is gone, I really cannot claim such a prestigious position anymore. Not that something as trivial as that matters..." His face took on a wistful look, as though recalling the days when he served the late king.

I felt the magic around us increase, as Nissim's gaze suddenly focused back on us. "I haven't much time..." the wizard announced. I sensed pain around him... physical and mental. "Ralston's power is growing stronger by the day. He has reached a point in his tyrannical rule, where he is about to expand further into the interior of Algernon. This must not happen! Do you understand me? Ralston is poison, for all that he touches dies and only an enormous amount of power can bring back anything he has destroyed." Nissim's mouth was set in a determined line. "I am appearing here at great personal risk... but I must be certain that the task appointed will be carried out. You do not understand just how much depends upon your success."

"But what if we cannot do it? What if we're not strong enough?" Emma suddenly shouted out, her face alive with worry.

Nissim gave a painful smile and coughed, "You will succeed Emma."

"Can you see the future then?" Clara exclaimed, her face flushed deeply with excitement.

A dark cloud seemed to pass over Nissim's eyes. "No, I cannot see the future. No one can do that, not even Ralston. The future is always changing, like the ebb and flow of the tides. All depends on what happens in the present. The outcome is never set in stone, so to speak. However, I truly believe we can win."

The image of Nissim began to flicker and the winds seemed to die slightly. "I... am fading..." Nissim's voice crackled. "You are on the right track. Head to Devona. Go straight to what remains of Dalton Castle and there you will begin your search for Prince Edric. All my senses say he will be located near the castle. I don't know anymore details than that. Your journey will be a long and hard one, but you mustn't give up, no matter what you encounter. Be careful, for Ralston's spies are everywhere. If he discovers your mission, he will seek to destroy you and I cannot provide protection, for I have my own problems to deal with. I am..." he faded then reappeared, "in the..." Nissim's image seemed to be growing weaker and weaker. His face was taunt, as he attempted to bring himself back before us. "Bravery alone does not accomplish great things. It takes a combination of virtues to succeed. One who is brave cannot conquer without the strength to do so, the wisdom to know how to control the strength and the heart to believe that it can be done." Then with a last blast of wind and crash of thunder, Nissim's image vanished, leaving us once again in the tranquility of the forest.

I let out a long breath and tried to soothe the shivers, which had taken control of my limbs. "He is very powerful," I whispered, but no one heard me. Up until this point I hadn't realized that such powers existed in the world, but now, I had felt his magic. It was strong... strong enough to destroy if he willed it and yet he could not defeat Ralston himself. This thought deeply disturbed me. There was so much I didn't know.

"He looked at me," Lily stated quietly. "He never addressed me, but he looked at me." She seemed very upset. "He said he cannot tell the future, but he knows what will happen." Though her voice was fearful, she never raised it above a soft coo. "And *I* know what will happen." Lily straightened her shoulders and gazed upwards. "Very well, I accept it and will go forward without regret."

Emma took Lily's arm gently. "Come along Lily, you are most overwrought. Clara has the map and Oliver is leading the way. We must go now."

Oliver shook his head. "Your wizard friend can sure make an entrance. Arvad could never do that. It makes his spells seem like cheap tricks."

Hey, those cheap tricks saved our lives, remember?" I told him, as I regained the use of my limbs.

"True!" Oliver smiled. "So shall we be off?" With a light-hearted whistle Oliver crossed the footbridge and disappeared into the foliage, with Clara nipping at his heels and pouring over the map. I followed Clara, while Emma and Lily brought up the rear.

Although the path had appeared well used and groomed, the farther we went, the more narrow and overgrown it became. At times I wondered if we were even on a path at all, for there was nothing but thick forest growth beneath our feet and low hanging tree branches above our heads.

"Are you certain this is the right way?" I asked, as a sharp branch whipped me in the face, leaving a stinging welt across my cheek. Tenderly I rubbed the burning pain, while hot tears leaked out of the corners of my eyes.

"Don't worry," Oliver called without turning around, "I know where I'm going."

"According to this map," Clara announced, "we must go south when we reach Petra. There appears to be some kind of retaining wall between the Forgotten Forest and the Plains of Algernon, but that shouldn't be a problem." She looked thoughtful, while allowing another branch to swish back towards me. This time I was quicker and caught it before I received another welt.

Clara continued her jabbering without notice. "The plains go on for a great distance, but it seems we just follow the main road straight southward. We will have to cross the Jade River, which runs through the city of Jadestone. Have you ever heard of these places?" She shook her head and didn't wait for an answer. "Beyond the Jade River, are the Sterling Hills. They appear to precede the Thea Mountains, which is where Devona is located. Hmmm... in the mountains. I wonder how we're to get through the deep chasms and rugged peaks? Devona is in a valley, so it looks as though we'll have our work cut out for us. How thrilling! I've always dreamed of the mountains!" Clara looked so alive that I couldn't help but share in her excitement.

"The mountains are very beautiful, I'm sure," I declared, wishing I could skip, but the foliage prevented me from doing so.

Clara raised her finger in a knowing fashion. "The stars are much brighter in the mountains too, mainly because we're so much closer to them. I bet if we wished on the stars while in the mountains, there's a better chance our wishes will come true!"

I clapped my hands together. "You really think so? Oh I can't wait! You and I will make a wish when we get there, right?"

Clara nodded vigorously as she rolled up the parchment tightly and slipped it into her satchel. "We sure will Alice. You can wish for your fairy prince and I for more adventure. I will be a great hero someday Alice. Crowds will chant my name and I will be made a knight."

"Girls can't be knights!" I giggled, ducking another branch.

"Then I'll be the first!" Clara replied with determination. "Sir Clara they'll call me. I can rescue damsels in distress!"

At this remark, Oliver, who had been listening amusedly, broke out into laughter. "You are a damsel!" he chuckled, to which Clara punched him in the back. "Careful milady, don't hurt me!"

"Maybe bringing you along wasn't such a good idea," Clara teased.

"I'm just joking Clara," Oliver laughed. "I do that a lot."

The sun was nearly overhead now and my growling stomach reminded me that we would soon need to stop for lunch. I was also starting to grow hot and thirsty. The spring sun, though not as warm as the summer sun, still had a drowsy effect on my body. "I'm hungry," I declared. "Maybe we can stop and eat something soon."

"It's still too early," Emma pressed from behind me. "We must keep going a little further. You'll be fine until then Alice."

"You will have to get used to irregular meal times," Lily added carefully. "On this quest, much will be thrown off balance. We must be strong and not lose heart."

I sighed and clutched my churning stomach. It was only the first day of our mission and already I was getting sick of people telling me what virtues I needed to have in order to succeed... especially when I knew I possessed none of them.

*   *   *

Despairingly I had watched the sun move from its midday position to its late afternoon position and we had still not stopped walking. My legs ached and my heels throbbed with each step I took on the uneven ground. I was beginning to wonder if we'd ever reach the main road which would take us through Petra, but at last Oliver let out a cry.

"Here's the main road! If we follow it south we'll soon be in Petra!" he announced triumphantly. "We must have come out just a little north of the village," he mused thoughtfully. "Well, no matter!"

"Can we take a little break now?" I asked, dropping down onto a large boulder, which was crumbling near the side of the road.

"I agree, now is a good time to rest," Emma sighed, wiping her forehead. "It is getting rather hot." She looked at pale Lily with concern.

"I feel so invigorated!" Clara cried, whirling around on the dusty road. She put her hands behind her back and smiled, "But I am a little hungry."

"Never fear my dear," Oliver announced regally, "for I am at your service!" With that, he opened his pack and revealed a large handkerchief filled with bread, cheese and dried fruit.

We all seated ourselves in a semicircle and dined on the fare Oliver offered to us. We had forgotten to fill our water flasks, but luckily, Oliver had not and so we shared his water. "We will have to remember to fill our flasks in Petra," Emma stated, as she munched on a piece of bread daintily. "I must say Mr. Renwick, you are coming in handy after all." For the first time, Emma cast young Oliver a genuine smile.

He grinned famously in return. "Call me Oliver."

Suddenly Lily's voice broke in. "Look, down the road. Someone's coming... can you see them?" She pointed a slender finger northward.

I stood up on the boulder and squinted. Sure enough, I could see a wagon coming our way. It was a funny looking contraption, with a brightly painted cover on top and bright red sideboards. A pair of healthy looking black mares were pulling the wagon, while their sleek coats glistened in the afternoon sun.

"Perhaps they'll give us a ride into Petra!" Clara exclaimed.

As the wagon approached, I realized that it was an old man and woman in the front seat. They both looked to be in their seventies, but I suspected that hard work had aged them prematurely. The woman's silver hair was braided and wrapped up around her head, with a few stray hairs straggling about her wrinkled face in a pleasing manner. She looked to be in her best clothing, for although her dress was a faded yellow, there was neither patch nor tear in it anywhere. The old man wore a brown leather cap and I could see no hair hanging out of it, leading me to believe he was bald. He wore a brown tunic and baggy breeches. Although he was missing many teeth, he looked to be very kind. There was something about these people's bright eyes that gave me confidence.

Once the wagon was before us, the old man reined the mares and stopped. "Good afternoon!" he smiled jovially at us.

Oliver stepped forward boldly. "Good afternoon sir!" He turned and bowed to the woman. "Good afternoon ma'am."

The old man smiled knowingly. "Do you need a ride into the village?" he asked with a twinkle in his eye.

"If it's not too much trouble sir," Oliver replied with a nod.

"No trouble at all!" the man laughed. "It's a warm day and a fairly long walk into Petra. Besides, that one girl there doesn't look too healthy." He stared sadly at Lily, who managed a weak smile.

"I'm fine, really," she replied softly.

"Nevertheless, just hop right on into the back and make yourselves comfortable. A lonely road like this is no place for a group of young people," the woman suddenly spoke up. Her voice was gentle and flowing.

Quickly we scrambled into the back of the wagon, which smelled of clean, fresh wood. It was obviously quite new. As if in answer to my thought, the old man called over his shoulder, "We're just on our way back from having this wagon made by an expert craftsman. He lives north of here on the border between Algernon and Hildegard... a city called Riordan."

The woman laughed. "It's a very poetic city. The arts seem to flourish up there." She then looked sad. "But it suffers because of the border being closed. They depended so much on trade with Hildegard." She shook her head with a 'tsk'. "It won't be long before this whole area falls into the dark shadow. So far we've been lucky to have been spared... or forgotten."

I settled my back against a couple of grain sacks and relaxed. It took a while, but my burning feet were starting to cool. Oliver settled himself against a sack next to me, while Emma and Lily leaned their backs on the other side of the wagon. Clara had her head out the back watching the scenery as we bumped along.

"By the way, we are the Deans," the man called back.

"I'm Alice," I replied settling deeper into the grain sack. Everyone followed with their names, though I noticed Emma seemed uneasy about giving away information.

"Where are you from?" questioned Mrs. Dean. "I don't believe I've seen you around Petra before."

I paused, unsure of what to say. The truth somehow sounded less than truthful. I however was spared having to reply, for it was Emma who spoke and she was looking at the map. "We are from the northwest... the village of Muir," Emma replied, as she quickly rolled the map back up.

"I have a great aunt who lives up there," Mrs. Dean continued on. "Her name is Ava Hulbert. Do you know her? She always has the prettiest gardens in the village. Nobody can grown roses like Auntie Ava. Red ones, pink ones, yellow, orange... She is working on blue and green ones. Won't that be pretty? Green roses?"

"You're boring them love," Mr. Dean told his wife with a chuckle. "They're asleep."

I listened to Mr. and Mrs. Dean chatter for a minute or two more. Emma had signalled for us all to shut our eyes, as though we were asleep, in order to avoid being asked the question we could not answer, "Why are you here?"

CHAPTER SEVEN

The Village of Petra

I STOOD ALONE in the darkness. Looking upwards, I could see grey clouds swirling together, against a pitch black sky. My mind couldn't think straight... The only feeling I had was a terrible emptiness...

I was completely alone. No, I was not completely alone. There was someone else with me, but most definitely not a friend. I couldn't see much, for there was a dark haze around... it wasn't smoke, but something thicker, more acrid. I began to cough as the haze thickened. My eyes burned and my skin crawled.

Then faintly, I heard someone calling my name. The voice grew louder and louder. Where was it coming from? I spun around, but it was all in vain. Suddenly, I could feel someone grip my shoulders hard.

"Alice! Alice!"

I opened my eyes and was greeted by the sounds of people talking loudly, children squealing gleefully and chickens squawking. Oliver's image gradually cleared before my eyes. His face was lit up with excitement, blue eyes twinkling. For a brief moment, I lay against the sack of grain in the back of the Dean's wagon, stunned.

"Alice, wake up already! We're here in Petra!" Oliver informed me with a grin.

Sitting up, I observed the backs of Emma and Clara, as they were both huddled around the back opening of the wagon, watching the scene before them with amazement. We had never been to a village before, so excitement was in the air. Already my dream was fading, as I jumped up and pushed my way between Emma and Clara to get a better view. Lily I had noticed, was still leaning against a sack, with a taunt look upon her face. Oliver was trying to coax her over to us, but she shook her head gently.

The village was abuzz with activity, for apparently it was market day. Dozens of little stands lined the narrow dirt streets, selling everything from blankets to chamber pots. There appeared to be many tiny stores as well, with living quarters located above them. I couldn't help but smile at the quaint yellow thatched huts. The streets were filled with shoppers... many more people than I had imagined lived in Petra, but then again, perhaps many had come in for market day only.

Emma turned around and announced, "We had better get off here. It won't due to overstay our welcome."

Oliver nodded and tapped Mr. Dean on the shoulder. "We'd like to get off here please sir."

Mr. Dean reined the black mares, which trotted to a stop in the village square. One by one, we exited the wagon, making sure that the sacks of grain were stacked as neatly as we had found them.

"We can't thank you enough for the ride," Emma curtsied politely, offering the Deans a few gold coins from our purse.

"Oh no!" Mrs. Dean waved her hands in the air. "We couldn't possibly!"

"Never mind about us," Mr. Dean added. "You keep that gold for yourselves! Who knows when you may need it. Take care now!"

We all waved goodbye as Mr. Dean started the mares moving again. As the back of the wagon passed by Emma, she tossed five gold coins into the back where we had been sitting, then turned her gaze to the village.

"I suppose we ought to get some supplies," Clara ventured. "You can't go on a quest without supplies."

As Emma and Oliver joined in the conversation about what exactly we needed to buy, my mind began to wander to the many stands nearby. Everything was so lively. Girls my age wandered through the narrow streets, arm in arm, laughing and pointing excitedly at the goods for sale. I had a sudden pang of longing to be just like everyone else... to have no worries about some stupid quest. I wished with all of my heart at that moment, to be just a regular girl out to buy some bread at the market for her mother. It was a hope and dream I knew I could never have.

"You look like a smart young girl," came a voice off to my left. I looked about, wondering if the voice had been addressing me. My gaze landed on a stooped wiry old lady, selling pottery at a small table. It was hard to tell much about her from a distance, but she was indeed beckoning to me. I glanced back at Emma, Clara and Oliver, who were deep in conversation.

"We need horses," Clara declared, crossing her arms.

"But we can't each have one," Emma pointed out. "It would cost too much and they would be difficult to feed."

"Do you even know how to ride a horse?" Oliver chuckled, trying to lessen the tension between my sisters.

Lily stood back from the conversation and appeared to be deep in thought. Her brows were deeply furrowed and her fists were clenched. I debated speaking to her, but the old woman called to me once again.

"Come and see my child, perhaps there is something at old granny's table you would like," she cawed like a crow.

With a final shrug, I stole away to her stand. "Hello!" I smiled warmly at the woman. Upon closer inspection, I could see that the woman was severely underfed and had long bony fingers with horribly gnarled nails. Her yellow eyes were sunk deeply into her head, which was covered with thin wispy white hair.

"Good afternoon precious. Aren't you a pretty little girl! I don't often see such loveliness around this little village. Just like a painting!" She licked her thin lips. "Are you new to these parts?"

"Not really," I replied absently, as I inspected her wares. "We just don't get out much."

"We?" the woman repeated. "Do you mean those three other girls and the young lad over there?"

I nodded. "Yes, those are my sisters Emma, Clara and Lily."

"What about the boy?" the woman questioned, as she handed me an earthenware bowl to look at. "Is he married to one of you? Or is he your brother?"

I laughed. "Oliver? Oh no! He's just a friend we met in the forest. He lived all alone, so we decided to let him come with us. How much is this cup?" I held up a dainty teacup.

"A boy of that age living alone in this wild forest?" The old woman looked sceptical, her eyes glued to my face.

Hooking a hair behind my ear, I pursed my lips. "Well, he didn't always live alone. A man name Arvad looked after him, but he died this past winter." I leaned in closer and whispered, "Arvad knew magic! And he taught some to Oliver! Ummm, how much did you say this teacup was?"

"Arvad?" the old woman whispered, a new sense of alertness about her frail form. "Are you okay?" I asked her with concern.

"I'm quite all right my dear," she replied and turned my attention to a flower vase, with a brightly painted design. "Where did you say you were headed?" she asked casually.

"I didn't," I answered fingering the smooth vase. "We're on our way to Devona."

The woman's gnarled nails bit down hard into the soft wooden table. "Did you say Devona? Why would you want to go to that awful place? What business have you in the great City of Ruins?"

Suddenly my stomach clenched and a fear crept across my skin. Why did this old woman ask so many questions? She was ugly... but that didn't necessarily mean she was evil. "I think I'd better get back to my sisters," I said nervously turning to leave.

She reached out quick as lightning and grasped my wrist with her cold hands and drew me back to her table. "Stay awhile and keep a poor old lady company," she cackled. "You can't be planning on walking the whole way to Devona," she grinned, revealing blackened teeth.

"Well," I began thoughtfully, taking pity upon the wasted woman and trying to ignore the pressure building in my ensnared wrist, "we were thinking of purchasing some horses."

She shook a finger on her free hand in the air and winked. "It's a good thing you passed by old granny then. For I know where you can find some good strong traveling horses."

"Really?" My fear dissolved. I would know something that my sisters didn't for once.

"There's a ranch, just to the west of Petra. A man named Xenos Sanderson runs it. It's just a short trip out there and very easy to walk." She sucked in a hoarse breath.

"Well thank you so much!" I gave her a bright smile. "I'll just go tell everyone now." The grip on my wrist did not waver. "You're still holding my wrist," I told her gently.

"Am I?" She raised a thin eyebrow. "I hadn't noticed." Then, with one powerful pull, she yanked me onto her table, sending pottery crashing to the ground. Her eyes clouded over with rage and she seemed to possess much more strength than her limbs suggested. "Do you take me for a fool?" she spat. "You miserable little brat! Do you actually think that I do not know who you are and what your purpose in Devona is?" Her words hissed with menace.

"Who are you?" My voice came out as a whisper and terror had weakened every muscle in my body.

She ignored my question and gripped my wrist harder, causing it to go numb. "Now listen here you wretched little girl! I don't know where you've been hiding all of these years, but I suggest that you get back there! As a servant of the Dark Lord Ralston, I can guarantee that if you continue on to Devona, you shall pay most dearly! In actual fact, with your life!"

"Let me go!" I cried, finding my voice, as I twisted painfully in the woman's grasp.

"Let you go?" She gave a chilling laugh. "You have a lot to learn my dear!"

"If you don't leave me alone," I threatened, "Nissim will appear and destroy you!"

"Nissim? Don't make me laugh! He's been dead for years! You are alone child! Do you hear me? Completely alone!" She squeezed tighter, digging her nails into my flesh. Ruby blood began to run from my wrist onto her rough skin and down my arm.

"Help me!" I screamed, feeling hysterics coming on. "Someone please help me!"

I could hear the villagers begin to cry out too, for black smoke seemed to be rising in the air around the woman's stand.

"Let her go witch!" came Oliver's voice behind me.

"Oliver!" I screamed. "Get me out of here!" I tried to control the sobs, which were now wracking my body.

The witch gave me a violent shake, causing my pendant to fall out of my dress and clang the table's surface. Her eyes widened at the sight of it. "This isn't over!" She glared daggers at me and in a poof of sooty smoke vanished, table and all, leaving me lying on the ground shaking.

I coughed and spluttered in the dirt, as villagers surrounded me. "Poor girl." One woman shook her head.

"Who would have thought a witch lived in Petra?" another commented with disgust.

"I've never seen her here before. This must have been a one time thing," yet another voice assured the worried people.

Oliver and Emma hauled me to my feet. "Alice, are you okay?" Emma examined my bleeding wrist with care.

"Oh Alice! That was terribly frightening and yet exciting all at once!" Clara popped up in front of me, her eyes a mixture of concern and amazement. "Tell me, did she cast a spell on you?"

Trembling and nauseated, I was helped to a shady spot to rest. The villagers backed off now and seemed afraid to come near me, for fear the witch had left some curse. Many made a sign against evil.

Lily gazed at me with wild eyes. "She was waiting for us," Lily commented. "The secret is out. Ralston knows."

"I said too much." I kicked at the dirt as Emma bound the finger marks on my wrist. "If Ralston didn't know before about us, he knows now. She said she worked for him."

Oliver drew in a sharp breath. "In that case, we'll just have to be extra careful. Don't worry about it Alice."

Emma glared at me sharply. "You should never have left my side! What am I going to do with you? You are so immature!"

"Emma." Lily put a restraining hand on our sister's arm.

Breaking into tears, Emma flung her arms around my neck. "I was so afraid we were going to lose you!"

"So was I..." I muttered quietly.

Straightening, Emma looked skyward. "The sun will set soon... we must continue on. I want to leave this place. Can you walk Alice?" She looked down at me.

"Of course," I replied, making an attempt to hide the shakiness in my voice. "But where are we going?"

"To a place called Xenos Ranch," Clara told me as she squeezed my hand. "A villager said that's the only place where we can buy horses."

The hairs on the back of my neck stood up. That was the place suggested by the witch. Was it safe? "I don't think we should go there," I told the group.

"Why not?" Oliver wondered. "It's not that far, honestly."

"No, it's not that." I shook my head and gulped. "The witch suggested that place too."

Emma paled and Lily hugged her arms. "What other choice do we have?" Clara asked, feeling the sudden chill of the oncoming evening.

"We could walk, I suppose." Oliver looked uncertain and kicked at the dusty ground with the tip of his boot.

"No." Emma's mouth was set in a firm line. "We must go... we'll be careful." She sighed. "We need horses and this Xenos is the one to give them to us, witch as a reference or not."

"Okay then," Clara agreed, "let's go."

I took Lily's hand, which was as cold as ice. "Are you alright Lily?" I asked, wincing at the pain still burning in my wrist.

She looked at me with huge mournful eyes. "Oh Alice, I wish the sun were rising and not setting. The sunrise is so much more beautiful than the sunset!"

"The sun will rise again tomorrow," I told her, attempting to be a comfort.

"Only for the living," she whispered.

CHAPTER EIGHT

Terror in the Night

*O*N A PLEA from Lily, we had given our best effort to find a ride out to Xenos Ranch, but whether it was because of the witch incident, or just unhelpful people, we could find no such ride. Oliver had made the suggestion we wait until morning to set out, but unfortunately, none of the inns would allow us to stay either. The villagers appeared to connect us with evil, for they always made a sign against it when we came near.

"I don't relish sleeping in the streets," Emma declared in distaste. "I don't trust the people here anymore than they trust us. I'd rather sleep out on a lonely road. My suggestion is that we start walking to the ranch tonight."

Staring up at the dusty rose coloured sky, I shivered. There was something odd about the way in which the villagers had suddenly packed up their market stalls and disappeared into the brightly lit thatched houses. As each door had closed tightly with a slam, I had heard the methodical bolting of locks echo throughout the empty streets. Somehow I didn't feel it was simply us the villagers feared. No, there had to be more to the story than that, for they had fled urgently and looked terrified.

"It bothers me that the villagers seem to fear sunset and darkness so much," Clara mused thoughtfully. "It seems so serene... almost unreal in the forest at night."

"That it may Clara," Emma replied, handing out the last bit of bread and cheese from Oliver's pack, "but we must move forward. I want to leave this place as soon as possible. We are clearly not safe here." She cast a glance over at me. She hadn't asked exactly what I had told the witch, but she could guess well enough... I had said far too much.

Unable to withstand Emma's scrutinizing gaze, I linked my arm into Lily's. She had been staring down the dim dirt path which led to Xenos ranch. The path was really more of a road, for it was quite wide and well used. Each side was lined with thick trees and vegetation which rustled gently in the evening air.

"I foresee a short and long night," Lily commented vaguely, without blinking her huge clear eyes.

I couldn't help but giggle. "Lily! Don't be silly! How can a night be both short and long? It's either one or the other!"

She reached up and smoothed my hair with a sigh. "Perspective dear Alice. It all depends upon whose point of view you see things from."

"Come along girls!" Emma waved to us impatiently. "Let's get moving! I don't like this lingering about... it makes me nervous." She shot a glance over her shoulder at an owl who watched us with a swivelling neck.

As we began our trek down the darkening path, I realized that everyone seemed to have found a position. Emma, ever practical, was the motivator, leader and dispenser of advice (some of it unwanted). Oliver and Clara appeared adventurous and more than willing to be on this quest. Every time I looked their way, they were either pouring over the map, pointing out something interesting on the roadside, or discussing our next move. I couldn't help but feel a pang of jealousy, for Clara and Emma took up most of Oliver's attention. For a boy younger than myself, he seemed so mature and I was envious. So it was that Lily and I walked together, both I suspected, feeling out of place and in the way.

The sun gave one last burst of light, before it was snuffed out entirely by the cool night. The moon rose high into the sky, bathing everything in its pure silver radiance. Crickets could be heard in the grass as a damp cold set in. A thin veil of mist appeared and swathed us in its folds. Above the mist, high in the sky, the stars *did* seem distant and cold as Lily had said, despite their merry twinkling. They cared nothing for people's suffering.

*   *   *

As the hours rolled by, I observed the moon creep across the sky, just as the sun had earlier. My legs were becoming heavy and I shuffled, rather than walked. Lily did her best to keep up too, but her features were drawn and tired; we needed to rest for the night.

"Emma," I beseeched my oldest sister, "please can we stop now? The path to the ranch will be there in the morning." I rubbed my burning eyes. "I'm so weary, I can hardly take another step," I complained, even though I continued moving at a decent pace.

"Just a little further," Emma pressed. "I don't like the feel of these damp glades."

"It's just a short ways to Xenos Ranch," Clara declared with triumph. "Perhaps they will put us up there for the night. Won't that be nice?"

"Actually," Oliver observed groggily, "the gates to the ranch will probably be closed and locked for the evening. Even if we get there tonight, we will be shut out."

I was about to put in another bid for us to stop and rest, when the road suddenly opened up into a strangely circular clearing. I held my breath as the moonlight trickled down between the tree branches, revealing an awesome, yet strange sight. In the very center of the clearing, there was a circular pond, with clear blue water rippling in it. Large white alabaster pillars, surrounded the pond on all sides. There were nine pillars in all and they supported a marble pyramid shaped roof, with various statues and carvings decorating it.

"What is that?" asked Clara with excitement, running towards the strange arrangement.

"It looks like some sort of shrine…" Oliver hesitated, then he too ran with Clara.

"It cannot be a shrine, for there are no priests or priestesses here," Emma pointed out. "A shrine must have a guardian… or at least someone to look after it."

"Perhaps its secrets guard themselves," Lily spoke softly. "Look how well it's groomed. Someone looks after it."

Curiosity was welling up inside of me. "Come on!" I tugged at Lily. "Maybe it's a wishing well or something!"

She remained fixed to the ground for a moment, but finally relented. Emma had already started to make her way towards the pillars, leaving a trail of footprints in the short dewy grass. As Lily and I approached the shrine, or whatever it was, I was deeply impressed by the immensity of it all. Placing my hand on one of the pillars, I could feel an energy flowing within it. Then, it sounded as if a voice were calling… a soft almost haunting sound. Gingerly I peered down into the depths of the water.

I felt Lily suddenly at my arm. "It's very deep," she commented, "and cold I should think."

"It looks like there's a door down there," I observed, watching the ripples lap upon the grassy shore of the pond, "but that doesn't make sense."

"If it's a shrine it does," Clara interrupted from behind me.

"Underwater?" I was sceptical.

"The ways of the divine are mysterious," Clara replied in a factual voice.

"Maybe there's some kind of mechanism for bringing it above water," Oliver suggested, "but it stays inaccessible to those who are not authorized to enter."

"An interesting theory," Emma nodded, "but I'd like everyone to back away from the edge right now. I don't trust this place." She pulled her cloak about her body tightly and shivered. "We shouldn't be here. Let's get going. The ranch isn't far now. We can camp outside the gates."

Ignoring Emma, I continued to stare into the hypnotic waters. I could have sworn I saw something move in the dark depths. "There's something down there," I whispered and felt Lily grip my arm. "A dark shape…

I can't make it out." I shook my head, but was unable to turn away. The hum of a voice seemed to fill my head once again.

"Alice, get away from there! You'll get your feet all wet and muddy," Emma demanded, impatience rising in her firm voice.

"But look," I murmured, feeling a strange sleepiness draining the strength from my limbs. My mind began to grow cloudy and I was scarcely aware of leaning farther and farther forward.

Suddenly, a small hand grabbed my arm and forcefully threw me backwards onto the damp grass. My vision cleared at once and I felt stunned. Lily was looking down at me with a grim frown. "Are you alright?" She extended a hand to me.

"I'm fine," I whispered, trying to think about exactly what had happened.

"Alice, you never listen!" Emma snapped. "You just about fell in! Now get over here and away from that water!"

"I think she's serious," Oliver laughed. "But really, you almost did fall in."

"Then I would have been forced to dive in and rescue you," Clara piped up, striking a heroic pose.

"I was just so tired," I explained, groping for some explanation to my behaviour. "You pulled me back, right Lil?" I smiled at my sister.

She nodded slowly. "It wasn't meant for you," she replied in a voice so soft I barely heard her.

Surprisingly, as we stood in the cool clearing, Emma embraced me. "You do seem rather flushed and weary. Perhaps we should go no further tonight."

"Please," I begged, "let's rest here."

"Okay," Emma relented, sagging her proud shoulders, "but we shall sleep far away from that... whatever it is. For goodness sakes Clara! What are you doing in the dirt?"

Clara sat cross legged near a pile of stones, a look of deep fascination and curiosity playing on her animated features. "Look!" she breathed. Oliver was at her side in a moment. "It's some sort of tablet. It has some writing on it, probably explaining what this place is."

The stones Clara referred to were crumbling into a pile of dust on the ground, but some of the words were still visible. "I don't understand those words," Clara furrowed her brow, "but I know these ones." She traced the letters tenderly with her finger.

"Those other words are ancient Algernonian," Oliver informed us, "the same as appears on your pendants." He hung his head. "Arvad was going to teach me how to read it, but he died before he had the chance."

"There's a year there Clara," Emma pointed out. "What does it say? 15..."

"1557... the summer of 1557 I believe," Clara finished. "That must be when this was constructed."

"It's so ancient!" Oliver let out a low whistle. "Let's see, if it's 4698 now... then you..." He worked the math out in his head.

"3130 years ago," Lily stated quietly.

"That can't be right," I declared. "How can anything be that old?"

"There are many things older than yourself Alice," Emma told me with a gentle smile.

"The words are all broken and chipped." Clara licked her lips in frustration. "It says 'Heart.' I can tell that much. Heart Tem... Heart Temple?" She looked questioningly back at us.

"Perhaps." Oliver shrugged his shoulders.

"Built by Nissim and O... and Cl!" Clara gasped. "Nissim helped to build this! I don't know who O or Cl is, but if Nissim was here, it must have magic."

"Well, then," I observed, "Nissim is on our side, so there should be no reason to fear the temple."

"Nissim has not been here for a long time Alice," Lily put in. "Anyone could have corrupted it in the meantime."

"But it looks so tranquil," I protested, crossing my arms.

"Looks can be deceiving, you know that as well as I," Lily remarked.

"For King... and Queen... I can't make out the names." Clara sunk down lower, until her face was only a short distance away from the rock. "And the young Prince Darius, may there be many more to come."

I smiled to myself. Darius was a very kindly sounding name.

"So this is some kind of temple for an ancient royal family," Emma concluded. "That's all fine and well, but it means nothing to us. If you're so insistent on us resting right now, let's get some sleep already."

A great splash startled us all and I felt the icy sting of water on my bare leg. Lily looked very worried. "It's okay Alice," she reassured me with a weak smile.

Emma looked slightly paler in the moonlight. "Let's rest by the edge of the forest." She motioned for us to follow her. "You see Alice," she told me, "there's fish in that pond. That was what you saw earlier."

I truly wanted to believe Emma, but something at the back of my mind told me it was not a fish I had seen and it was definitely not a fish that had jumped. I suddenly felt uncertain about staying in the clearing, but my thoughts were interrupted by an enormous yawn. I had to sleep, temple or not.

Using our satchels as pillows, we curled up near a low hanging bush along the edge of the clearing. Oliver slept slightly apart from us, using his cloak for warmth. Emma huddled on one side of Clara and I on the other side. Lily lay in front of me and I had a feeling of great warmth and security snuggled amongst my sisters.

*   *   *

"Alice!" came a menacing voice from above.

I was lying face down on a pile of sharp rocks and as I tried to stand, my body ached with bruises. Heavily I lifted my head and stared up into the impenetrable darkness. The clouds in the pitch black sky were moving faster by the second, with flashes of lightning illuminating them every so often. I screamed in agony as I forced myself to my feet. For some reason, I knew I had to stand up... I could not just lay there and rest.

"Who are you?" I screamed into the wind, which chaffed my lips until they bled. My mind was a blur of thoughts. Once again the overwhelming loneliness swept over me and I could feel hot tears streaking across my cut face. With a cry of anguish, I fell to my knees and wept. "I let them all down! It's all my fault!"

My body twitched violently and I found myself on the ground in the clearing, still huddled by my sisters. Touching my face gently, I found it to be tear stained. As I sat up sweating and trembling, I realized with a start, that Lily was no longer lying beside me. Pushing the terrifying dream out of my mind, I scanned the clearing, fully illuminated now by the moonlight. I spotted Lily sitting by the edge of the pond, staring into its depths. Quietly, so as not to wake anyone, I stood up and crept across the grass towards her.

"Hello Alice," Lily greeted me without turning around. I stopped a little ways away from her surprised she had heard me. "Don't come any closer," Lily warned me in a gentle voice.

"Why," I questioned before continuing my interrogation, "were you having trouble sleeping?"

This time Lily did turn to face me and I saw that her eyes were red and swollen as though she had been crying. I started to rush towards her, but she held up a hand. "Please stay where you are Alice," she pleaded, then smiled weakly. "You are right, I could not sleep." She paused briefly. "You must know that I sometimes have visions or glimpses of the future... premonitions."

I nodded. "Emma told me that you have a special power."

"Well, I don't know about that," Lily replied as a soft wind caressed her dark hair, "but tonight, I will meet my destiny. I cannot run from it... I cannot change it. I must accept it as the will of the Power."

An eerie feeling entered my heart. The hairs on the back of my neck stood up as I stared hard at my sister, trying to make sense of what she was saying. "Is it something bad?" I managed to squeak out.

"Bad in one way, but good in another," Lily told me, her large eyes unblinking. "I don't have much time… Oh how I wish I could embrace you little sister! You are so very dear to me!" she cried.

"Well let me come over there." I tried to step forward, but she shook her head.

"No Alice, stay put. No matter what happens you must continue on, do you hear me? Every one of us has a destiny and when it calls to us, we must be courageous. We cannot always understand it at the time, but that is part of what makes life worth living… the unpredictability."

A small seed of panic had started to grow inside of me. "Lily I don't follow what you're saying. Why must you speak in riddles?"

"Even though our destinies do not run side by side, they serve the same purpose in the end." Lily seemed unfazed by my confusion. "You're still young Alice, though so am I… but I've aged 20 years in the past few hours as far as understanding goes. But *you* my little sister, have much learning and understanding left to do. Someday, you will see child." She smiled sadly. The water in the pond before her seemed to be bubbling as though it were boiling in a pot above a fire.

"What's going on Lily?" I stayed rooted to the spot, only this time it was out of fear and not Lily's request.

Suddenly, a great black tentacle shot out of the pond, sending icy crystals of water all the way over to where Emma, Clara and Oliver slept. The tentacle swiftly flew towards where Lily was standing and hit the backs of her legs, causing her to fall to the ground with a yell. Then, in a flash, the tentacle wrapped itself around Lily's neck and lifted her high into the air.

At the sight of this, I found my voice. "Lily! Lily!" I screamed, though I still did not move. "Let her go! Help! Emma!!!"

Lily's eyes had grown larger and her face was turning a sickly blue. Behind me, I heard the rush of footsteps. "Lily!" came Emma's voice as she grabbed my shoulders tightly.

"By the Power we have to get her out of there!" Oliver exclaimed, grabbing a nearby stone and throwing it with all his might at the arm, which waved Lily triumphantly in the air. The stone hit its mark and stuck in the slime which coated the creature… though it did have some effect, for its grip momentarily loosened on Lily's neck.

"Run," she called weakly. "Get away. Keep me in your hearts as you are in mine." She could say no more, as the tentacle resumed its death grip on her neck.

"We won't leave you!" Clara screamed as she followed Oliver's lead in pelting the tentacle with rocks, which simply stuck to it.

With her last ounce of strength, Lily reached up to her chest where her pendant hung and ripped it off. She tossed it hard towards the shore, where it landed at my feet. Her body then went completely limp.

"Lily!" I stepped over the pendant and tried to run towards the pond, but Oliver and Emma grabbed my arms tightly.

"Don't be a fool," Emma told me, "it will catch you too." The look of anguish in her eyes was enough to tear my heart out.

"NO!" I dropped to my knees in tears. "We have to do something!"

Oliver's mouth was set in a determined line and suddenly he ran full speed towards the pond.

"Oliver no!" Clara exclaimed running after him.

As if sensing the impending attack, the tentacle rapidly descended into the bubbling water, dragging the body of Lily with it. Still, Oliver did not stop running. I caught the glint of a small dagger in the moonlight. With a great yell, he dove into the pond and disappeared beneath the water.

"May the Power help him," Emma whispered and I realized that her face had gone completely white. She looked like a ghost, just standing beside my pathetic figure clawing at the neatly groomed grass. Clara stood at the water's edge, head moving frantically as she tried to catch sight of Oliver.

"He's coming up!" Clara cried out as Oliver's form burst through the surface of the water and swam to the edge. Clara grabbed his hand and dragged his soaked body out onto the damp grass.

Breathing heavily, Oliver spluttered, "I'm so sorry... but there's nothing down there save a locked door with no handle." He heaved another great breath and my stomach tightened. He didn't have to say it, Lily was dead.

CHAPTER NINE

Xenos Ranch

I THREW MYSELF onto the wet grass and wailed in anguish... something I had never done before. If someone had beaten me or cut my heart out, it would not have hurt as much as the pain of seeing Lily's limp body, plunge beneath the crystal water of the temple. At first no one comforted me. I felt no hand of reassurance, nor gentle word to ease the suffering, but it was not because no one cared. No... everyone else was as pained as I. A new thought then entered my foggy mind... but not by my own design. It was a voice, the soft one I had heard earlier while gazing into the hypnotic waters. However this time, the words were clear.

"It is your fault," came the voice. It sounded as though it were right inside of my head, for no one else seemed to notice... or perhaps they agreed. "You did this. You Alice, are responsible for your sister Lily's death. Her blood is on your hands!"

"It's true!" I fell to my knees clutching my head. "It *is* all my fault! If I hadn't wanted to stop for the night this never would have happened!"

Emma softly touched my shoulder. Her voice was deep and husky, "No Alice, this is not your fault. It is no one's fault."

I forced myself to open my swollen eyes. We were still caught deep within the clutches of the night. The air was calm and the stars above still twinkled as merrily as they had when we lived with Ms Craddock. Oliver was wrapped in a thick cloak, shivering slightly, his wet dark locks stuck to his forehead. Clara stood a ways off and was flushed a deep red, while her eyes rained tears upon the dewy grass. Emma kneeled beside me and lifted my chin; forcing me to look into her eyes. They were different somehow... still the same clear blue... but empty... very empty.

I flung myself into Emma's thin arms, which wrapped themselves protectively about me. "I'm so sorry Emma," I whispered into her shoulder. "I couldn't save her. I... I just stood there."

She tightened her grip around me. "There was nothing you could have done," Emma choked. "Had you tried, we would have lost you too."

Inside I knew this to be true, but it did not ease my suffering. "Oh Emma, it's not fair," I sobbed.

"No, it's not," she replied tightly and sucked back a breath. "If anyone has failed, it's myself. I am the eldest, therefore I should have been there to protect her. I will not fail again."

"Oh yes you will!" screeched a voice from above the temple. Jerking my head up I gasped, for it was the Witch from Petra, who was now hovering above the marble roof. A dusty black robe flowed about her skeletal limbs, as she threw back her head and laughed. "Poor little children! I advised you to run home, but did you listen? No! You continued to stick your noses into other's business! Well," she gloated, "let this be a lesson to you!"

"You old hag! Leave us alone!" Oliver cried and jumped to his feet, a menacing glare shining from his icy eyes.

"Stay out of this boy!" the Witch spat angrily. "This is none of your concern!" She narrowed her eyes slyly and reached into her cloak.

Emma stepped protectively in front of me. "Watch it Alice," she warned.

With a look of triumph, the Witch withdrew a lock of dark brown hair. "This is a symbol of my victory!" She tied the hair onto her belt. "And if you don't stop your pathetic little quest now, I'll have to add to my collection!"

"You monster!" Oliver grasped a large stone in his hand and was about to cast it at the Witch, when a soft voice from the edge of the forest called out.

"Flee sisters! Run away while you still can!" There was no mistaking the voice… it was Lily. "You mustn't give up! We can still win, now run!"

Oliver looked over his shoulder at us. There was a look of anguish in his handsome young face. "We must go," he said with a grimace.

Emma nodded towards him, as did Clara. I could say nothing as Emma took a tight hold of my hand and with a deep breath, turned and ran, pulling me behind. I was hardly aware of my surroundings when we reached the continuation of the road to Xenos Ranch, at the west end of the clearing. The Witch, for some odd reason had not pursued us, but I still sensed her presence, hovering… watching.

"Do not look back," Emma instructed us as she set a fast pace down the trail. Oliver and Clara hurried to get up front, neither one speaking a word nor making any move to look back.

Despite Emma's order, I couldn't help but take one last glance back and even though I was far away from the old hag, she stared directly into my eyes. She spoke, but it seemed that I was the only one to hear her voice and it was as though she were whispering into my very ear.

"Everywhere you go, I will be watching and waiting for the opportunity to strike, little one. When you close your eyes at night, beware, for I am skulking in the shadows, creeping about your nightmares, just waiting for you to let your guard down. I am the cold wind, the unnerving noise, the foul smell, the choking mist... I am part of what you fear most. And what's more... I serve the indestructible." I could fairly see the Witch licking her lips eagerly before her prey. "I know you Alice of Algernon. I know you. We have met before, but this time, you shall not win. This time, you shall die."

As the voice faded into the night, I slowly felt the Witch's presence drift away into a nightmare. "She's mad," I whispered.

"Shhh, Alice." Emma linked her arm with mine. "You..." She had trouble getting the words out. "You must be brave. We all must be." She stopped in the middle of the dirt road. "Do you understand?" she asked shutting her eyes tightly. "We cannot turn back now."

Clara nodded. "We know Emma. We must avenge the murder of Lily."

I noticed that Lily's pendant was now around Oliver's neck. He was starting to dry off, despite the cool of the night, yet still he shivered. "Though I only knew Lily for a short time, I cared deeply for her. I share your grief and desire to avenge her. I pledge myself to all of you, to the bitter end." He thrust his hand out, blue eyes glistening.

"To the bitter end," Clara placed her hand on top of his.

"The end," Emma nodded, as she lay her hand above Clara's.

Everyone stared expectantly at me, as I stood alone in the moonlight. My nightmare flashed before my eyes. I was alone... abandoned... forsaken. My mind cowered at the thought of being alone. It was my worst fear. Yet silently, I stepped forward and put my cold hand on top of Emma's. Raising my eyes to look into everyone else's solemn ones, I whispered hoarsely, "To the end."

*   *   *

I awoke with a stiff neck, slumped against the high wooden fence of Xenos Ranch. We had reached it just before dawn and as Oliver had earlier predicted, the gates were closed and bolted shut. Having no choice but to wait until morning, we had fallen asleep next to a stack of musty hay, just outside the doors. As if to suit the mood of the day, the sky was a mass of solid grey clouds and the smell of rain hovered in the air. Emma, Clara and Oliver were just standing up and stretching. They spoke of horses and the weather... but not one word about Lily. We couldn't... I knew I couldn't. I wanted to deceive myself, if only for a little while, into believing that Lily was still alive. Anything to ease the emptiness I felt inside.

"Come along Alice." Emma reached down and helped me up. "The gates are open now, so we must hurry and not tarry." She did not reveal any pain... the only evidence of loss was in her eyes... they had lost their sparkle.

"Xenos must be the owner of the ranch," Clara remarked evenly, as we entered the yard. It was a spacious ranch, with several stables lined up in rows and stacks of sweet smelling hay piled neatly against the stable walls. To our immediate left, was a large chateau, built carefully with smooth brown stone. A narrow chimney protruded from one end of the chateau and thin wisps of smoke curled softly skyward.

"Where is everyone?" I asked, surprised by the emptiness of the ranch.

"It's still early," Oliver noted. "Perhaps they are eating breakfast."

At the mention of food, I was reminded sharply of just how hungry I was from the long and arduous night. "Do you think they would spare us some food?"

"Let's find out. I'm sure they are nice folks. Surely some people around here are decent," Emma tried to convince herself.

As we approached the tall chateau, an old spotted dog came lumbering up to us, offering kisses all around. His soft deep eyes seemed to sense our sorrow and he offered what condolences he could. The smell of sizzling bacon wafted out of an open window, mingling with that of fresh baked bread. My stomach tightened painfully. Standing before the door, we could hear the sounds within quite plainly; pots and pans banging, a baby jabbering cheerfully and a woman humming softly.

Emma dusted off her dress which had ripped in one corner and rapped twice on the sun faded door. "We look like common beggars," she sighed, but held her shoulders back proudly.

There was a muffled sound of footsteps and soon the door opened, revealing a pretty young woman with curly red hair. She stood before us wiping her hands dry on her apron, which protected a soft green dress.

"Hello and what have we here?" she exclaimed in a loud but kind voice. Her sparkling green eyes scanned us over quickly and I detected a hint of pity.

"Good morning ma'am." Oliver stepped forward, flashing her a winning smile. Then with a bow, he continued smoothly, "My name is Oliver Renwick of Muir." His eyes laughed as he recalled where we had told the Deans we were from. It was a good village to claim connection to, since it was far enough away to be safe, but close enough to be believable. "These are my cousins, Emma, Clara and Alice." He indicated towards us. "We've come here to purchase some riding horses." Oliver held his smile.

The redheaded woman nodded knowingly. "Oh that's my husband's business. He's out doing chores right now, so why don't you all come in and wait for him. Breakfast is ready to be served, if you'd like something to eat." Again I saw the pity in her eyes. My stomach gurgled at the thought of food.

"Oh we couldn't impose," Emma graciously waved her hands in the air.

I sucked in a sharp breath. What was she doing? We were being offered food and she was trying to be polite! My panicking thoughts were cut short as the woman motioned us through the door.

"Nonsense! You're not imposing at all! I get visitors so rarely that it would be truly an honour to have you in!" She winked at me when she saw the relieved look on my face.

Oliver cleared his throat. "If it's all the same to you ma'am, I'll just go have a word with your husband in the stables." He clutched the sack of gold coins, which we had found in the chest from the orphanage.

"Whatever you wish," the woman nodded pleasantly, "so long as you promise to come eat afterwards."

Oliver grinned. "I wouldn't dream of passing up such an offer!" With that, he sprinted off for the stables.

"Come along my dears," the woman beckoned. "My name is Matilda Sanderson."

She led us into her cheerful and bright home. It was sparsely furnished, but welcoming just the same. There was an extremely large hearth in one corner, where the delicious smelling food sizzled and popped. Underneath a window was a long table, laden with various cooking utensils and ingredients. A number of dried herbs hung from the roof just above this table, releasing a pleasant aroma. There was a round eating table towards the center of the room, with six chairs around it. In the shadows I saw a flight of stairs, leading to the next level of the house where the bedrooms must be. On the other side of the room was another bright window, with an old woman seated in a willow rocking chair. She had her thin hand placed on a baby cradle, which she slowly rocked back and forth.

"What a lovely house!" Emma exclaimed, genuinely enthralled by the serene atmosphere. It was our first experience in a real home and I wished deeply that we could have been raised in such a lovely place.

"This is our happy little abode," Matilda smiled. "My husband Xenos works hard to look after it. It's been in the family for generations. His father, who was also named Xenos, inherited this ranch from his father, Xenos. The line stretches back for many generations," she declared proudly, as she indicated for us to be seated at the table. Matilda then continued jabbering away, as she got the breakfast ready. "I used to live in Petra, but I moved out here when I married Xenos seven years ago. I have found myself to be much happier out here than in Petra. No one trusts anyone there it's just horrible. I try not to go into town often, but when old man Xenos died a few winters ago, I was forced to meet up with the villagers at his funeral."

"We noticed that people are not very friendly in Petra," Clara stated as Matilda placed heaping plates of food before us, complete with a steaming fresh bun.

"It's a close knit community," Matilda sighed, "and they tend to be hostile towards outsiders." She walked over to the old woman and handed her a warm bun, which the woman took feebly. Matilda reached down into the cradle and withdrew a smiling baby with a tuft of red hair. "This is my child, Julia." She displayed the girl proudly, then indicated to the old woman. "That is my mother-in-law, Isadora." Then as she approached the table she lowered her voice, "Isadora hasn't spoken a word since her husband died. It's so very sad."

"Yes it is," I whispered quietly and Matilda looked sympathetically into my face. For a moment I felt warm inside, but it faded quickly.

"You have experienced great loss yourself," Matilda stated gently.

Emma stiffened, but replied, "Yes, we just lost our sister Lily last night. It happened along the road to your ranch, by a strange pond with white pillars and a marble roof."

Matilda's face paled and her grip on Julia tightened. "You went to the Heart Temple?"

"We just stopped there for the night," Clara explained as she took a small nibble at her bun.

"Oh mercy!" Matilda almost looked faint. "I would die of fear before I even came close to that accursed place!"

"You mean it is known to be dangerous?" I asked, feeling my throat tighten. I was glad I was almost done eating, for now I had lost my appetite.

"By the Power! You must have led a sheltered life!" Matilda ran a hand through her curls. "It is one of the most dangerous places in all of Algernon, probably in the entire land of Fadreama! Mind you, it hasn't always been like that. I can still recall the days when people used to make pilgrimages to the temple."

"I'm sorry to interrupt," Emma cut in, "but we are quite lost on this whole idea of temples."

Matilda raised an eyebrow in wonderment, but elaborated on her information. "The Heart Temple is one of the four sacred Virtue Temples in Algernon. They were build thousands of years ago by The Three—"

Clara cut in, "Who are The Three?"

Matilda shook her head in disbelief. "The Three, were the most powerful wizards of all time. One was Nissim, the other was Octavius and the last was Cloud Li. They served the monarchy of Algernon. Legend has it, that they built the four Virtue Temples to honour a great Queen and King. Each temple was said to house a virtue that the ruler was to possess." Matilda leaned back in her chair. "They were mostly used to connect the ruler to his people, especially those in the far reaches of the kingdom like us."

"If Nissim built that temple, then he would be thousands of years old..." I mused quietly to myself. "But it couldn't be the same Nissim then... could it?" No one had heard my soft whispers, but I felt as though the old woman... Isadora, had heard.

"When I was still young," Matilda explained as she broke a small piece of bread for Julia to munch on, "the Heart Temple was a place of healing. However, after King Alfred died, evil seemed to invade the sacred waters. Death came to all who ventured too close to the temple, or even walked about after sunset. There are corrupt beings in this forest, who prey upon the people of this land. Mind you, we're not as affected up here by Ralston Radburn," she shivered at the name, "as the people in say, Jadestone. But the evil is creeping farther and farther north. Someday, darkness will envelope us, as it has the south." A tear slipped out of the corner of her eye and splashed on Julia's tiny head. "I fear for my baby's future. What will the kingdom be like when she is my age? I don't like to even imagine. Everyone in Algernon is a prisoner, sentenced to death, though some more severely than others."

There was silence after this last piece of information had been revealed. There was so much suffering in the world that my pain seemed insignificant, although that did not make it hurt any less. A question formed in my mind and before I knew it, I felt myself asking, "What are the other temples?" Matilda blinked. "You said there were four, but you only named one," I clarified.

"The next one I believe is the Temple of Strength," Matilda mused. "It's located somewhere in the Plains of Algernon." Julia began to cry and Matilda rocked her softly. "The other one is the Temple of Wisdom... I think that one is in the Sterling Hills. The last is located in the capital city, Devona. It is the Temple of Courage. The Power only knows how corrupt those southern temples have become. I shudder to think of it."

"If only we had known this information before, perhaps Lily would still be alive." I felt regret flood my mind once again. "It's all my fault you know."

Matilda and my sisters stared at me with a mixture of pity and sadness. "Child," Matilda began, "you need to move on. I know the grief is still fresh in your memory, but it will destroy you if you let it. Think, is this what Lily would have wanted?" I shook my head and fought back tears. "Now come on," Matilda said briskly, "I'm going to make you a basket of food for your journey... you're going home to Muir I assume?"

"Yes of course," Emma replied quickly. "We are indeed heading home."

Clara and Emma began to help clear away the breakfast dishes, while Matilda handed Julia to me. "You can look after her while we get things cleaned up."

I took the tiny child in my arms and looked down at her miniature features. Her eyes were a faint green like her mother's and judging by what little hair she already had, I predicted that Julia would be a replica of Matilda Sanderson. I walked over to the window where Isadora sat in silence. "If we succeed," I told the baby, "you will not have to grow up in a world of evil." She was so innocent and unknowing. Something stirred deep inside of me at the injustice of a child being born into a world without peace... a world that was on the brink of destruction. Julia fixed her gaze up at me and cooed softly. "What will happen to you if we fail?" I asked quietly, smoothing back the tuft of down on the baby's head.

"Then... we... will... all... die..." came Isadora's croaky voice beside me.

I stared in wonderment at the wizened old woman. She was as fragile as Julia, though she was no longer innocent. Her deep set blue eyes revealed much pain and suffering. "You spoke," I found myself whispering.

"Of course I spoke," she replied, chuckling silently. "Now that I actually have something to say, I will speak. I have seen many things in my lifetime... both good and bad." She coughed painfully. "I don't believe I will be seeing much more in this age, but before I go, I want to know that this is not the end for our world." Her withered hand grasped my arm. "I want to know that my granddaughter will have a chance to grow up."

I stood speechless. I didn't know what to say to old Isadora. She was dying and pleading on behalf of her granddaughter's future... so did she know of our mission?

"I know very well what you are thinking Alice," came Isadora's weak voice once again. "I have powers too you know." She shrugged her thin shoulders and continued, "Old age doesn't dim my abilities, no, rather it enhances them. I know who you are and where you are going. I only wish I could go with you... and help in any way possible." She sighed and looked unhappy. "However, that is impossible now. I am old and weak." Her brow creased slightly. "But I am *not* senile. My mind is as sharp now as it ever was." Isadora beckoned for me to lean closer. "You must beware of the other three temples child! I see only pain and suffering anywhere near them... especially for you Alice." Though her eyes were fixed on me, she was not seeing my face. "I see fire... flames and smoke in a storm."

"What do you mean?" I panicked. "What's going to happen?" Julia reached up and grabbed a lock of my dark hair, before stuffing it into her drooling mouth.

Isadora grabbed my hand and I felt something cool slip around my middle finger. "You are so confused, I know," she sympathized, "but in time it will all pass. In time, you will come to understand things. It may take a lifetime to learn, but that is part of what it means to be human. It is a journey of understanding our place and purpose. May the Power guide and protect you."

As she lapsed back into silence, I looked down at my finger. It was a seal ring, for pressing into hot wax when sealing a document. I gazed at the beautiful and intricate carvings with awe. There was a heart with a quill pen and sword forming an 'X' across the front. Above the heart was a beautiful crown, covered in jewels. Written underneath the carving were the words, '*Oc Jykpea Yh Focohla*'. I looked up and whispered, "It is the same as our pendants."

"It means, 'All Virtues in Balance,'" Isadora told me with a glint in her eyes.

There was a knock at the door and in stepped Oliver, beaming with pride. "I got us four beautiful ponies!" he exclaimed happily.

"All our horses are of excellent quality," Matilda smiled, as she drew him to the table and placed a plate in front of him. "Eat up young one."

"Xenos praised your cooking skills highly," Oliver told her with his usual charm.

Since Isadora had become silent again, her eyes had clouded over. I knew she would never speak again. She wanted peace... I wanted to reassure her, but somehow the words wouldn't come out. Besides, if peace was to be brought about, it certainly would not be by my hand. No, my sisters and Oliver were in charge. I was just in the way and once we found Prince Edric, he would set everything right, without any of our help.

*   *   *

When Oliver had finished eating, he brought us outside to view his purchase. The ponies were truly beautiful. They were all a soft shade of grey with a silver mane. Although they were mostly the same size, the pony I was given, was slightly smaller than the rest and had four black spots on its rump. I hugged the pony's large head and looked into her soft eyes, which stared gently back into mine.

"I shall call you Moondancer." I smiled as I ran my fingers through her silky mane. Somehow Oliver had managed to get us saddles and bridles for the beautiful ponies, although my sisters and I had no idea how to put them on or take them off. In fact, we had never ridden a horse before, but Xenos had assured Oliver that his ponies were well trained and gentle.

"Oh how exciting!" Clara exclaimed as she sat in the saddle proudly. "My darling pony is called Storm and together we shall have many adventures!"

Emma sat uncertainly at first in the saddle, but soon her back was straight and her head held high. "My pony will be called Lady and I should like for everyone to refer to her as such."

I turned to face Oliver who was looking pensive as he sat upon his mount. "What name did you give your horse?" I asked him, amused by the look on his face.

"I'm just thinking of that now..." He snapped his fingers. "I've got it! Nightflame!"

"Very mysterious and intriguing," I mused to myself.

Matilda reached up and handed a basket to Emma. "Take care of yourself," she smiled kindly. "I hope you reach home soon." She was holding baby Julia in her arms. "If you're ever in Petra again, be sure to come visit!"

Emma smiled. "We will Matilda and thank you so much for breakfast. You are truly a kind soul."

I had been curious to see what Xenos looked like, but he was still out in the stables working and it wouldn't be appropriate to make him come bid us farewell. At any rate, Oliver had told us that he was a very kind young man.

Matilda took baby Julia's hand and moved it up and down. "Wave goodbye to everyone Julia," Matilda giggled.

Oliver led the way out of the ranch, followed closely by Clara, then Emma and finally myself. As we passed through the gate and onto the road, I cast one backward glance at the Sanderson home. Although I couldn't be certain, I thought I saw Isadora standing in the window, her hand over her heart in a gesture of goodwill. I hadn't told anyone of our conversation and I didn't intend to... although I wasn't quite sure why. Maybe I feared being scolded or laughed at, but somehow I felt as though the conversation between old Isadora and myself, should go no further. Her warning echoed in my head with painful clarity, "*I see fire... flames and smoke in a storm.*"

I shivered. What could it mean? She hadn't said where, or when or even why. There were so many unknowns... including the possibility that she was just a rambling old woman, but I knew in my heart that she wasn't. Only one thing was certain; danger lay ahead and we were moving straight into it.

CHAPTER TEN

Charon's Gate

*A*LTHOUGH RIDING on our beautiful grey ponies was a quicker way to travel, it was not the most comfortable. None of us were used to having our bottoms bounced up and down and so despite the soft saddle, we soon found ourselves in pain. However the thought of stopping was never once voiced, as we would rather have sore bottoms, than risk any more tragedies on the side of the road. Overall, purchasing the ponies had been an excellent investment, as there was a great deal of room for carrying supplies in the leather saddlebags. Either Xenos was very generous, or Oliver was an excellent bargainer, for we still had many gold coins left in our money satchel. This was a great relief, considering how far we had to travel yet.

Following the road back to Petra, we soon reached the Heart Temple. Unfortunately, since the road went straight through the clearing, we had no choice but to pass by it. Oliver reined Nightflame at the edge of the clearing and looked pensive. In the daytime, with golden sunlight streaming through the trees, the temple did not look quite so mysterious as it had in the silver moonlight.

"Do you think the Witch is still nearby?" I rode up beside Clara and Storm.

Clara pursed her lips tightly and pushed a strand of hair behind her ears. "I don't know Alice. Everything seems quiet... but... it's hard to tell."

"I say we ride hard and fast through the clearing." Emma's face was hard with determination. "We are in more danger standing around here, than we are riding like the wind. Let's make haste!"

Oliver nodded. "I'll lead the way! Let's go!"

Spurring Nighflame into action, Oliver sped across the clearing, with Clara on Storm nipping at his heels. Emma and Lady stayed behind Clara, if only to make sure that Moondancer and I followed. I lowered my head down onto my pony's neck, burying my face in her soft silver mane, all the while praying that she would follow the others' lead. As we sped through the clearing, I had expected to sense the presence of evil, but I felt nothing but a deep sadness... Lily's sadness. The Heart Temple now had a guardian... and it was my dear sister Lily. "Oh Lily, watch over this sacred place. Someday, I'll return and build a memorial for you, I prom-

80

ise. Until then, all I can offer you is my love." I squeezed my eyes shut and let Moondancer run, as tears streamed down my cheeks.

*   *   *

When we arrived in Petra, the people were once again out and about, selling their wares and doing daily errands. Unfortunately they were no friendlier today, than they had been before. As we rode through the village square, everyone seemed to stop and stare at us with huge eyes. I supposed it must be an odd sight; four young people on ghostly ponies, returning alive from a much feared path.

"They actually returned!" a bearded man exclaimed to his wife.

She shook her head. "No, no! Look, they are missing one girl... the pale one is gone."

I bit my lip angrily and suddenly reigned Moondancer in front of the couple. "That right!" I cried. "My sister died at the Heart Temple and now she is its guardian. Because of everyone's 'kindness' she is dead!" I held back a sob. "When Algernon is free and the Heart Temple once again sacred, it is the Priestess Lily, through whom you shall make pleas. Remember that name in the future!"

Surprised by my outburst, the bearded man stepped forward with a look of awe on his face. "Where are you going?"

This time it was Emma who answered, "We are heading to Devona, where we shall locate Prince Edric!"

I had expected the villagers to laugh, but instead they stared solemnly at us. "Bless you!" one woman cried.

"May the Power protect you!" shouted another.

"Save us!" called a voice from the back.

To my surprise, villagers crowded around us and filled our saddlebags with supplies. I could not believe my eyes! They took us seriously and actually had faith in our mission!

"Go now!" ordered a burly man. "Ride on for freedom!"

Taking this as our exit cue, we trotted down the road, leaving Petra and its villagers behind. I awaited Emma's scolding for my outburst, but instead she said gently, "I am proud of you Alice." She pulled Lady up beside me. "I was shocked to see you standing up for something you believe in. No offence darling sister, but bravery is not exactly your strong point."

My grip on the reigns tightened imperceptivity. "I just couldn't stand to see them whispering about something they knew nothing of. If only someone would have taken us out to the ranch, we wouldn't have had to stop and Lily would still be with us."

"There is nothing we can do to change the past. It is the future we need to shape." Emma looked at me sideways. "Do you really think Lily is now the guardian there?"

I looked up at the sparkling sunshine which filtered through the canopy of trees. "I don't know actually. I felt something as we rode through there… it was very sad."

Emma did not reply and I knew that the conversation was over. "The growth is very thick through here," she commented more so to Clara, who rode just a little ways in front of her.

"And it seems to be getting more and more overgrown," Clara agreed as she ducked a low hanging branch.

"It's probably because no one in the Forgotten Forest travels south anymore," Oliver hypothesized. "For the northerners, the south means only one thing and that's Ralston Radburn." He lowered his voice as he spoke this name. "They have no reason or desire to go in this direction and as a result, the forest has begun to take back the road."

"The leaves are just starting on these trees and yet the branches are so thick and tangled that I can hardly see the sky." Clara tipped her head upward.

"It does make things rather dark," Emma mused, as she scanned the odd assortment of plant growth. "Look at all the mushrooms!"

"Such colours!" I breathed with delight. Ms Craddock had educated us somewhat in herbs, but Emma especially had been interested in learning about it. The dim sunlight and moist ground, had created the perfect conditions for a vast population of mushrooms to flourish and I could tell that Emma was eager to pick some.

When we stopped for a lunch break and to rest our aching bottoms, Emma set off with a saddlebag to collect various specimens for our journey. "We can sell some to people outside of the forest and use the rest for food or medicine," she told us with great excitement. It was a relief to see something of a sparkle in Emma's eyes again, if only for a short time.

"I think I shall collect some firewood," Clara declared, grabbing the saddlebag off of Storm. "Wood might be scarce beyond the forest."

Oliver and I were left to finish eating the food Matilda Sanderson had packed for us. I leaned back leisurely, as Oliver nibbled on a piece of cheese and studied the map carefully.

"Are you going to miss the forest?" I asked him suddenly.

He looked up. "Eh? Miss the forest? I suppose so… I never really thought about it actually." Oliver put a hand behind his head and laughed. "Never coming back here didn't really cross my mind, but I suppose that's always a possibility. Are you going to miss it Alice?"

"I think so," I replied, shifting my back against a moss covered boulder. "I grew up here and this is all I know." I plucked at a blade of grass absently. "Trees, trees and more trees. That's all I've ever seen... and unlike Clara, I don't crave adventure. The world beyond the forest scares me."

"You might change your mind later." Oliver smiled charmingly. "Who's to say? Maybe you'll like the world beyond the forest. We still have to travel through the plains, a river valley, foothills and mountains. Wouldn't you like to see mountains?"

Wrapping my arms around my knees I sighed. "I guess so. But we're going to be in so much danger, that it's not even going to be enjoyable."

"Well *I* want to see the mountains," Oliver declared. "I've only ever heard Arvad describe them. I don't really care for the danger part either though." Then glancing sideways at me, Oliver asked, "Hey what's that on your finger?" He pointed to the seal ring from Isadora. "I never noticed you wearing that before."

"Oh this? Uh..." I paused. "Don't tell anyone Oliver," I lowered my voice, "but Xenos's mother gave this to me. I don't really know why. I gather she took a fancy to me..." The words I had exchanged with the old woman would not leave my mouth. Our conversation was locked away in the recesses of my mind.

Oliver took my hand to get a closer look at it. "It's very pretty. I wonder where she got it." Releasing my hand he grinned, "Don't worry, I won't tell your sisters. They seem to keep a close eye on you, especially Emma."

"She worries about me," I laughed and smoothed my brown hair back. "She thinks I'm too dreamy. Maybe I am a little," I confessed, "but I maintain that someday I'll mature."

"There's no point in growing up too fast," Oliver observed with a laugh. "We're only young for so long." He then focused his attention back on the map which he had absently set in his lap. "You know Alice, there's something about this map that bothers me."

Moving over to his side, I looked down at the parchment. "What are you looking at?" I asked.

He pointed to a strange line, which jutted across the entire span of the Forgotten Forest and divided it from the plains. "What do you think that line could mean?"

I stared for a moment at the strange markings. "Well, if you look right here," I indicated to where our road crossed the line, "it says..." I squinted. "Charon's Gate... Charon's Gate? What does that mean? Is there a wall across the kingdom?"

"Now what would be the point of that?" Oliver mused.

"Protection." Emma came up from behind us. "The wall is probably used to protect the people of the north. It may be one of the reasons why these northern people have evaded Ralston's grasp for so long." She traced her finger on the map. "Look how the line almost attaches to where the mountains come up on both sides of Algernon. Denzel the Dark Coast surrounds us on three sides, right? However the mountains protect us up until a point. Then there is a gap, where the Denzelians could enter Algernon from the north through the forest. But look, with the dividing wall, the Denzelians are kept out of Algernon completely... or at least have a harder time getting in."

"That makes sense," Oliver agreed thoughtfully. "I just hope it doesn't cause problems for us getting out."

All too soon, our break was over and we found ourselves painfully back in the saddle. "I may never be able to sit down again," I muttered to myself, as I bounced up and came down hard.

We rode without breaks and almost in total silence. Any words that were exchanged had either to do with supplies, the map or the weather. Emma was concerned about us being out on the open plains without shelter. My mind recalled Isadora's warning about storms once again, but the idea scared me so much that I pushed the thought out of my head. The weather was fair now, although the sun was on its downward path... and soon we would be in the darkness once again.

The forest cooled down rapidly and I clutched my cloak about my shoulders, while keeping one hand on Moondancer's reigns. At this time yesterday, Lily had still been alive. I shivered and decided that I would not ask to stop for the night, as that would only lead to trouble.

Glancing up at Oliver, I saw that he was trying to read the map in the fading light. "I think we can reach the wall tonight," he announced optimistically.

"Excellent," Emma approved. "I should like to be out of the forest soon. There are too many places for *things* to hide." She cast a glance nervously over her shoulder and into the dark bushes.

I heard the flapping of wings overhead and just caught a glimpse of an enormous raven, passing overhead. The bird's yellow eyes glared suspiciously at us from above. Clara frowned. "I saw that same bird when we were coming back from the ranch."

"Nonsense Clara, there are many ravens in the forest. It can't possibly be the same one," Emma contradicted, though nervously. "We just tend to blow things out of proportion when darkness falls. Let us continue on without scaring ourselves."

It wasn't very long after, that we saw a massive stonewall looming across the road in front of us. "There it is," Oliver pointed out, "right where it's supposed to be. Who could have built such a thing?"

As we approached the magnificent structure, we found that the stones used to build it were impossibly large, as though pieces of a mountain had been lopped off and fitted together perfectly. The wall was obviously very ancient, as moss grew heavily upon it and trees pressed sharply into its sides. However not one stone was cracked nor crumbling and the structure stood firm against the push of the forest. Where the road met the wall, there was an impressive wooden gate, which also showed no signs of aging. The wood smelled new, as though freshly hewn. Elaborate carvings covered the wooden gate, depicting vast fields of farmland, with lush crops blowing in the wind. Two torches were mounted on either side of the door, but not surprisingly, were unlit.

"So how do we get through?" I asked, scanning the wall for some form of lever or handle, with which to open the great gate.

Oliver and Clara dismounted and began to search the wall. "There's nothing to open the door with." Clara looked confused as she blew a hair out of her face.

"The gate is locked shut too," Oliver confirmed, as he banged his shoulder hard into the solid wood.

"Just stay calm," Emma warned, without getting off of Lady. "There must be a way through. One doesn't just build a gate that cannot be opened. If we have to, we'll burn the gate down..." As these words left her lips, the two torches mounted on the cold stonewall burst into blue flames with a crackle.

Oliver laughed nervously. "I guess the gate doesn't like the idea of being burned down." He slammed into the carved wood once again. "It's still locked though."

Sliding down off of Moondancer, I felt a strange presence in the air. It was one of great frustration, arrogance and anger. The blue flames gave us some light, which was comforting, for now the sun had set and we were once again at the mercy of the night. I inspected the grey stone around the edge of the gate. It had been concealed in the shadows before, but now with the torches, I was able to see the grooves where each stone had been fitted together. Hoping to find a lever, I was shocked when the crawling vines attached to the stone, drew back when I touched them. I held in a frightened gasp as words carved into the stone were revealed beneath the vines.

"I'm telling you, there has to be a switch or something!" Clara crossed her arms stubbornly as she faced Emma, who had finally dismounted.

"The doors are just stuck Clara," Emma replied firmly. "Oliver," she ordered, "keep trying to open them. We may all have to push... maybe get the horses to help," she mused.

"Maybe we should try pulling?" Oliver joked, but quieted after Emma shot him an annoyed look.

I turned my gaze back to the writing on the wall. The first section was written in ancient Algernonian, which I could not read, but beside it, were words written in modern speech. I hesitated. It seemed like instructions of some sort. Suddenly, I felt a compelling urge to say the words out loud and so quietly I began:

"If you dare to go outside,
You must first prove your worth inside.
Charon's tasks you must complete,
For she is the appointed gatekeep.
To call upon this tormented soul,
This chant you must speak in whole:

Spirits, ghost and those long gone,
I call upon you, as I sing this song.
The special trials I will complete,
If only with Charon I can meet.
So come forth now from your eternal rest,
And put my courage to the test."

As I finished speaking these words, my mouth suddenly felt dry as parchment and I could almost taste the magic I had just spoken. I stood straight up and glanced over my shoulder at the others. They were still discussing the gate situation. For a moment, I didn't think that anything was going to happen, but I then noticed that our horses were pawing anxiously at the ground. Moondancer's eyes were rolling back in panic as she suddenly reared and let out a neigh of terror. Swiftly I was at her side, jumping at the swinging reigns and trying to get a hold of her.

"Alice!" Emma cried sharply. "What did you do now?"

"Nothing!" I exclaimed as a gust of wind swept up a cloud of dust and swirled it around mercilessly. The two torches mounted on the sides of the wall, suddenly glowed brighter than before with a crackle. The eerie light cast misshapen shadows across the forest floor.

"Alice!" Emma called out again in a tight voice. "Tell me what you did! Don't lie because I know you must be behind this somehow!" She ran for shelter beside Lady. Both Clara and Oliver scurried wordlessly to their own horses, wild looks of fascination in their eyes.

"Whatever you did Alice," Clara cried half gleefully half frightened, "we're going to get some action!"

"The flaring torches were impressive," Oliver joked but only received a mouthful of dust.

"All I did was read some words carved into the wall!" I shielded my eyes against Moondancer's heaving body.

"And you didn't think to warn us before you spoke?" Emma was indignant. "You have to learn to think before you act sister!"

There was no time to defend my actions, for suddenly there was a brilliant flash of blue light in the air before us. My teeth chattered in the cold which followed the blinding blueness. As the light dimmed slightly, my hand flew to my mouth in shock. Floating in the air just a short distance from where we stood, was a tall, slender lady of undeterminable age. Her beauty was unparalleled, with her high cheekbones and dainty, slightly upturned nose. However without a doubt, the most striking feature of this lady, was the fact that she was completely blue, from her flowing metallic hair, to her graceful bare feet.

She did not speak at first, but instead stood eyeing our party, with narrow icy eyes. The cold wind fluttered through her long glittering dress, which had revealing slits on each side. Perhaps the only part of her that wasn't blue, was the thick silver belt pulled tightly about her tiny waist. She toyed with a strand of hair behind a pointed blue ear and then pursed her lips tightly.

As she opened her mouth to speak, I suddenly had a vision of the ocean, with its glassy dark waves, crashing over sharp rocks. "I am Charon," she stated while crossing her arms, which had a soft blue aura about them, "and I dislike mortals." She glared at us again carefully. "Actually," she smiled coldly, "I dislike mortal girls."

I felt my feet sliding backwards slowly, taking me farther behind Moondancer. I didn't *want* to be a coward and run away. After all, it was me who had called this lady from beyond. Yet a fear that was almost too strong to fight, was trying to make me as small as possible.

Charon hovered near Oliver and smiled arrogantly. She put a long finger under his chin and looked into his eyes. "Much too young, but he will be a handsome man no doubt. A real heartbreaker!" she laughed, causing frost to cover an overhanging tree branch. "You look so much like someone I used to know," she told Oliver with a sad look and then almost immediately, her attitude took over once again.

Oliver gulped and tried to step back, but Charon caught his wrist tightly. "Um... miss, your hand is really quite cold." Oliver's unruly black hair hid his blue eyes, along with the fear, which I knew had to be in them.

She stuck out her lip in a mock pout. "Oh poor baby." She threw back her head and had a good long, oceanic laugh. "Now," she turned her attention back to us, a mischievous grin plastered across her elfin features, "which one of you summoned me?"

My fingers clawed into Moondancer's flesh, as I broke out into a cold sweat. What would she do to the person who had called her?

Charon placed her free hand on her hip, giving Oliver a brutal yank.

"Look, someone obviously wanted to attempt, notice I said attempt, my trials, so they had better speak up."

Clara shot me a look and winked. Stepping forward she smiled, "It was I Charon, who summoned you here to us."

For a moment Charon just hovered there, staring into Clara's face, while keeping a firm grip on poor Oliver's wrist. "How dare you!" Charon suddenly shrieked. "Do you think you can deceive me? Me? Charon?" She stretched out her arm, palm facing out and let loose a mighty blast of ice cold air, sending Clara flying into the base of a tree. Lines appeared in the corners of Charon's eyes, as she narrowed them to little more then a slit. With a tremendous swoosh, she back flipped onto the top of the wall, bringing the unwilling Oliver with her.

Emma had run over to Clara and was just helping her to stand, when Charon began to speak once again. "Do you see what's over this wall boy?" she asked Oliver, who was staring wide-eyed at whatever lay before him. "You and this little group, obviously want to go onto that side, for that is why I was summoned from my peaceful rest. I find this waking world torture every second I'm in it!" She massaged her temples. "I want to go back to my rest as soon as possible, so let's just get this over with. Whoever spoke the sacred words had better step forward or else," she grabbed Oliver with amazing strength by the neck and dangled him over the edge of the extremely tall wall, "this mortal boy has a little fall and breaks his cute neck!"

It felt as though something inside of me was coming loose. A rope of fear had begun to fray and I ran out from behind Moondancer. "Stop! Stop!" I screamed. "It was me!"

Charon gave a small half smile and set a breathless Oliver back on the top of the wall. "I know," she gritted between blue teeth. "I despise cowards," she sniffed and floated down to us, holding Oliver by the wrist and dropped him a short distance from the ground. He landed with a grunt and gingerly touched his red neck.

Emma approached my side and put a protective arm around me. "What do you want us to do?"

Charon raised a well shaped blue eye brow and cocked her head to the side. "Us? What do you mean us? It was this girl here, who spoke the awakening spell. It is she who must face my trials in the Land of the Undead."

I caught a sob in my throat before it could escape and betray my mind numbing fear. What a foolish girl I was shaping up to be! I could not cry... I would not cry. Oliver had not cried, even when he was in the clutches of this arrogant gatekeeper. I sighed inwardly... I was not Oliver...

I was not strong either and the tears slipped down my cheeks, despite my efforts.

Emma squeezed my shoulders tighter. "We are a team," she told Charon. "Wherever Alice goes, we go and whatever she must do, we also shall do."

Charon was not looking at Emma, but at me... and her gaze was one of disgust. "A weak wretch," she muttered and then looked up at Emma. "So you all wish to suffer?"

Emma nodded resolutely. "A great adventure," Clara added, now recovered from her smash into the tree. "Something history will remember us for."

"We stick together," Oliver finished off, folding his arms tightly, Charon's finger imprints still clear around his neck.

"You're even more stupid than I though!" Charon laughed. "But, no matter. You shall all perish then, for no one has ever overcome my trials before."

"Probably because no one has tried," Oliver whispered, as he came to stand beside me. I giggled in spite of my tears. "Don't worry Alice. This lady is all talk."

"I'm also all ears!" Charon was suddenly only a handbreadth away from us, her icy breath cold and fresh on our faces. "Joke all you wish mortals, because soon you shall be no more. When you fail and are brought before me on your knees, it is I who shall be doing the laughing! For my name is Charon and I mock thee!"

With that said, she thrust her hand out behind her and a great black portal seemed to rip through the fabric of the air. Feeling the presence of Clara behind me, I felt slightly strengthened, as I stared into the impenetrable gloom.

"I don't like the looks of this," I told Emma as I grabbed onto her cloak with white knuckles.

"Great deeds, heroism, fame, glory..." Clara repeated over and over to herself. "Surely we will be recognized in history for facing this trial."

"Time to go!" Charon laughed, as the portal began to suck everything towards it.

We all fell forward onto our knees as the portal pulled us inwards, ready to either devour or transport us. I didn't even have time to be terrified, for all too swiftly we were swept up into the air and tossed like dry leaves into the suffocating darkness. The last image I saw before my mind was engulfed by the nothingness, were the bright yellow eyes of a raven, sitting high upon a tree branch, watching as we spiralled out of sight.

CHAPTER ELEVEN

The Land of the Undead

I HELD MY BREATH and shut my eyes tightly, as we whirled headlong in the abyss. When I finally worked up the courage to crack my eyes open, all I saw was complete and total darkness. I could not see my sisters or Oliver, but their screams informed me that they were near... Clara's sounded almost excited... almost, but not quite. Emma's screams were of terror, which matched my own nicely. My thoughts turned to Lily and I wondered if we would soon be meeting up with her again. I didn't get very much thinking done, for soon we crash landed painfully upon sharp rocks. My eyes had shut upon impact, but once I opened them again, I quickly wished that I hadn't.

A nauseous sensation welled up in my stomach, as I surveyed our new surroundings. It was truly a barren and desolate place, with jagged cliffs jutting out as far as the eye could see. It appeared to be some sort of mountain range, except that the cliffs were an ugly combination of black and red. It seemed to me that we had landed upon the summit of the tallest mountain, for we appeared to be presiding over the entire landscape. Wisps of dark clouds encircled the peaks of all the other mountains, but did not seem to touch the one we were on. The air was clear, but very thin, making breathing a painful struggle. It wasn't long before my throat began to burn. None of us had spoken or moved, for it was all we could do to catch our breath.

I leaned back on my hands and felt the ground give way slightly. Searing pain shot through my wrists and a numbing coldness penetrated my fingers. Taking a closer look, I realized that the ground was covered with what looked like old snow... but was so black that it couldn't possibly be. Yet my hands were freezing cold and my wrists were cut from breaking through the icy surface. Wiping the blood on my dress and trying to hide my tears, I attempted to speak.

"Emma, my wrists," I managed, but the thin air did not carry sound well and I only succeeded in making my throat raw. Fortunately, Emma had seen my mishap and weakly crawled towards me, tearing long strips from her dress to bind my wounds. Tilting my head skyward, my stomach turned again at the sickening green hue in the sky. How I longed for the bright sapphire blue sky of Algernon! Emma hugged me gently and dropped a kiss on my head, before standing up and raising me to my feet. Clara and Oliver followed this lead, albeit, painfully.

"So you finally decided to get up!" Charon spoke suddenly, as though she had been there the entire time. "I was beginning to think you were beaten already... especially the one who summoned me! She isn't even here five minutes and she's already injured! I mock thee!" Charon doubled up in a very unladylike manner.

"Oh mock yourself," Clara muttered and clutched her throat.

"Let's get on with it," Oliver gasped, a look of impatience playing upon his handsome features.

"So anxious to end your life!" Charon smirked. "Well, whatever! I'm just the gatekeeper! When King Alfred ruled, anyone could pass in and out of the gate, but that was no fun! Now at least I can make others suffer as I do!"

I felt a brief moment of sympathy for Charon, as she was obviously very unhappy, but the gravity of our situation quickly dissolved that emotion. Emma squeezed her eyes painfully and asked, "Please, what do we do?"

"Wouldn't you like to know!" Charon chuckled, as she touched her sparkly blue cheek playfully.

This time, is was Oliver whose anger had boiled over. Blue eyes flashing, he stood right underneath Charon. "Look, I don't know who you think you are, but we've come a long way and we still have a long way to go. Stop wasting our time and just tell us what we have to do, so we can get out of this world and be on our way!" I could tell his throat was in agony at that moment, for his face was twitching in pain, but he seemed to have authority in his voice. He reminded me of myself when I had yelled at the villagers in Petra. There was only so much a person could take before they had to release their anger.

"Oh I *do* like you!" Charon smiled tightly and licked her lips. "Very well! Inside of that cave over there," she pointed to a small tunnel on a sharp outcrop nearby, "there is an item called the Diamond Rose. It is a very special, very magical item, created by The Three, long ago. There were once many, but now only this one exists and I have possession of it!" Charon did a gleeful jig in the air. "Now, my trial is quite simple. One of you, just one of you, must touch the rose before it reaches full bloom. If someone can do this, which I highly doubt, then everyone gets to go free and..." Charon's eyes narrowed further, "as an added bonus, you will get to keep the Diamond Rose!" She waved her hands in the air. "But there is really no chance of that happening!"

"We will not fail," Emma stated hoarsely.

"Oh believe me you will," Charon seethed, "and when you do, everyone will be forced to spend eternity here! Your souls will be trapped in this land, lost between life and death! Haven't you noticed how the thin air is sucking the life out of you right now?" She inspected her bright blue fingernails. "The Rose takes 20 minutes to bloom, incidentally the amount of time a mortal can stay alive in the Land of the Undead." She calculated something on her fingers. "Let's see, you've been here for 10 minutes already, so that leaves…" she clapped her hand facetiously, "10 minutes left before the Rose blooms and your souls become trapped!"

A look of horror spread across Emma's strained features and grabbing my hand, she began racing for the cave entrance, with Clara and Oliver close behind. I felt as though I were suffocating, for each time I drew in a breath, hardly any air seemed to come out of it. The black 'snow,' sliced at our ankles as we plodded through it, leaving a trail of scarlet blood in the dead world. Emma didn't even hesitate when we reached the dark entrance. Running headlong into it, I realized that there were blue fire torches mounted on the stonewalls, giving us a minimal amount of light.

We stood in the middle of a perfectly round chamber, with great stalactites and stalagmites protruding from the ceiling and floor. The cave smelled rotten, damp and utterly disgusting. I shuddered at the thought of spending an eternity here.

"Look," Clara choked and pointed in front of us. There were five different tunnels, each with blue torches to illuminate the passageways.

"We can each take a route," Emma mused clenching her fists, "but one of them could be the wrong. There are only four of us… and five tunnels."

"There's no time to discuss this," Oliver winced.

"We must split up and hope the Power guides us," Clara affirmed, while clutching at her throat.

"Let's go!" Emma declared, as Clara and Oliver each took off down a tunnel. Emma turned to me. "Be brave Alice." She offered no more advice and left me standing alone in the circular chamber.

I gasped. Only one of us had to touch the Rose, but how much time was left? I stared at the remaining two passageways. Which one? I wanted to just sit down and hope that either one of my sisters or Oliver reached the Rose… but there was the chance that the correct tunnel was one of my choices. Therefore I couldn't just sit, waiting for the others to save us… I had to at least try. Sucking in a painful breath, I raced into one of the tunnels.

From the moment I entered the stale smelling corridor, I knew that I had taken the wrong one. Something about it just didn't feel right… Suddenly I felt a airy hand on my right shoulder, jerking me backwards. I stopped just before the edge of a jagged pit. I peered into the ebony hole, which I had nearly fallen into. What had stopped me? I was completely alone and yet, I could have sworn a hand had stayed my shoulder. Lily?

"Don't give up Alice..." a ghostly voice echoed off the moist stone.

With a little yelp of fear, I raced back to the circular chamber and without hesitation, entered the other passageway. I silently offered a prayer to the Power, for now I was running so fast that if there were another pit, stopping would be impossible. I finally did have to slow my pace however, for the tunnel was becoming smaller and smaller, as well as terribly twisted. Before long, I found myself crawling through the tiny space, all the while cutting my knees and ripping my dress on the slime coated floor.

My fingers started to go numb with cold and I fumbled as my coordination faded. The passageway was now too small for torches and my heart nearly thumped out of my chest as I moved forward in the darkness. I could have died when I felt cold wet sludge hanging from the ceiling slap me in the face. The sludge was sickening and relentless. It hung in sheets from the roof and I was forced to push my poor face through every one of them.

The tunnel began to slope sharply upwards and before long, I found myself struggling to crawl uphill. Once or twice I lost my footing and slipped a little ways, but instead of crying as I normally would have, I felt myself grow more and more determined to keep going. Then suddenly, without warning, a glowing green bat appeared before me. The tunnel was too small to go around him and too steep to retreat. I froze in terror, cramps clutching my insides...The bat's face was human! Fringed in wiry black fur and glowing with a green aura, the creature glared hard at me and revealed it's fangs with a hiss. Poison glistened on the ends of the pearly white teeth and I resisted the urge to scream with hysteria. The walls suddenly felt so close, the rocks so sharp and my position so hopeless.

"Do... you... feel... like... flying?" the bat hissed, red eyes glaring coldly into mine.

Weakly I responded, "But I can't fly, I have no wings." What else could I say?

"You had better grow some quickly then," the bat replied as the stones beneath me began to crumble. Vainly I clawed at the air, as I fell rapidly into the darkness, leaving the bat to hiss and cackle to himself. I didn't want to scream, for that would only please Charon and her disgusting bat, but I couldn't help myself. The pain of screaming only made me want to shriek louder. Pulling myself into a fetal position, I prepared for a deadly impact, but it wasn't long before I could see a faint blue glow before me.

The light rapidly grew brighter and I realized that I was falling into a large room. My heart gave a jump as I wondered whether it would lead to a miraculous escape or a crushing blow on a stone floor. There wasn't much time to think or wonder, for I was falling extremely fast. My brown hair was violently ripped out of their braids and flew in a dark stream above my head.

As I entered the room, the enormity of it was breathtaking… but there was no time for gawking, for I realized with a start, that my fall would take me straight through the room! The pit continued down, down, down… deep into the bowels of the earth. Yet for the moment, I was only near the very top of the brightly lit chamber. Tearing my gaze away from the blackness that awaited below, I spotted a brilliant chandelier of sorts, suspended from the roughly hewn stone ceiling. Blue candles surrounded it on all sides, giving off a tremendous amount of light. My panic stricken mind set to work as I estimated the distance between myself and the light… my descent would take me right beside it! There was no time to think! As I flew by the long length of rope that held the chandelier in place, I reached out and grabbed it, feeling myself continue to slide downward… but firmly holding on. I could feel my hands flame and burn, as the rope fibres scrapped my hands, but I would not let go! I landed with a brain rattling jolt on the center of the chandelier. Realizing I had shut my eyes, I slowly opened them, only to be dazzled by the dozens of flicking blue flames which now surrounded me. "I'm alive," I whispered to myself and gingerly peered downward.

There was something of an island in the center of the murky pit, which I had been falling towards. My eyes widened, for there, floating upon a marble pedestal, was a gleaming crystal rose… and it was nearly in full bloom! The Rose caught the blue light and reflected in all directions, giving it a truly mystical appearance. Briefly mesmerized by the beauty of the object, I almost failed to see the figure who came hurtling through a tunnel on the side of the wall and screeched to a halt at the edge of the chasm.

I blinked my eyes, trying to clear away the blue spots before them. "Clara!" I screamed, feeling my throat constrict with the effort. My head was starting to become light and dizzy from lack of fresh air.

Clara looked perplexed and short of breath. "Alice?" she managed weakly.

"I'm up here!" I leaned over the candles as far as I dared, feeling their sharp heat upon my cold cheeks.

She wasted no time and I could see she was gauging the distance between herself and the floating island. "What can I do? There's no bridge and the Rose is nearly full!" Irritation and… perhaps a bit of panic, were flashing through her eyes. Even from my height and limited view, I could sense her growing fear and it was not like Clara to be fearful. As for Emma and Oliver, there was no sign.

Clara moved swiftly to the surrounding wall, searching, no doubt, for a lever, switch, or inscription. There simply *had* to be a way across. Charon was not that unfair, was she? Suddenly Clara stood straight up and I could tell she had found something, but oddly enough, she did not seem pleased.

"Clara, what is it?" I called down to her and narrowly missed catching my skirt on fire.

"It's an inscription." She stared up at me with woeful eyes.

"And?" I pressed, beginning to sweat.

"The Undead," she began, clutching her arms tightly, "require a living sacrifice in order for the bridge to appear."

It made sense… that was why no one had ever passed Charon's test. Everyone had tried to reach the Rose individually and in the end, could not complete the task because a sacrifice was needed and there was only one of them. My heart leapt, as there were four of us, but that meant… I nearly got sick right there. Lily had said we would recognize our destinies when we saw it… but this certainly was not the destiny I had envisioned for myself. Perhaps I would truly die and not be trapped with the Undead… I could be with Lily once again, but even she did not seem to be resting peacefully.

I looked down slowly. The Rose was growing closer to full bloom by the second and Clara was wavering from side to side. I burst into a choking sob. It wasn't fair! With an anguished scream, I tore at the rope which I still clutched tightly. I had to make a choice, but why did it have to be so hard? Below, Clara fell onto one knee and the blue lights before my eyes had grown foggy. It was over. I let go of the rope and jumped through the flames. Strangely enough, my skirts did not catch fire, but that didn't matter now, for I was falling to my doom.

With amazing swiftness, I descended through the room, passing into the darkness far below the floating island. The last sound I heard was Clara's muffled scream. The suffocating blackness seemed to draw me in and down. I could feel it at my neck, closing off all air. An empty silence filled my ears with an unbearable ring. I thought of Emma… Clara… Oliver and Lily. I closed my eyes tightly. Oh Ms Craddock, it wasn't supposed to end this way!

I continued to fall deeper and deeper… but still, no cold hands reached out to claim their prize. Was I even truly conscious anymore? I couldn't tell. In fact, my mind had almost gone blank. Who was I? Where was I going and why did it matter? Then, all at once, a light appeared below me, pure and white. Surely this was the end… or was it another room? Or had I even been in a previous room? The light grew brighter and brighter until it completely blinded me. Covering my face with an arm and curling up tightly, I prepared myself for the worst.

Part Two

The Plains of Algernon

CHAPTER TWELVE

The Lone Hill

*I*T WAS DARK, cold and terribly windy. My ears rang with the whistle of wind, relentlessly blowing against them. All around me were piles upon piles of boulders and smashed rock, as though some impressive structure had been destroyed. In the darkness behind me, I could faintly see the outline of a castle, with crumbling down walls and an incapacitating sadness about it. Above the wind, I could hear screams of agony and wails of torture.

"Alice!" came a dark menacing voice from above. "You have escaped me for the last time!"

I felt my left leg buckle and I fell hard to one knee, feeling the sharp rocks cut through my flesh. "Who are you!" I called out vainly, only to have my words stolen by the wind. "Why is this happening? How could I have let it come to this?"

My shoulders began to shake and I felt something cool on my forehead. A voice from beyond the darkness called out with a ghostly air, "Alice, Alice. Wake up dear."

Still the darkness held me fast and the evil voice which hovered in the air just above me, began to materialize into a shadow. I squinted, trying to see who my tormenter was. Then another ghostly voice spoke, though it was not addressed to me. "Is she breathing?"

"Yes," came the first voice. "She is just unconscious... I think. A little delirious though. Quick, fetch me some water!"

A soft hand held mine, but all I could see was the dark shadow becoming clearer and clearer. "You are mine now!" the evil being cried.

"No! No!" I screamed and began to struggle, only to find powerful arms restraining me.

"Calm down Alice," the soft voice soothed, "you'll hurt yourself."

"Why won't she wake up?" asked a concerned voice that was slightly deeper than the rest.

"Have her smell this," the first voice suggested and I immediately smelled a strong, pungent odour.

The darkness around me began to dissolve into sunlight, but the menacing figure stayed long after my surroundings had gone. Then, it was nothing more than a fleeting shadow, gone back into the night and I numbly cracked my eyes open. The first thing I saw was a bright shining blue sky, with thin wisps of white clouds, streaking across the blueness. Then a face suddenly blocked out my view. "Emma?" Yes, that was her name. My thoughts were jumbled.

Emma's face broke into a smile. "Thank the Power! You're awake!"

Oliver appeared at my other side with a flask of water. "Here," he propped me up on his arm, "drink this, you'll feel better." As I gingerly took the cool liquid into my mouth, he grinned. "You're the deepest sleeper I know!" he laughed. "And by the sounds of things, you must have had one wicked dream."

"Shush Oliver!" Emma shook her head. "The poor girl is confused enough as it is."

Feeling a rustling at my feet, I saw a puffy eyed Clara watching me with a smile and her hands clasped under her chin. "My dear little Alice," she whispered. "So brave."

Pushing aside the water flask, I tried to gather my thoughts and shake the last of the cobwebs from my head. We had been in the Land of the Undead... attempting the trial of... Charon? I recalled seeing the Diamond Rose... then falling, or rather, jumping.

The world around me slowly steadied and soon I was able to sit up on my own. Everyone sat patiently in the soft green grass, while I composed myself. Between the three bodies which were closely huddled around me; I could see...the horizon! Never before had I been able to view the horizon, for the trees in the forest has always been so relentlessly thick. Here I could see everything around me and it wasn't much. There was not a tree in sight, only fragrant heather and lavender waving gently in the warm breeze.

"What happened? Where am I?" Questions tumbled out of my mouth as I swivelled around to get a look behind me. Charon's wall loomed a ways back, the tips of the very tallest trees peeking out from behind it.

Emma smiled. "Slow down dear. You're still weak from all you've been through and," she touched one of the numerous bandages on my body, "it seems as though you sustained most of the injuries." It was true, for there were thick wrappings on my hands... rope burns and several bandages on my arms and legs from crawling through the tunnels.

"There's not much to tell really." Oliver stood up and dusted himself off. "You're now on the northern most edge of the Plains of Algernon. A very original name," he joked.

"And we are here thanks to you sweet sister," Clara told me with shining admiration. "You sacrificed yourself so that we could live. Such a hero! I never knew you were so brave."

"Neither did I," I replied, nervously recalling my plunge from the chandelier into the pit below. I shuddered in the open air, thinking of the terrible fate that could have awaited us. I felt my cheeks grow hot with shame, as I realized that had I been in a more stable state of mind, I probably would *not* have jumped. They called me a hero, but I knew that I was nothing more than a fraud.

"Are you alright Alice?" Emma asked, feeling my forehead. "You look a little flushed."

"I'm fine," I replied quickly, trying to squelch my shame. Absently I pulled at a blade of grass near my side. "So what happened after I fell... er... jumped?"

"There was a brilliant flash of light," Clara confirmed. "I thought that perhaps it was the end, but when the light faded, there was a swinging bridge out to the floating island. All I had to do was run across it and touch the Rose."

"You are the real hero," I told Clara, as I cast my eyes downward. "I would have just collapsed and cried at losing another sister."

Clara touched my bandaged hand. "Believe me, I wanted to Alice. But sometimes..." she paused, "we have to put our grief aside and do what we must for the sake of everyone. It's tough to be strong mentally. So many people are physically strong, but that is not where real strength comes from." She sighed. "When I reached the Rose, Emma and Oliver were transported to my side."

"I had been trapped in some sort of water chamber," Emma announced. "I may never feel dry again." She squeezed her slightly damp hair for effect.

"I must have been in some sort of stone maze," Oliver added. "I just kept running into dead ends and disgusting bats with human faces."

"I saw one of those too," I told him and then turned to Clara. "What happened after Emma and Oliver appeared?"

Clara looked thoughtful. "This part is confusing and difficult to explain... it was all so unrealistic. Charon appeared and said we were worthy to pass through her gate... grudgingly I might add. The next minute, we were standing out here in the middle of the night, with you laying fast asleep at our feet." She reached into her cloak and withdrew a rich velvet purse. "Look, we have the Diamond Rose!"

I gaped at the beautiful object. It was as clear as fresh spring water, but cut in such a way that it caught every last ray of light and scattered it into every colour of the rainbow. "What does it do?" I wondered, feeling a strange warmth being emitted from the magical object.

Clara shrugged. "Charon didn't say, but I'm sure we'll find out when the time is right."

"Charon's not so bad really," Oliver shrugged and stared off into the distance. "She's just doing her job… and I think she has experienced some great sadness in the past."

"I think somebody likes Charon!" I teased, feeling my strength return, as Emma handed me a steaming mug of powerful brew.

Oliver blushed crimson. "I don't think so Alice. She tried to throw me off a wall, remember."

As my thoughts returned to the previous night, I suddenly gasped, "The horses! Oh Moondancer!"

"They're all here," Emma confirmed and pointed to where our grey ponies stood grazing peacefully, obviously delighted by the abundance of grass. "Charon must have transported them here." With this said, Emma stood up and made her way back to where a small fire crackled. There were various pots and pans surrounding the fire and it became evident that Emma was cooking. "Do you feel strong enough to travel today?" she called over to me.

I nodded. "Yes I think so. I just need something to eat." It was still early morning, but the sun's intense rays reflected brightly off the green grass, which was dotted with purple blossoms here and there. A scarcely traveled trail wound its way south, presumably towards Devona. There was nothing but wide open spaces on every side of us. If the Witch should attack, there would be no place to hide. Oliver strolled over to where Emma was cooking, while Clara seated herself beside me.

"What were you dreaming of?" she asked, breaking the silence.

Startled, I tried to remember. "It fades so fast," I sighed, trying to recall the images, but only saw blackness. "I think I've been having this dream since we started our quest, but I've always just brushed it aside."

Clara nodded, listening intently. "It's different from the one you used to have at the orphanage?"

I nodded vigorously. "Yes it is. In fact, I haven't had *that* dream since the morning we confronted Ms Craddock." A gentle breeze blew a stray hair into my mouth. Brushing it away, I continued speaking as Clara pulled my hair back and began to braid it. "This is a different sort of dream. Before, I think my dream was of the past, but now…"

"You think it's of the future?" Clara pulled my hair back tightly.

"Maybe… but I hope it doesn't mean anything. I can't recall the details, but it was horrifying. Everything was so dark and I was so alone. There was a figure… a shadow that called my name."

Clara leaned over my shoulder with a concerned look on her face. "I don't like the sounds of that. But perhaps it's just a nightmare and nothing more." She tied the end of my hair with a string of leather. "Still, just to be on the safe side, you should really pay attention to everything, okay?" She stood up and began to walk over towards the fire. "Come have some breakfast now, you must be very hungry. I know I certainly am." Clara stopped and turned to face me once again. "And despite what insecure feelings I know you have, you were truly brave last night."

*   *   *

Our breakfast was brief, but with the infusion of food in my system and a generous amount of Emma's herb brew, I felt energized and ready for a day of riding under the warm sun. Our ponies seemed absolutely delighted with their wide open surroundings and fresh grass to nibble at every turn.

I discovered with relief that there had been no serious effects on us from being in the Land of the Undead. Cuts and bruises seemed to be the extent of our injuries and those would heal with time. I gave the Forgotten Forest one last glance before I fixed my eyes on the scarcely used road ahead. "Goodbye," I whispered softly. "I know not when, or if I shall see you again." The tangled mass of trees which extended above the wall seemed to wave a sad goodbye.

"With every ending, there is always a new beginning," Emma stated as she trotted Lady up beside me. "You'll see the forest again someday."

"So what lies on the road ahead?" Clara asked Oliver, who was trying desperately to read the map, while at the same time keep Nightflame on the road.

Oliver grunted as Nightflame attempted a trot. "Well, it looks pretty empty for a while. Most of the villages fall either east or west of this particular road. They build near the rivers, which makes sense."

"But what is the next village we will come to?" Emma pressed, as she adjusted her position.

"Verity," Oliver told her. "A farming community is my guess. It's just a ways west of the Felda River. Very fertile with good soil I should think." Oliver looked wistful. "I sure do like the plains... there's something awe inspiring about them." He shook his head and turned his gaze back to the map.

"Sounds fairly straightforward," I commented, as a pleasant whiff of lavender came my way. "Oliver, what's wrong?" I asked, for his face had suddenly gone very pale.

"We need to stick close to the road," he told us tightly. "Just to the west of Verity, is the Temple of Strength."

My hands involuntarily gripped Moondancer's reigns tighter. "A Virtue Temple," I breathed. That could only mean trouble and suddenly I had vision of danger ahead.

Clara broke the tension with a laugh. "Well that's easy! We just have to stay on the road! That's not difficult!" And with that, she spurred Storm on, overtaking us all, leaving a cloud of choking grey dust. As I looked up at the sky through the grime, I was certain that I spied a dark shape circling overhead. The Raven.

*   *   *

We rode on in the hot sun for three uneventful days, each night realizing that we had less and less water. Our flasks were running dry and it was becoming more and more evident, that soon there wouldn't be enough water for both the horses and ourselves.

"We could go off course a bit to the west and gather water from the Hazel River," Oliver suggested one morning as we trotted along, parched and weary.

"But you said we had to stay on the road to avoid the Temple of Strength," Emma pointed out, a sudden shadow lowered across her lovely features.

"The temple is further south," Oliver assured us. "We can go west here and not have to worry."

"We can't hold out until Verity?" I asked, the dark foreboding gathering strength. I had experienced my darkness dream, as I had come to call it, each night we had been out on the plains. Every time I saw the shadow in the air, he became more and more real. I had begun to fear the worst, but surprisingly enough, I no longer had the urge to run away from him. No, rather, I wanted to confront the shadow... to find out who he was (for indeed it was a he) and why he called out to me.

"We need water, dear Alice," Clara smiled at me. "Besides, what's a little detour?"

"Well, if you're certain we're still a ways north of the temple," Emma considered, "I suppose we have no choice."

"Don't look so concerned," Oliver grinned. "I know exactly where we are on this map. Now let's just alter our course slightly." He grabbed Nightflame's reigns and steered him west.

We hadn't been on this course long, when a strange round hill appeared ahead of us. As we approached, I realized that the strange landform was sheltering a weather beaten house, which was partially engulfed by the hill. Petite round windows dotted the shelter, each covered with delicate blue curtains. Around the far side of the dwelling was a large vegetable garden and sparkling pond, with an array of tiny orange fish swimming around in the weeds. A strangely bent chimney protruded from the top of the house, with swirling smoke puffing out. Grass had grown overtop of the dirt covered roof, causing it to blend into the plains so perfectly, that from a distance, one could hardly recognize it for what it was.

"What a funny little house!" I giggled, not thinking that perhaps the owner was listening.

"It seems pleasant enough... besides the fact that grass grows out of the roof. It's as though the hill is growing over the house," Emma commented with a light-hearted smile.

"Are you thinking what I'm thinking?" Clara asked Oliver excitedly.

"Water!" Oliver laughed. "So we may not have to go to the Hazel River after all!"

"Let's just calm down and talk to the owner first," Emma advised wisely. "We mustn't assume we are welcome."

"But you are more than welcome," came a high pitched voice from the door, "you are expected!"

CHAPTER THIRTEEN

Keenan's Predictions

MY HEART JUMPED at the sound of another voice, but quickly
relaxed when I saw who had spoken. Standing in the doorway
of the house, was a wizened dwarf of a man, with a long grey
beard that curled about his toes. His skin sagged with wrinkles and was
peppered with liver spots all the way up his tanned bare arms. He peered
at us with bright dark eyes from behind tiny round spectacles that sat
perched upon his long pointed nose. The little old man, with his bright
green and red tunic, seemed to be a beacon in the middle of nowhere.

"Come in, come in!" he exclaimed excitedly, beckoning us into his
home. "I have waited so long for you to come by and patience is not one
of my strong points, although I do have many." He turned and hobbled
into the house with glee.

We all looked at each other in confusion. "Emma?" I asked uncertainly. I wasn't sure what to make of the dwarf, except that he seemed
very glad to see us.

Emma looked pensive. "Well, we don't want to seem rude... and he
appears hospitable. We do need water from here, so perhaps if we humour
him?"

Clara giggled and walked swiftly towards the faded door. "He's a lonely
old man Emma. Come on, we won't stay long."

"I could take him out if things got nasty," Oliver boasted proudly. He
grabbed my arm. "Come on Alice, let's go!"

I nodded, feeling my old sense of curiosity rising, the likes of which I
hadn't felt since the orphanage. "Please Emma!" I laughed as Oliver steered
me to the door.

Emma sighed. "Very well, I can see no harm." We peered into the
little home from the doorway, before Emma gave us a soft shove from
behind. "If we're going in, just go. Lingering by the entrance is very rude."

Stepping into the house, which was half covered by a hill, I felt overwhelmed by the coolness inside and the smell of fresh soil. Grass roots
dangled from the ceiling, along with various dried herbs. The floor was
pure black dirt, but packed so that it was firm and smooth. Sturdy wooden
bookshelves lined most of the walls and were packed with ancient volumes that had an almost magical quality to them. There was a small table
in the room, as well as a lovely stone hearth with a willow rocking chair

beside it. The dwarf man was humming to himself as he poured us all drinks of what smelled like tea. As we stood dumbly watching, a sleek white cat curled herself around my bare legs.

I started at the tickling feeling on my ankles and then laughed. "Why hello there sweetie," I cooed while reaching down to pet the cat.

"Her name is Gimra," the dwarf told me with a lopsided, loose smile. "She seems to really like you young Alice."

My eyes widened in amazement, rather than fear. "How did you know my name?"

He motioned for us to have a seat near the hearth. Seeing no chairs, we sat upon the cool floor, setting the teacups he handed us on the hearth-stones. "Like I said," he chuckled, "I've been expecting you!" With a delighted smile, he seated himself down in the willow rocker. Silently he surveyed us, maintaining his unwavering smile. Folding his hands in his lap he sighed. "Emma, Clara, Alice and Oliver. What a sight for sore eyes, eh Gimra?" The cat mewed softly and sprang into his lap. "This is truly an honour."

"Excuse me," Emma cut into the dwarf's glee, "you know our names, but we don't know yours."

"Oh, of course! Silly me! I often forget it myself! Hee hee!" he laughed for a moment before falling silent.

"So what is it?" Clara asked, drawing her knees up to her chest.

"What is what, dear child?" inquired the dwarf, taking a noisy sip of his tea.

"Your name!" Oliver hid his own chuckle by taking a drink.

"Oh right!" The dwarf stroked his long beard. "Let's see now... I knew it early this morning..." Gimra mewed helpfully into his ear. "Oh thank you Gimra! My name is... is... what was it again?" The helpful cat mewed twice. "I knew that," he laughed. "Keenan. My name is Keenan. I knew it all along." He scratched Gimra's ear affectionately.

"Pleased to meet you Keenan," Emma smiled politely.

"Who's Keenan?" The dwarf looked confused.

"You just said that was your name!" Clara clamped a hand over her mouth to keep from laughing.

"I did? Of course I did," Keenan mused into his cup and then cleared his throat with a rattling hack. "But now, down to business, which is why I was expecting you. You see my young lassies and lad, I am a seer... possibly the most powerful in Algernon." He winked at us from behind his spectacles.

"What's a seer?" I asked dumbly.

"The future child." Keenan leaned forward. "Yes, the future! I have the power to see it!"

I gasped. "What a marvellous talent! You must never make mistakes then!"

Keenan settled back into his willow rocking chair with a proud smile on his face. "That's right Alice. I am basically perfect." Gimra let out a low mew which could have easily passed for a sarcastic remark.

"So you knew we would be passing by then?" Emma pressed, as she watched a beetle scurry across the earthen floor.

"Indeed I have Emma," Keenan nodded. "For a long time in fact... six... no eight..."

"Mew," said Gimra with a yawn.

"Seven years!" Keenan stated with triumph. "I've know of the quest you would be undertaking for seven years now."

"So how do you do it?" I asked eagerly, kneeling towards the dwarf. "How do you see the future I mean?"

Keenan extended a short thin finger towards the fire in the hearth. "I see it in the flames," he replied almost softly. "Visions... images. Even smells and sounds. I can experience them all in the fire."

For a moment his comical countenance faded and he stared long and hard into the brightly dancing flames. None of us dared move or scarcely breath while his gaze was riveted to the fire. Even Gimra sat like a stone statue upon Keenan's lap. He continued to stare like this for several minutes and before long, I could see the sweat pouring down the sides of his wrinkled face. The graceful flames reflected off of Keenan's eyes, giving them an unearthly glow, but not once did he blink. Then, he began to tremble violently and his already drooping mouth dropped open even more. "May the Power save us all," he whispered and finally closed his eyes.

"Is he asleep?" I asked Clara uncertainly, wondering if perhaps he was dead. Gimra stood up and put her paws on Keenan's chest. Tenderly, she licked his long nose with her rough feline tongue.

Keenan's eyes opened, but were full of water... tears? He looked down at us; dirty, ragged and confused. "I have just had another vision," he announced, as if to clarify things. "I saw what was, what is and what is yet to be." He shook his head slowly. "Sometimes this gift is not worth the pain of knowing. Knowing only brings about anxiety."

"What did you see?" asked Oliver, forcing a smile to lighten the atmosphere.

Keenan eyed Oliver carefully and raised an eyebrow. "Tell me Oliver lad... do you like fairies?"

"Fairies?" Oliver chuckled and rubbed the back of his neck, "Well I don't know... I've never met one."

"Fair enough," Keenan nodded. "But I see fairies as being *very* important in your future."

"I don't see what's so disturbing about that Keenan! You look so upset!" Oliver laughed nervously.

Keenan did not answer Oliver, but instead turned to Clara with a look of pity. "You miss Lily, don't you?" Keenan asked.

Taken aback, Clara gripped the edges of her skirts. "Well, yes of course. She was my sister and I loved her."

Then suddenly Keenan reached forward and patted Clara on the head. "Be strong my child. There is no easy way to say that I see flames and smoke in the midst of a storm for you."

I tensed. Flames and smoke? That was what Isadora had prophesied! Nervously, I fingered the seal ring she had given me.

Clara let loose a howling laugh. "Of course you saw flames, Keenan my friend! You were gazing into a fire!"

He gave her a momentary blank look and with a sigh, stroked Gimra. "So I was Clara, so I was." Next he turned to Emma. "You are a very remarkable lady," Keenan smiled approvingly at my oldest sister, who sat with her back straight on the hard floor. "I saw you in the flames making some very tough decisions, Emma my dear. Very tough indeed." Emma looked as though she were about to speak, for she took a breath and opened her mouth. Then, as if having second thoughts, she abruptly halted and folded her hands in her lap.

Keenan removed his spectacles and using the bottom half of his tunic, wiped them clean. Any hint of absent mindedness or humour, had left his face. Perching his spectacles back on his nose, Keenan faced me sternly. "I saw much in the fire of you little Alice. A pretty little 15 year old girl, with great curiosity but also, great fear. You seem tormented little one." He eyed me carefully. "You are haunted by more than just dreams of the past and future. I would not wish to be in your place." Keenan shook his head sadly and Gimra mewed mournfully. "No indeed. There is a shadow... you know the one I speak of. That will be the end, for it is written in the stars."

"The end!" I cried. "No, it cannot be true! There will be no end!" I cried, suddenly on my knees clutching the old dwarf's tunic.

"I am sorry child, but that is what I saw and it is my experience that you cannot change what is written in the stars." Keenan looked upon me with pity. "You must accept what is to come and face it, for that is your destiny. I did not understand all that I saw though." Keenan attempted a smile. "At least make an attempt to be brave, if nothing else Alice. You're young... and simply not strong enough to succeed."

I sat stunned, a terrible feeling in my heart. Keenan, the strange dwarf had basically predicated my doom... at the hands of the shadow in my dream. I shivered and felt Emma take my arm as she stood up swiftly.

Keenan had been right about one thing though... I was a coward... but I had thought I was getting better. Perhaps not, for I could literally feel my self-confidence draining away and soaking into the dirt that was his floor.

"Come along everyone," Emma announced to Clara and Oliver. Her eyes were both sad and angry at the same time. "Thank you for the tea Keenan, it was a pleasure to meet you." She fairly gritted out the last two words. "Is there a well outside where we can fill our water flasks before we depart?"

Keenan staggered to his feet, obviously drained from his flame gazing efforts. A shiny bead of sweat hung off the end of his nose. "Indeed, there is a well on the south end of my land. You may take all you need." He escorted us to the door with his hobbling hunched over gait. "I bid you farewell now. We shan't meet again I predict, but that's all right. I don't expect much will be left of the land in the future anyway." He gave Emma a penetrating look.

Emma narrowed her gaze and swept out the door, with Oliver and Clara following closely. I paused as Gimra encircled my ankles once again and gave a mournful mew. Keenan picked her up and placed her in my arms. "What are you doing?" I asked in wonderment.

"Take her with you," Keenan told me softly. "You may need a friend to comfort you someday. She is young and healthy yet, unlike myself, who is nearing the end. It is in fact, the end of an era."

"No," I found myself saying firmly, "it is not the end. We will not fail."

Keenan gave me a strange look and I thought I saw a faint spark of hope in his eyes. "Perhaps I was wrong about you. Perhaps the vision was wrong. Maybe, just maybe, your destiny can be altered... but alas, I know not." He sighed dejectedly. "It is beyond my power to see the future exactly as it will unfold... I think it is beyond any earthly power and I am not what I used to be." He touched my shoulder gently. "You have great abilities Alice, if only you have the courage to use them."

"Alice come on, we're leaving!" Emma called impatiently from around the hill.

"Coming Emma!" I shouted back. "Goodbye Keenan."

The dwarf gave me a lopsided grin and scratched his grey beard. "Keenan? Who's that?"

Shaking my head, I walked away. I found the others already mounted and ready to go. Emma had her arms folded when she saw me approach. "Alice, just what were you doing? That old dwarf is crazy..." She looked at my arms. "Why are you carrying that cat?"

"Her name is Gimra," I corrected, as I kissed the top of her silky fur, "and Keenan gave her to me."

"We don't need another mouth to feed on this quest," Emma replied crossly.

I placed Gimra on Moondancer's saddle and then mounted behind her. Emma's strange mood was exceedingly annoying. "If Lily were here," I replied, "there would be another mouth to feed."

Emma scowled and gave Lady a little kick. "Well then, the cat is your responsibility Alice. Let's get back to the road! I don't like the looks of those approaching clouds." She set Lady off in a swift gallop.

Clara rode beside me with a sympathetic look. "Don't mind Emma. She's just upset over Keenan's predictions. She believes too much in that sort of thing. Though our destinies may be partially set out, it is we who decide the outcome. What I mean is, we determine whether we succeed or fail. The shadow Alice, in your dream... if it is your destiny to confront him, then you will. But only you," she pointed at me, "will determine the results of that confrontation." Clara's tone then lightened, "Gimra's such a sweet kitty. I'm glad she's with us."

I smiled happily and tapped Gimra's pink nose. "So am I. It's nice to have a little companion."

Oliver grinned, "And if we get low on food..."

"Oliver!" Clara smacked him playfully in the shoulder. "You're awful!"

Just then, a mighty gust of wind flew by, nearly knocking us out of our saddles. The flat world around us suddenly darkened, as the looming black clouds snuffed out the sun. Moondancer reared when a bolt of lightning flashed across the sky, followed almost immediately by a tremendous crack of thunder.

"This sure came up fast!" Oliver shouted into the wind, black hair whipping violently.

"We must go back to Keenan's for shelter!" I cried, just as another fork of lightning struck nearby. "It isn't safe out here!"

"She's right Emma!" Clara agreed, attempting to soothe Storm. "We're not that far away yet!"

I felt an icy drop of rain land with a sting upon my nose. Within seconds it was pouring so hard that I could scarcely make out the others, who were only a few meters away. Gimra let out a pathetic mew and I tucked her under my cloak. "Hold on little one," I spluttered.

"Come on then," Emma cried, "this way!" With Lady in the lead, we began to follow Emma through the worsening storm.

The wind increased and the rain came down harder and more painfully. It was then I realized that it was no longer raining, but rather hailing! Thousands of little ice pebbles were blown forcefully into our skin and I could feel tiny welts forming. The wind continued to increase and as

I turned my gaze skyward through the ice, I could see a strange object descending from the clouds, towards the ground. It was long and slender... almost like a finger, but grey in colour. I continued to watch it rapidly snake towards the ground. When it touched the flat land, dust was suddenly swept up in every direction.

"It's a twister!" Clara cried out as Storm let out a heart wrenching whinny.

"I don't know what direction we're facing!" Emma revealed with a note of panic in her voice. "I... I... don't know which way to go!"

"It's headed straight for us!" Oliver exclaimed with a squeak in his voice. "Move move move!"

We needed no more coaxing. At that moment, it didn't matter which way we were headed. All that matter was that we got away from the twister... which, odd as it seemed, appeared to be chasing us. Overhead, the lightning continued and the thunder rumbled. It seemed as though the very earth itself was trembling.

We rode long and hard and I could feel poor Moondancer tiring. Her body was sticky with sweat and there was froth at her mouth. No matter which way we veered, the twister followed, though it stayed at a constant distance. It almost felt as though we were being herded, like common cattle! The wind screeched in my ears like twisted laughter and my eyes, nose and mouth were filled with gritty dirt. I could feel dear Gimra's claws clutching me through my dress. The poor cat probably was wishing she was sitting by the hearth with confused Keenan.

Suddenly Moondancer stopped, as though we had reached an impassable obstacle. With a scream, I found myself flying through the air, head over heels. I landed painfully face first on the ground. I tasted dirt and blood in my mouth, but my most urgent concern, was the twister that had followed us so relentlessly. Yet oddly enough, it had disappeared, leaving us under a clouded sky with thunder and lightning, but no rain or hail. Emma, Clara and Oliver were lying on the ground nearby, all looking as shocked as I. Gimra crawled out from underneath me with a dazed but uninjured look upon her feline features. Then suddenly, the hairs on the back of her neck stood up and she hissed.

As I looked up to see what was wrong, I could feel my heart quicken and the colour drain from my face. Off to my right, Clara was breathing heavily in disbelief. "No, no, this can't be right! It's the Temple of Strength!"

CHAPTER FOURTEEN

Trapped!

T HERE WAS A SCUFFLING noise as Emma scrambled to her feet in a panic. Pulling at her disarrayed hair she screamed, "What have I done? I've led us right into danger!" As she spoke these words, the thunder rumbled loudly overhead and the air crackled with static.

"No," Oliver groaned, lifting himself onto one knee, "it wasn't you Emma. That twister... it was unnatural! It forced us to go this way! This is the Witch's doing!" he growled, getting to his feet. During our long days on the plains, we had discussed extensively the dangers of the corrupted Virtue Temples with Oliver. Our coping strategy had been to avoid them, but that plan had failed miserably.

I grabbed Clara's hand in a fright, for she was nearest to me. "Clara," I trembled, "let's get out of here!"

Holding me close she soothed, "Don't worry Alice, everything is going to be just fine." She said this with a steady voice, but I could feel her inwardly shudder.

Gimra pawed at the hem of my dress comfortingly. I scooped her up into my arms and nuzzled my face in her silky fur. Then tearing myself away from her, I gazed intently at the Temple of Strength. It looked exactly as the Heart Temple had, with the same circular clear pond, surrounded by alabaster pillars and a pyramid roof. "I want to leave," I declared, attempting to move my gaze away from the scene before me. There was something about the temples that was hypnotizing... almost mind controlling. At any rate, I didn't like how my mind worked around them.

Oliver and Emma made their way over to where our ponies were pawing nervously at the ground. They were loyal creatures, that was for sure, for they hadn't bolted away into the wildly blowing grasses. Clara attempted to pull away from me to help the others check for damages, but I held her fast.

"Alice, I'm just going to check the saddlebags on Storm. You should look over Moondancer," Clara told me as she tried to pry her arm away.

"Listen Clara..." I paused, every muscle in my body full of tension. I had heard it again... a haunting voice, just like at the Heart Temple before I had nearly fallen in. "A voice!" I cried. "Can't you hear it singing?"

Clara stopped struggling and listened, her grip tightening suddenly on my arm. "I hear it all right." Pursing her lips together, she set off in a run towards Emma and Oliver, dragging me along with her. "Don't worry about checking things!" she exclaimed. "We must leave this minute!"

Emma jumped at the urgency in Clara's voice, her blue eyes widening. "Well, of course we have to leave immediately—"

Clara cut her off. "I don't mean immediately, I mean NOW!"

Emma swung herself up onto Lady, a mixture of fear and confusion in her face. I had just put Gimra onto Moondancer's saddle and Oliver had just placed one foot in his stirrup, when there was a tremendous 'whoosh' behind us. I felt an intense heat on my back and the acrid smell of smoke filled the air. Behind us, where the circular pond had been, flames now shot up high into the air, blackening the pyramid roof. These were not ordinary orange flames either, or even eerie blue ones like Charon's. These flames were green, black and yellow claws, which scraped away at the beautiful white pillars.

Moondancer threw her head back in fear, eyes rolling wildly, while Gimra dug her claws into the leather of my saddle. "Mount Alice! Mount!" screamed Emma. "We must ride!"

The flames began to reach out, setting the dry grass around us ablaze. Overhead, the lightning flashed and the thunder crashed, but no icy rain fell to help us. With a cough, I swung myself up into Moondancer's back and grabbed the reins. At the same moment, Nighflame reared, almost sending Oliver tumbling to the ground, but he held on, eyes wide with fear.

"This way!" Oliver shouted, pointing towards the open field that was as yet untouched by the devouring flames. The fire was spreading quickly and our ponies were still tired from the twister. Hopefully fear would give them speed and with speed, escape. It was fear that gave me the ability to act quickly, for I was the first one to follow Oliver.

"We can outride this fire!" Oliver called loudly. "It will be okay!"

His words almost comforted me, but just then, an enormous wall of flames shot up in from of him, causing Nightflame to give a shrill whinny. I turned around to go back, but only received a staggering blast of heat upon my soot covered face. There was now a wall of flames behind us and no sign of Emma or Clara.

"Our escape route is blocked!" Oliver turned Nightflame around angrily and then started, as he saw the second wall of flames.

"We've lost Emma and Clara!" I exclaimed, as my head started to feel light. Sparks that seemed to have a life of their own flew towards us, catching more and more grass on fire. Moondancer bucked and began to spin wildly in a panic, her hooves thudding dully on the fiery earth. I lowered myself in the saddle to keep from falling off, covering Gimra protectively with my breathless body. "We must find the others!" I coughed out to Oliver, who was turning his head about rapidly looking for somewhere to go.

"I can't see anything in this smoke!" Oliver spluttered through the heavy air. With great difficulty, he navigated his way towards me and I felt the warm side of Nightflame against my leg.

My eyes and throat stung painfully from the sooty smoke, which was completely unlike that of a campfire. This smoke was very thick and almost gritty, like a black liquid. It smeared its darkness on everything and filled our lungs with noxious fumes. I felt as though I were underwater and unable to reach the surface. Still, the merciless green fire continued to grow and consume all in its path. "We can't just stand here!" I rubbed my eyes. "We must move... somewhere!"

Oliver didn't reply, but I felt Nightflame move slightly. "Over there! I see an opening! Follow me!"

Slowly we made our way through the tiny break in the wall of flames, all the while calling for Emma and Clara. They hadn't been far behind, but someone had wanted to separate us. There was no doubt in my mind that it was the Petra Witch. A dull ache began at the back of my head and I started to feel woozy. Oliver continued to lead us, but in complete silence. I supposed it was too smoky to speak... after all one could hardly see. Then I finally did see something... and I almost wished for the thick smoke again, for it was the Temple. We were heading straight for it! We had got turned around again!

"Oliver!" I coughed. "We need to change directions!"

"We can't," he replied weakly. "The flames are pushing us this way... we have no choice but to be burned unless we continue."

Then a flicker of movement on the ground caught my eye. It wasn't much, but it was definitely a movement. "Oliver!" I called out to him. "I see something!" To my relief and joy, it was Emma and Clara. Both girls were seated on the charred grass, with their ponies standing nearby. My joy quickly turned to fear though, when I realized that Clara had been injured. Emma was kneeling over Clara, who was clutching her stomach and lolling from side to side in pain.

"Emma! Clara! What's wrong?" I cried fearfully.

Emma looked up mournfully. She had hairs straggling in her face, but made no attempt to them brush away. "Clara's hurt..." Emma's voice died off as tears rolled down her face, leaving black trails in the soot. Her sad face reminded me of someone, but I couldn't recall who, or when.

"Put Clara on my horse and I'll carry her," Oliver offered, glancing over his shoulder at the flames, which were creeping towards us.

"No," Clara coughed, attempting to raise her head. "I don't think that will be necessary…"

"So you're strong enough to ride yourself?" I asked hopefully, as the sweat roll down my back.

Emma held Clara's hand tightly and turned towards Oliver and I. "Storm bucked her… She flew off and was trampled. The hooves hit her stomach pretty hard…" There was a strange look of hopelessness in Emma's eyes.

"So she can't ride?" I pressed, still not understanding Emma's meaning… or perhaps trying not to.

"Alice," Emma began, but was interrupted by a strange cool glow behind Clara.

Instinctively I turned my face towards the freshness and was surprised to see a translucent image of Nissim! He stood still, long robes flowing like a white ghost, shimmering amongst the searing heat. Though his face was as kindly as before, he looked considerably older or perhaps fatigued, was a more accurate description. There were great bags under his eyes and he stooped over slightly, leaning on a twisted staff.

"Nissim!" I cried. "Please help us!"

Leaning even more heavily on his staff, Nissim took a weary breath. "I wish that I could help young ones, but I am very weak right now. I have been in the sacred Wizard's Realm, trying to hold back the full force of Ralston's evil." His tired eyes locked on mine. "I'm losing strength dear children, so I cannot physically assist you without sacrificing all of Algernon in the process."

My face fell in bitter disappointment and I felt hot tears stinging on my cheeks. Nissim had been our only hope and now that hope was gone, like so many others, fleeing into the night. "It is all over, just like Keenan said," I whispered.

"Don't despair Alice. I expect so much more from you than that," Nissim told me kindly. "Though it's true I cannot physically help you, I can tell you how to escape on your own. I have great faith in everyone's abilities."

I was shocked momentarily. How could this powerful man have faith in us? *I* didn't even have faith in us. We must have looked positively pathetic; trapped in a fire, covered in soot and hardly able to sit upon a horse without wavering from side to side. Only Emma seemed to be in control, for she sat on the ground beside Clara with an unreadable expression on her face. As for Clara, I thought she might be getting better, for she had stopped writhering in pain and now lay still, breathing heavily. She was too tough, too adventurous and too full of vibrant life for anything to bring her down.

"So Nissim, what do we do? Just name it!" Oliver nodded towards the wizard, while stealing another quick glance at the approaching flames. A bead of sweat trickled down his temples.

"Your deliverance from this evil lies in the mystical item you received from the Land of the Undead. I speak of the Diamond Rose, naturally." Nissim's image faded slightly. "The Diamond Rose has the power to transport all who touch it from one place to another. Be sure to focus on your destination, because the Rose was designed only for one time use. Oh and another thing, it doesn't move you very far, but it should be enough to escape the flames."

"Thank you Nissim!" Oliver clapped his hands together joyously. "This is almost too easy!"

Nissim looked grim. "You know not what you speak of lad. You all must hurry to Devona, for things are becoming worse by the hour." Nissim scowled, causing deep furrows to form in his forehead. "Ralston's power is growing and mine is diminishing. Time grows short for Algernon and indeed all of Fadreama. I cannot hold back these malignant forces for much longer... I have grown far too weak. This battle will soon no longer be mine. You mustn't quit!" He fairly glared at me. "I implore you, don't quit!" With that, the cool white image of Nissim dimmed until it completely faded out.

"The Rose..." Clara whispered weakly, "it's in my belt..."

With nimble fingers, Emma opened the dark pouch which hung at Clara's side and carefully removed the Diamond Rose. Its crystal pureness glowed, as though it knew it would fulfill a purpose.

Emma stood up and brought the Rose over to me. "Here, take this and stand by Oliver." She then grabbed the reigns of Lady and Storm. Slowly, so as not to frighten the ponies she walked them over to stand beside Moondancer, who was pawing impatiently at the ground.

Oliver dismounted swiftly and made his way to Clara's side. His eyes were full of pain as he looked at her face. I could not see her properly from where I stood and since Emma had burdened me with holding the horses, I could not get down to comfort her.

"We... we have to get you up," Oliver told Clara, while placing a hand under her head and trying to raise her up. He lifted Clara enough for me to actually see her face... and immediately I wished I had not! Her skin was death itself... no colour remained, save the blue in her lips. Even her eyes seemed to have become devoid of the life she had so abundantly possessed. From where I sat upon Moondancer, I could see that her skin was clammy and probably ice cold, despite the inferno around us. Reaching out to my right, I grabbed Nightflame's reign. I was now in control of all four ponies and the Diamond Rose, for Emma was busy rummaging in one of the saddlebags.

"We have to go now!" I called, feeling the heat creeping up from behind. I couldn't help but stare into the flames... There was something there... My stomach turned. We were right beside the Temple... I could reach out and touch the stone! It was the great alabaster pillars I was seeing and they looked awfully unsteady, for the fire seemed to claw at them.

"Come on Clara, work with me!" Oliver shouted, still trying to lift her limp body.

Emma turned and was about to assist him, when a loud noise made her stop sharply. The ponies all shook their heads and stamped their feet fearfully. "Steady," I told them with gritted teeth. The pillar... it had moved... and it seemed to be leaning outwards.

It all happed so quickly and yet it seemed like slow motion. One of the alabaster pillars crumbled at its base and began to fall sideways, straight towards Oliver and Clara. Oliver too had heard the noise and looked up to see the impending disaster. Instead of running, he continued to desperately pull a frightened Clara out of the way, but her body was too weak.

"Get out of the way!" Emma screamed and ran forward only a few steps. She dared go no further than that.

For the briefest moment, Clara looked straight into my eyes and the vacancy left them. She now had a look of sudden clarity, as of a baby discovering something for the first time. With her mouth set in a determined line, she pushed Oliver roughly backwards. It seemed to sap the life right out of her, for she collapsed back onto the ground and didn't move. There was no time left, for the Temple of Strength's pillar came crashing down.

I felt a sharp pain in my chest as I watched the dreamlike scene unfold before my shocked eyes. Clara was gone... ? Emma rushed forward to where Oliver sat stunned and hauled him quickly to his feet. He seemed disoriented and stunned, but I couldn't see his face, for he kept his head bowed.

"The Rose Alice! The Rose! Hold it out now!" Emma ordered, not looking back at the flaming white pillar. Her face revealed nothing of her feelings.

Numbly I held out the Rose, while keeping a tight grip on the horses' reins. Shaking slightly, Emma placed Oliver's hands on the Rose and closed her own over his.

"What's going on?" the words came out of Oliver's mouth in a jumble.

"Concentrate," Emma replied without emotion. "Concentrate on leaving this place."

Concentrate indeed! My mind was a whirl of thoughts and emotions, uncertainties and fears. How could I ever focus my mind? Another pillar crashed down behind us... We were running out of time. "I can't concentrate!" I screamed in anguish, only faintly aware that Gimra, my sweet kitten, momentarily forgotten, was nuzzling my chest encouragingly, but stayed under my cloak.

"Don't give me that!" Emma shouted angrily back. "Concentrate or we'll die!"

Surprised and horrified by the sudden anger in Emma's voice, I closed my eyes and tried to block out everything. I blocked the loss of Clara. I blocked the loss of Lily. I blocked the image of the little boy screaming as he was taken down the hallway. I blocked the tired image of Nissim, fading into the night. I blocked out Keenan and his predications, one of which, had come true already. "Please work," I whispered desperately. The only thought I could not block, was that of the shadow who tormented me in my dreams. He hovered above me still, with a menacing laugh as I felt the searing flames engulf my body.

CHAPTER FIFTEEN

The Choice

ROSES. All around me wafted the fragrant smell of fresh roses, with the clean scent that only comes after a spring rain. This sensation broke through the darkness that enveloped me… and banished the ever present shadow that hovered in the air. There was a bright light behind my eyelids, beckoning me to open my stinging eyes. With a great effort, I cracked my lids open and found an unearthly blue sky directly overhead, with the sun hanging like a great golden orb in the eastern sky. Unlike the stormy night before, not a single cloud marred the sky's perfection. I drew a breath in slowly and my chest convulsed painfully as though a fire were still burning inside of me. As I sat up, I gingerly felt my face. It was dirty, but unburned, thank the Power.

As I sat in the long fragrant grass, trying to adjust my eyes to the sparkling light, something wet brushed against my hand. "Gimra!" I exclaimed, as she licked the back of my hand again. I scooped up the silky white cat and hugged her close. "Oh you darling! I bet you're wishing Keenan had kept you…" I trailed off. Keenan. Isadora. Both had prophesized a fire in a storm. Now their predictions had come true. "Oh Clara," I sobbed quietly into Gimra's fur.

Suddenly Gimra jumped out of my arms and bounded a short distance away to something hidden in the long grass. Crawling over to Gimra, I realized that it was the Diamond Rose! Tenderly I held it up in the early morning sunshine. The Rose glistened with its pure crystal light, creating spots before my eyes. Then in an instant it was gone, disintegrated into crystal dust and blown away by the uncaring wind.

"One time use only," came a voice from behind me.

With a start, I turned around. "Emma," I breathed. She was covered in black soot and looked extremely weary. I ran into her waiting arms and she held me for a very long time. "Why Emma?" I asked her suddenly. "Why did she have to die? Clara never hurt anyone in her life."

Emma stroked my hair gently. "These…" she paused as if thinking and began again, "these things happen Alice. It is a part… a part of life."

I pulled away from her tight embrace and stared up into my sister's face. "Not like this Emma. People shouldn't have to die horrible deaths. All people should live long full lives and die of old age. In fact," I bit my lip to keep from sobbing, "people shouldn't have to die at all. It's simply not fair!"

Emma held my shoulders tightly and studied me carefully. "You know that can never be."

Looking away I suddenly asked, "Where is Oliver? Is he alright?"

Emma nodded grimly. "Yes, he is alive, but still sleeping. I let you sleep as well. We've had a long and arduous night. One I wish never to repeat."

"Who would want to repeat that?" I shook my head and picked up Gimra, who was nuzzling my ankles, as she was in the habit of doing when she wanted attention.

Emma turned away from me and began to make her way over to where our ponies were grazing peacefully. They seemed completely serene and unfazed by the previous night's events. "Alice, this night will be repeated if we continue on our quest. Of the final outcome I cannot be certain, but of the danger that lies ahead, I am."

I followed her closely, unsure of what she was hinting at, all the while attempting to control my tears. We passed by Oliver, who was sleeping peacefully on his side in the heather. "What are you talking about Emma? We were warned of danger before we started—" She cut me off.

"But not like this Alice!" Emma retorted sharply. "I have been the leader throughout this quest, have I not?"

Shocked by the strange tone in her voice, I took a step back. "Well of course Emma. You're the oldest and wisest of us all, therefore you made the natural leader."

Emma crossed her arms tightly against her chest. "And just what has my age and wisdom done for us?" She said these words with such venom that I was almost frightened.

"Emma!" I started towards her, but she put out a hand to stop me.

"Don't Alice. Don't even attempt to offer comfort. I have failed the mission. Two of the most important people in the world to me are dead. This is not saving Algernon! This is suicide!"

I blinked back hot tears, as my feelings erupted inside. Suddenly I was full of so many different emotions, that I didn't know what was truly in my heart. "Emma what are you saying?" I could feel Gimra's claws tighten ever so slightly on my arm.

"Alice, I don't want to lose you and Oliver too." She silenced me with a glare before I could protest. "We will all die if we continue on... We were stupid to think that we could reach Devona, let alone find Prince Edric!" She gripped Lady's saddle with pale hands. "We cannot go on Alice. We will not go on. It is over." In one smooth motion, she was atop Lady, ready to ride. "Wake Oliver now, we ride north."

I stared dumbly at my sister, proud and beautiful, despite the soot. Her lovely dress was now nothing more than tattered rags, blowing softly about her erect body. "You mean, go back to the Forgotten Forest?" I asked, clutching my pendant suddenly.

Emma nodded viciously. "That's exactly what I mean. We will go there and live out the rest of our days hidden, forgotten, as we always were meant to be. There is no great destiny awaiting us as Lily would say, or some wonderful adventure as Clara liked to believe. Our little company is breaking apart Alice! Look at us! To go on to Devona is... is..." she groped for words, "ridiculous!"

I had a terrible sick feeling in my stomach, as though I had been struck. My head was suddenly light and I broke out into a feverish sweat. There was a choice before me now... a choice I never dreamed that *I* would have to make. Yet here it was before me, whether I expected it or not. I had always wanted out of this expedition, in fact, I had never wanted to go on it in the first place. All I had desired was an explanation of our past, not... not this. The entire way I had secretly wished and hoped and prayed for an escape. Now here it was in front of me, shimmering like a mirage in the desert. I had but to reach out... I had but to wake Oliver and mount my horse. It was as simple as that. So why did I not move? Why did I continue to stare mutely at the ground? Why did I not reach out and take that which I most desperately desired?

"Alice," Emma pressed impatiently, "I am not going to wait around all day. Let's get out of this haunted wasteland! Soon we'll be back within the shade of the forest! Come sister!" There was something of a challenge in her eyes...

My mind cried out to listen, to follow, to obey, but my body did not respond. No, in my heart, I consciously *chose* not to respond. "Emma," I began quietly, "out of all of us who began this quest, I have been the most unenthusiastic. I, more than anyone else, wished to give up and leave everything alone." I finally met her hard blue gaze. "And yet now, when handed the opportunity to fulfill my greatest desire, I find myself unable to do so. Even as I quiver with fear at the thought of what lies ahead, I know that deep down inside, I cannot waver from this course." I gulped back tears. "Besides, stopping now would not bring back Clara or Lily. They died for this quest... we owe it to them to finish."

Emma narrowed her gaze and replied through tight lips, "Wake Oliver and mount."

I took a step back. "No Emma, I will not!" My insides quaked. What would she do in the face of my defiance? What was I doing? I should just listen, but...

"Fine then!" Emma cried, blue sparks in her eyes. "If you insist on continuing, you shall do so without me!"

"What!" I screamed and ran over to her. Clutching and pawing at her skirts I wailed, "Please sister, don't leave us! We need you to lead! I will be lost without you to guide me!"

"Get off of me!" Emma cried, angrily kicking me away with her leg. "I try to protect you and you throw it back in my face. Fine! You have chosen your path and I mine. I just hope Oliver feels the same way you do! Goodbye *sister*!" With that, she turned Lady around so quickly, that the pony reared and let loose a whinny that echoed across the plains. Then without so much as a backwards glance, Emma and Lady took off northward, dust flying up behind them. I watched in silence, until their dark figures disappeared on the horizon and into memory.

Stunned, I kneeled in the waving grass for a long time, unable to move, or utter a sound. It had all been so abrupt, so unexpected. Immediately I began to regret my decision. Why hadn't I just mounted and gone with her? Now I was alone. Gimra sat facing me, a look of concern playing across her small features. She nudged her cool pink nose under my hand, in an attempt to get me to stroke her. "This is it Gimra," I finally spoke. "I have signed our death warrants and I am truly sorry. I picked a horrible time to decide to have a spine." She looked up at me in a very understanding manner and I knew that *she* would never leave me.

Suddenly off to the side, Oliver let out a loud groan and sat up stiffly. The long locks of hair which used to fall over his eyes were singed and burned together in a black lump. His eyebrows were completely burned off, as were his eyelashes. My stomach turned as I looked at his blue eyes, which were badly burned and terribly swollen. My mind went back to the flaming pillar that had consumed Clara. She had pushed him out of the way, but perhaps not fast enough.

Slowly I approached Oliver, with Gimra at my heels. I reached out to touch him, but pulled my hand back at the last moment. Something wasn't right, for he was staring in a very blank manner. "Oliver?" I asked softly.

He turned his injured face in the direction of my voice. "Alice? Where are you? It's so dark…"

Gulping, I replied, "Come over here Oliver."

"Do you have a… a torch or something? It must be very late still, but I can't see any stars, so it must be cloudy too. Yet," he turned his face upward, "I can feel heat, like the sun…" He crawled towards me, clutching at my skirts. "Oh there you are Alice… Alice?"

Bursting into tears, I flung my arms down around his neck. "Oh Oliver!" I sobbed.

"What's wrong? Is it Clara? She's gone, isn't she?" He didn't wait for a response. "I knew it. But don't worry, it's going to be okay," he tried to comfort me.

Releasing his neck from my grasp, I whispered, "Oliver, it's morning. The sun is high in the sky and there is not a single cloud overhead." I bit my lip hard, for I hadn't the heart to tell him...

Oliver sat in silence for a moment, unblinking and unmoving. Finally using my skirts, he staggered to his feet. "This darkness... if it's not night, that means..." He felt for my hand and I turned him to face me. "I'm blind, aren't I? I mean, it's so obvious isn't it? You must have had a good chuckle watching me. Imagine, thinking it was still the night..."

"Oliver," I began, but he silenced me with a hand.

"No Alice," he drew in a deep breath and smiled painfully through his burns, "it's okay, really. Clara saved my life by pushing me away, but I guess the fire decided that if it couldn't kill me, it may as well maim me. I'll manage though." There was a determined look upon his face, but I could see and feel his torment. "Are you okay?" he changed the subject abruptly.

"Other than feeling ripped apart inside?" I asked.

"Yeah," Oliver nodded, as Gimra mewed at his leg.

"I'm fine, but..." I trailed off and looked into the distance.

Puzzled by my voice, Oliver touched my shoulder. "But what? Is something wrong... I mean other than the obvious loss of Clara?" He had some difficulty speaking Clara's name. My tears then betrayed me, as they fell like rain onto his outstretched arm. "Alice?" he inquired again with great concern.

I looked up into his blank blue eyes and covered my face with my hands. "I'm so sorry Oliver! I don't know what came over me! You must forgive me!"

Cocking his head to the side, he gazed unseeingly at me. "For what Alice?"

"Emma is gone!" I blurted out. "And I let her go!"

"I don't understand." Oliver shook his head. "What do you mean gone?"

"She decided that the quest was too dangerous and that we should return to the forest. I... I... told her no... that we couldn't stop now, even though that is what I truly want to do! I am sorry Oliver! Now we are lost... all of Algernon is lost and it's all my fault!"

Oliver linked his arm into mine and tightly held on. "You sure do take credit for a lot of things Alice," he told me with a teasing note in his voice. "I hardly think you're responsible for the loss of Algernon, keeping in mind that it's not lost at all."

"But it's just us Oliver! We're alone now," I pointed out sadly. "I don't know why I stood up to her. I should have just listened, for now I am filled with regret."

"Do you feel though, deep down, that you made the right decision to keep moving on? In spite of all the uncertainties that lie ahead... do you feel that this is *right*?" Oliver was looking slightly past me, into the distance.

I closed my eyes and thought for a moment. Did it feel right? Frightening, yes. Uncertain, yes. Dangerous, yes. Suicidal, definitely. But right? Somehow... "Yes, Oliver. It does feel right, despite everything else."

"All right then!" Oliver smiled. "Never regret a decision your heart knows is right. So Emma left, okay. I'll miss her terribly it's true and her abandoning us upsets me, but I promised to see this through until the end and I mean to do so...even if it's only the two of us." By our ankles, Gimra gave an annoyed mew. "Oh, I mean the three of us!" Oliver chuckled to himself.

"There are three horses left as well," I informed him. "Moondancer, Nightflame and Storm."

"Good," Oliver nodded. "At least we won't have to walk. Perhaps it would be advisable to stop somewhere for awhile." He touched his swollen face tenderly. "I am actually in an extraordinary amount of pain."

"The map," I whispered. "Did Clara have it?" Panic swept through me, for without the map, I truly would be lost.

"Actually," Oliver replied, "I have the map. My guess is that we're not that far away from the temple."

"No," I squinted. "I can just make it out in the distance."

"Good," Oliver mused. "Then it's just a matter of heading east. There should be a village called Verity right along our route. Hopefully we can find a place to rest there and recover."

"Stay right here with Gimra," I told Oliver. "I'm going to hook the ponies up together... that way, we won't lose one another." I took another step and my foot hit something solid. "What?" I bent down. It was Clara's pendant!

"Alice?" Oliver asked hesitantly. "What is it? I can hear you breathing all the way over here."

I brushed away the soot and dust, revealing the undamaged gold beneath it. "It's Clara's pendant," I replied, stringing it around my neck. It gave off a metallic clang when it rattled against my own pendant.

"But how did it get all the way out here?" Oliver mused.

I shrugged. "Don't worry about it. I'm just glad to have it as a... keepsake. I am not going to start crying again," I whispered softly to myself, as I grabbed Nightflame's reigns and tied them to Moondancer's. Storm's eyes were sad and down turned, as though she knew her mistress had gone forever. I tied her tightly to the other side of Moondancer, who continued to placidly chew grass. One thing was for sure, the ponies had plenty of food. My stomach growled at the thought. I was hungry once again. We could eat in Verity... it shouldn't be too far off.

As I continued to secure everything for our journey, a soft wind swept by. It seemed to speak my name... "Alice," the wind whispered almost inaudibly. "Danger, there is danger nearby..." These words I heard quite clearly despite their softness. Without thinking I turned around. There was nothing. Oliver stood a ways off, cuddling Gimra, but other than that... wait! Far up in the sky, descending lower was a black speck. As it moved closer towards the ground, the hairs on my arms stood up. It was the Raven! Evil wouldn't be far off! I braced myself for action, but the bird simply let out a shrill shriek and was gone as quickly as it had come.

"Whew!" I wiped my forehead nervously and turned back to the ponies. Immediately I wished that I hadn't, for the Witch stood before me, only a footstep away. I could smell her hot foul breath blowing into my terrified face. Her black robes hung on her thin frame, making her look like a sinister skeleton with skin. She was wearing a hooded cloak, but thin wisps of grey hair escaped and blew into the soft breeze, which was flowing protectively about me.

"Greetings Alice," she hissed, taking a step towards me with an almost amused look upon her grisly features. "It has been a while, did you miss granny?"

"You are not my granny!" I shouted at her, although she was very close. I could hear Oliver draw in a sharp breath. I prayed he would stay put and not do anything stupid... I couldn't bear to lose him too.

"Why child, you're shaking," the Witch feigned concern. "Could it be fear? Or sorrow? Or perhaps a little of both?" She reached her gnarled hand out towards me.

"Don't touch me!" I screamed, but remained rooted to the spot. My feet wouldn't move and I knew that it was not out of fear.

"Your company seems to be shrinking child. Could that be because of you? So many sorrows are your fault you realize..." The Witch shook her head disapprovingly. "So much blood is on your hands... Lily... Clara... the Sandersons..."

"What!" I exclaimed, my hands flying to my mouth. "What did you do to the Sandersons? They have nothing to do with this quest!"

"Oh I know," the Witch examined the back of her hand, "but I was in the neighbourhood and decided to stop in for tea! Even Isadora could not foresee *that* visit!" she laughed, sending shivers up my spine. "Now enough talk girl! I came here to show you something!" She indicated to her belt. There hung two locks of nearly identical brown hair. "One from Lily and now, one from Clara! My collection grows!" she cackled and spittle flew from her mouth.

Anger surged through my veins, but I found that the angrier I got, the more I was unable to move my body. "You are horrible!!" I screamed venomously.

"I'm truly flattered you think so!" The Witch bowed slightly and then shuffled closer to me. She ran her thin fingers through my long hair and inspected it carefully. "So soft and lovely, though a bit sooty. Soon this will hang from my belt as well, a symbol of my victories to show the Master!" Tightening her fingers in my hair, she yanked my head back. "But first, I'll relieve you of those pendants!"

Suddenly I heard the sound of tiny paws bounding at full speed through the long grass and before I even knew what was happening, Gimra was on the Witch's face, clawing at her eyes. "Gimra?" I breathed, hardly recognizing the enraged animal, which was now mauling the evil one. Black blood oozed from a slice across the Witch's paper thin cheek. Finding that I could move again, I made a dash for our ponies, who although were frightened, had not bolted, which was absolutely astounding. Gimra let loose one last scratch, before leaping clear of the bloodied Witch.

"Ack!" the Witch screamed into the air, her voice crackling. "A white cat!" She put her arms in front of her protectively. Glaring at me from a distance, with her glowing eyes, the Witch pointed a long finger at me. "You little *white* witch! This isn't over! Don't think for a moment that it is! When we meet again, you'll be sorry!" She spat into the dirt and with a toxic cloud of thick black smoke, disappeared.

I hadn't realized I had been holding my breath until I finally released it. Gimra stuck her petite wet nose in the air and sauntered over to me with a protective look in her eyes. Almost immediately I had her in my arms and was covering her fur in kisses. "Oh Gimra, you brave kitty!"

I noticed Oliver groping his way towards us and doing quite a good job of following my voice. "I take it the cat saved you?" He managed a grin, though quickly winced in pain.

Putting Gimra down, I ran to his side and helped him over to Nightflame. "Yes indeed, Gimra saved me from that woman... She's not even fit to be called a woman. 'Thing' is a much better name." I smiled at my cleverness, then turned sullen once again. "She is sick, Oliver, very sick. I don't look forward to seeing her again, though I'm certain we will. I must be honest though, just the thought of confronting her again, makes me feel like curling up into a ball and screaming!"

"Well," Oliver began as I helped him up onto Nightflame, "it seems to me, that she has trouble dealing with white cats, despite her evil power."

"I know, it did seem that way," I agreed and mounted Moondancer. "I don't quite understand what role Gimra will play in all of this, but I was sure grateful for her today!" I nuzzled the white cat, who was seated proudly in the saddle before me, claws digging into the leather.

I unrolled the map and studied it carefully for the first time on our quest. Shielding my eyes, I gazed up at the dazzling sun, attempting to make out directions. It was so hard to tell and I hadn't paid much attention before, since my sisters had been in charge. I chided myself silently for not paying closer attention when I had the opportunity to learn. I let out a slow breath. "Well, I guess I'll have to learn the hard way."

After a lengthy debate with myself, I finally decided that heading left would lead us back to our road and the village of Verity. Gimra let out an approving mew and so I set the ponies in motion with slightly more confidence.

Trying to hide his suffering, Oliver attempted another grin. "Alice, I may not be able to see, but I can tell you're worried about what we're doing. I know it's not much, but I have faith in your abilities. Arvad used to say that sometimes all it takes is one person who believes in you, to help you succeed." He paused. "Do you have faith in yourself?"

Taken off guard, I stumbled over my words without giving a real answer. Finally I managed a weak, "I don't know."

"Well," Oliver straightened himself in the saddle, "I hate to say this, but unless you learn to have faith in yourself, we don't have a chance."

I gulped and stared straight ahead.

CHAPTER SIXTEEN

The Flower of Verity

*T*HE JOURNEY TO Verity lasted several gruelling hours under the hot
sun. I missed the shade of trees desperately during these hours, but
luckily other than the heat, we experienced no misfortune. The wild
fields of grass disappeared into freshly ploughed soil, with fresh green
shoots poking their heads out into the open air for the first time. We had
most definitely entered the farming district of Algernon. Waist high stonewalls divided the fields into different sections. The walls appeared to be
in dire need of repair, for in some places, entire sections had crumbled
into heaps, with weeds growing on top of them. I described this all to
Oliver, who seemed absolutely fascinated by the entire concept of farming.

"There's a sign up ahead," I declared, as I slowed the horses into a
leisurely walk. "It says that Verity is just up ahead."

"Good thing too," Oliver wiped his brow. "I'm hot, hungry and tired...
not to mention this sweat! It makes my burns sting even more. I hate to
complain Alice, but this is pure torture."

"I'll find us someplace to rest," I assured him, while squinting into the
distance. The heat shimmered up off the road in waves. I saw buildings
up ahead, though not many and not very large. All of the houses seemed
widely spaced out, but it was a tall narrow house made out of bright white
wood, that we came to first. The surrounding yard was well taken care of
and the flowerbeds were magnificent, especially for this early in the year.
Climbing sweetheart roses were creeping their way up the side of the
house, like a great pink curtain. Various other types of flowers splashed
every colour imaginable about the front steps and around the base of the
home. I spied a large garden in the back, with healthy looking vegetables
well on their way to maturity. Judging just by the exterior of the house, I
decided that the owners must be very pleasant people... which would be
a welcome relief.

"There's a lovely white house just up ahead Oliver. I think it's a good
place to stop." I reached over and gave him a reassuring pat on the back,
as I stopped our train of horses and dismounted. Dust flew up around my
feet as I walked toward the steps. The ground was so dry, I wondered how
they managed to grow their crops. Back on Moondancer, Gimra mewed
loudly. "I'll only be a moment Gimra!" I smiled, though my heart had

begun to beat rapidly. What would the people say when they saw us? We looked dreadful. Hesitantly, I rapped on the wooden door.

There was no answer, though I distinctly heard quiet footsteps from within. "Who's there?" came a female voice.

At first I was struck silent, but Oliver urged, "Just say friendly travelers or something! Don't hesitate too long, it looks bad."

"Travelers!" I called back, placing my mouth very near the door. "We need—" My plea was cut off as the door swung open.

There stood a young lady of about 16 or 17 years of age. She appeared to be a few years older than myself, though not quite as old as Emma. I stood there in mute awe, for she was absolutely beautiful, like a prairie rose! Her golden blond hair was held up in a loose bun, from which many wispy strands straggled gracefully over her slender face. The lady had a small nose, tiny rosebud mouth and deep blue grey eyes, which matched perfectly with her simple blue dress. A crisp white apron was tied around her waist and the pockets were filled to the brim with fragrant wildflowers. I felt so dingy standing before this beautiful lady, that I unconsciously bowed my head in shame.

She drew in a sharp breath as she surveyed the dirty scene before her. I looked up in time to see her face scrunch up and her hands fly to her cheeks. "Oh good gracious! What happened to you two?" Not waiting for an answer, she swept past me and went to help the wavering Oliver from his saddle.

"We were, uh, caught in a fire," I stated simply, though she didn't seem to be listening.

"Don't worry," she told us, though it was more to Oliver, who she supported with an arm around his shoulders. "I'll have you both feeling better in no time." She delivered Oliver into my care. "Just go on into the house and I'll get your horses settled in the stables." As she said this, Gimra suddenly leapt down off Moondancer and scurried under my skirts. With great skill, the lady gathered up all three horses' reins and led them around the house.

"She sounds very nice," Oliver commented lightly, as I led him into the cool house that was heavy with the scent of flowers.

"Yes," I agreed, "and she is very beautiful! I've never seen anyone like her before. I wonder if she lives here alone? I don't see anyone else."

"How old would you say she is Alice?" Oliver asked, gingerly touching his burned eyes.

"Don't touch," I instructed, pulling his hands away from his face. "Oh, I'd say she is 16, maybe 17. Not Emma's age though, but older than myself." I cringed at saying Emma's name. I still didn't understand how she could have just left us. The anger and shock was so fresh in my mind that I couldn't think about it just yet.

Oliver nodded strangely. "That's what I thought." He seemed pleased with himself.

I quickly scanned our surroundings. I didn't want to be a snoop, but I was curious about this lovely house, as it was quite possibly the most feminine home I had ever seen. The room we were presently in, seemed to serve as a sunroom. There was a bay window directly off to our left, where dried flowers were hung upside-down in the sun. As well, there was a firm looking wooden chair, with a sweet patchwork cushion on it, positioned so that anyone who was seated, had a view of the path which led into the village. There were various pairs of shoes lined up perfectly by the door, as well as shawls, cloaks and bonnets, hung on hooks mounted on the wall. All articles looked very much like those that belonged to a lady. Oddly enough, nothing appeared to belong to a man.

"I think she lives alone," I whispered to Oliver, attempting to sneak a peak into the next room, which had the look of a parlour. My spying was interrupted as the lady reappeared in the doorway.

"Go in, go in!" She smiled warmly. "Don't be shy." She ushered us in with a gentle push. "By the way, my name is Carrie Lynn Huxley, but you can just call me Carrie."

Remembering my manners and feeling relaxed at once in the cozy parlour, which was decorated with flowers, I replied, "My name is Alice and this is Oliver." I twirled around the room in awe. The walls had wildflowers painted on them in the same colours as we had seen in the flowerbed outside. There was a stone fireplace in one corner, but no fire, since it was a terribly warm day. There were also various decorative tables and chairs placed strategically about, giving the room a very warm and inviting look. There were two windows, with long flowing curtains that nearly touched the floor and were the colour of lavender in full bloom. For a little farmhouse on the plains, it was very refreshing.

Carrie seemed amused by my amazement. She covered a giggle. "I like to decorate," she offered in explanation to her frilly abode. "My mother liked to paint and my father liked to work with wood and the result is this magnificent parlour, which I like to call the Flower Room. Has a nice ring to it, don't you think?"

I nodded vigorously. "My sisters would have absolutely adored your house as well..." My voice lowered at the end and Carrie, sensing my discomfort, cleared her throat.

"I can see you have both endured a lot and I shall do my best to help you in any way possible." Carrie offered a gentle smile and guided Oliver over to a chair. I cringed at the black sooty marks he would leave in it, but noticed much to my relief, that the chair had no fabric on it. Carrie turned back to me almost hesitantly. "So are you brother and sister?"

I paused, unprepared for such a question. The truth at this moment appeared much too far-fetched, so I found myself nodding. "Yes, Oliver is my dear brother."

Carrie seemed somewhat relieved by my answer and gave a light-hearted laugh. "When I first met you, I thought you might be husband and wife! How silly of me!"

The statement made me recoil with distaste. Oliver, my husband? Somehow that idea didn't sit well with me. He had become far too much like a brother for that to ever, ever, be a possibility. I noticed that Oliver himself looked awfully amused, but said nothing.

"Well now," Carrie stated, as she disappeared through a door and into what I assumed was the kitchen, "the first thing both of you require is a bath." She re-emerged from the kitchen carrying a small trunk, lovingly cared out of redwood. "I've set some water to boil for washing." Placing the trunk on a pentagonal shaped table, she unfastened the lock, using a tiny silver key. "I have some clothing in here that I hope will fit properly, seeing as your... um... your present clothing is quite beyond my skill to repair."

I flushed crimson at my ragged dress... the dress I had been so proud of when Ms Craddock had presented it to me. That seemed like another lifetime. Now it was time to leave behind yet another tie to the Forgotten Forest. "I guess our clothes have seen better days," I admitted sheepishly. I shot a glance over at Oliver, who was listening intently to Carrie's prattle, but making no attempt to join the conversation.

"Here we are!" Carrie exclaimed proudly, holding up a royal blue tunic and a slightly larger scarlet one. "I believe these will fit okay, but if not, I can always make alterations, so not to worry. They are much better suited for traveling, which I assume is what you were doing." She gazed inquisitively at me. "By the way, if you don't mind my asking, where are you headed?"

I shifted uncomfortably. Should I lie or tell the truth? My mind went back to Petra and the Witch, taking advantage of my loose tongue. Perhaps if I was vague, then I could elaborate later if it seemed safe. At the moment, it was so hard to tell... Carrie seemed like a lovely lady in a gorgeous farmhouse, but... perhaps it was best not to rush into things, as was my habit. However, I was spared having to say anything at all, for it was Oliver who spoke up.

"We're heading south." He smiled with conviction. "But it seems that misfortune is waiting for us around every corner." He paused, with Carrie seeming to hang upon his every word. "But perhaps our misfortune has ended, since we've come across your refreshing kindness." His charm was indeed captivating, I had to admit. I thought I spied a twinge of a blush play across Carrie's delicate cheeks, as she quickly folded the tunics across the back of a chair.

"You are most welcome here," she replied, while locking the trunk once again and turning towards the kitchen. "Follow me Alice. You can take your bath in the back room. Oh and grab that blue tunic," she told me.

I grabbed the soft tunic and tucked it hastily under my arm. "But what about my brother?"

Carrie wavered it off as nothing. "Not to worry, I shall take good care of him. He needs bandages on those nasty burns. I have another washtub upstairs he can use. You just relax and—" Carrie was cut short by a rather loud and demanding mew.

"Oh Gimra!" I exclaimed, seeing her leap out from underneath a table. "You have a knack for hiding don't you?" I laughed as the sleek cat sauntered up to me.

"I guess she wants to go with you!" Carrie smiled. "She is indeed a beautiful cat."

I almost added 'and very useful against witches', but decided quickly against it. I was finally learning to think before speaking. "Will you be okay without me Oliver?" I asked hesitantly, wondering briefly if he resented being left under the care of a complete stranger... especially when he had just lost his sight.

"Don't worry Alice!" Oliver grinned from his chair and waved me away. "I will be fine. You and Gimra just relax."

Without further protest, I allowed Carrie to lead me into the next room, which was indeed a spacious kitchen. It was adorned with the usual wooden cupboards and cooking instruments, though the walls were painted very cheerfully. In one rather dark corner, was a steep staircase that led upstairs. The door to the back room Carrie had referred to, was directly across from these stairs.

"I use the back room for bathing most of the time, since it is convenient to heat the water up right here in the kitchen," she explained and opened the door. A quaint wooden washtub sat in one corner, underneath a small window with a lacy curtain. A bowl with dried flower petals sat on a corner shelf, along with various coloured bottles. "I like to make my own soap with herbs and such," Carrie explained. "Feel free to use anything in here." She added one more kettle full of steaming water.

I stood admiring the room, with Gimra at my feet. "I won't be long," I assured Carrie as she backed out of the room.

"Oh no. Take your time, please," Carrie smiled and shut the door with a click.

There was a little round mirror hanging on the sidewall, mounted on a silver hook. After I peeled off my dirt encrusted dress, I stood for a moment and simply stared into the silver mirror. It had been a long time since I had seen my reflection and what I saw didn't look at all familiar. My long brown hair was a mat of dirt and tangles, which I instinctively knew would take some work to get clean. The sad face that stared back at me was soot covered, except for the pink trails where tears had fallen. I hadn't even realized just how sad my face looked. At the orphanage, my mouth had nearly always been smiling and now it was a straight line. Even my eyes once had a brilliant sparkle, but that too had disappeared. Where was the pretty little girl who had started out on this quest not so long ago? With a sigh, I removed my pendant, as well as Clara's and set them on a shelf.

Testing the water with my index finger, I slid down into its warm embrace. Gimra stared strangely at me for a moment, before plunging herself into the steamy water. She came up spluttering, resembling a white rat and looking very unamused. I laughed in spite of myself. "How is it that such a simple act can make me feel warm all over?"

I then leaned back and closed my eyes, allowing the cleansing water to wash away not only dirt, but also guilt and terrifying memories. I wondered briefly how Oliver was faring under Carrie's care. She acted very strange towards him, very strange indeed.

CHAPTER SEVENTEEN

Recovery

*A*FTER A RELAXING and rather lengthy bath, I was in much better spirits. Upon gazing at my appearance in the mirror after washing, I was relieved to see my familiar self staring back. The sadness was still there, but was not nearly as visible. As I tidied up the little bathing room, I glanced outside at the sun and to my surprise, it was plunging downward. The day was nearly over! I shook my head sadly; we were not making very good time to Devona and Nissim had said he was becoming weaker. Would I even have the courage to complete the quest? Gimra shook herself and licked her paw, now seeming quite pleased that she had taken a dip.

Upon exiting the bathing room, I found Carrie busily working away in the cheerful kitchen, humming happily to herself. The table was all laid out for supper and there was a little dish on the floor for Gimra. Carrie brought a steaming platter of corn muffins to the table and looked up with the biggest smile.

"I see you've finished," she commented brightly. "And you look so much better! Does the tunic fit all right?"

I nodded and stretched my arms out to model my new garment. The undertunic dress was a deep beige colour and a nice contrast to the dark blue overtunic, which extended to just above my knees, as well as above my elbows. The skirts of my undertunic flowed about my ankles and covered my arms all the way down to my wrists. "Yes it fits perfectly," I told Carrie, "and I love the colours. Are you sure you want to give this to me? I could pay you some money for it…" I offered uncertainly, as I seated myself at the table.

"Nonsense!" Carrie shook her head. "It's nothing really." She wiped her hands on her apron and stole a quick glance towards the stairway.

"Where's Oliver?" I asked, rearranging my eating utensils nervously. There was something… I wasn't quite sure what, that was going on. I wished that I could understand, but it was beyond me at the present time.

Carrie began pouring water into mugs at the table from a large clay jar. "Oh he's still upstairs. I dare say that his burns will heal completely, but I don't think his eyes will." She looked sad. "He wouldn't say much, except that there was a terrible fire and that you lost a sister in it." Carrie touched my hand lightly. "I truly am sorry. I too, know what it is like to

135

lose family." She didn't elaborate any further, but instead strode towards the stairs. "I'll go fetch Oliver for supper. You can start filling a plate."

"That's okay," I offered, starting to stand up, "I can go get Oliver. You can finish up whatever else needs to be done."

"That's fine Alice, I'm all done anyway. Besides, you're my guest. It wouldn't be proper. Relax! Eat! I'm sure you haven't had anything nourishing all day," Carrie told me and there was no room for arguing, for she was already halfway up the stairs.

"She sure is eager to please, especially when Oliver is concerned," I muttered and threw some bits of meat into Gimra's little bowl, which she pounced upon hungrily. "Oh well." I shrugged and helped myself to some roast with rich brown gravy, as well as carrots and lettuce.

I was just biting into a hot corn muffin, when Carrie emerged with Oliver. She was holding his arm and helping him down the creaking wooden stairs, with a look of concern across her striking features. Oliver clutched at the railing as though in fear, but something about his expression told me that he wasn't the least bit afraid. I made a face, as Oliver was pretending to be helpless for some reason. I was positive that he was perfectly capable of getting down the stairs himself and yet he was letting Carrie fuss over him like a child.

"Careful Oliver," Carrie warned softly, "this is a big step."

"Oh please," I sighed and turned back to my food. Gimra greeted Oliver as he walked by and sat down at the table, or rather allowed Carrie to seat him. At last I looked up at him and blinked, for he was completely changed. Oliver was his handsome self again, for his burned black locks had been trimmed and even his eyebrows appeared to be okay. The deep scarlet tunic fit him perfectly, outlining his developing muscles and shoulders that would one day be strong and broad. The breeches he wore were nearly the same colour as my undertunic and so, we matched. I had to also admire the expert bandaging job Carrie had done to his eyes, for it didn't look half bad. She had used clean white cloths and bound them across his eyes as well as around his head, but in such a neat manner that it almost appeared stylish.

"Hello Alice!" Oliver greeted me with a warm smile. Feeling Gimra against his leg, he laughed, "Greetings to you too Gimra!"

"You certainly look and sound a lot better," I commented, cutting a piece of roast. I watched as Carrie passed Oliver a pre-filled plate.

"Here you go Oliver," Carrie gushed. "I cut up the meat too… Here's a fork. Can you manage?"

"Yes Carrie, thank you so much. You're very helpful." Oliver flashed her his winning grin.

This time, there was no mistaking the blush on Carrie's face, even though she quickly tried to hide it by looking at her plate. "Oliver can't see if you blush," I told Carrie with a stifled giggle, but wished I hadn't said anything, for her shade darkened and she looked pained. Perhaps I still had a lot to learn about what to say and what not to say, especially on matters I didn't fully understand.

Oliver cleared his throat. "Well, this food sure is great! I'll have to eat lots now, because we sure won't get meals like this on the road."

"I could try and cook like this," I offered. "Maybe Carrie could give me some recipes."

With a slight chuckle, Oliver took a long drink of water. "No offence Alice, but I don't see you as the cooking type."

My mouth dropped open, but I quickly closed it and went on, "When I lived at the orphanage, I used to cook all the time!"

"The orphanage?" Carrie repeated, suddenly looking inquiringly in my direction. "But Oliver told me your parents lived in Muir and that you were going to visit your uncle in Jadestone." There was no accusation in her voice, only confusion.

I felt a sharp kick in the shins from Oliver and I bit my lip. "Well, that is, I worked in an orphanage... volunteered really. My... um... our... cousin was the headmistress and sometimes I would do some chores for her."

"Really?" Carrie raised an unbelieving eyebrow.

"Yes, really," I confirmed quickly, "but we're off to visit good old Uncle... Uncle... Guy."

"I though Oliver said it was Hadwin." Carrie looked very puzzled now.

"Oh!" I scratched the back of my head nervously. "Well, his name is Hadwin of course, but sometimes I call him Uncle Guy... like a pet name and he calls me little Al." I could feel Oliver's desire to bang his head into a stonewall. How did I ever get myself into these messes? Lies only add up to more lies...

Suddenly Oliver stretched his arms in the air and yawned loudly. "Well, I'm done! What a *good* meal! But I am very tired, so I think I'm going to turn in. We're leaving tomorrow morning I take it?" He addressed this question to me, although he did not look in my direction.

Grateful for the change in subject, I confirmed Oliver's statement. "Yes, we really must not wear out our welcome."

"Tomorrow?" Carrie's head shot up suddenly, as she dropped her fork with a clatter. "But you've only just arrived and Oliver is in no condition for traveling! I insist, you must stay tomorrow as well."

"I'm sorry Carrie," I told her apologetically, "but we really must continue on as soon as possible. We don't have a lot of time..." There was no point in trying to make her see our urgency when she didn't know the full story.

"I guess I understand." Carrie stacked our empty plates together doubtfully. "Will you... ever be coming by this way again? On your way back home perhaps?"

"I don't think so," I replied as truthfully as I could. "At least not for some time."

"But that doesn't mean never," Oliver quickly put in. "I'm positive our paths will cross again." The smile never left his face, but he stood up abruptly and pushed his chair in. Feeling his way towards the banister, he began to mount the stairs.

"Let me help you!" Carrie began to rush forward.

"No, no," Oliver replied quickly. "I'm... I'm fine. The first door on the left, right?"

"Yes, that's right," Carrie confirmed and dropped her arms lifelessly to her sides. She remained silent as she swiftly carried the dirty dishes off to a washbasin and covered the leftover food with a red checked cloth.

There was a certain tension in the air that made the delicious food I had just ingested sit poorly and I suddenly had the terrible urge to bury my face in my hands and cry. The sun had now set, leaving the kitchen in dim shadows and Carrie had not yet lit any candles. At this moment, as I helped a stranger, lovely as she was, I was struck with such earth shattering loneliness that it literally hurt to breath. Carrie's silence only added to my grief and despite my best efforts, I felt my breath quicken and my shoulders begin to shake. The tears fell unbidden and unwelcome, but nevertheless, they flowed. Gimra sat silently under a chair watching me with sorrowful eyes, but not moving.

As Carrie placed the last clean dish upon a high shelf, she turned to me with glistening blue eyes. "Shall we take a walk outside Alice? That is, if you're not too tired. It's a lovely evening."

I wiped my eyes quickly on the sleeve of my undertunic, leaving dark stains in the soft fabric. Without a word, I followed Carrie out into the cool night air. She looked very thoughtful, but remained silent. I decided to let her initiate any conversation. Light paw sounds in the grass gave away Gimra's presence. She followed like a shadow and only appeared when she deemed it convenient. I felt comforted by her presence, since she appeared to be a powerful ally against the dreaded Witch.

Carrie took me out to her large garden and bending down to touch the dry soil, sighed. "Without moisture, everything will dry up and die soon. This area lives off of the crops. If they fail, we shall all starve." Her face took on a sudden look of defiance. "It wasn't always like this. No, when I was a child, things were always lush and green. Ever since we lost our

King, things have slowly begun to fade away. The sun shines hotter and the rain comes less often." She watched me carefully for a reaction, but I remained expressionless... a skill I had learned from Emma.

The moon rose high into the sky, bathing everything in soft silver light. It was the same silver light that had witnessed so many tragedies. If the moon had a memory, I was certain it would be weeping constantly. Around the moon, the stars flickered and danced. A particularly bright one caught my attention, but suddenly flared and went out completely. Even stars had to die...

Carrie pointed out a rickety shed, possibly the only building on her land that looked rundown. "I never come out to this building," she explained, fiddling with the lock. With a groan, she flung open the heavy door.

I gasped at the sight before me. Piled from the dirt floor to the roof, were weapons of every sort. Some where so terrible looking that I could not even imagine how they worked, but there were others I was sure I had seen before... but only in nightmares. "Where did you get these?" I finally broke my vow of silence.

Carrie leaned against the wooden doorframe and looked out into the distance. "It's a long story and though I'm sure you'd listen to it, I do not want to get into details. When Ralston Radburn... I think you know who he is," she gave me a sideways glance, "first took over Algernon, he was overly ambitious. He tried to gain control of everything at once. He sent his forces as far north as our little village of Verity." She made a fist and held it up in the air, shaking slightly. "However Ralston is fallible and overestimated his own power. Devona, I have heard, proved difficult to restrain and so Ralston had to withdraw his forces from here in order to maintain his power in the capital. But still, for many of us, it was too late." Carrie's fist dropped quickly and her face convulsed in sorrow. "I was just a little girl at the time, but I remember that night so clearly... I was in my trundle bed when the attack came. There were horrible green flames everywhere..."

My mind flashed back to the scene at the Temple of Strength. Those clawing green flames had engulfed poor Clara and maimed darling Oliver. I couldn't imagine the trauma poor Carrie had undergone as a child.

"My mother came rushing into my room, out of breath and coughing terribly," Carrie recalled. Her eyes seemed blank as she witnessed all the tragic events again. "She grabbed my hand and concealed me in the root cellar under the kitchen. Mother told me, 'Now be a good girl Carrie and stay down here until we come get you. Do not move or make any noise. That's my flower, mummy loves you.' Those were the last words my mother ever said to me. I never got to even see my father that night."

I stared in horror at Carrie as the wind tugged at her wispy blond hair. For all her beauty, for all her lovely possessions, she bore a past unlike any other I had heard. "And your parents?" I asked. "What happened to them?"

Carrie broke off her distant stare, but to my surprise, her eyes were dry. "They never came to get me in the cellar. I waited and I waited and I waited. Finally my aunt found me, hungry and cold. She raised me until I was 12, then got married and I have lived alone ever since, supported by the kindness of the other villagers. As to what happened to my parents, I have no idea. They simply vanished, like so many other villagers that night. No one knows if they are dead or slaves... but I know they're dead. Ralston takes no prisoners."

I couldn't help myself from saying, "You are so strong... You tell that story, yet shed no tears."

She smiled gently at me. "That's only because I have no tears left to shed. From the amount I have cried, I could water the entire Plains of Algernon for a decade. But now, to the weapons. When Ralston's army retreated, they dropped everything except their food in order to move more swiftly. My aunt gathered up the weapons and stored them in this shed. I don't know why she did it, but she did. I think... I think you may want to pick something out... for your journey."

She knew. She knew we had lied to her and yet had played along with it all. At that moment, I decided that telling her the truth was the right thing. So, I slumped down into the grass against the shed and took a breath. "Carrie," I began, "you know we didn't tell you the real reason we are heading south."

With a nod, she replied, "I gathered as much. But I also respect your reasons for silence. Let me assure you," she took my cold hands into her warm ones, "your secrets are safe with me. I would never betray you."

For a brief second, I had a strange feeling of uneasiness, but it was soon gone and I was left with no feelings of danger. "Okay," I sighed, "here goes." My story was a long one and was made even longer by my sobbing. I was not as strong as Carrie when it came to recalling past events. Still she listened patiently and soothed me when I required it. The moon was high in the sky when I finally finished.

"So you and your brother must find Prince Edric," Carrie remarked, letting out a low whistle. "That sounds difficult."

I started when she referred to Oliver as my brother, but recalled that I had forgotten to say he was anything else. I decided to leave it for now, since she obviously liked the idea of him being a relation of mine. A small inkling at the back of my female mind had been awakened and things that had previously been unknown to me, were starting to become clear.

"So which weapon would you like?" Carrie inquired, as she put her hands on her hips and surveyed the pile of ghastly instruments.

"They all look so... so... evil," I remarked, gingerly touching the hilt of a sword. "And I don't think I could even lift some of them." Gimra suddenly appeared from behind the shed and bounded inside. Crawling into the pile of weapons, through various crevices, she re-emerged dragging a medium sized bow and quiver full of golden arrows. I picked up the bow and was amazed by how light it was. The string let out a healthy 'twang' when I plucked it and I slung the quiver onto my back. "I guess I'll take this one!" I laughed in spite of myself. "Gimra, you've done it again!" She purred softly and sat down on my foot.

"Give this to Oliver." Carrie handed me a smoothly polished walking stick, with a sapphire embedded in its top. It fairly glowed in the moonlight. "It will be... of great use to him I think. It's not one of these weapons... It was my father's actually. I removed some of the jewels from the weapons... Ralston apparently spared no expense and I mounted them onto the walking stick long ago. I would like very much for Oliver to have it."

Even in the dark, I could see her blush. It was becoming quite clear now, though the emotion was still rather foreign to me. "You like him, don't you?" I asked softly.

She nodded slowly. "But it's not meant to be," she whispered sadly. "I'm just so afraid... I wish I had never met him and yet my life is fuller now that I have. Something is going to happen in Devona, I just know it. And remember the predictions you told me Keenan made. He said that fairies would play a major role in Oliver's future. He made no mention of farm girls."

"Carrie, if old Keenan's prophecies are completely correct, then that means I am going to fail and darkness will cover everything. I choose not to believe that... I have to believe that everything will turn out, or I won't be able to continue day after day. I need all the strength I can get. You must believe that things will work out Carrie, you must," I found myself begging.

"You are so much braver than you think Alice." Carrie's face lit up. "When you speak, I believe you... I have faith in the future. There's something about you that shines so brightly, yet you try so hard to smother it. Keep that inner light close to your heart and in your darkest hour, it will not fail you." She stood up and brushed the dry grass from her skirt. "Come now, it's late."

CHAPTER EIGHTEEN

Mysterious Rescue

"*A*T LAST YOU ARE MINE!" shouted a dark shadow, as his long black cloak flapped like raven wings in the wind.

"No!" I shouted, scrambling to my feet and running away, rock chips flying into the air as I went. I threw myself behind a rather large boulder and leaned against it, trying desperately to catch my breath. The Shadow Man... Who was he? I should know... but my mind was racing with thoughts all too quickly.

"Come out Alice! There is no one left to save you!" the Shadow gurgled in his throat.

"How can that be?" I whispered, clutching my chest in agony. Where was everyone else? Oliver? Emma? Surely they would help me... Little Gimra? Why had they left me all alone in this wretched place? Had I been forsaken by everyone... or had the Shadow already finished with them? I was the last... the last hope... That thought awakened something deep inside of me... but I was no hero.

"This is the end!" squealed the Shadow in glee and I felt painful bites all over my body. "NO!"

I opened my eyes and found myself staring at a ceiling with stencilled flowers. The bed beneath me was soft and my head was resting gently upon a pillow filled with heather. I was in one of Carrie's guest rooms. I sat up quickly and shook my head. The dream was getting more vivid. No, it was a vision, not just a dream. It was a vision of things to come, it just had to be. The bites I had received in the dream still ached and yet I could find no marks upon my body.

There was one window in this guest room and it faced east. The sun was just creeping up over the horizon, its pink rays painting the dark sky with its softness. A sudden sense of urgency stole over my body. I sensed that Nissim was growing weaker and Ralston was growing stronger. Soon Ralston would attempt to take over the rest of Algernon and possibly all of Fadreama as he had tried before, but this time, he would not fail.

Then there was a small voice at the back of my mind, reminding me that I could still turn back. Emma couldn't have gone far. I could catch up with her and beg for forgiveness. Oliver could stay with Carrie and I could live peacefully in the forest. Absently I fingered the seal ring Isadora had given me. Her last wish had been for baby Julia to grow up in a peaceful world. Were they truly all dead? Somehow I thought that if such a thing had happened, I would have sensed it... and yet I sensed nothing.

I shook my head violently. No, I could not quit and I knew it. Algernon would not be peaceful unless something was done. Already I owed many people at least an earnest attempt. "I had better get up before I change my mind again," I muttered and jumped out onto the cold wood floor, just as Gimra poked her nose out from under the down filled quilt.

*   *   *

"Thank you for everything Carrie," Oliver stammered nervously. He was seated atop Nightflame, who was tied behind Moondancer. In exchange for her kindness, I had insisted that Carrie keep Storm. Besides, it would be too much trouble to keep three horses. "You have done so much for us... We'll never forget you." Oliver bit his lower lip as if deciding something and then added, "I won't forget you. That is a promise."

Carrie's hand was resting atop Nightflame's head as she gently stroked the pony's silky mane. "I shan't forget you either Oliver and *that* is a promise," she whispered almost inaudibly.

He reached out and found her hand without the slightest bit of groping. With a slow bow, Oliver raised Carrie's hand to his lips and brushed it ever so lightly with a kiss. "Here's hoping that when we meet again, it will be under more joyous circumstances and I've no doubt that we will indeed meet again." Had there been no bandage across his eyes, Oliver would have been staring intently into Carrie's.

She made no attempt to withdraw her hand, or cover the fierce blush that coloured her flawless features. "Please Oliver, no matter where you go, or what you do... or what you become, don't forget about me." She pressed a fresh blue flower into his palm; a Forget-Me-Not.

"Nothing could make me forget anything about you," Oliver told her gently.

"Then I shall take your word for it," Carrie stated quickly. "Farewell!" She withdrew her hand swiftly and fled some distance away. "Goodbye dear Alice!" Carrie waved her hand at me.

I waved back at her, feeling slightly uncomfortable at the exchange I had just witnessed. That same inkling of turning back was creeping up again. "Goodbye Carrie and thank you!" I called out before I could think too deeply. Gimra let loose her own sound of gratefulness, as she sat upright in the saddle before me.

"Remember what I told you Alice," Carrie reminded me. "Even when everything else has been plunged into darkness, your own light will guide you. If only you believe, then you shall never be alone!" She brushed a stray strand of hair from her face and smiled hopefully at me.

At this, I decided it was time to take our leave. There was no use in extending the obvious pain that both Carrie and Oliver were in. The road stretched before us far into the distance. The last time we had been on this great path, our company had been much larger. With one last glance back at Carrie's figure standing alone in front of her house, we departed. It wasn't until Verity was left far behind, that I spoke.

"Oliver, are you angry that I didn't let you stay with Carrie?" I asked the question that had been on my mind since our departure.

"Let me stay with Carrie?" Oliver repeated, startled and confused. "What are you talking about? My place is by your side, helping in any way I possibly can." He clenched his fists. "I know I'm blind now, but that doesn't make me useless and I won't be a burden, I promise!"

"Oh Oliver!" I exclaimed. "That wasn't what I meant at all! It's just that you seemed so fond of Carrie..." I trailed off, feeling my foot in my mouth.

Keeping his bandaged eyes on the road, Oliver replied in a tight voice, "Yes I am fond of Carrie, but I do not let my feelings distract me from my purpose. I have a task to complete and so help me, I'll finish it before I do anything else."

"I wish I had your determination Oliver," I sighed. "You and Gimra will have to keep me motivated. I must admit that second thoughts have been eating away at my mind."

"Alice, there's not always going to be someone there to prop you up. I've said this once before, but I'll say it again. You must learn to believe in yourself. Even with a great army, you cannot win unless you have some faith in your own abilities. Do you understand my meaning?" Oliver sounded slightly frustrated but then brightened, as though a cloud had lifted from his face. "Enough lecturing, I'm starting to sound like Emma!" he laughed and couldn't see my frown.

Trusting Moondancer to follow the road, I carefully unrolled the map. "Jadestone isn't all that far away. We can reach it sometime tonight, if we ride hard," I commented, scarcely paying any attention to the shadow that passed in front of the sun quickly. I glanced up... There was nothing in the sky, but perhaps it had been a wisp of cloud...

"There's a river in Jadestone, right?" Oliver mused thoughtfully. "I think it is called the Jade, hence the city's name."

"Yes indeed, there is a river," I confirmed, tracing my finger along the yellowed parchment. "And it's a great river from the looks of things. I hope it won't be difficult to cross."

"Well there must be ferries or something we can take," Oliver suggested helpfully. "People have to cross it all the time."

"But remember," I replied as Moondancer stumbled slightly, "Jadestone is getting awfully close to Devona. What if Ralston's army didn't withdraw from that city? We might have more trouble there than we expect."

"I think you worry too much Alice," Oliver grinned, shaking his freshly trimmed black locks out of his face. "We'll find someway through Jadestone, you'll see." He stopped speaking abruptly.

"I don't know—" I started, but was promptly shushed by Oliver. He had his finger to his lips.

"Do you... hear something?" he asked, cocking his head to one side. Our ponies tossed their heads fretfully and Gimra's body tensed up.

"Hear something?" I repeated and shook my head. "No, everything seems quiet, but there is a foul scent in the air." A tiny sweat broke out above my lip and I had the strong sensation that we were being watched. "Hold on Oliver!" I called back to him. "We're going to try and outrun whatever it is that's following us!" Our ponies needed no urging to get them to run and within minutes, we were practically flying across the plains.

"If nothing else, we're making good time!" Oliver called up to me. He was bent low in the saddle and clutching Nightflame's mane for dear life. I decided that it must be terribly frightening to be moving so swiftly and unable to see anything.

My teeth rattled and our rapid pace jarred my bones. I watched the passing ground beneath us for a moment, but the blur only made me dizzy. Poor Gimra had her claws extended into the saddle their full length. Still no matter how fast we went, the sensation of being watched did not diminish. The terrain gradually became rougher, with more loose rocks and the vegetation seemed to transform from waving prairie grass, to slightly denser greenery. The only explanation I could think of, was that we were on the outer rim of the Jade River Valley. The land did seem to be sloping downward, but that aided us in our flight.

The sun disappeared for a split second again, as it had when I was studying the map. This time though, I saw a shadow cast on the ground. It appeared to be the outline of a great bird... Suddenly, there was an ear piercing shriek above our heads. The sound was one of pure agony and it made my blood run cold.

"Alice!" Oliver cried out. "What's going on?"

"I don't know! I think... ahhhh!" I felt something strike me hard from the side and I flew through the air briefly, before smashing into the hard ground. I could hear Oliver's cry of anguish as the ponies continued to run, with him blindly in the saddle. Groggily I shook my head and looked up, just in time to dodge a pair of skinny hair covered legs with enormous pointed talons. "It's a bird," I whispered, but nothing could have prepared me for the creature I saw circling around in the sky.

This was no ordinary bird... It wasn't even the sinister looking Raven that had so often followed us. This creature was at least 10 times the size of any bird I had ever seen before. My thoughts went back to a bedtime story I had once heard at the orphanage, about a great bird called the Harpy. This, I decided, was definitely that creature, which up until now, I had believed was a myth.

Bronze in colour and with an immense wingspan, it was obvious that the Harpy was very powerful. However the aspect of this formidable creature that terrified me the most, was her face; it was that of a woman. Though her features were dark and contorted, it was still very clearly a woman's face. Her eyes were glazed and black, but they held an emotion that I had no words to describe. It was somewhere between anger and torment... It made me feel like weeping. The Harpy opened her golden lips and let loose another squealing shriek. As she did so, I spied a set of razor sharp fangs, glistening against her metallic skin.

"This," I gasped, "is the Witch's doing! It has to be!" I screamed and stumbled into the grass as the Harpy made another dive for me. Wincing, I felt something poke sharply into my side. My bow! It wasn't much, but it was something to defend myself with! I knew quite well how a bow worked... but I had never actually shot one before. Perhaps I should have considered this before accepting it from Carrie! The Harpy was circling around for another attack! There wasn't any time to decide! I had to do something!

Quickly I drew an arrow and prepared to take aim... but to my astonishment, the Harpy had vanished! "What the... ?" I muttered, turning around nervously. There was no sign of it... or of Oliver and our runaway ponies for that matter. A terrible feeling clutched at my insides... What if the Harpy had got Oliver! I was about to scream out his name when suddenly a figure appeared on the road from the south. It was hard to tell from this distance, but I could just make out our two ponies with Oliver seated on one and Gimra on the other. But who was the mysterious figure leading them?

There was no time to ponder this, for the Harpy's deadly shriek sounded behind me. Feeling the rush of wings, I ducked, just in time to avoid the jagged grasping talons. With trembling arms, I held up my bow, but found it difficult to take aim at a moving target. Even the string was more difficult to pull back and keep back, than I had expected. The Harpy swung around in midair and came at me with full speed. There was no time to move and as I hit the ground, I felt my bow go skidding away.

"No," I moaned and started painfully crawling towards my lost weapon. My sides felt bruised and battered, but I knew that if I didn't get to my bow, I was going to feel a lot worse pain. Just as I was about to clasp my salvation, I felt a sharp, searing pain in my back. The pain did not stop there, but rather increased dramatically. I was pressed downwards into the uneven ground by the weight of the Harpy, who was now perched upon me. At least I was lying on my stomach and thus protecting my vital organs somewhat, but I knew *that* wasn't going to save me. Every time I drew in a breath, my head felt as though it were going to explode. The weight was crushing the air, no, life, right out of me! So this was the end...

Suddenly the Harpy screamed in agony! Then again! I could feel her grip on me slacken ever so slightly, allowing me a tiny bit of air. I heard an odd 'whiz' above me, but I was unable to lift my head to see exactly what was going on. The Harpy let loose another painful shriek and swiftly took flight, leaving me dazed and confused. Finally able to lift my head, I saw the figure who had been leading our ponies, shooting arrows at the mythical bird, who was flying dangerously low.

I couldn't see much detail about the strange person from where I lay, except that the figure wore a dark grey cloak and held a magnificent look-ing bow. The arrows being shot were no ordinary arrows either! They glowed with a bright green aura and flew faster and straighter than any-thing I had ever seen before.

"Either those arrows are magical, or the shooter is," I whispered to myself, while crawling to my knees.

It didn't take many more hits, to send the unhappy bird crashing to the ground, only to disintegrate as soon as it made contact. Without a shadow of a doubt, the Witch had sent this monster to kill us, seeing as she was so frightened of our little white cat. Upon seeing the destruction of the Harpy, my mysterious saviour rushed to my side, leading our ponies.

I couldn't see the figure's face, for a large hood had been pulled up, so that all features were completely shrouded. It was difficult to tell if it was a man or a woman, but I decided that it must be a man.

"Who are you?" I asked in wonder. "You saved my life!"

"Not to mention mine," Oliver added from Nightflame's back. He was breathing heavily and his knuckles were white. "One minute I'm riding like the wind, the next I'm being led by someone who won't speak!"

"My name," came the figure's rich voice, "is Io." He reached into his belt and produced come clean cloths. Bending down, he began to put pressure on my back wounds, which burned most dreadfully.

"Well Io, thank you so much for stopping that creature," I replied, in an attempt to initiate some sort of conversation that would lead to more information. Poor Oliver was even more confused than I. Gimra appeared calm and almost regal, still clinging to the back of Moondancer.

Io produced three bottles of clear liquid and popped the corks off with his gloved thumb. "I did it for the good of Algernon. Now hold still while I heal you." He poured some of the sweet smelling liquid into his hand and after rubbing them together, held them on my back, while whispering under his breath.

"You... know of our quest then?" I inquired, when Io finally removed his hands from my back and bid me stand up. To my surprise, my back was completely healed. Aside from the claw marks in my tunic, there was no evidence that I had ever been attacked.

"Your quest?" Io repeated in an amused tone. "Yes, you might say that I know about it Alice."

"And my name!" I took a step back, as it seemed rather strange for Io to know such things.

"I know many things," Io explained, packing the bottles and extra cloth back into his belt.

"But how?" I pressed, as Io led me to Moondancer.

"Get back on your horse and hurry on your way. There is no time or need for introductions or unnecessary questions. You must move more swiftly than you have ever moved before, lest the Witch should unleash another attack. You are too close to Devona for the evil one's comfort." Io pulled his hood up closer about his face.

"But I would like to know more about you!" I complained, mounting Moondancer stubbornly. "You owe me at least that much."

"*I* owe you nothing, little one. Time is growing short! Can you not sense the change in the air? Ralston's power is growing in the mountains and soon he shall break free! Find Edric the heir! There is no other way!"

"Will we ever see you again?" I asked, taking up the reins and turning the ponies south once again.

Io looked so mysterious, swathed in his dark cloak. Was he good or evil? "I am bound by a different mission, therefore I cannot say. You must keep up your courage Alice. Algernon's fate hangs by a thread now and if you give in to fear, that thread will be broken."

"Nothing like a little pressure for motivation," I muttered under my breath.

"Go now and perhaps our paths will cross again! Good luck to you!" Io slapped Moondancer's rump, sending her off into a run, dragging Nightflame and Oliver behind.

"And Alice," Io called out, "beware the weak minded and be careful whom you trust!"

I turned for one last look, but saw only a fading cloud of purple smoke.

Part Three

Jadestone and the Sterling Hills

CHAPTER NINETEEN

Jadestone

"**H**ow in the world do people disappear so quickly in this land?" I blinked my brown eyes in surprise, but there was no time to contemplate Io's abruptness, for Jadestone was already looming in the valley below us. It was a large city, which spread along the mighty Jade River. From our elevated point of view, we... that is I... had a good view of the river itself. My first thoughts were of its incredible width, for I had never seen such a wide river. Its flow was not particularly swift, but the deep muddy hue that coloured it, was enough to discourage me from attempting a swim.

The main road began to develop deep wagon ruts, evidence that we were entering a major center. There were obvious impressions in the road where horses had trod, but everything was dried out by the sun and solid as rock. Evidently moisture was hard to come by here as well. A few farmhouses appeared off to our sides, but the further we traveled, the closer they clumped together, until they ceased to be farmhouses, although they still had rather large yards.

Every so often I would spy a peasant out in their garden, or trotting by on a horse, but despite my smiles towards them, they kept to themselves. Perhaps city people were like that. I didn't really know, since I had never been to a city before. Small villages were very different, for everyone knew everyone else, as well as their history and everyday business. In the city, as far as I could tell, that was simply not the case.

"I'll bet that when I was a baby, Arvad took me through a city," Oliver stated proudly, slapping his knee as though recalling something of importance. "I seem to remember being in a city when I was just a wee lad. Can't recollect much though..." He looked thoughtful. "I must have been terribly young, but I do seem to remember tall buildings." He laughed hysterically. "Nothing like being vague, is there?"

I chuckled nervously, for the city was nearly upon us and fear of the unknown had begun to creep over me. It made me so angry that I still could not get rid of my paralyzing fear. Oliver didn't seem too concerned, despite all the warnings we had received. He hadn't even flinched when I told him the whole story of my encounter with the Harpy. In my opinion, Oliver was far too easy going, but maybe that was his way of dealing with stress. I supposed that everyone needed a method of coping. I wondered what mine was... Screaming perhaps?

Presently, a large sign appeared on the side of the road. Carved in flowing script, were the words, 'Welcome to Jadestone'. In smaller script below this, was a brief amount of information about the city. 'Nestled on the banks of the Jade River, Jadestone is the second largest city in Algernon and the number one supplier of fish'. The sign was in great disrepair, for the wood was rotting away at the edges and peeling off in chips from the sun's rays beating on it day after day. I described these sights to Oliver, but he urged me on.

"Move into the city itself! Tell me everything you see! Are there tall buildings? Throngs of people? Streets lined with every shop imaginable?" He squirmed in his saddle with excitement. I felt a pang of guilt that I could see it all and he could not, when it was obviously so important to him. Oliver had Clara's sense of adventure, though perhaps not in the same proportion. No one could have as much spirit as my late sister.

The dirt road suddenly merged into hard cobblestone streets, chipped and caked with mud from years of use. And yes, there were tall buildings. After telling Oliver as much, he fairly shouted with glee. The buildings were in fact, very impressive, as they towered up on both sides of us, nearly blocking out our view of the sky. I found it to be rather shocking, since I had become used to seeing the horizon. I had found great joy in this simple pleasure and I was sorely disappointed to have it taken away. Being in the city was almost like being in the forest again, though much louder... I didn't like it at all.

Still more of Oliver's predictions came true, as there were indeed, throngs of people and shops selling anything a person could ever want, including pottery, weaved baskets, fish, fruit, cloth, rope, jewellery and so much more. As I continued to lead our little party deeper into the hive of Jadestone, the citizens swarmed even more thickly about us. The streets were packed with people of every age, from children, to seniors and they were around every turn, sitting, standing, walking and running. It was all I could do to keep Moondancer from stepping on them. The hum of voices melted into a 'buzzing' sound, not unlike that of bees. Smoke curled out thickly from so many chimneys that I lost count. Petra and Verity were *nothing* compared to the magnificence of Jadestone. I was left speechless, much to Oliver's dismay.

"Describe it Alice!" Oliver pleaded. "I can only pick up so much from sound and smell! I don't want to miss this splendid experience!"

"All of the shops along the street have brightly coloured awnings over them," I informed Oliver. "It makes the street look like a patchwork quilt! There are some flimsy stands without awnings, but for the most part everything is covered." The people didn't seem to care how large or small the market stalls were, for they pushed and shoved equally at every outlet. My mouth could scarcely keep up with the activity I witnessed and Oliver I feared was becoming a bit overwhelmed. He sat bewildered upon Nightflame, with a dumb looking smile plastered across his face.

"Isn't this amazing?" he breathed, as we entered a large square where there was slightly more breathing room.

"It's more than I ever dreamed," I agreed. "So many people... I just can't get over it." I dismounted Moondancer and led our party over to a round marble fountain, which stood bubbling in the center of the square. "Stay on Nightflame," I told Oliver. "It's much too easy to get lost around here."

I sat down on the edge of the fountain and stared into the rippling water. As I did so, a strange reflection perched upon the statue in the middle of the fountain caught my eye. It was the Raven! However when I looked up at the real statue, the Raven was gone... or had it ever been there at all? I shook my head... How strange. The statue in the fountain was very beautiful indeed, something I hadn't noticed right away. It appeared ancient, for it was badly chipped, but retained its charm just the same. The statue was of a regal looking woman, with hair that touched the backs of her knees, bound in two loose braids. Delicate fairy wings protruded from her back and her hands were outstretched, from which the water poured. A delicate crown sat upon her head, but the stone on her face was badly broken. I wondered how this statue survived Ralston's attack on the city long ago... It seemed to me that he would have destroyed anything beautiful.

Oliver abruptly broke my train of thought. "Do you think we ought to stock up on supplies while we're here? Carrie gave us some, but it's not enough to last us through the mountains... and if my memory serves me correctly, once we leave Jadestone, there won't be any other villages to pass through. The next major center would be Devona... Is that not correct?"

"Yes, you're right of course Oliver," I agreed. "I just can't get over how few settlements lie along our path."

Oliver shrugged. "Remember, our road does not pass through easy terrain. There are better routes across Algernon, I'm sure, but this is the path Nissim suggested, so we should stick to it." Then, changing the subject, Oliver continued, "Do you see any stores where we can stock up? We still have a few gold coins left." He produced the satchel and shook it.

"There are a few stores in this square," I mused, allowing my eyes to wander. They rested upon a rather ancient looking establishment, with two long windows in front. The windows were heavily shuttered, but that was most likely for security purposes. The sign hanging above the door read, 'Dragons Plus'. It seemed like as good a store as any to buy supplies at and I was really quite intrigued by the name.

I tugged at the fringe of Oliver's crimson tunic. "I'm just going to run into a store nearby, I won't be long. Here, let me take the gold coins." Along with the coins, Oliver handed me Lily's golden pendent.

"Here," he offered it to me, "you are the one who should be wearing this. I have no right to it."

Giving Oliver an odd look, I replied, "That's okay Oliver, you can keep it on for now."

"No Alice," Oliver persisted, flushing slightly. "I really must insist. Besides," he fidgeted with Nightflame's reigns, "I feel sort of... you know... less of a man, wearing a pendant that says Lily."

"People would just think it a token from a fair lady," I told him with a grin, "but if it bothers you so much, I shall take it."

"I would be most grateful," Oliver acknowledged and handed the pendant over.

"Okay, I'll be right back. You just stay here. Don't go anywhere," I instructed giving Gimra a reassuring pat on the head. "Watch over him Gimra," I whispered in her ear.

"Honestly Alice, where would I go?" Oliver scratched his dark head, as Gimra leaped from my saddle to his. She knew exactly what I had told her.

As I approached the Dragons Plus door, it seemed like the air had grown stiller... as though it were listening to my breathing. For some reason, I hesitated before heaving open the creaking wooden door by its rusted handle.

Inside, the air was musty smelling and I suppressed the sudden urge to sneeze. Because of the shuttered windows, not one drop of sunlight filtered in, leaving only a few candles to provide light and they must have been low or of poor quality, for they gave off puffs of sooty smoke. There was no sign of the shopkeeper, or any other customers for that matter.

"Hello?" I called out into the dark store, hearing my voice echo eerily. I was uncertain as to what this store specialized in, though I had come to the conclusion that it was nothing we'd be interested in. There were high shelves all lined up in rows, similar to a library, but books did not occupy these spaces. Every nook was filled with glass jars; big ones, small ones, skinny ones and fat ones. I squinted into a cloudy jar at eye level, as I stopped before one of the shelves. It appeared to have something floating in it and I had a very bad feeling that it wasn't food. Shivering, I backed away from the jars, cringing at the thought of touching them.

"May I 'elp you?" asked a croaky voice behind me.

Giving a startled yelp, I spun around to see a frightfully pale and withered old man. His one eye had a patch over it made of red cloth and his right ear was much larger than his left. The affected ear protruded from his head in a deformed manner. He held his right hand close to his body, cradling it with his left. The favoured hand appeared to be made out of wood. The old man glared suspiciously at me with a bloodshot eye.

Not wanting to know what was in his creepy jars, I decided on the spot not to say I was shopping. Thinking quickly I replied, "Hello... I was wondering if you could give me directions to the river crossing area? Is there a ferry to get across in?"

He crinkled up his already wrinkled face. "Now why would ye be needing to know that? 'Ardly anyone crosses the Jade River anymore. Everyone in the city knows that... 'less you not be from the city." He glared at me with an almost menacing gaze.

"Well actually, I'm not from the city," I admitted. "I'm just passing through. So if you could just give me directions..."

"Just passing though lass? What an odd concept that be... just passing through," he mused. "So where be a pretty young thing like yourself be going?"

It was as though a warning bell had gone off in my head. This man was not to be trusted... just as Io had warned me. "If you don't know the way across the river sir, I won't trouble you any further and just be on my way."

"Didn't say I didn't know, now did I," he chortled in his throat with a rasp. "But 'for I give you information, you must be buying something from me shop."

"With all due respect sir, there doesn't appear to be anything in here that interests me. I'm looking for food and traveling supplies and you don't appear to have anything of that nature."

"You're a might jumpy lass." The man hobbled a step forward, his eye gleaming with a light of its own. He was standing between the door and me... I was trapped!

"Please sir, I don't want any trouble. I just want to be on my way." I boldly pushed my way past him for the exit and surprisingly, he made no move to stop me. I tried the handle left, then right. I shook it violently, but knew that it was locked. The panic had begun, but it was mixed with anger that this shopkeeper thought he could intimidate me! "Let me out!" I screamed, half frightened, half frustrated. "I don't have time for any of your warped games!" It occurred to me suddenly that Oliver wouldn't even know that anything was wrong, therefore he wouldn't think to come looking for me. Gimra on the other hand might sense something, but there was no other way into this building from what I could see.

"If you not be going to buy something, then you better be making a wee donation my pretty lass." The old man was right next to me, his good hand twitching. "Gold be hard to come by these days."

Fighting to stay calm, I backed up towards the rows of shelves, but stumbled over a loose floorboard. "I... I don't have anything to give you," I stammered. We only had a few gold coins left! I couldn't give them away to this disgusting sack of bones!

The old man looked amused and as he attempted what I guessed was a smile, the corner of his mouth drooped. "Oh but you do have something," he told me, a sinister look stealing over his deformed features. "And if you're ever wanting to be seeing the light of day again, I suggest you be giving me what I ask for."

"And just what is that?" I asked, a note of defiance seeping into my voice.

"I don't be caring much for your tone," he growled angrily, scratching his protruding ear.

"What do you want?" I asked again, trying to ignore his threats. "Money? Well I can tell you this, I don't have any. If you'd like, I have some herbs and mushrooms from the Forgotten Forest. They are very rare... should bring in lots of gold." If he took the bait and allowed me to go outside, I would jump on Moondancer and lose the man in the crowd.

Licking his parched lips he replied, "I'm afraid none of those will be doing lass. You have something that be fetching me far more gold than any herbs."

Surprised, I straightened. "Like what? I don't have anything else of value." There was something strange about the way he looked at me... It was very unsettling.

Hobbling another step forward, he pulled at a silver chain around his neck. "I be referring to jewellery lass. I likes pretty jewels myself, but I know someone who likes 'em even more."

The realization hit me like a slap in the face! What a fool I had been to wear all three pendants on the outside of my tunic! I nearly always tucked them inside my undertunic, but for some reason, I had not today! My hand closed around the cool gold tightly. "Back off!" I exclaimed defensively.

"Be a good lass now and give 'em here! I'll not 'arm you if you do!" he hissed, spittle flying everywhere.

"They are of no use to you and of great importance to me!" I exclaimed, dodging behind a shelf as he made a grab for me. "You don't understand!"

"Oh but they be of great importance to me too!" he contradicted, edging his way towards me again. "I be knowing someone 'ho will pay a great deal to get 'er 'ands on it she will! A reward to anyone 'ho brings me the golden pendants says she! Announced it in the square yesterday she did!"

It had to be the Witch! She must have alerted Jadestone of our impending arrival! But that didn't explain why this man was acting so horribly! It didn't seem natural! Still, what I had trouble understanding, was why the Witch wanted our pendants so badly in the first place. Were they that powerful? Ms Craddock had mentioned that when used together, they would open things... but what? Deciding to test my theory, I asked, "Did a witch instruct you to get my pendants? And how do you know these are the right ones?"

The old man snorted, his pinched nostrils suddenly flaring. "Don't you get it lass? Jadestone be ruled by Ralston the Shadow! Be you blind... 'is soldiers are everywhere! 'Twas 'is top advisor, the wise one what told us: be on the lookout for a strange little lass, with dark 'air an' golden pendants. You be matching the description nicely." He chuckled deeply. "As for the one 'ho be wearing the pendants, we supposed to kill 'em and toss 'em in the river!"

"But why?" I found myself pleading with his insanity. "Why do you listen to such terrible people? Ralston... the Witch... They are pure evil! Can you not see that? They are trying to destroy your world!" Defiance burned inside of me. "They slaughtered your King and Queen... and their children!" I fought the urge to shake the old man who was truly fragile, despite everything.

His ancient face remained like stone; completely expressionless. He blinked his good eye a few times, but there was no hint of emotion in it. "Once I be a good person, least I likes to think so. It's 'ard to remember... but things be different now. I wants to survive, seeing as I can't live. I 'ave me orders and so does the city. No one be the disobeying type, not anymore."

"I feel sorry for you," I whispered, as I stared at this pathetic excuse for a human being. Any hint of hope or compassion was completely gone from him and yet I couldn't help but wonder if somewhere, deep down inside, his true self was screaming for help. Hope was a strange thing I was coming to believe and I had difficulty accepting that it could be completely driven out of people. This man was tormented and hated Ralston, even if he couldn't show it... of this I was certain. Ralston somehow forced the city people to obey him.

Still even if deep down the man had some good left, that was not going to save me. I had to escape somehow, but the door was locked and the windows were barred. He was advancing quickly, real and wooden arm outstretched. There was no doubt in my mind that he had every intention of fulfilling the Witch's command, no matter how much he hated doing her bidding.

"Now there lass, be still," he warned, eyes on my neck, "and give me the pendants. Then," he cackled, "prepare to die." His laugh echoed throughout the sealed building, reverberating in my ears like the drums of doom.

CHAPTER TWENTY

On the Run

THE OLD MAN advanced swiftly, but I was ready for him. In the blink of an eye, I disappeared among the rows of jar lined shelves. For once, darkness was my ally, allowing me to slip undetected between the man's wares. The dust was awful, swirling up into my nose steadily. Trying to suppress the urge to cough only made me feel like gagging, so I allowed myself to choke freely.

"I 'ears ya lass!" the man cackled, seemingly unaffected by the filth in which he lived.

Desperate and tired, I pressed my back against the end of a wobbly shelf. I had to think of something fast, for it was suffocating in the store! I knew that I was moving farther and farther away from the front door, but what else could I do? Besides, it was locked and knocking down a door was far beyond my strength.

It was then that a faint gleam of light caught my eye. It wasn't much... a sliver of life giving sunshine, cutting through the darkness. Cautiously I peered around the shelf, attempting to make out exactly where the light was coming from and if it was a possible escape route. My eyes were blurred and unfocused, but the light looked to be coming from underneath a back door! What if that was locked too? I could hear the man's footsteps in the aisle to my left, so I slipped around to the opposite side. There wasn't any time! I had to try!

As I began to tiptoe down the aisle, I heard the man's heavy breathing directly across from me. Startled, my shoulder bumped the shelf, which wobbled unsteadily. "So there ye be! I'm a coming lass!" His shuffling footsteps picked up speed across the rough floor.

A plan formed in my mind though I did not want to execute it... but, there was no other way. With a great grunt, I slammed my shoulder into the unsteady shelf, sending it and all of the glass jars upon it, crashing onto the old man in the next aisle. The wood groaned as it snapped and ripped, while glass shards shattered everywhere. The old man screamed in pain and anguish, as he lay pinned beneath the twisted shelf. I could not see him for the dark, but by the amount of cursing he was spouting, I knew he'd be okay.

With my mind at ease, I sprinted towards the precious sliver of light, not wanting to wait around and see if the old man could wiggle out of his predicament. My hands brushed against a heavy wooden door... much heavier than the front. Grasping the handle and holding my breath, I turned it. To my relief and joy, it opened to reveal a narrow alley leading back to the square. Before fleeing, I turned back into the darkness and cupping my hands to my mouth, called out, "Don't worry sir! I'll find a way to set you free from this enslavement! One day you'll be a good man again!"

Angrily and with surprising strength for a frail man trapped beneath that much weight, he spat back, "You won't be getting far lass! All of Jadestone be looking for you! I may 'ave failed, but the others will not! You won't be finding your way out of the city alive!"

Ashamed of the fear he ignited in me, I slammed the door hard and fled down the alley. Could everyone in Jadestone really be looking for us? No one had done anything before when we passed by... Perhaps he was exaggerating. Maybe he had simply been one insane, lonely old man. "Ugh!" I muttered stepping around heaps of garbage, piled high against the backs of the buildings. A trickle of foul smelling water slunk by my feet, meandering its way towards a gutter. "This place smells like a chamber pot!" Plugging my nose, I plunged ahead, making a particular effort to avoid the rather large rats that scurried into my path. This was a different side of Jadestone and somehow, it didn't seem so magnificent anymore. Along with all the wondrous sights in the city, there were so many horrible ones hidden in the corners, pushed out of sight, but they were still there, flourishing in the dark. It seemed to me that if unpleasant things were dealt with, rather than concealed, there would be a lot less problems. But then, who was I to judge? I could do no better had I been in charge of the city.

When I finally emerged breathless back in the square, I had to shield my unadjusted eyes from the bright sunlight. After a moment my vision returned to normal and I spied the fountain with the fairy lady where I had left the others. However to my utter horror, there was no one there! Oliver, Gimra and the ponies were gone! I raced towards the fountain, not wanting to believe my eyes. They had disappeared without a trace!

"Okay," I told myself in a vain attempt to slow my breathing, "relax, take it easy. They probably just went shopping... a blind boy, a cat and two ponies? This is not good," I whispered under my breath.

Strangers strolled about the square, seeming innocent enough at first glance, but now I could sense something else about them. Their innocence was feigned, for they were watching, waiting. We had not entered Jadestone unnoticed as I had proudly thought. I had been careless and foolish in thinking we could just walk into a city occupied by Ralston and exit unharmed. This was entirely my fault! The Witch was right when she had said blood was on my hands! A passing mother and child gave me a strange glare as they walked by carrying a bag full of fresh vegetables. There was something in their eyes that unsettled me... a fire that seemed to say, 'I know who you are'.

"I can't stay here." I clutched my arms around me, but dropped them quickly. I had to look casual and confident. I spied a rather wide street exiting the square up ahead. It headed south, which was probably the best direction to go until I figured out what I was going to do. Oliver could still be alive... After all, there was no indication that he wasn't. Keeping my head down, I slipped in amongst the crowd, keeping close to the street edges in case I had to duck for cover.

As I passed a particularly dark alley shrouded by garbage, a strange hissing sound caught my attention. I paused for only a fraction of a second, but that was long enough for a hand to swiftly reach out and roughly yank me into the foul alley. I strained to see who my captor was, but it was impossible in the shadows. Gloved hands were firmly being held over my mouth, as I was dragged deeper into the rank corridor and behind a load of fishy smelly refuse. The air was stale and heavy, in addition to being laden with all sorts of unpleasant smells. I could feel the sticky ground beneath my feet, as I was dragged along.

"For goodness sakes girl, use your feet! I can't drag you about like this!" came a familiar voice. A small ray of light drifted to the bottom of the alley, like a ray of sunshine breaking through the treetops.

"Io!" I exclaimed, recognizing the dark cloak and masked face. Behind Io, pressed firmly against a dank wall, was Oliver, Gimra, Moondancer and Nightflame. "Everyone!" I could feel tears of joy, wet on my hot cheeks. "You're alive!"

"Of course they're alive," Io's voice was tart, "but no thanks to your foolishness! Whatever gave you the idea to just leave them in the middle of the city and wander into a store! Surely you have more sense than that?"

"I know now that it was the wrong thing to do." I bowed my head in shame. My tears of joy were turning bitter. Twisting the hem of my overtunic, I blubbered, "I was stupid! I... I didn't think! But then, I'm not cut out to be the leader of anything! This just goes to prove it! Like Keenan said, my fate is to die at the hands of the Shadow in my dreams and there's nothing I can do to change that! So I don't even know what the point of this whole dumb quest is, if it's doomed to failure anyway!" There, I had said it.

Io seemed unfazed by my outburst and made no move to comfort me. However, he offered these words of condolence, "Just because something is predicted for the future, that doesn't mean it's going to come true."

"Yes, but everything else Keenan predicted came true," I pointed out.

Io sighed with frustration. "This is really not the time to be discussing such matters. The future is what you make of it. Don't let anyone else tell you what is going to happen, for that is in your hands alone. Now enough of this prattle!" Io held his cloak tighter about his face.

Softly I edged to Oliver's side, giving his ice-cold hand a reassuring squeeze. "You alright?" I asked.

"Confused, but uninjured," Oliver replied. Even in the dark, I could see his pale face.

A soft nuzzle at my neck alerted me to Gimra's presence. She purred gently in my ear, seeming to say, 'I'm so glad to see you'.

Io's impatience grew steadily. "I thought you two might need some assistance getting through the city... alive that is. I know now that I was right to come." He cast an accusing glance at me. "When I heard that the Witch had alerted the entire city, I knew you would be in the greatest of danger. She wants your pendants Alice, though even I do not know why. You must guard them with your life. I shudder to think what would happen if she got a hold of them."

"That man in the store," my voice trembled and I tightened my grip on Oliver's hand, "he tried to kill me and take the pendants. I... pushed a shelf onto him and ran away. I was afraid of killing him, but he was alive when I left."

"You have mercy in your heart Alice," Io stated, though I couldn't tell whether he thought this a good thing or a bad thing. Loud voices echoed out on the main street, followed by a great deal of feet stomping along the ground.

"They are looking for us," Oliver whispered coldly.

"Ralston holds this city not only by hidden Denzelians soldiers, but also by the people, which makes our chances much slimmer, for we are terribly outnumbered. But fear not my friends, for I have a plan. You will get out of this city, you have my word, even if I die in the process." He seemed to glide, for he walked so quietly up to our faithful ponies. Lifting Gimra from Moondancer's saddle, he handed her to me. "Place Gimra in your cloak. That's right. These noble ponies will go no further with you on this quest."

I started to protest, but knew that Io was right. It was too dangerous for both the ponies and ourselves to travel together. Oliver and I could easily slip onto a ferry without the ponies' bulk. However that meant we would have to carry the supplies ourselves. Io began to empty our saddlebags into two satchels.

"I will find these ponies a good home, you can be certain of that." He fondly patted Moondancer's nose. "But this may well be the last time you see them."

Oliver and I took up the heavy satchels Io handed us. I found it awkward carrying a satchel as well as my bow and quiver, but there was no other choice. Hugging Moondancer's head, I looked into her huge watery eyes. There seemed to be understanding and compassion within them. "Please don't forget me my friend. You have borne me a long ways and we have been through much together. You are relieved of your duties now, so relax and don't worry." The fact that I was speaking to a horse did not seem to make any difference to those present. Oliver spoke a similar phrase to Nightflame and then relinquished the reigns to Io.

"Tonight you make your escape," Io told us gravely. "It will not be easy, but I *will* get you out or die trying." Io began to cautiously lead us back to the clean cobblestone street. His steps fell so silently, it was as though he wasn't there at all. "I know it's hot out, but I advise you to pull your cloak hoods up. Soon it will be dark and cool anyway." Io paused a short distance from the street, hiding in the last shadow. "We must part here my friends."

"Do you think it is wise for us to be on the streets of Jadestone at night?" I inquired, suddenly afraid to leave Io's protection.

"On the contrary, I believe night is the very best time of day to travel. Less people will be on the streets at night. Think of the darkness as a delicate blanket. When it is used for warmth, it protects, but become too wrapped up in it and you will be strangled. There is a time for darkness and a time for light. The truly wise individual can make effective use of both."

"Well Oliver, do you mind night travel?" I turned to face him, as he was clutching the fabric on my cloak.

"Everyday is night travel for me," he replied tightly.

"Oh Oliver, I'm sorry!" I bit my tongue. "I don't think before I speak."

"A useful skill to learn," Io commented. "But wisdom does not come overnight. It must be learned through experience and mistakes." Suddenly Io broke off and became his impatient self again. "But enough talk! Honestly, your endless chattering can cause even the most serious of conversations to stray!"

"I'm truly sorry Io, but I—" I began to apologize, but Io put his hand over my mouth swiftly.

"Take heed now Alice and Oliver. Go straight down this road until if forks. Then you must take the path on the right. Got that? Go right. Follow that route until you approach the ferry docking platform. Be very careful there, as some Denzelian soldiers may be about. Hopefully they will all be drunk by nightfall, but even a drunken Denzelian is a very real danger."

"Yes of course," I interrupted rudely, "but which boat do we take?"

Io massaged his temples wearily. "Patience Alice, I was just getting to that. Honestly child!" He stroked Moondancer's nose absently. "You are to board the ship called Nova. The name will be painted on the side in blue lettering. If memory serves me correctly, it is usually docked in the east harbour, which suits your purposes grandly."

Now it was Oliver's turn to interrupt Io's instructions. "But surely we will be discovered wandering about the ship's deck!"

"My dear boy, I'm afraid you are picking up some very rude habits from Alice. You shall conceal yourselves of course. Use your heads! There will be someplace to hide," Io told us with a firm nod. He then added, "There should be a lifeboat hoisted on the main deck. There is only one, so you can't miss it. Hide there."

"But what if things should go wrong?" I pressed, feeling a knot of fear in my stomach, the one that never seemed to completely go away. "What if we must face death tonight?" I shuddered at the word 'death'.

"Be resourceful my dear child! I have great faith in you, so don't spoil it by becoming nervous on me. I don't know what else to say besides good luck. May the Power watch over and protect you tonight. Now go!" Io gave Oliver and I a slight shove towards the street, but I dug my heels in and turned around.

"Why are you helping us?" I eyed the hooded figure carefully. "I just don't understand why you'd be willing to die for us... two young people whom you hardly know."

Io was quiet and thoughtful, but only for a moment. "Let's just say that your cause is something I believe very strongly in... and that my very existence depends upon your success." There was no opportunity for further questioning, for Io sent us out into the street with a mighty push and we were swept away with the crowd.

I adjusted Oliver's cloak so that the hood concealed his face and bandages completely. He hid his jewelled walking stick within his robes, for I believed it would only draw unwanted attention. As for myself, it was difficult enough trying to keep my own face covered, but I also had a cat clinging to my tunic underneath my cloak. Gimra absolutely refused to follow us on foot, so I had to bear her sharp claws on my skin.

Though it was hot at first, darkness came rather quickly... almost abruptly. So far no one had spoken to us or attacked and I took that to be a good sign. This time my pendants were tucked safely underneath my tunic, so they were completely out of sight. Still I could not shake the sensation that our every move was being monitored... a most unsettling feeling.

"I'm hungry," I complained to Oliver, who clung tightly to my right arm.

"I am too, but can we really afford the chance of buying something?" Oliver wondered, tightening his grip on my arm as a stocky bald man brushed his shoulder.

"No." I shook my head. "We cannot chance it and our food from Carrie is all but gone. We could eat the mushrooms from the forest, but they may come in handy later on." I grimaced as my stomach growled. "But even if I dared to purchase some food, it wouldn't be possible, for all the shops are closing up. The streets are emptying out, just as Io said they would." The faint smell of bread filled my nostrils as we passed a closed bakery. In the twilight, I saw half a loaf of dried up bread on the ground. Pretending to drop something, I swiped up the bread and broke it in half. "Here Oliver," I handed the crumbling loaf, "this will have to sustain us until... until..." I didn't know how to finish the sentence.

"Here's to the fine food of Jadestone," Oliver joked, biting into the dry bread with a smile. "It's not *that* bad. Not that good either. Hey, why are we stopping?"

"Oliver," I kept the excitement in my voice low, "it's the fork Io told us about! She said to go right." I began to pull Oliver in the appropriate direction, when suddenly he spun around and sniffed the air.

"Something smells odd Alice," he whispered in a tight voice.

"Well it should," I gulped back, fairly digging my fingernails into his hand. Behind us stood a fairly large crowd, composed of men, women and even small children. Their eyes glowed with cold hatred and their faces were twisted with contemptuous greed. The old man with the patched eye stood at the head of the mob.

"That's 'er!" he shouted and pointed an accusing finger in my direction.

"Get 'em!" came a woman's shrill voice.

"They're here to destroy us!" a deeper voice stated with a roar.

"Get the pendants from the bodies!" another screamed in a frenzy.

Armed with blazing torches and glinting knives, the mob proceeded to advance on us, with murderous fury. Flames from the torches flickered in the darkness, casting eerie shadows onto the cobbled ground. The sun was gone and we were alone. Only the distant stars aloofly observed our dire situation. I was staring at Death and his face was that of my own people.

"What's going on?" Oliver asked me nervously, head turning from side to side, even though he could not see.

"Remember when Io said to be resourceful?" I asked tasting bile in my mouth.

"Yeah." Oliver could no long hide his trembling.

"Well now would be a really good time to start doing so," I gasped, as the crowd suddenly plunged forward.

"You're the leader Alice!" Oliver cried. "Think of something resourceful then!"

"Run!" I screamed.

CHAPTER TWENTY-ONE

When Plans Work Too Well

WITH FUMBLING HANDS, I held tight to Oliver as we raced blindly down the street, which Io had told us to take. We seemed to have a slight advantage over the mob, as the large group could not coordinate their chase efforts effectively. I could hear them cursing at one another as they all tried to burst forward, but only got in each other's way. However that did not stop their advance, for we were still well within their sight.

"We must make it to the docks," I puffed, as the mob rained stones down upon us. Most fell short of their mark, but a few hit me hard in the back.

"But even if we get to the docks, how are we going to sneak onto a boat will all of these people following us? Ouch!" he cried, as a sharp stone struck the back of his head.

"I don't know what to do just yet, but I'm sure we'll think of something... We have tooooooo!" My foot had caught a loose cobblestone, sending me stumbling to the ground. Lucky for Gimra, I managed to land sideways and lucky for Oliver, he had released my arm just in time to avoided tumbling with me.

"Alice are you okay?" Oliver asked, as he waved his arms around in an attempt to locate me.

"I'm fine," I muttered. I was just getting to my feet, when a sharp kick from behind, sent me tumbling back down. One of the faster runners in the mob had broken free and caught up with us. He had a rather large slab of wood, which he waved precariously in the air above my head.

"Take that! Little demon troublemaker! You won't have a chance to terrorize our city again once I'm done with you!" the man taunted in a husky voice. His cloths hung off of him in dirty rags and the odour he gave off was repugnant.

I glanced desperately at Oliver, who was trapped in his dark world, but there was no fear in his face. Instead, there was hard determination and courage beyond his 14 years. I noticed him reach beneath his cloak and reveal his jewelled walking stick. He seemed to be judging the distance between himself and my attacker. I had to get the man to speak again, so that Oliver could locate him!

"Me, a demon? Have you looked at your fearless leader Ralston? He is the true demon who has destroyed your city! Don't you remember?" I asked loudly.

The man shook his head in disbelief. "You lie sorceress!" he wailed and brought his weapon down towards my head.

My muscles had been tense, awaiting this inevitable move and the man was flustered, so I was able to dodge the blow. The slab of wood struck the cobblestones hard, splintering the end into a sharp point. Now I was in an even worse position. "Leave me alone!" I tried to project my voice, in hopes that it would guide Oliver further. Perhaps he could do something against this one man, but as soon as the rest of the mob caught up, neither one of us would have a chance.

"Hand over those pendants!" the man spat, extending a dirty hand with blackened fingernails. "My mistress needs it for her master."

"No!" I tried to scramble backwards. "I'll... I'll die before I give you anything!" Had I just offered to die? What was I becoming?

"Suit yourself!" he shrieked and raised the now pointed wooden slab above his head, preparing to bring down a fatal stab.

What was Oliver doing? Was he just going to stand there? I could feel Gimra's claws on my chest nearly drawing blood. She was prepared to die too. I closed my eyes and was ready for the worst. Lily had confronted her death with courage, so I would too. A split second later, I heard a hollow echo, but felt no impact. Opening my eyes, I cried with surprise, for Oliver was standing before me, blocking the man with his walking stick.

The man displayed shock at Oliver's bravery or perhaps stupidity, but the shock melted quickly into rage. However before he could retaliate, Oliver delivered one swift blow to the man's head with the solid walking stick he had received from Carrie of Verity. The man stood for a moment, then his eyes rolled back and he crumpled to the ground with a moan. His lighted torch flew out of his hand and extinguished with a hiss, as it landed in a puddle of water.

Shaking with excitement, Oliver held out a helpful hand. His hand was not pointed in my direction, but I reached and took it, allowing him to think he had pegged my position correctly. "Let's get going before the rest of that mob catches up. I can feel their footsteps rumbling through the ground!" he told me.

Grabbing Oliver's arm, we broke into a run, unlike anything we'd ever done before. Our problems weren't over yet, as there were hundreds of men and women, just like my attacker and they weren't far behind us. My head was starting to become foggy, a sure sign that fatigue was beginning to catch up with me. If Oliver was tired, he never voiced it, but instead continued to be a strong arm linked with mine.

"The docks Oliver!" I cried exuberantly. "I see the docks up ahead!" Sure enough, there were ships lining the shore of the Jade River, bobbing lazily in the slow current. None of them however, had their gangplanks down, much to my dismay, until I recalled Io saying that our ride was on the east dock. But there wasn't time to get there! I slowed our pace, unsure of what to do.

"Alice, why are we slowing down?" Oliver demanded, breathing heavily.

"Oliver, I can see the mob approaching. We could make it to the east dock and find the ship... Nova was it? But there would be no point, because everyone would see us and follow. We need to stall them somehow," I mused, "or better yet, stop them completely."

"We don't exactly have a lot of time to formulate a plan," Oliver told me with impatience in his voice.

It was then that a fleeting vision flashed in my mind... The vision was of my attacker with the wooden slab. I saw before my eyes, his lighted torch flying into a puddle with a sizzle. Supposing that it hadn't burned out and had caught fire right there? The flames would have blocked the crowd and we could have escaped.

"Fire!" I exclaimed jubilantly. "That's the answer!" I eyed the multitude of dry, seaweed-encrusted crates piled around us. All we needed now was fire... It was as though someone had been reading my mind, for there, mounted to a little shack beside one of the great ships, was a burning torch. Letting go of Oliver's hand, I fetched the torch praying that it wasn't too late.

"What are you doing Alice?" Oliver inquired, suddenly shying away at the sensation of flaming heat. His hands went involuntarily to his eyes.

Squatting low, I held the torch up to a particularly dry crate, which, after only a moment, whooshed up in flames, causing me to fall backwards. Ignoring Oliver's rampant questions, I continued to do this until entire rows of crates were crackling in devastating flames.

"Fire worked against us once," I called out to Oliver over my shoulder, as I set another lot of crates aflame, "but now, it shall work for us!" I almost added, 'I hope', but decided at the last minute not to.

"It smells like rotten fish," Oliver commented wryly.

"Who cares!" I exclaimed as the fire spread viciously on its own, eating up everything in sight. "It's just like at the Temple of Strength..." I whispered quietly, catching a glimpse of Clara's anguished face as a pillar fell on top of her.

Oliver was fidgety and obviously uncomfortable. "Let's go!" He tugged at me. "I think you've done enough damage!"

"Yes," I replied vaguely, "I think you're right." The fire had spread and grown much better than I had expected… perhaps too well. The entire riverbank roared and crackled as more crates and storage sheds were consumed. I could hear the mob stop and start screaming in terror. Women yelled and men cursed angrily, but they could not pass beyond the protective wall of flames. I was horrified by my actions and hoped that no one would be injured.

"Alice!" Oliver was pulling hard at my arm.

I stumbled to my feet in a daze, but somehow managed to lead us to the far end of the east dock. The fire had not made it this far yet, so all was dark and quiet. The chaos further down the harbour was barley audible, but the red glow against the sky revealed the chaos *I* had caused. Guilt overpowered my mind.

"Oh Oliver, what have I done?" I asked, feeling tears in my eyes, an all too familiar sensation.

"You did what you had to," Oliver replied, for the first time sensing just how distraught I was. "They'll have the fire put out soon, so not to worry. It was either start the fire or die and if we die, so does the kingdom. Sacrifices have to be made sometimes."

I shot him an angry glance, but he could not see it. "I don't believe in sacrifices." I wiped my eyes with the back of my hand. "No one should have to suffer in order for good to be accomplished."

"Things don't work that way I'm afraid," Oliver sighed, kicking at the dock, which was made out of cracked grey wood. I was half afraid it would break, sending us into the murky water below.

Gimra gave a soft mew and stretched, her white coat shimmering in the moonlight. She turned and gave me a look that seemed to say, 'This is no time for tears.' She then bounded further out onto the dock and gave a sharp meow.

"That's it!" I exclaimed grabbing Oliver's arm so suddenly that he almost fell over. With a sniffle I told him, "This is the ship Io told us about. The name 'Nova' is written on the side."

"Is the gangplank down?" Oliver questioned in a low voice, while sniffing the air.

"Yes." I dropped my own voice, realizing just how loud it had been before. The ship Nova, appeared to be an older vessel, but still in working condition. Its sides were well encrusted with barnacles and dry seaweed, not unlike the crates I had set fire to. A rusty chain was hanging into the water, securely anchoring the ship to shore. It was hard to tell exactly what the deck of the ship looked like from here, but there was a cabin up top at one end, with dim candlelight filtering out through the curtained windows. "Let's board." I entwined my fingers with Oliver's.

"Lead the way," he whispered back, firmly squeezing my hand.

Oddly enough, it was not I leading the way, but Gimra, with her keen cat eyes. As we stepped up onto the deck, I could still hear the peasants yelling far down the river. The only thing I could do now, was try to shut out of my mind what I had done.

Gimra made a soft noise and began to creep stealthily along the deck. "Stay low," I told Oliver, as we passed by the lighted cabin. I could hear low voices inside, but I couldn't make out what they were saying.

"Do you see the lifeboat yet?" Oliver plugged his nose, as the smell of fish was overpowering.

"No," I breathed, still following Gimra's lead. "I'm trusting Gimra to find it."

"A cat?" Oliver raised his voice slightly and then lowered it once again. "Gimra's smart I know but..." he stopped talking and clenched my shoulder, which I took as an indication to stop moving.

"Oliver what is it?" I scarcely dared breath.

"I think I hear footsteps," he whispered in my ear.

"You sure?" I glanced around at the lonely ship deck and heard only the wind amongst the ropes.

"Of course I'm sure. We need to find that lifeboat fast," he hissed, just as Gimra poked her head out from around a corner and mewed.

"Gimra's found it, I'm sure," I informed him with confidence. We followed Gimra around the cabin and there, right up against the ship's rail, was a lifeboat, covered with some sort of strong tarp. "There it is Oliver. I knew Gimra would find it." The sleek white cat crawled up the side of the boat and with a tiny 'mew', disappeared underneath the tarp.

"I'm telling you Alice, I hear footsteps," Oliver pressed again.

This time I heard them too and they were walking briskly towards us. Without a word, I roughly dragged Oliver over to the lifeboat and lifting the corner of the tarp, pushed him in headfirst.

"It stinks," he gagged from inside, wriggling around.

"Here goes nothing." I held my breath and dove under the tarp, only to have Oliver's knee strike me in the chin. That however, was the least of my problems, for it *did* stink with a mixture of fish and damp wood. It was also unbearably hot under the tarp, so I was forced to leave the flap open just enough to get some fresh air. Hopefully no one would walk by and look in the boat, for they would surely see us. I couldn't get comfortable, but at least we were on the ship. It wouldn't take long to cross the river, so we would just have to be strong.

*   *   *

I must have dozed off despite my discomfort, for Oliver was kicking me gently with his foot and saying, "Alice wake up! The ship has started to move! I can feel us bobbing up and down!"

"Wha... ?" I mumbled sleepily, rubbing my eyes. I could see nothing but the dark tarp.

"We're on our way across the Jade River! Soon we'll be in Devona!" The Oliver I had first met seemed to re-emerge, with his lust for excitement.

Now fully awake, I was able to comprehend what he was saying. We were one step closer to Devona and that meant, one step closer to Prince Edric... and one step closer to being done this quest! But I had a sinking feeling, for the Shadow in my dreams was nearer now. He knew I was coming, for he was waiting...

Footsteps outside the lifeboat took me by surprise. In no time at all, they were right beside our hiding place! A deep, strong voice, announced suddenly, "We've left port Captain Wyston sir, but it may take us a little longer than usual to reach the opposite shore, as there are some obstructions we must sail around."

"Whatever you say Barlow," the Captain answered back good naturedly. "So long as you get us to the other side before dawn, I won't complain, for we are in dire need of fresh herbs."

"Will do sir," the man known as Barlow, answered back loyally. Footsteps could be heard rapidly tapping away.

Although it seemed quiet on the ship's deck now, I could sense that the Captain was still standing where Barlow had left him. I peeked out of the corner of the tarp, but could see nothing. What the Captain was doing, I couldn't tell, but I felt certain that he was listening. I heard a few more footsteps draw nearer and halt. I drew in a breath and held very still. Just then, the smothering tarp above us came flying off and I found myself staring into the face of a white bearded man.

CHAPTER TWENTY-TWO

The Good Ship Nova

"**H**ELLO AND WHAT have we here?" boomed Captain Wyston in a jolly voice, his merry aqua eyes dancing.

Startled, I sat up quickly, nervously pressing the wrinkles out of my tunic. The Captain was an older man, I guessed to be in his sixties. Unlike the other citizens of Jadestone, his eyes looked quite merry and not at all empty or forlorn. He had plenty of silky white hair, partially hidden by a very official looking navy blue hat. The Captain's beard matched his hair and was cut short so that it was really no more than long whiskers over his chin and cheeks. Broad shouldered and strong looking, Captain Wyston wore a blue suit with shiny golden buttons, which matched those on his hat. There were various patches and medallions sewn onto the front of his jacket. Was he evil like the rest of Jadestone? It was so difficult to tell whether I should run or speak.

"Don't be afraid my dear." Captain Wyston smiled gently, revealing glistening white teeth. "I shan't hurt you. What are your names?" he asked encouragingly.

Hesitantly, I replied in a hoarse voice, "I'm Alice and this is Oliver." Picking up Gimra and holding her in front of my face I added, "This is my cat, Gimra."

With a deep laugh that seemed to come from the depths of his belly, Captain Wyston took Gimra from me and held her against his chest. "Well, it's a pleasure to be making your acquaintances. Ah, but where are my manners? Please, please, come out of that old tub. I doubt it would float on water anyway. I really ought to get a new one made," he mused, extending his hand to me. Once I was clear of the stinking lifeboat, the Captain assisted Oliver in exiting the craft. Oliver caught his foot on the way out, but recovered himself before falling, his face scarlet with embarrassment. "Oh I've forgotten to introduce myself!" the Captain laughed. "My name is Captain T. Wyston of the good ship Nova."

"It's a lovely ship." I offered up the compliment in hopes that it would somehow spare us any wrath that was to come, although I didn't sense any.

"An old ship," Captain Wyston nodded, "but she is indeed lovely." Leaning over towards my ear he asked, "Is your brother blind?"

"Yes sir he is, but... he's not my brother," I admitted. I had decided quite suddenly, to give up the whole 'brother ruse' after we had left Carrie. Besides, I didn't feel that lying to this impressive man was right.

"Not you brother?" Captain Wyston raised an eyebrow.

"He's a dear friend," I added quickly to avoid any confusion on the matter.

"Well," the Captain cleared his throat and gave Gimra a squeeze before handing her back to me, "now that introductions are out of the way, perhaps you'd like to tell me exactly what you were doing in my lifeboat?" He paused, "Alice, why are you staring at me like that?"

Turning my head to the side in puzzlement I replied, "I'm sorry sir, but you just don't seem like someone who's under an evil spell."

"Call me Wyston, my dear," he smiled, then looked briefly confused. "Evil spell you say?"

"You know, the spell that's made everyone in Jadestone lose the will to think for themselves," I explained, feeling my tension begin to melt away by the positive aura of Captain Wyston.

A look of recognition washed over the Captain's kind features. "Ahhh... *that* spell. There are so many nowadays, that you really must be specific when referring to one. I assume it is the mind control spell you speak of?"

Nodding quickly I cried, "Yes, that's the one! The people lose their identity, their hopes, their dreams... everything!"

"And a powerful spell it is." Wyston scratched his beard. "It's one of Ralston's more potent and long lasting magical scourges. Yet he still must send his 'advisors' around to keep the power strong."

Oliver broke his silence suddenly, "So if it's so powerful, how come you're not affected?"

Wyston threw his head back and gave a booming laugh that echoed off the water. "What makes you think I'm not?"

I jumped and stepped back. Had we been fooled into trusting once again? So if he was evil, why did I not sense it?

"Relax young ones! I didn't mean to scare you," Wyston chuckled, pulling me forward the space I had jumped back. Then lowering his voice, he continued, "No I'm not under Ralston's spell and there's a very good explanation for it, just as I'm sure there's a good explanation for you three being on my ship." He glanced around as if he had heard some unseen enemy. "However, I think it would be in our best interests to take this conversation elsewhere. We'll go to my private quarters." He clapped his hands loudly and a voice from the ship's helm answered.

"Yes Captain?"

"Barlow, please have some tea and buns brought into my cabin... Three servings! Oh and a saucer of milk!" Wyston ordered.

"Will do Captain!" the deep voice replied back.

"It shall be a while before we reach the other side of the Jade," the Captain explained, ushering us along the deck towards his lighted cabin. "The waters are always changing and shifting... New obstacles lurking beneath the surface are always appearing. It's been this way for 13 years." He stopped to push the heavy cabin door open. "Right this way, if you please."

Oliver hung back uncertainly, his mouth a tight line of suspicion, but I saw no danger and so, taking his hand, we entered the spacious quarters. Once inside Captain Wyston's cabin, I came to realize that he was no ordinary man. There was shelf after shelf in the large mahogany room, lined with thick, ancient volumes of books, not unlike those of Keenan. Was this man a seer as well? A glass cabinet on one side of the room, was filled with glowing crystals of every colour and shape. The very atmosphere of his room suggested mystery and magic... but for good or ill was the real question. The room's colour scheme was a deep navy, which matched the Captain's uniform splendidly... probably the desired effect. I noticed the Captain watching my face with a rather amused look, which crinkled his eyes at the corners.

"You seem to be judging my character, based on the looks of this cabin." Wyston twisted the side of his beard. "Have you decided whether I'm a good person or a bad person yet?"

I blushed deeply and felt Oliver's grip on my tunic tighten. "Actually," I put forth boldly, "I was wondering whether you were a seer or a wizard?"

"You're a young girl to know of such things, but," he toyed with a golden button on his uniform, "you are wrong on all accounts. I am no seer, though my mother was. Nor am I a wizard," he chuckled. "That is, I've never had any formal education in wizardry. In the old days, it used to be a very prestigious profession, though now it is nearly forgotten. I've never even had an apprenticeship with a wizard, but I have taught myself a thing or two." He winked, putting his index finger in the air. "Sometimes, the best education is derived from experience. But now tell me, how is it that you know of such things? You speak of it as naturally as one speaks of the weather."

Deciding to take a risk, I told the Captain, "We are, I guess you could say, friends of a wizard, though neither of us are apprentices to him. You may have even heard of him, for I have been told he was once very well known."

"Yes yes?" Wyston's eyes twinkled merrily in anticipation.

"Nissim of Quinn," I revealed, gauging his reaction carefully.

Wyston's cherry red mouth dropped open in awe. "You know Nissim?

He is a *very* powerful wizard indeed. He is one of The Three, from thousands of years ago. He still lives? Amazing!"

If the Captain had been under a spell, he would have turned on us by now. Somehow, he had escaped Ralston's grasp... how I wasn't yet sure, but he seemed trustworthy and we were in dire need of a powerful friend. "Yes Nissim still lives," I began, but Oliver interrupted.

"But he's not within this world right now. He's sort of between worlds you see," Oliver attempted an explanation. "He's trying to hold off Ralston's forces."

"I see." Wyston looked thoughtful, as he indicated for us to sit down upon a deep blue seat, with images of foamy white waves upon it. "Nissim has great power, while I only know a handful of spells and a healing remedy or two. Still, even he will not be able to hold off the power of Ralston forever. I wonder if he's waiting for something?" Wyston gave me a hard gaze.

It was time to reveal the truth. Lily had once told me that you could only avoid a topic for so long, before you had to simply come out with it. Now was the time to confide in this eccentric captain.

"Nissim has actually employed us to do a job," I began my explanation in earnest.

"Children? How old are you?" Wyston cut in.

"I'm 15 and Oliver is 14," I replied, slightly annoyed by his early intrusion into my tale.

"Interesting." Wyston covered a smile with his hand, as he seated himself in an oversized armchair.

"He has employed us," I repeated, "to locate the heir to the throne, Prince Edric. Nissim believes that the prince still lives and is somewhere within Devona."

"Just the two of you he sent?" Wyston picked up a long pipe and began to puff on it rapidly.

"Well, no," I admitted uncomfortably, picking Gimra up and placing her on my lap for comfort. "He actually asked my three sisters and I to find the prince, but two of them died and the other quit. Oliver here just volunteered to come along."

"I see," Wyston puffed. "And you are, boy?"

Oliver stumbled around for words, but only for a moment. Finding his composure and straightening his back, he replied, "I am Oliver Renwick, as Alice told you. I lived in the Forgotten Forest with a *wizard* named Arvad, up until he died." Oliver emphasized that Arvad was a wizard, no doubt to impress Wyston.

"Now *that* is something boy." Wyston pointed his pipe at Oliver. "Did you know that Arvad was an apprentice to Nissim a long time ago? Nissim was rumoured to dislike apprentices... He hadn't the patience for their mistakes, but he did have one who never completed his training. Arvad was an exception. He was more like a son than anything else and there were enough stories regarding *that* issue. So you see, Arvad was not a full fledged wizard, since Nissim never formally proclaimed him one."

Oliver sat very still, as one who has just been struck. "Well, he was a good man at any rate... like a father to me."

"I've no doubt about that boy." Wyston smiled apologetically. "Now don't get me wrong, I wasn't denying Arvad's character." Clearing his throat, Wyston turned to me, "Continue please young Alice."

"There's not much else to tell." I folded my hands neatly in my lap. "We have traveled all the way from the Forgotten Forest and needed to cross the Jade River in order to get to Devona. Your ship had its gangplank down." I decided that to keep the story short, I would not mention Io. Besides, I didn't understand him enough to explain anyway.

"I see," Wyston smiled. "So you were hoping to stowaway aboard Nova, eh? Well, that's a fair reason and I take it you feared the captain would be just as crazy as the rest of Jadestone?"

"We had no reason to believe otherwise," Oliver told Wyston in a curt voice, still offended by his words about Arvad. Oliver had taken great pride in the fact that Arvad was a wizard and being told that he wasn't, hurt his ego greatly.

"Well, you chose the right ship." Wyston looked pleased with himself, as though it were he, who had invited us onto his vessel. "Though my powers are not very strong, I did manage to cast a spell over my ship, to protect it from Ralston's grip. With a little luck, I've been able to slip through his fingers for over a decade. As long as I stay on this ship I am safe, but as soon as I step off, I become susceptible."

"Don't you get lonely?" I wondered while stroking Gimra.

"Sometimes," Wyston admitted. "I only have one other crew member and that is my First Mate, Barlow. He seems a rough man at first... a bit intimidating perhaps, but he's an old softy underneath!" The Captain laughed heartily. "By the way, where did you get that splendid cat? A gift from Nissim perhaps?"

"Actually, a gift from the seer, Keenan," I explained and at Keenan's name, Gimra mewed.

"Keenan? Keenan?" Wyston mused looking upwards. "A little dwarf man?" I nodded. "He used to live in Jadestone long ago, but headed north just before Ralston's men arrived. Foresaw it I assume. His predictions are fairly accurate, but as with all things, the future is never certain. One can guess and predict as much as they like, but no one will know the outcome until it happens."

Presently there was a knock on the door and a giant of a man with messy brown hair, entered carrying a tray. "Your food Captain," the man boomed. "I see you have guests."

"Indeed Barlow." Wyston stood up to receive the tray. "This young lady is Alice and her friend Oliver."

Barlow *was* a rather intimidating man, simply from his sheer size and bulk. He must have been younger than Wyston, for he was in much better physical shape, though probably from doing all the ship work. Barlow had a tiny brown moustache that matched both his hair and his eyes. "Greetings!" he bowed. "Barlow at your service. Welcome aboard the good ship Nova! If I'd known a lady was coming, I would have made appropriate quarters. Are you enjoying your ride so far?"

I nodded enthusiastically. "Yes, it is proving to be most interesting."

"I'm so glad miss. You must excuse the mess around here. I try my best, but sometimes it's hard to stay motivated," Barlow apologized. He seemed so eager to please that I couldn't help but like him.

"Barlow," Captain Wyston began, "please go pack a sack full of food and hiking supplies. Keep it light, but don't be cheap."

Barlow nodded, bowed and quickly exited the cabin with extraordinary grace, for a man of his carriage. Wyston looked gravely at me. "When I leave you on the other side, you'll need all the help you can get. There are no villages along your particular route to Devona. There are more settlements in the mountains, but not along the road you will be taking."

"I'm afraid," I said suddenly and quite bluntly.

Wyston gave me a deep look of sympathy. I expected him to give me the usual words of encouragement, but he simply said, "I don't blame you. There are beings in Devona that I have only seen in my nightmares. You must have great courage to have come this far."

"I don't think so." I hung my head. "I honestly don't know how I've made it this far. I certainly have wanted to turn back… I even had the opportunity to."

"Well that proves great courage!" Wyston slapped his knee. "You could have turned back, but you didn't! That is worth a lot! You don't give yourself enough credit."

"Too much has been sacrificed already." I clenched my fists. "Lily and Clara, my dear sisters were killed at Virtue Temples. I want to avenge their deaths."

"Don't be doing this out of revenge," Wyston warned. "If your intentions are not good, then your purpose will not be pure. When that happens, you become no better than the evil one himself." Softening, he added, "But I sense you are not continuing for the purpose of revenge. You honestly want to make a difference."

"I don't know…" I muttered. "I don't know anything anymore. I feel like I've lost who I am."

"Perhaps you're not losing yourself young one, but merely finding who you really are. I know it seems frightening, but… it's like, well," he groped for an analogy. "Sometimes you must be frightened, in order to get rid of the hiccups."

I gave him a confused look. "All I know is that I am terribly lonely and confused."

"You never told me that," Oliver whispered quietly.

Wyston reached underneath his chair and withdrew a dusty red book, whose cover was falling off. "Algernon has faced difficult times before, since the beginning of civilization. There have been many 'Ages of Darkness' all over the Fadreaman continent, but they have always given way to an 'Age of Light'. There are many heroic tales, but I haven't the time to tell them to you now. We are at the present in a Dark phase, but I sense that light is hovering just below the horizon. All we need is for someone to break through the darkness. That time is now."

"What are you saying?" I leaned forward in my seat.

"I don't know what your role will be when this all plays out young Alice. But I do know this, you are much more powerful than you think. You may be going to Devona to locate Prince Edric, but things never work out as we plan. You may end up playing a very unexpected role. I do not know details, so please don't ask. I will however, give you two things." Getting up and walking over to his glass cabinet, Wyston returned with a tiny bottle of green liquid. He handed it gingerly to me.

"What is it?" I wondered, quickly describing it to a curious Oliver.

"I noticed you have a bow," Wyston observed. "I am going to guess that your shooting skills are less than accurate?"

"I was never taught how to shoot a bow," I defended myself.

"I'm not criticizing," Wyston held up his hands, "but I think this potion will aide you. It is poison, so you must be very careful. Coat the tip of your arrow in it and even if it only grazes one's skin, it will kill."

"Kill!" I exclaimed. "I don't want to *kill* anyone! Who am I to decide whether someone lives or dies? That is the Power's job!"

"Nevertheless, I insist you keep it." Wyston frowned worriedly. "Who knows where it will be useful."

"What was the other thing you had for us?" Oliver inquired, rubbing his bandaged eyes.

"Ah!" The Captain flipped open the dusty book before him. "You are very lucky to have met me, or you never would have found Devona, even if you had followed the road to it." Turning a yellowed page and muttering to himself, he exclaimed, "Here it is!"

"What is it?" My curiosity was definitely aroused.

"It is a spell," Wyston explained in a low voice, licking his lips. "It will reveal the infamous Hidden Valley of the Fairies." He whispered this last part in a voice so low, that I could scarcely hear him.

Staring blankly at the Captain I asked stupidly, "But why should we need to know that?"

"Arvad once spoke of it," Oliver mused, mostly to himself.

"The Hidden Valley, is one of the main reasons that the people of Algernon are so isolated from one another. It's similar to Charon's gate, in that you cannot get to Devona without first passing through it, no matter which route you take!"

"So it's a gate with a test?" I offered.

"No, not exactly," Wyston told me without taking his eyes off of the yellow paper. "It's not quite as obvious as a gate. You see, you cannot pass through the valley unless you know it is there."

"I don't understand," I sighed, my head beginning to ache.

"Okay," Wyston took a deep breath, "you need a spell to *see* the valley. It simply doesn't exist in our world without it. You could try to make it to Devona without reciting the spell at the appropriate time, but you'd never find the city. Many have tried and all have disappeared without a trace."

"So everyone must know the spell then," Oliver concluded, attempting to make sense of Wyston's prattle.

"When King Alfred reigned, he had a wizard guard stationed where the valley would appear. This guard was in charge of opening and closing the portal for travelers, so there was never any need for ordinary people to know how to access it. Ralston however, had the wizards killed, so only a precious few people recall how to pass through the valley. I," stated the Captain, "am going to grant you two... er... three... the power to open the portal."

I held up my hands quickly. "Okay, let me get this straight before you go any further. To get to Devona we must pass through this hidden valley?" Wyston nodded. "But the valley is invisible without this spell?" Again the Captain nodded. "So we get the spell, we say the spell, go through the valley and end up in Devona?" I summarized.

"Exactly," Wyston approved, "except you don't *say* the spell. It's actually a tune called 'Requiem of the Invisible'. Its purpose is to reveal all things that are there, but unseen."

"Like ghosts?" Oliver suggested, sitting up straighter.

"I suppose," Wyston sighed. "Now, listen carefully. You must either hum or whistle this tune, when you feel the time is right. And," he held up his hands, "don't ask me when, because you'll know the time is right somehow. Now listen!" With that, the aging captain began to whistle a strange, haunting tune. It stirred me right to the depths of my soul and yet there was something familiar about it. It was like something out of a dream... as if I'd heard it before, in a time and place long forgotten. The tune went on for a few seconds more and when it ended, stayed firmly planted in the fields of my mind. "Did you get that?" Wyston asked, taking a drink of now cold tea.

"Yes sir!" Oliver and I answered at the same time. We gave each other a strange look, even though I was the only one of us who could see.

"That tune," I began, "there was something familiar about it, as though it has always been inside my head and I just needed to be reminded of it."

"Indeed," Wyston mused taking a long drag of his pipe and emitting perfectly circular smoke rings. "It is fortunate that I don't have to repeat it, for we have arrived at our destination." The Captain rose swiftly and we followed him to the cabin door. Outside, the sun was just rising in the eastern sky. I must have slept longer than I thought in the lifeboat, for we hadn't been talking to Wyston for very long. In any case, I found that amazingly, I was no longer tired. Such was the magic of Nova.

Barlow approached us from behind, with two medium sized sacks flung over his enormous shoulders. "Here are some supplies miss." He handed me one sack and after a moment's hesitation, gave the other to Oliver. "Are you okay with this sir?" he addressed Oliver.

"I can handle it. I may be blind, but I'm not lame." Oliver's voice was almost tart. He wanted to make it very clear to everyone, that although he couldn't see, he was far from useless.

With Oliver in tow and Gimra at my ankles, I stood at the gangplank and stared out at the rolling foothills before me. Never had I seen such a landscape before. I gulped, for I knew that the majestic and unforgiving Thea Mountains lay just beyond the hills.

"Those are known as the Sterling Hills," Captain Wyston explained, placing an encouraging hand on my shoulder.

I continued to gaze in wonder at the land before us, trying to describe it all to Oliver. We were so close to Devona... I could feel the evil closing in and a strange sense of urgency coursed through my veins, stronger than anything I had ever felt before. I turned to the good Captain. "Thank you for everything. Your kindness will not be forgotten." Not knowing what else to do, I shook his hand.

"And thank you for the supplies," Oliver put in. "I'm sorry I was snappy about Arvad."

"No harm done son," Wyston assured him. "My old heart is at ease, knowing that Ralston will soon meet his match."

"Edric will be very strong, I am sure," I declared positively, as an uncertain wind whipped my loose hair about.

Wyston frowned. "A word of caution dear ones. There is a place called the Temple of Wisdom located within these hills. You must be very wary of it, for evil has consumed its sacredness and caused it to be a place of untold suffering."

"We've dealt with temples before," I commented dryly.

"But you don't understand. The Temple of Wisdom is unlike any of the other temples you have encountered," Wyston pleaded urgently.

Oliver cocked an eyebrow from beneath his bandages. "How so?"

"This temple is never in the same place twice. It is always moving about at will. It disappears and reappears in a matter of mere seconds," Wyston explained, gesturing wildly. "No warning is given when it is about to appear, therefore avoidance is practically impossible! All I can really say is, be aware and use caution."

With a shiver, I replied, "We will Captain and thank you." We began to descend the gangplank, which sagged under our weight. Even little Gimra seemed on edge.

As we set off into the unknown, Wyston waved and called out, "Good luck my friends… good luck."

I looked up into the early morning sky, just in time to see the Raven, black as the night itself, swoop into the trees which covered the rolling hills.

CHAPTER TWENTY-THREE

Into the Sterling Hills

NE OF THE FIRST sensations I felt in the vast, forest covered Sterling Hills, was a sense of isolation. The fact that Jadestone was straight across the river meant nothing… It could have been another world away. There was no real port on this side of the Jade and not a single building. Obviously no one had come to this side for a very long time, for even the path leading steeply upwards, was overgrown with ferns and trees. The ground beneath our feet was littered with sharp needles and crunchy cones, which, despite the hardships that lay ahead, created a beautiful setting.

Oliver reached out and touched a prickly pine tree as we trudged up a sharp incline, using protruding roots as a staircase. "It's times like these I really miss my eyesight," he stated. It was not a complaint, nor self pity. It was simply a statement. Still, I felt terribly sorry for Oliver in his dark world. The sight of the enormous hills and towering trees took my breath away and yet, I could not fully enjoy it, for Oliver could not share the awe.

"We still have a long journey ahead," I told him, unrolling our weather beaten map. "But Devona is getting closer… and so is the Shadow. He's watching me Oliver, I can feel it." I felt goosebumps rise on my arms, in spite of the warm breeze.

"Tell me about this… Shadow," Oliver inquired, inhaling the fresh air deeply.

I hugged Gimra close to my body, for she was not presently in a walking mood. Her warmth against my chest seemed to give me strength. "I don't know what to say really," I shrugged. "He's always in my dreams…"

"You don't dream about the nursery and children anymore?" Oliver wondered. He had heard the tale of my strange dream, which had started our inquires and ultimately, our quest.

"No," I answered vaguely. "I haven't dreamed of the nursery scene for a very long time. Now it's the Shadow. I'm all alone in it… Everyone I care about is gone." I recalled the emptiness vividly. "I carry a tremendous amount of guilt with me and grief," I added. "I'm also in physical pain too." I recalled with a shudder, the sharp biting sensations.

"Do you think… it's a prediction?" Oliver asked hesitantly.

"I don't know," I admitted. "Right now I'm not sure what to think.

183

There are always so many things going through my head that I can't seem to keep anything straight. I just know that the Shadow is real and that the closer we get to Devona, the more control over my subconscious he gets."

"Do you think we will face him?" Oliver couldn't help but question, scratching at the now dirty bandage across his eyes.

"I know that at least I will," I replied softly, pulling the hair off my neck, which was sweating profusely. "Don't ask me who will win the confrontation either, because I don't know and I don't want to think about it."

Changing the subject, Oliver went on briskly, "Can you see the mountains from here?" His voice betrayed a hint of excited anticipation, despite all of the danger.

I squinted in the sunlight through the trees. "No, not yet," I replied, "though its difficult to see with the thick foliage."

Oliver nodded quickly and we lapsed into silence, content to listen to the various birds sing their cheerful songs. It was so hard to believe that evil in its second purest form was in control here. The purest evil being of course, Ralston's ultimate master, the Fallen. This was who I was certain had given Ralston the ability to terrorize, in exchange for his soul.

I shuddered, for it was generally considered taboo to even think of the Fallen One, who ruled all things that were dark and evil. He was the greatest enemy of the Power, who lived beyond the stars. This however, was the extent of my knowledge... there were good forces and evil forces in the world, each one active in people's hearts. This knowledge was basic and Ms Craddock had not gone into depth during our classes. Still I had the general idea; the Power protected and the Fallen tried to lure people out of that protection.

Gimra's claws suddenly released my tunic and she leaped down onto the trail with incredible stealth. Large white ears erect, she took the lead, walking as softly as leaves drifting from trees in the autumn. As we rounded a sharp corner, I could see something blocking the road up ahead. It was quite large and light brown in colour. Gimra stopped suddenly and listened. I could see her muscles tense and the hairs on her neck rise.

Upon closer inspection, I came to realize that the brown creature up ahead was only a deer... a doe to be precise. She looked up curiously, as we stopped upon the overgrown path and blinked her soft brown eyes. The doe acted as though she had never seen a human before and sensing no danger, quickly returned to her munching on a low growing bush.

"Oh Oliver," I leaned close and whispered in his ear, "there is a lovely doe just a few steps in front of us. She is such a soft shade of brown too and her eyes... they're so... so... innocent," I breathed.

"I wish I could see her," muttered Oliver dejectedly. "Is she anything like the deer in the Forgotten Forest?"

I studied the noble creature for a moment, ignoring Gimra's sudden hisses. "Well, she's sort of like the Forgotten Forest deer, but a little tamer I think. Smaller too perhaps... She looks a little thin," I responded thoughtfully, but Oliver wasn't listening, for he was focused on Gimra.

"Hey," he asked suddenly, "what's wrong with Gimra? She's hissing and spitting like something's wrong..."

"I don't know," I replied back puzzled. "Everything seems fine..." Just then, the doe's head shot up in fear. Her ears pricked up as she swung her head around in all directions. There was a wild fear in her large eyes, as though she sensed a mortal enemy. In the blink of an eye, she bounded away in terror, white tail flying up as she went.

Oliver grabbed my elbow tightly. "What happened? Did we scare her off?"

In a confused, but edgy voice I answered, "No, I don't think so. I mean, we were being so very quiet and still... except for Gimra here. Her hissing is loud enough to wake the dead." A bird in the distance let off a series of rapid twitters.

"I don't like this." Oliver looked around, despite the fact that he could see nothing. "Something's not right... but I don't sense evil." He took a deep breath and seemed to be sensing the layout of our surroundings, which was a lot to take in, even for a person with their vision. However I had noticed that ever since Oliver had become blind, his other senses had seemed to be heightened. For instance, he smelled odours that I could not and heard sounds that were beyond my capabilities.

Suddenly heightened hearing was no longer necessary, for an ear shattering scream, like that of a terrified woman, rang out through the trees. There was no time to contemplate or react, for Oliver quickly lunged towards me, knocking me roughly to the prickly ground.

"Oliver!" I began angrily, but was unable to finish my sentence, for right where we had been standing, stood an enormous jet-black panther. His yellow-green eyes narrowed and stared hungrily towards me. I felt my breath quicken at the thought of what would have happened, had Oliver not been so quick. "We're in trouble," I murmured to him, as he lay tensely on the ground beside me.

"Don't worry," he reassured me in a strong voice, "I'll distract it, while you get your bow ready." Oliver seemed very much in control of his fear and I felt it cowardly to disobey, but nevertheless, I protested.

"But Oliver—" I began, only to be cut off sharply.

"No buts Alice! Don't quit on me now!" His voice had taken on a note that was definitely not to be argued with. There was a certain sense of leadership in Oliver that I had never seen before. He seemed to conceal this ability with an easy going nature, but now things were quite desperate.

The panther glared at Oliver strangely, curling his black lips into a menacing snarl. Oliver slowly got to his knees and seemed ready to spring into action at any moment. The panther appeared uncertain of whether it should pounce upon this bold creature who dared challenge him, or run back into the dark undergrowth. Getting to his feet and standing protectively in front of me, still sprawled dumbly on the ground, Oliver brandished his walking stick.

"Hurry Alice! Your bow!" he hissed, never turning his bandaged face from the panther's direction. Without fumbling, Oliver began to move back and forth, keeping the panther's attention fixed solely on himself. His face hardened with determination. The panther's growling grew louder, as though realizing that Oliver was at a disadvantage.

Gimra pawed impatiently at my leg and nudged the bottle of poison potion hanging loosely from my belt. Of course! Captain Wyston's potion! If I could at least scratch the panther with an arrow laced with the potion, we would be okay!

"Alice," Oliver's voice was still as steady as ever, but there was a note of uncertainty in it, "anytime now." He swung his walking stick through the air in an attempt to push the panther farther away. The giant cat let out a scream and took a step forward instead... now too close for comfort.

My hands were shaking so badly that I could scarcely draw an arrow, let alone dip it into the tiny bottle. A drop of the thick green liquid hit a small weed on the dusty ground, causing it to wither into a pile of black ashes. A wisp of foul black smoke rose from the ashes and found its way to my nose, turning my stomach. As swiftly as I could, I corked the bottle and got to one knee. What now? The fact that I couldn't shoot a bow, hit me hard and I wiped the sweat, which was stinging my eyes.

Oliver and the panther were circling around me, so getting a clear shot even at this distance would be difficult, for Oliver was directly in my line of sight! Gimra let out a sigh of frustration and meowed at Oliver, just as the panther suddenly struck out with his dagger-like claws. Hearing Gimra's warning, Oliver was able to roll in the undergrowth, thus missing the shredding claws. "Run Alice!" he gave a muffled bellow.

Although it was good that Oliver had avoided being killed, I was now left facing the angered panther alone. His eyes were focused solely on me, as brave Oliver was currently caught in the roadside brambles. Instead of shooting the poisoned arrow, which I had so carefully drawn, I threw back my head and screamed. It was cowardly I knew, but I found that my hands were unable to take orders from my mind. Everything in me had gone numb except for my lungs, which were now working to their full capacity. Gimra stood protectively in front of me, a tiny white dwarf, compared to her enormous cousin of the wild. Finally heeding Oliver's advice, I found my feet and fled down the road, the weapon in my hand forgotten.

I was running uphill, so the going was difficult and it felt like I was hardly moving at all. It was then that I realized no one was following me; not Gimra, not Oliver, not even the panther, who was supposedly chasing me. I bent over in an attempt to catch my breath. From where I stood, I had a perfect view of the little hollow where the panther had found us. Now to my horror, the wild creature had Oliver and Gimra backed into a thick bush, from which there was no place to run! Oliver waved his walking stick in a defensive manner, his eyebrows furrowed in determination... with not a trace of fear.

The panther was crouched down low, his sleek black body a shadow, edging closer and closer to his victims. There was no way Oliver would be able to fight such a creature and Gimra hadn't the slightest chance either. There was no one else who could save them besides myself. I was their only hope! The very thought made my knees tremble. I shook my head violently. No! I would not let Oliver die! Oliver, who had been my unwavering companion throughout this entire miserable journey! And sweet Gimra! Keenan had entrusted her to me! I couldn't let her be food for some wild animal! As much as I dreaded it, I had to stop that panther somehow.

There was no time to run back down to the bottom of the hill and yelling would be no help at this point. I gazed downwards and caught sight of my bow and the poisoned arrow, dangling in my hand. I had to shoot from here and it had to hit its mark on the first try.

"Maybe if I got just a little closer," I muttered, shuffling down the slope a little way, sending pebbles rolling down the hill. The panther took a sudden swipe at Oliver and I heard him grunt in pain.

Oliver's cry tore my heart as painfully as if the panther had done it himself. I planted my feet firmly into the ground with a sudden surge of anger, though I wasn't certain who it was directed at. Almost without thinking, I aimed my arrow and with a whispered prayer to anyone who was listening, let it fly. For a moment, the world stood completely still and I wasn't even sure that I had actually done anything, for no one was moving. The wind had stilled and the leaves no longer rustled. Far off bird's cries were silenced, as though they had never existed.

Then slowly, the world started to reawaken and the eerie moment passed. The panther suddenly dropped to the ground with a thud at Oliver's feet and I found myself running downhill towards him with incredible speed. Upon reaching the bottom of the hollow, I skidded to a stop and saw my arrow, protruding from the side of the panther.

"He's dead," I whispered, feeling dizzy. I had not wanted to kill the majestic creature, no matter how much it had wanted to kill us. The scent of blood and death hung heavily in the air, clouding over the peacefulness we had experienced thus far in the Sterling Hills. This sensation, I knew, would not disappear, for it was not the death of the panther that had caused it. Devona. The smell of death was wafting from Devona. Ralston had seen what had happened here… He knew I had killed and he delighted in it.

"Alice?" Oliver found his way to my side. "Are you okay?" He was clutching his arm tightly, where the panther had scratched him.

"Yes," I answered, feeling a chill creep into the air. "Are you?" I inspected his wound and with relief, found it to be nothing more than a scratch.

"I'm fine," Oliver assured me. "You saved us… Gimra and me, I mean."

"The panther was not evil you know," I said suddenly and sadly. "He was not sent by the Witch to kill us… He was just following his instincts. I didn't have a choice."

"Alice, you can't regret shooting it? It would have killed us!" Oliver winced as I bound his arm with a piece of my blue overtunic.

"That's just it Oliver," I wiped a hot tear away, "I do regret. I regret it with all my heart. I have killed something and it wasn't for food. I am stained… and the Shadow knows it. He is calling out, can you hear him?" I stared off into the direction of the Thea Mountains.

"I think you've been out in the sun too long," Oliver told me in a concerned voice. "We are still too far away from Devona to be within Ralston's direct reach."

"No," I shook my head, "he has grown stronger, I can feel it in the air. We are *losing* Oliver and Ralston is mocking us. He thinks we are a joke!" I didn't know where these desperate words were coming from, but I knew in my heart that they were true. Ralston really was watching our every move closely and we were in a great deal of danger.

Nervously Oliver tugged at my sleeve. "Let's just get going. I think we had better leave this place immediately."

"Yes, you're right," I admitted. "Just let me get my arrow." I turned to the panther's carcass and saw nothing more than a heap of ashes and dust, drifting away in the wind. Swallowing the lump in my throat, I turned back to Oliver and said, "Forget it. Let's just go."

Neither one of us spoke another word about what had just happened, for we were both eager to put it all behind us. Oliver, Gimra and I, covered a great distance in the Sterling Hills, stopping only twice to eat and catch our breath. The farther we went, the quieter and more sinister the forest became. No longer did cheerful birds chirp in the tree branches over our heads, nor did we see the busy squirrel gathering food in the underbrush. The forest about us seemed unchanged, but at the same time it had. The familiar aura of the trees had altered and lost its protectiveness. I had always felt in my heart that the trees were watching over us, but now all I felt was malice.

A dark shadow passed overhead, stopping me in my tracks. "Wait here Oliver," I whispered, concealing my rising fear. I cautiously stepped forward a few paces, looking for a break in the heavy spruce branches. Suddenly I discovered that I didn't have to search hard to find what I had seen. The Raven, the Witch's familiar, was perched upon a branch, just above my head. His eyes glowered at me from above, as if challenging my soul. Gimra began to climb the base of the tree with great stealth.

"You!" I seethed. "You have been informing the Witch of our progress!" Instinctively I reached for an arrow, but was cut off by a loud splash from behind me. The Raven flapped off, leaving a dejected Gimra at the base of the tree. I spun around and to my complete horror, saw Oliver floundering around within the waters of the Temple of Wisdom!

There was no mistaking it… this was the temple Captain Wyston had warned us about. It appears at will, he had said and now here it was! What a fool I had been in my carelessness! Everything about the temple was identical to that of the others, except that it hadn't been on the road a few seconds ago! I rushed to the edge of the pool and grasped the edge, unsure of how to help Oliver. The cold water lapped at my fingers, turning them bright red.

"Alice, please don't tell me I'm in what I think I'm in!" Oliver cried in a panicked voice. His boldness with the panther seemed to have vanished in the face of this mystical threat.

"Oliver! Oliver!" I called to him, reaching my hand out in vain. "It's okay! Just follow my voice to the edge of the pool!" I tried to sound encouraging, but in truth, it was all very déjà vu. Oliver was quick to comply with my order and began to paddle towards where I was leaning forward. "That's it Oliver! Keep it coming! Almost there!" I had to keep talking until he was within my reach. All the while my gaze kept darting about, waiting for some deadly assault to be launched, but so far, there was nothing but the sounds of Oliver splashing blindly about.

"Alice," Oliver spluttered, "where are you?" He was within my grasp at last.

Ignoring the icy splashes I got in the face, I lay on the ground and reached for Oliver's hand. It was as cold as ice when I finally grabbed hold, but just as I did, the image of the temple began to fade into translucence, until it disappeared altogether, leaving Oliver flopping in the dirt.

He stopped moving suddenly and spit pine needles out of his mouth with disgust. "Huh? What just happened?" Oliver wondered in a confused voice, as his teeth chattered.

Unable to help myself, I flung my arms around the sopping wet boy, soaking my own tunic in the process. "I'm so glad you're okay!" I nearly sobbed. "I thought I was going to lose you like I did Clara and Lily!"

Oliver sneezed and hugged my shoulders. "Not to worry, it takes more than a little water to get me down. I swam to the bottom of the Heart Temple, remember?"

"I know," I sniffled, "but I saw the Raven and that means the Witch is nearby."

"We'll just have to be more alert, that's all," Oliver sighed and removed the sack which had been on his back. "All of the supplies in my bag are soaked. I hope we can salvage them."

I removed a warm blanket from my own pack and wrapped it around his trembling shoulders. "Your bandage is falling off." I tried to fix the soaking bits of cloth that Carrie had so expertly bound his eyes with.

"Take them off." Oliver pulled at the bandages. "I don't need them anyway." He tossed them to the ground in frustration. "If only I could see, I wouldn't have fallen in!" There was no mistaking the bitterness in his voice now. Oliver had gone through many emotions today, from excited, to bold… to bitter frustration. I missed his joking charm, but could hardly expect that from him considering the circumstances.

The burns around his eyes were nearly all healed… to the point where you couldn't tell that anything was wrong. His blue eyes were still vibrant and alive, but unfortunately, also very blank.

I pulled Oliver to his feet and attempted to brush the needles and leaves off of his tunic. "The Temple of Wisdom is very dangerous…" I bit my lip. "It may reappear, so we have to be extra careful. Where is Io when you need him?"

"Io is a long ways away." Oliver looked grim. "We have to take care of ourselves now." He paused then asked, "Where's Gimra?"

"She was attempting to attack the Raven, but he flew off." I led Oliver over to the tree where the evil bird had been perched. Gimra suddenly mewed from atop one of the tree branches, as if indicating something. "Come on Oliver." I tugged him along to the top of the hill and sucked in a breath.

"What is it?" he inquired, pulling the blanket around his shoulders tighter.

"I see the mountains," I whispered, staring at the rocky ledges and snow capped peaks before us. Wisps of cloud swirled around the mountain summits, an indication of just how high they were. Everything was very dull and very grey, but the clouds towards the south were black and ominous.

"Is it beautiful?" Oliver wondered, wringing out his tunic.

"It should be..." I breathed, still in awe by the great chasms, ledges and valleys in the distance.

"Should be?" Oliver repeated. "What is it then?"

"Dark..." I mused. "Foreboding..."

"How lovely." Oliver folded his arms sarcastically.

"I think we're in for a storm," I stated solemnly and proceeded to lead us forward, in search of shelter.

CHAPTER TWENTY-FOUR

A Muddy Vision

THE STORM I had predicted moved in with extreme swiftness. The black clouds swirled rapidly overhead and the sound of thunder echoed throughout the hills. Although the Thea Mountains loomed just ahead of us, we were still technically within the Sterling Hills and I wondered how they would react in a downpour.

"I can smell the storm coming," Oliver sniffed the air, "but it's different from the one at the Temple of Strength. This one seems... I don't know, just different I guess." He was at a loss for words.

"You're right," I agreed, pulling up the hood on my cloak. "It's darker and more powerful, perhaps because it's coming straight from the south. We need to find shelter soon." I glanced over at Oliver who was still soaked.

"But where Alice? Captain Wyston said there were no villages along this route!" He kicked at the air in frustration.

"It's going to be okay," I told him, although I didn't sound very convincing. My eyes were fixed on the menacing clouds gathering overhead. "Maybe there's a big tree we can take shelter underneath," I mused, feeling Gimra crawl up underneath my cloak. She must have sensed the rain coming, for even I could smell it in the air.

"Well we can't just stand out here," Oliver chattered. "If there's lightning in this storm we aren't safe up on top of this hill."

I shrugged and replied, "I can't see any lightning, so we should be quite safe." Just as I concluded my sentence, a huge fork of brilliant light lit up the darkening sky, followed almost immediately by an earth shattering crash. I couldn't help but jump in fear. "Okay, now we have something to worry about!" I exclaimed, grabbing Oliver's hand and breaking out into a run. It didn't matter in my terror stricken mind that I was leading us further up hill.

"Why are we fleeing Alice?" Oliver tried to wretch his hand out of mine. "We can't outrun a storm!" He dug his feet into the loose soil and pulled me to a grinding halt. "You can't just run away from everything that scares you!" he scolded. "Sometimes you have to stand your ground and think of a solution!"

Bewildered by his sudden defiance, I was left speechless. Feeling a sudden sting on my face, I wiped my cheek absently; it was a rather large raindrop. "The rain has started!" I tried to urge Oliver onwards, but he stood stubbornly where he had stopped.

"I felt it too." He rubbed a drop from the tip of his nose, but still made no effort to move. "But we're not just going to start running without knowing where we are going! You have to *do* something!"

A spark of anger jumped inside of me and I cried indignantly, "What do you mean me? Can't you think of a plan for once? Why is it always Alice this and Alice that! I'm getting sick and tired of everyone always depending on me! I can't handle it!" I was nearly screaming now, for the wind had picked up and the raindrops were falling more rapidly. Though our argument was not over, any further words were drowned out by the raindrops, which had quickly turned into a horrendous downpour. Neither one of us had been prepared for this drenching, which was much worse than what we had experienced at the Temple of Strength.

Hardly able to make out Oliver's shadow, which was only a few steps away, I groped for his hand. At the moment, I was just as blind as he was. Fearing that Oliver was still angry with me, I half expected him to shove away my hand, but when it brushed his, he grasped it tightly. I could barely see him draw his cloak hood up and pull the now soaked blanket around himself.

There was nothing to do but press on, for the trees around us had thinned as we reached the hill's summit, leaving us quite exposed to the elements. The wind blew sheets of freezing rain directly into my face, which felt like a million tiny knives were being stabbed into my skin. Our feet sloshed about in the ankle deep mud, which had formed from what had been dust only minutes earlier. The black clouds had blocked out the evening sun, sending us into an early darkness, which was only illuminated by the occasional flash of lightning. I couldn't tell where we were going, except that it was south... towards the Shadow.

"Do you know where we are going?" Oliver spluttered out.

I gritted my teeth against the incredible pain and shouted back, "To Devona!" I shifted my weight backwards as we began to descend the slick muddy hill.

With a little cry, Oliver's foot slipped out from under him, as the mud suddenly got deeper. He fell backwards, landing in the rapidly deepening mud. Oliver had nearly pulled me down with him, but at the last minute I had released his hand, saving myself from the mud bath.

"Are you okay?" I choked and attempted to help him up. However I soon discovered that it was difficult to move towards him, for the mud seemed to be flowing against me.

"I'm fine!" he grumbled. "But the mud's getting deeper!" There was a note of rising fear in Oliver's voice, which, as of late, had been so defiant.

I decided that his changing moods would be something to ponder at a later date.

The gritty muck was now up around my waist and through the rain, I could see that Oliver was into it up to his neck! Sloshing my arms around, I tried to make my way towards him, but the ground beneath my feet was slippery. The mud clung heavily to my tunic and it felt as though hands were trying to drag me under.

"Alice! I can't brea—" Oliver's voice was suddenly cut off, but before I could react, something hit my legs, sending me flying down into the suffocating mud.

For a moment, all I felt was the cold gritty mud, filling my eyes, ears, nose and mouth, but then came the pain. There were sharp stones, twigs and pine needles in the mixture! I felt them scraping and slicing my exposed skin without mercy. I could hardly breath and the panic had set in. I tried desperately to claw my way to the surface, but soon discovered that I no longer knew which way was up and which way was down! Stupidly I tried to call out, but only received a mouthful of disgusting slime.

If only... if only I could hold out until the mud carried me to the bottom of the hill... then perhaps the slide would stop and I would be free. But what of Oliver? Where was he? My thoughts were a jumble as I felt myself being carried rapidly down the hill, like a branch caught in a fast moving river. My mind briefly passed over Gimra, who had been hiding underneath my cloak. There was no way to check if she was still there or still alive! I felt so helpless! If Oliver and I died in this mudslide, our last words to each other would be those of anger and frustration! The regret I then felt, was enough to equal the pain my poor body was being subjected to.

Gradually I felt the pace of the mud begin to slacken and I suddenly found my head above the slime. Although I could scarcely open my eyes, for they were so caked with dirt, I saw that I had reached the base of the hill and was coming to a stop... but, I gasped, for although *I* had stopped, the rest of the mud had not. A new horror struck me; I was going to be buried alive by the remainder of mud and water still flowing down the hill! The brief reprieve I was currently receiving was soon going to be gone! Out of the corner of my eye, I caught sight of another blob in the mud, gasping for air.

"Oliver!" I gagged, trying to wrest my arms free of the mud, but it held me fast.

It was indeed Oliver, for he called back weakly, "Alice!"

"I'm sorry!" I managed to call out, before another wave of mud washed over my head, cutting off all air. Now I was no longer moving, but instead, held prisoner within the mud, which was building up in layers above my head. This was indeed the closest I had ever been to death throughout the entire journey and there was no conceivable way for me to escape. I was trapped and there was nothing I could do! In the far recesses of my mind, I stood screaming for help, since I could not physically do it.

My eyes were closed and so everything was quite dark, but now I felt things going dim in another way. I was losing my sense of being... Was I dying? I still felt as though I were standing alone in the dark, when suddenly there was a sparkling flash before my eyes. That beard... it was Nissim! He looked old, tired and horribly weak, but his eyes still looked kindly upon me.

"Alice," he spoke my name in a smooth flowing voice. "You've nearly reached Devona. It won't be long before you face the source of evil in Algernon."

"I've failed Nissim!" I cried out in my mind. "The company you created has fallen apart! I am truly sorry!"

Nissim smiled gently. "You are so afraid and confused my dear Alice. It saddens me to have to see one so young, go through so much." He cast his gaze downward for a moment and then looked back up at me. "While at least two people remain true to each other and the quest, then there is yet hope."

"But Oliver and I fought," I told Nissim dejectedly.

He chuckled slightly to himself. "Oh Alice, everyone has fights, especially in times of great stress. You mustn't take Oliver's anger too seriously. He's just as confused as you are, though he's too proud to admit it. The boy came looking for adventure, but discovered that it was much more than he expected. Try to put yourself in his place child. But," Nissim added quickly, "do not regret bringing him, for Oliver's destiny lies in Devona, just as yours does, so never blame yourself for anything that happens to him."

It was only then, that I recalled just where I was. "Nissim! Please help us get out of this mud! Oliver and I shall both be dead soon if you don't!"

"Have no fear Alice, as your destiny does not include death by a mere a mudslide. There are bigger things planned for you."

I was unsure if this comment was a good one or a bad one. Did he mean bigger things, as in better things, or bigger things as in a more horrible death?

"Just remember Alice, that no matter what happens, the power to save Algernon lies within you, if only you have faith. True power lies on the inside," he placed a withered hand over his heart, "not in any potion or form of weaponry. A weapon is only as good as its wielder. Listen to your heart child, for it is there that you will find the strength to triumph. Your mind has expanded considerably with the experiences you have had and already you have begun to change. You now have the wisdom to utilize your newfound strength and I know that you are courageous, for I have seen it in your eyes." Nissim turned and had already begun to fade away. "But none of this will matter unless *you* can reach deep inside and truly believe. Only then, will Ralston and his minions finally go crawling back to the Fallen One."

With that, Nissim was gone and sunlight was left in his stead. I blinked the dry mud out of my eyes. There was a hole in the top of my mud tomb and dimly, I saw a figure digging on the surface. Gradually the hole widened and I could see the pink sky of dusk.

The figure who was digging spoke deeply, "Can you get your arm free?"

I pulled hard and wriggled until it hurt, but I finally managed to release my left arm.

"Here," the figure continued, "I'll pull you out. Give me your hand."

Using my left arm, I succeeded in freeing my right arm. Stretching stiffly upwards I winced, as I was painfully jolted from the hardening mud. Despite all of the pain, it felt absolutely heavenly to be in open air again. Everything smelled damp and clean, in spite of the fact that I was standing on a heap of hardening mud. The rain had stopped and the last of the storm clouds were quickly dissipating. The aura around me was still menacing as it had been before, but without the clouds, it was a great improvement. I coughed a few times and tried to clear my throat so that I could speak. Who had saved me? And where was Oliver? I rubbed my gritty eyes and took a better look at my saviour.

There stood Io, with his mysterious cloak flowing in the wind and entire face concealed amongst the shadows. In one gloved hand, he gripped Oliver's jeweled walking stick and in the other, my bow. Oliver sat, head between his knees, beside Io's feet... muddy, but very much alive. Io took a step towards me, reaching into his cloak as he did so. I tensed suddenly, but he simply withdrew a brown cat... Gimra, covered in mud. She leaped into my arms and licked my mud caked face.

"That," Io told me sternly, "was a close call. Very close indeed." He stood straight and stiff, like an unbending tree in the wind.

"Yes," I scraped the dirt on my tongue with my fingernails, "I know. I can't thank you enough for saving us... again."

Io handed me my sack of supplies from Captain Wyston. Though it was slightly wet and mucky, it seemed to be in good condition. How it had gone from my possession into Io's, was beyond my comprehension. "Algernon needs you Alice... that is something you must come to understand. You are young so it is forgivable, but in the future, you must learn to be more careful, for I won't always be around to save you. There will come a time when the only one you have to rely on is yourself."

"How could I have possibly avoided the storm?" I questioned. "Or foreseen a mudslide?" I added defensively.

Io made something of a chuckle, as he pulled Oliver to his feet. "Fair enough young Alice. It was unexpected and with your limited knowledge, unavoidable. But that is in the past! Let us deal with the present."

"What of the future?" Oliver piped up suddenly, in a voice louder than his ragged condition would seem to permit.

Io gave him a light slap on the back. "The future, my friend, will take care of itself." Io then made his way over the edge of the mud hill where we now stood and gazed out into the distance, all the while mumbling to himself.

I took this opportunity to speak with Oliver. Making my way over to him, I quietly took his arm. "Oliver, listen, about before… I'm very sorry. I need to stop doing this leadership thing only half heartedly and though it's difficult, I'm honestly going to try to put forth a full effort." I paused and fidgeted with a lock of dirt encrusted hair. "When I was down there… under the mud I mean, my greatest fear was not losing my life, but leaving this world on poor terms with you."

Oliver stared blankly out into the distance for a moment, then spoke haltingly. "I… It's actually me who should be apologizing Alice. I snapped back there… I don't really know why… Oh I suppose I do. It's been very hard for me, but I… I don't like to show it. I guess everything just finally got to me and you were the convenient… nay… the only person around I could get angry with, despite the fact I wasn't angry with you at all." Putting his hand behind his head, he suddenly broke out into laughter. "Guess I really blew my easy going image, huh? The ever laid back, ever charming Oliver Renwick loses his temper!" The grin I had grown to know and love was seeping into his features once again.

I embraced him tightly. "Oh Oliver!" were the only words I could get out. I cared so deeply for him that I would rather die than lose his friendship.

"Are you two quite finished back there?" Io asked, with his hands on his hips, not even turning around to face us. "It's enough to make one sick! Everyone argues! It's a sign of good terms! Just because you yell at someone, or act crossly with them, doesn't mean you stop loving them!" Io spoke these words quite passionately.

"What would you like us to do Io?" I asked patiently, feeling so overjoyed at my reconciliation with Oliver.

"Just follow me," Io ordered. "It's getting late and there are too many dangerous creatures around these parts… much worse than mere panthers. Besides, you must both be very hungry and tired."

"I want to get cleaned up," I said, just as I spit out another chunk of rock.

"That too." Io nodded in agreement. "Now come along, darkness falls faster this close to Devona. We don't want to be out in the open when the lights go out, for that is when everything breaks loose."

Part Four

The Thea Mountains and Devona

CHAPTER TWENTY-FIVE

The Mystery of Io

*I*O KEPT A BRISK PACE that I found difficult to keep up with and he was merciless in pressing us forward. The amount of ground we covered in those few evening hours was unbelievable, for we cleared the Sterling Hills altogether. Gone were the mud swept hills, and before us was a terrain of solid, unforgiving rock. Bits of grey stone protruded from the ground here and there, with hardly any grass to cover its rough baldness. The thick trees had thinned substantially and although there was no more grass, the rocks were covered with a thin coat of fuzzy moss. The road had begun narrowing a ways back, but now, it was nothing more than a tiny ledge, with a towing mountain on one side and a sheer drop on the other. We had finally entered the realm of stone castles... the mighty Thea Mountains.

I held Oliver tightly and kept him near the mountain wall, while I braved the ledge. Well, I wasn't actually the one along the edge... that spot was Gimra's, who had insisted upon taking the outer rim. Along with the darkness had come a bitter and lonely chill that hung heavily in the air. I wondered when we were finally going to stop... for I wasn't sure how much longer I could continue to go on. It was then that Io led us around a sharp corner and halted. In the side of the mountain was the mouth of a dark cave. It was not quite as large as the entrance we had seen in the Land of the Undead, but it was without a doubt, the perfect size for a human to walk through.

"We shall rest here for the night," Io told us, as he reached into his pack and withdrew a stick of dry wood. Turning his back to us, he muttered a few words under his breath and the end of the stick burst into bright orange flames. There was nothing eerie about this fire, for it was neither green nor blue. The flames were simple and cheerful. "Right this way." He motioned us to follow him into the cavern.

"What a strange place," I murmured, as we entered the damp cave. There were several pools of clear water dripping into hollows on the ground. Beside these depressions sat dusty water jugs, teetering precariously on the uneven surface. I could see a tiny spider's web woven into the cracked handle of one jug. Obviously no one had used them for a long time. On the other side of the cave, a few worn straw mats were strewn about, creating some sort of sleeping area on the cold stone. The corners of the mats were chewed by mice and the weaving had become loose and messy, but they would offer us at least some protection from the sharp rocks.

I let go of Oliver's arm, allowing him free range in our new surroundings. He gingerly felt his way along the rock walls, accidentally knocking one of the jugs over into a hollow of water. "What is this place?" Oliver asked, as he sloshed his hand in the water trying to locate the upset jug.

"This," Io held out his arms extravagantly, "is all that remains of a once popular rest stop for weary travelers. At one time, this very cave was alive with laughter and merry conversation. There are many happy memories within these ancient stones." Io put his hand on the rough rock, as if sensing times long gone. "Now," he sighed angrily, "this cave is merely a place for dust to collect and mice to nest. It is all but forgotten by the citizens of Algernon... Amazing what 13 years can do. It doesn't seem like much and I suppose it isn't... and yet, it is." Io clenched his fists together.

I seated myself on a large slab of stone near one of the deeper pools and without wasting another moment, had my shoes tossed off to the side. The water was surprisingly warm upon my bare feet, leading me to believe it was a hot spring of sorts. Then thinking ahead I asked, "Are there more rest stops like this one?"

"I believe so," Io answered, unpacking a load of firewood and arranging it into a pile, "but I'm unsure of their condition. Whenever a hot spring flowed near a road, a place like this was created. However without people to keep up the maintenance, the quality and safety of the caves deteriorates quickly. When I discovered this particular cave, I was surprised at its relatively excellent condition. Time has been kind to this resting area." Io blew on the soft red sparks he had created amongst the dry wood. He clapped his hands in front of the rising flames and rubbed them together briskly. "But enough talk! You two must get cleaned up and fed. Then, rest! Yes, lots of rest! Tomorrow you will begin your trek in the mountains, which will be unlike anything you've experienced before."

"You mean we've left the Sterling Hills already?" Oliver inquired with amazement, his blank blue eyes staring straight ahead.

"The Sterling Hills... at least where you crossed them, are a rather narrow band," Io confirmed. "Now Oliver, you wash in the pool you're beside and Alice, you wash in the one your feet are in. I shall prepare some food. Be quick about it." Io's commands were not to be ignored.

*   *   *

Hours later, I found myself clean of all mud, well fed and lying restlessly on a bed of straw and moss. The bed smelled of must and mould, which rather gave me a headache. I turned over onto my side, only to have a sharp rock prod at my ribs from under the padding. With a grunt of frustration, I returned to my previous position of lying on my back. I knew we would be up early the next morning, so I needed to fall asleep right away, but the harder I tried, the more sleep evaded me.

As I lay there, I realized that I had been asleep, but for how long, I had no idea. Yet now I was awake and it only stood to reason that *something* had awakened me. One didn't just wake up out of a deep sleep for no reason... The entire cave was still pitch dark and silent, except for the soft trickle of water dripping into the hot springs.

Oliver was resting peacefully on his own mat, which was opposite mine, but no better as far as padding went. What was truly amazing, was that Io had consented to spend the night with us. I had half expected him to disappear in a puff of smoke as soon as we were down. He now lay some distance away from both Oliver and myself, right on the edge of a pool. Io had gone to sleep with his oversized hood pulled far down over his face and to be doubly certain that we wouldn't sneak a peek at his identity, he lay with his back turned towards us. I longed to see Io's face out in the open, away from that awful cloak he always wore. The cloak and hood hid more than just his face, but his entire character as well. This was our third meeting with Io and we still knew nothing about him.

Gimra, who had been curled up next to my knees underneath my blanket, suddenly stirred and crawled out into the open, her eyes gleaming in the darkness. She nuzzled her face against mine, as if sensing my unease, but it brought me no comfort. Something had removed me from my dream with the Shadow, so it must be very significant if it could break the dream's powerful hold on my mind. I stared up into the darkness, blinking rapidly. I could feel a disturbance in the energy of the cave...

Involuntarily I sat up suddenly, digging my nails into Gimra's soft coat. My heart began to beat so rapidly that I was sure it was echoing off the cave walls. Deep within me, something was screaming out in terror at an apparently non-existent threat. What was wrong? Surely there was a foul scent on the air? I shook my head. Perhaps I was going crazy or still dreaming. That was it, I had to be dreaming still.

At that moment, Io shifted in his sleep and with a rustle, turned to face me. "Alice, is something wrong?" he asked sleepily, the only time I had heard his voice soft and without alertness. It didn't have its usual deep snappiness to it.

Awakened by Io's voice, Oliver mumbled something and rolled over. "What's going on?"

Before I could answer, Io reached into his cloak and withdrew a handful of some sort of glowing substance. "Luminescent mushrooms," he

204   *Candace N. Coonan*

told me in a low voice. "I don't want to light a torch just yet…" He propped himself up onto his elbow and listened intently.

The panic was growing inside of me by the minute. "Something's not right," I forced myself to keep a low tone. "Can't you feel it?" There was a heavy darkness in the room, hanging all around, waiting for the right moment to strike.

Io did not answer me, but instead seemed deep in thought, as he attempted to sense what was wrong, if indeed anything was. He stayed silent for five minutes and neither Oliver nor I dared to speak, lest we should break Io's trance. Suddenly Io's head shot up and if I could see his face, I'm certain it would have registered alarm and fear. "You're quite right Alice," he told me in a tight voice, "there is an odd air in here. Quickly, grab your things. We must leave immediately."

I nodded and was rapidly on my feet gathering our supplies, which had been partially packed the night before. Oliver, in spite of being half asleep, was just as swift in getting up to assist me.

"Here Alice," he handed me my sack, "this bag is done and ready to go. My stuff is all packed too." He slung the sack onto his back with a groan and then suddenly gripped my arm. "Did you hear that?" he asked in a tense voice.

I paused… I did hear a faint noise. It was almost like the rush of a million leathery wings. The noise continued to grow louder over the course of a few brief seconds. The hair on my arms began to stand up and Gimra whimpered in a pathetic voice.

"We must go now!" Io shouted and pointed to the exit.

I started to move, but felt a strange 'whoosh' near one of my ears. In my confusion, I just stood there for a moment, until all at once, hundreds of tiny things were flying into me from behind. "Ahhhh!!!" My screams nearly rocked the cave.

"Bats!" Io exclaimed, grabbing my arm. "Run! We must get out into the open where they will no longer chase us!" He yanked me into action and I had just enough time to reach back and grip Oliver's sleeve.

Disgusted, we ran in an unorganized train out into the pre-dawn air. Io stopped us quickly when we emerged on the outside, so as not to run over the side of the deadly cliff. "Duck!" He threw us onto the ground, before casting himself downwards and covering his head.

Although Io and Oliver were lying with their faces smashed into the ground, I could not help but look up. I had expected to see the bats fly off into the night in search of food, but instead, they continued to swarm before us, like a mass of blood sucking mosquitoes. These were not normal bats! That must have been why I woke up. The only force authorized to disrupt the Shadow's tormenting of my dreams was… .the Witch! It had to be and Gimra's sudden angry hisses confirmed this. But where was the wretched woman hiding?

"They're not flying away!" I cried, while holding the back of my neck.

Beside me, Io rose to his feet, seeming to realize just what was going on. He clenched his fists at his sides and growled, "They are the creation of the Witch! We cannot escape them… We must face them. On your feet!" he commanded us.

The bats began to tighten their swarming formation, until they melded into one huge black mass. I couldn't even tell the individual creatures apart anymore. They swirled faster and faster into a dark stationary twister.

"I don't like the sounds I'm hearing!" Oliver took a step closer to my side.

Io stood rigidly beside me and though I wasn't certain, if seemed as though he were shaking. Io, afraid? Now this *was* puzzling. Breaking the tension, he spoke in a solemn voice, "This is it. I knew this was coming, but I didn't think it would be so soon. Well, if this is how it has to go, so be it… but they won't get me without a fight!"

I stared unbelievingly at Io. "What are you talking about?" A tiny prick of fear and uncertainty tugged at my heart.

Perplexed and frightened all at the same time, Oliver asked, "Do you know what's going on here?"

Io did not turn his head in our direction and instead answered, "Not exactly. All I know is that this is my destiny and it is time to fulfill it. We shall be parting company sooner than expected."

Though it all sounded very familiar, I still didn't comprehend what Io was going on about, though it disturbed me very deeply. Since Io made no attempt to speak anymore on the subject, I turned my attention back to the glowing twister, which had gained speed and taken on a black aura. The black mass was neither blowing air, nor sucking us in… It was simply spinning. It was then that I saw the image beneath the shadows begin to materialize.

"No," I whispered. "Please no. Anything but that." It was no use pleading, for the Temple of Wisdom continued to materialize.

"Just as I thought," Io murmured beside me.

"Please tell me what's going on!" I tugged on Io's robes, forgetting my awe of him. "We need to flee!"

Io shook his head. "No. There are two reasons for that. Number one, you cannot escape destiny and number two, the Temple is blocking our path."

"Then we will run backwards!" Oliver cried out suddenly. "I don't like running away either, but this time I have no problem with it! You don't understand what these temples can do."

"Oliver," Io replied fingering the edges of his hood, "you can never go back once you've started something. You must always finish what you've begun," he paused only for a moment, then added in a somewhat choked voice, "and yes, I know exactly what these Temples do to people."

The Temple was now nearly fully materialized and I could see the eerie ripples on the surface of the pool. "Io, Io I don't understand!" I was nearly crying now. "I don't understand why we can't leave!"

At last Io turned slowly and faced me. "You must give me your solemn promise that you will not try to stop me when I reveal what must be done."

I hesitated, not liking the way things were sounding at all. However what alternative was there? "Io, I can't promise anything when I don't know what you're going to say."

"This is not the time Alice!" Io cried impatiently. "This is for your own good! Now promise!"

There was no time left for arguing, for the Temple glistened before us like a mirage in the desert. "I promise," I whispered in a hardly audible voice.

"This promise binds you," Io told me sternly and then grasped his hood. "Now I must be honest with you, for my hour draws near." He swiftly removed his grey shroud, only to reveal that he wasn't a 'he' at all, but a 'she'!

I nearly fainted at the sight before me. "Emma!" I screamed and threw my arms out to embrace her. Oliver had begun to do the same upon hearing my exclamation.

Emma held up her hands to stop me. "Please don't. It will only make things more difficult."

I drew back in wonder. "What do you mean? We are together again! The company is back together... well, nearly."

Emma grasped my shoulders and gave me a little shake. "Listen to me Alice, for I haven't much time. When I left you and Oliver in the plains, I did it to protect you." She faltered only slightly. "As Io, I gained unimaginable skills, the likes of which could fill a book. But also, the Witch paid no attention to me and so I was free to watch over you. I'm sorry for the deception... It was cruel, but necessary for my plan to be successful. I have learned so many things as Io that I will never be able to relate and for that, I am most sorry."

"Oh Emma, don't be sorry!" I cried in anguish. "But tell me, what's all this talk about destiny?"

Emma looked pained and uncomfortable. "Alice, what I am about to tell you won't be easy to understand, but you must trust me. As Io, I did a lot of thinking over the events of the quest. At last, I came to realize that you and you alone Alice, are destined to face Ralston."

I paled. "Emma, what are you saying? My only job is to find Prince Edric!"

Emma shook her head slowly. "No Alice, that is only part of the quest. I don't know how, but you are going to have to confront the Shadow in Devona." She sighed wearily. "Look at the pattern Alice! There are four Virtue Temples and originally there were four of us... four sisters that is. Three were meant to fall at a Temple, while the final sister would triumph in the end. My fate lies in this Temple... The Temple of Wisdom."

"How can you be so sure I will not die in the final Temple?" Tears gathered at the corners of my eyes. "Remember what Keenan said..."

"That is one prediction Alice and predicting the future is a risky business. So he said that the end would come... change that Alice. Change the future! Shape it into your own dreams of peace! The past cannot be altered, but the future can, based on what you do in the present! You can triumph, no matter how small and insignificant you believe yourself to be!"

"But Emma," it was Oliver who spoke, "what about you?"

She smiled gently. "This is where my path leads. This is my destiny, can't you see? This Temple is mine... I shall be its guardian." She turned back to me. "Alice, the fourth and final Temple is where all of the darkness expects you to fall. When the world says you can't, that is when you must stand tall and say 'I can and I will'. Don't ever look backwards! Always look forwards, my darling sister!" She carefully removed her golden pendant and place it around my neck, along with the other three. "Guard these. They have some part to play, though I know not what." Emma then began to walk steadily towards the awaiting Temple.

That did it. I began to cry uncontrollably and would have run after her, had Oliver not held me fast. "But I can't go on alone!" I cried through my sobs.

Emma paused and looked over her shoulder. "You are never alone my dear Alice. All of my wisdom, Clara's strength and Lily's kind heart go with you. No one can take that away. Please be courageous and keep going. Everything we've fought and suffered for depends on you now."

"Emma!" I screamed hysterically and fought against Oliver's strong grip.

At the very edge of the Temple, Emma stopped and began to speak and though she did not turn around, her voice was loud and clear. "Alice, I just want you to know that I've always been on your side and I always will be. You are near Devona, so beware! When faced with a challenge, look deep inside yourself to find the answer. Oliver, please take care of her and always remember that the darkest hour is just before dawn." With that, she stepped over the pool's edge and with hardly a ripple, vanished beneath the water's glassy surface. Suddenly the black cyclone appeared around the Temple once again and spun rapidly before disappearing... taking my last sister... the new guardian, with it.

CHAPTER TWENTY-SIX

Ancient Bridge

*I*T WAS A LONG TIME before I ceased my fervent struggling and finally stood still in Oliver's arms. My terror dissipated without words and a sort of numbness took over. Every one of my limbs felt drained and weak, as though something had sucked the life right out of me, leaving just enough to keep my heart beating. A few minutes ago, Emma, my eldest sister, the woman who acted as a mother to me, had been standing by my side. Now she was gone forever from our world and into the spirit realm beyond... yet she had said something about being the guardian of the Temple. Would her spirit truly now be the keeper of the Temple of Wisdom? No, only when the Temples were free from Ralston's control, would she be able to preside over the third Virtue Temple.

My shoulder sagged tiredly. I was weary in body, mind and soul. Now I truly was an orphan... Sure her sacrifice had been noble, but how could she just leave me again? Sniffling softly, I felt a great sense of loneliness and betrayal. I had no one... Oliver released his grip on me and placed a reassuring hand upon my shoulder.

"It's okay Alice, I'm here," he told me gently, his empty blue eyes fixed on my tear streaked face.

I took his hands into mine and managed a sad smile. "Thank you Oliver, for always being there for me." I hugged him tightly, burying my face in his shoulder. "Please don't ever leave... you are like a brother to me."

Oliver held very still for a moment and then replied, "That means more to me than you realize Alice."

"Why Oliver?" I asked him suddenly. "I mean, why did Emma do it?" Above the towering mountain behind him, I could see the first rays of pink sunlight seeping across the sky. It was dawn and somehow... it was comforting.

"I don't know what to tell you Alice," Oliver replied quietly, releasing me from his embrace. "She had it all planned out... She knew more than she ever let on."

"She *could* have run away." I looked off into the sky. "She *should* have run away. I should have made her run, but Emma never was one to take orders." I sighed and muttered again, "She could have run away, but she didn't. I guess sometimes you have to face what you fear the most."

"Emma was a truly wise and brave individual. I feel privileged to have known her," Oliver told me with genuine feeling. "Someday perhaps we'll fully understand why she did what she did. I guess all we can do right now, is trust." He gave me a kind smile, which just barely crinkled the corners of his mouth.

I reached down to pick up Gimra, who had been sitting solemnly at my feet. She sensed my sadness and licked my nose. "What have we got you into kitty?" I asked her, wiping the last of my tears away into her soft whiteness. "There's no longer any option of turning back. We will go forward to Devona," I announced distantly. "That is where the answers we seek lie."

"Answers?" came an insane shriek. "Don't you mean graves?" The Witch appeared on schedule, in the sky just above where the temple had been. Her dark robes seemed even blacker than before and I could feel that her powers were stronger... This was probably because she was nearer her master. Placing her skeletal hands upon bony hips, she cackled. "So, this is what we're down to; one worthless little girl, an interfering boy and a..." she shuddered, "*white* cat." Throwing her head back she let loose an ear splitting laugh that caused a few pebbles to fall from the side of the mountain. "Ah, this is too easy! You're not even a challenge!"

Stepping slightly away from Oliver, I pointed a mocking finger at the Witch. "Too easy? Hah! That's a pack of lies if I ever heard one! If we're so easy, how come you haven't destroyed us yet? We're just a couple of children and a cat!" I folded my arms and looked sideways at the hag. "I think *you're* having a might bit of trouble getting rid of us."

"Why you little impudent wretch!" The Witch clenched her hands in the air as though strangling someone. Then as though she heard a voice calling, her head swivelled southward and I could see her mouth moving softly. Violently she turned her gaze back to me and pointing to her belt she seethed, "Do you see these three locks of hair? They belonged to your precious sisters! This fresh one here is from your darling Emma! I will have *your* hair for my trinket next and the pendants for my master, make no mistake about that!"

Oliver shook his fist in the air, just about the only action he could perform without actually being able to see the Witch. "You're nothing but an incompetent lackey for Ralston! You try to act powerful but you're not! It's all just a farce to cover up your own shortcomings!"

The Witch glowed black and her eyes seemed to sink into her head leaving dark pits on her face. "So, Alice's little puppy dog speaks! You pesky brat! If you're not careful, I shall have your pretty boy locks upon my belt as well! You'd be wise to turn back now boy and leave this girl to me. I have no quarrel with you."

"Forget it!" Oliver shouted defiantly. "If you want Alice, you have to get through me first!"

"You know not what you say boy!" the Witch retorted. "But be aware that you have just signed your death warrant! I always get what I want in the end!"

"Leave us alone!" I screamed running towards the Witch, with Gimra hissing in my arms.

The Witch flinched visibly and shielded herself with her robes. "Disgusting creature! Keep that animal away!" she wailed. "This isn't over yet! You've entered the Shadow's territory now! Soon, no white magic will be able to protect you, not even Nissim's! Welcome to your nightmares come true, the most miserable place in all of Fadreama! And when the final act is done, it shall be the darkness that stands victorious!" With another bout of maniacal laughter, the Witch vanished into thin air.

"Is she gone?" asked Oliver, making his way unsteadily over towards me.

"Yes," I stared upward vacantly, "she is gone, but she will not leave us alone. The Witch will not give up until we... at least I... am dead."

"Alice, don't take her threats seriously. She is powerful yes, but not nearly as powerful as she'd like us to think. Ralston keeps her on a very short leash. I think... well, I think Ralston has told her *not* to kill us. He probably wants that pleasure for himself. If he had willed it, we'd both have been dead long ago. Alice? Alice?" Oliver repeated my name, for I had not acknowledged his words, even though I had heard them.

I was looking up into the sky and the fading stars of the night. "Clara once said that when we got to the mountains, we'd wish upon a star together. We'll never be able to do that... at least not the both of us together as planned." I continued to stare up at the sky. "But even though Clara's gone, I'm not. I'm still very much alive. I can wish, hope and dream, so long as there's a breath in my body... and I mean to do so Oliver. Just because my sisters have died, that doesn't mean I have to as well!" I turned to face the bewildered Oliver. "I don't care what that old Witch says, in the end, it shall be us who triumph!" What inspired these words, I didn't know, but something inside of me had begun to sparkle. I knew not if it was my own inner light, but it felt warm and gave me strength and would continue to do so, so long as I believed.

*   *   *

The mountains seemed to grow into tall rugged peaks over the next five days. Some were so high that I couldn't even see their summit. If it weren't for the ever pervading sense of malice and darkening clouds on the horizon, the scenery before us would have been beautiful in its majesty. Unfortunately, every stone and patch of moss was permeated with

Ralston's evil. It was as though everything he touched became twisted and corrupted.

"I sense that the view is distorted somehow," Oliver commented on the sixth day following Emma's death, as we entered a narrow passage, carved through solid rock. Two enormous mountains towered above us on both sides, creating the sensation of being deep inside a well.

"You're quite right," I answered, glancing nervously up for falling rock. "The evil from Devona has warped nature's beauty, so don't feel too bad about not being able to see. Whoa," I stopped abruptly. We had cleared the narrow passageway, but now our journey had brought us to a rickety swinging bridge. It stretched over an enormous canyon, with a rough, fast moving river flowing beneath it. The roar from the water, even at our altitude, was loud enough to force Oliver and I to yell out our conversation.

"How do we cross?" Oliver asked, brushing a damp lock of hair from his face.

"There's a bridge!" I yelled back, looking nervously at the scene before us.

"Does it look safe?" Oliver wondered, obviously unnerved by my hesitation to move forward.

"It doesn't look as though anyone has used it for some time," I answered truthfully, not wanting to frighten him with the entire story.

In fact, the bridge did not look safe at all. The ropes that held it up looked frayed and the floorboards were splintered and warped, not to mention the fact that several boards were missing altogether, creating great gaps along the way. With a slight gulp, I shook the rope railing gently. It sent tremors throughout the entire length of the structure, causing it to sway back and forth. Gingerly I place my foot on the first floor board, which was still above the ground. With a great 'snap' it broke in half before I even had my full weight on it. "Not a good sign," I muttered, discouraged.

"Well?" pressed Oliver. "Is it safe?"

"Not exactly," I replied nervously, peering over the edge of the canyon to the frothing water below. There was no possible way we could cross the river at another point, even if we had a boat or raft of some sort.

"Do you think we can make it?" Oliver took a blind step forward, only to have me grab him violently and pull him back. "Must be quite the drop down…" he mused.

"A fair distance," I told him, hiding a nervous laugh. There was no need to worry him with details. I was terrified to cross the bridge with eyesight… I couldn't imagine doing it blind.

"So are we going to do this or not?" Oliver gave me a challenging look that suggested he knew how dangerous it was, but didn't care.

Did we have a choice? I placed my foot on the second board... It didn't break. Reaching back for Oliver's hand, I pulled him forward, just as Gimra raced up my leg and curled herself around my neck. "Gimra," I muttered, "move your tail, I can't see a thing!"

I paused before taking another step and turned back to Oliver. "Okay, we must go very slowly and use a great deal of caution," I warned.

"Hey, no problem, we're always careful," Oliver chuckled to himself. I couldn't believe he was so calm.

"Yeah right." I grasped the rope railing tightly. "Hold on to the back of my tunic. I'll try to describe the bridge as we go along, so you'll know where to step... and where not to."

"Got ya!" Oliver agreed grabbing my tunic roughly and tightly. Despite the calmness in his voice, his grip suggested something else.

"Ummm... Oliver, could you hold on a little less tightly? I do need to move you know," I commented, seeing a slight bit of humour in a humourless situation.

"Oh, sorry!" He grinned, but did not release his hold.

With a sigh, I slowly began to lead us across the creaking and swaying bridge. It was tedious work describing every step to Oliver, who although listened intently, had trouble making out my words above the roar of the water below. To make matters worse, my voice was becoming weak and hoarse from shouting, which garbled my instructions. One wrong step could potentially be fatal. The bridge swayed dangerous as we passed the halfway mark. Pausing for a brief second, I looked ahead to the opposite bank and held in a gasp, for perched on the post where the supporting rope was tied, sat the Witch's Raven. He did not move, nor make a noise, but simply stood there glowering at me with a chilling stare.

"Oliver," I attempted to still the swinging bridge's wild swaying, "the Raven is here. But don't worry," I added, "we're almost across."

"Great," he grunted. "Just keep going. I don't know how much more of this I can take."

As I took another hesitant step forward, the bridge suddenly began to shake more violently than before. In fact, it felt as though the ropes that tethered it to the ground were coming loose! Still the Raven sat like a carving, watching our every move. I tried to speed up our pace and told Oliver, "Hurry up! I don't think this bridge is going to hold out much longer!"

"I'm going as fast as I can!" Oliver protested. "You try doing this with your eyes closed!" After a moment he added, "On second thought, maybe you'd better keep your eyes open!" I risked a quick shoulder check to see how he was making out and at that very moment, Oliver's foot caught a weak board, which snapped in half! With a sharp cry, he released his hold on my tunic and fell forward onto the rest of the rotten boards. My hands flew to my mouth in horror as he struck the planks. I hardly dared look, for fear he was spiralling down towards the river.

I breathed a sigh of relief. "Thank the Power," I muttered, for only one other board had broken and a few had cracked upon his impact. Now I was afraid to move, in case I upset the tedious balance that was supporting him. He couldn't lay there for long… We had to get back onto solid ground. Taking a deep breath, I reached out my hand slowly. "Oliver, grab hold," I told him, as the bridge began to sway once again.

He thrust his hand out blindly for my aid. "Where are you?"

As I grabbed Oliver's ice cold hand, I distinctly heard a snapping noise, echoing off the canyon walls. Something was afoot! Throwing caution to the wind, I heaved Oliver to his feet and fairly began to drag him over the dying bridge. "Come on!" I urged, breaking into a light-footed run. The boards creaked and groaned under our weight, but for the most part, held up.

"Alice!" Oliver called out to me. "I don't feel so well… I feel dizzy and sick!" He clutched his stomach with his free hand.

"We don't have time to stop Oliver!" I cried, as we suddenly lurched forward. The bridge had begun to sag slightly towards the left. Now I was certain that the ropes were coming apart, even though the Raven had not moved. Another loud snap rang in my ears.

"Don't tell me, the bridge is breaking?" Oliver called. His face was a deadly shade of white. "We're not exactly level anymore." He had pointed out the obvious.

I slowed down, for we could no longer run, as the bridge was too unstable and uneven. "Almost there!" I tried to sound encouraging and not let on just how bad everything truly looked. I found it odd that although the Raven sat on the side we were heading towards, the ropes were breaking on the side we had departed from. Was the Witch hiding nearby?

"At least I can't look down," Oliver mused in a sickly voice.

But *I* certainly could look down and I had many times. The more I told myself *not* to look at the jagged rocks and dark cold water, the more I did. Gimra shivered around my neck, obviously very frightened, for I could feel her little heart pounding into my shoulder.

Suddenly there was another loud snap and before I could even comprehend what had happened, the left rope completely ripped in half. I felt myself fly forward and hit the bridgeboards hard, with Oliver just behind me. Then although it seemed like a dream, I started to roll to the left, for there was only the right rope supporting the bridge from the side we had come from. Hardly realizing what I was doing, I grabbed hold of one the boards and held on for dear life. On the side we were heading towards, the two ropes were still firmly tied to their posts... with the Raven roosting on one. Would the last rope on the other side hold out?

I could sense that Oliver was clinging right behind me, although I couldn't even begin to comprehend his fear at the moment. There was only one thing to do. "We're going to have to crawl the rest of the way!" I called back to him and started inching ahead. "You're going to need both hands, so you can't grab my tunic. Just crawl forward!" I instructed.

"Are you serious?" came his reply, laced with uncertainty and disbelief.

"What else are we going to do?" I knew he wouldn't have an answer for this, but the naïve part of me was really hoping that he would. Now would have been a great time for Io or Nissim to show up and save us, but it seemed that we were completely on our own.

Carefully we began to move forward, holding onto the rotten boards and rope as though it were life itself... and perhaps at this moment it was. The going was slow and though I couldn't be certain, it felt as though the right rope was now nearing its breaking point. Fearfully, I hollered back to Oliver, "If that other rope breaks, hold onto the bridge as tightly as you can and brace yourself. The worst that can happen is that we swing into the cliff and have to climb the bridge like a ladder."

"That's a good plan," Oliver gulped back, "but what if the other two ropes break as we're climbing up?"

"Then I guess we're up the creek... literally," I answered, grabbing hold of another board only to receive a painful splinter. I could almost hear Oliver frowning at the answer I had just given him.

"Somehow that wasn't what I wanted to hear," he told me with a little grunt as his hand slipped slightly, causing the bridge to tremble.

"Well there's always—" I was cut off by hysterical laughter from behind the Raven. It was the Witch.

"Looks like you children are in a bit of trouble and there's no one around to save you this time!" The Witch spoke in a diabolically mocking voice that seemed to emit a cold wind in our direction. "Oh how I crave trouble!" She smacked her dark lips together.

"We're not in any trouble!" I called back, though it seemed a stupid reply considering the circumstances.

"Such denial Alice!" the Witch cackled. "And I'm sure it wasn't your fault that your sisters died either!" she laughed. "But now I have you just where I want you! Go my pet!" she ordered the Raven. "Bring me those pendants!"

216 Candace N. Coonan

Obediently the Raven spread his dark wings and glided towards where I lay clinging helplessly. He dove for the golden chains, which glinted about my neck, but Gimra was ready for him. With a hiss, she let loose a scream and leaped from my neck and onto the Raven. She hit her mark with deadly accuracy and black feathers mingled with white fur and blood. There was nothing I could do, but watch helplessly as both Gimra and the Raven disappeared down... down... down into the canyon below.

"Oh Gimra..." I whispered. "I'm so sorry..."

"My pet!" the Witch screamed and pulled at her frizzled hair. "You little brat and that... that... *white cat*! You shall pay dearly!" she threatened me with her fist in the air. "The end draws near! Nissim is nearly dead and soon you shall be as well! Then... then all of Algernon shall pay for your insolence!" She revealed a long twisted staff with a strange red ball on top. With death in her eyes and anger in her heart, she aimed the tip of the staff towards the remaining rope on the far side of the canyon. What looked to be a streak of red lightning shot out and slice the rope completely in half. "Die!" she shrieked and disappeared, leaving us to plunge straight into the side of the rocky cliff.

CHAPTER TWENTY-SEVEN

White Out

*T*HERE WAS NO TIME to scream, as the bridge ploughed head on into the side of the cliff. I felt my bones crunch and my insides jolt upon the violent impact. Although I was too stunned to cry out, Oliver yelled loudly in pain, which was a good sign, as that meant he hadn't lost his grip and fallen into the canyon below. Somehow, both of us had managed to hang on to the dangling bridge. The only thing keeping us from falling to our deaths, were two lengths of rope tied around some rotten wood posts at the top of the cliff... that thought was not reassuring. The Witch obviously expected those ropes to give out, for she had vanished into the air, back to the darkness where she kept her counsel. A cool wind swept by and swung us back and forth, like a cat batting at a string... Cat... Gimra...

"Oooohhhh..." moaned Oliver down below me.

Risking a gaze, I turned my head so that I could see him, as he dangled precariously. There was a fresh gash on his forehead, but other than that, he seemed all right. Nevertheless I inquired, "Are you okay?"

"I'll live," he replied, while trying to get a tighter grip on the splintered board from which he hung, "and you?"

I looked down and saw a trickle of ruby red blood running down my tanned arm. To my horror, the bottle of poison potion which I'd kept hanging from my belt, was shattered and covered in blood as well. The foul green liquid was completely drained, with only a few drops clinging to the shards. It was my blood that covered the broken glass... When I had hit the canyon wall, my arm must have smashed up against my belt, thus breaking the phial. My heart began to race as I wondered if any of the poison had entered my body through the cut... Just a scratch would be enough to kill!

"Oliver!" I called down to him. "I cut my arm on the bottle of poison potion! It's all drained...my arm... crushed it..." I spoke in a halting voice, though without really noticing it.

"Are you okay though? I mean, did the poison get into your wound?" Oliver asked in a concerned voice.

"I don't really know..." I felt my grip on the bridge loosen almost imperceptivity.

"We'll bandage it up after we scale this cliff. I assume climbing up is the plan?" he asked, his voice slightly tinged with amusement.

"First we should climb the cliff," I replied distantly, forgetting every word he had just spoken.

"I just said that! Weren't you listening?" Oliver reached up and gave the fringe of my tunic a little pull.

"I'm sorry Oliver," I apologized. "My mind is just a little mixed up right now."

"That's okay Alice, I completely understand. My mind's been doing some funny things lately too," he reassured me. "Now, about climbing up, I think I can do it just by following your voice and…Alice?"

I had begun to feel woozy and light headed, for the poison had, without a doubt, entered my body. The world seemed to swirl into a blur of shapes and colours… Nothing was distinct anymore. To make matters worse, there was a terrible ringing in my ears that blocked out all other sounds. I just managed to stammer weakly, "Oliver…I feel a little strange…" I could feel myself begin to sway, thus causing the bridge to move unsteadily as well.

"Alice!" I could barely hear Oliver's voice. It sounded panicked. "You have poison in your arm! We have to get you out of here! Alice!"

I was unable to answer him, or even acknowledge that I had heard him. Nothing seemed to matter anymore and slowly, I felt myself letting go of whatever it was that I had been holding onto so tightly. I could still hear the muffled sounds of Oliver… He was shouting now… questions that didn't make any sense. Then, all at once, my body went numb. I could feel my hands open and release… but there was nothing I could do. I began to fall, but suddenly something caught me sharply around the waist. My stomach lurched at the impact, but I couldn't see or hear anything now. I was a rag doll, scarcely conscious of being alive.

Slowly I felt myself moving… going upward, although in a very awkward fashion. I thought I could hear garbled muttering and groaning, but I wasn't certain. After what seemed like an eternity, I was heaved onto an uneven surface, with sharp points protruding into my sides. There was a loud 'thump' beside me and then silence.

Before my eyes swirled a picture… a vision of sorts and it was of a… a… a mushroom! Now where had I seen it before? We had picked them a long time ago… in a forest. The Forgotten Forest? Yes, that name seemed familiar. The mushroom loomed even larger before me, so that I could see every last detail. The top was a bright red, with large yellow dots peppering its surface. Even the stem was bright red, but the underbelly was pure white. Yes, we certainly had picked that mushroom, though I wasn't sure who 'we' was. I had grabbed a great handful of the fungus and stored it in my satchel. I wondered if I still had it...

*   *   *

I opened my eyes and blinked at the quiet surroundings. I was lying atop a cliff between two wooden posts... bridge posts. A cloak was rolled up underneath my head and the sun was in the western sky. Without sitting up, I felt my arm and discovered that it was bound with strips of cloth. As the memories began to flash before my eyes, I sat up slowly, only to discover that I felt... quite well.

A short distance away, Oliver was sitting before a tiny fire with his back turned to me. I ran my fingers through my hair in an attempt to comb it out and then stretched my arms slowly... only the injured one hurt, but very slightly. "Hey Oliver," I said simply.

His head jerked up immediately and he turned around on his hands and knees. "Alice?" he exclaimed. "You're alive! So the poison didn't kill you after all! I was pretty worried there for awhile... at least once I caught my breath that is."

I gave him a questioning look, for all I could recall was feeling woozy while we were hanging above the raging river. "What are you talking about?" I wondered, noticing for the first time, that I could faintly see my breath in the air, which was quite cool.

"Don't you remember?" Oliver stood up and took a drink from the water flask. Then wiping his mouth with the back of his sleeve he continued, "No, I guess I can't blame you. You were poisoned Alice and you fainted."

"While we were on the bridge?" I asked in shock.

Oliver nodded. "That's right. You fell and I," he looked proud, "caught you."

"So you carried me up that bridge?" I stood up and brushed the dirt off of my tunic. Surprisingly enough, I felt quite well balanced, without the slightest bit of wooziness.

"Indubitably," Oliver replied, casting some dirt onto the tiny fire to put it out.

"Thank you," I smiled, "for saving my life."

"Hey, no problem," Oliver grinned, rubbing the back of his neck. "Although you were quite heavy mind you. Have you ever considered losing some weight?" he teased.

I cast a glance down at my slender figure and good naturedly threw a pebble at him. "You're crazy," I laughed. Oh how good it felt to laugh!

"And don't you forget it!" Oliver joined in the merriment.

Then wiping the tears of laughter from my eyes I asked, "So how come I didn't die from the poison?"

"Because I gave you the antidote, that's why," Oliver replied, as though it were the most natural answer.

Amazed, I stared at him, mouth agape. "But how?"

Smoothing back his hair, Oliver cracked his knuckles. "Well, I do know a thing or two about healing. After all, I was raised by a wizard. Oh and I'm a clever one, able to think fast in emergency situations and I have been known to perform a miracle or two."

"So what did you really do?" I folded my arms and tried to suppress another bout of giggles.

Oliver blushed and replied, "You talked in your sleep about some sort of a mushroom. So I took a chance that it was the antidote. After all, you're always having visions and such, so I thought…"

"But you can't see!" I interrupted him. "How could you know it was the right mushroom?"

"I didn't." Oliver looked sheepish. "There was a lot of guess work involved on my part, I must admit. But hey! You're alive, so I must have guessed right!"

"I could have died!" I smacked my forehead in disbelief. Thank the Power, for he must have been guiding Oliver's hand.

Oliver pulled out his walking stick and felt his way over to me with a light tapping sound. "Don't get me wrong Alice. I really truly was worried about you."

"I know," I assured him, then changed tones. "Well, we had better get going." The sun would soon be setting and as Io… Emma had said, that was when everything broke loose.

"Are you sure Alice?" Oliver raised a worried eyebrow. "I mean—"

I cut him off. "I'm positive Oliver, really. I actually feel quite good! My arm is a little tender, but that's about it. Besides, we can't stay here."

"I know that, but are you certain?" Oliver still looked uneasy.

I nodded and then realizing that he couldn't see me nod, spoke up, "Whatever was in that mushroom healed any ill effects the poison had on me. I feel fine… I wouldn't ask to go on if I didn't. You know me better than that."

Finally convinced, Oliver handed me my pack. "Well then, here you go. I carried *that* up the cliff too," he grinned.

"Just one moment Oliver." I turned back to the edge of the cliff and stared down at the raging rapids. Poor little Gimra… She had come a long way with us, only to meet a terrible end. The pure white cat had saved the pendants and possibly the kingdom because of her bravery. It simply wasn't fair. Why did everyone I love have to die?

"Alice?" Oliver spoke my name softy and as if guessing what I was thinking said, "Gimra did what she came to do. She gave you the most precious gift... her life. Don't let it go to waste."

I closed my eyes tightly for a moment, then turned around and opened them once again. "I don't intend to Oliver," I replied. "I don't intend to." My breath hung frostily in the air. With a shiver, I made my way towards Oliver and took his arm. "Come on, let's get moving... it's becoming quite cold."

So we set off, following the road indicated on our map. The going was rough, for the path was steep and uneven. Several times I lost my footing and stumbled, but Oliver was always there to hold me up and likewise, whenever Oliver stumbled, I was there to help him. We were very much a team and yet somehow at the back of my mind, I recalled that I had to face the Shadow alone in my dream. Where was Oliver then? Did something unspeakable happen to him or was Ralston simply toying with my mind? Never once did I voice these concerns to Oliver, for even speaking of the Shadow in my dreams frightened me beyond imagination.

Onward we steadily trudged, until there were no longer any trees around us. The forest had been left behind and now we were surrounded by cold stone and looming grey clouds. Even the sky, when a small patch peeked out from behind the cloud cover, looked different. It wasn't its normal blue colour, but somehow changed, somehow stained. I told Oliver this much and he simply declared that it was a sign our destination was fast approaching. Prince Edric, where are you now?

As night approached, the temperature began to drop drastically. I had expected as much from a high altitude, but I was not prepared for just how fast and how cold it became. Even though spring was nearing an end, in the Thea Mountains, if felt as though winter were on its way. My cloak offered some protection from the elements, but it was a spring cloak and subsequently, not made for the mountain drafts. I noticed that even the hardy moss dared not grow in this desolate environment, poisoned by evil.

"It smells like snow," Oliver declared with a shiver and pulled the hood up on his cloak.

"That would be just our luck," I muttered. "We've had enough rain, why not snow too?" My tone dripped with sarcasm. I didn't doubt that Oliver was right though, for there was the familiar scent on the air that comes just before a snowstorm. Although the clouds farther south were black, the ones above us were grey and low, almost like a heavy mist. The air was damp, sending a permeating chill straight into my bones. It honestly made me wonder if I would ever be warm again.

"It'll be an experience," Oliver ventured, in a lame attempt to make the best of things.

"One we could perhaps do without right now," I replied, as I stared up at the sky. The clouds were moving faster now, as though they had a mind of their own. Knowing the magic we were up against, it wouldn't have surprised me if they did. "It's getting sort of misty," I told Oliver, slowing our pace. "Maybe we should stop for the night... I can't see very well."

"As long as there are no temples around, I'm with you." Oliver rubbed his numb hands together briskly.

"But where... ?" I mused thoughtfully. "If only there were one of those travelers' caves around, but I don't see anything except solid stone."

"I've had enough of caves, thank you very much." Oliver looked cross. "Every cave we've ever been to along this quest has been nothing but trouble."

"We'll be in even more trouble if we don't find shelter for the night," I pointed out, just as a snowflake fluttered softy in front of my eyes. I stretched out my hand and the snowflake landed gently in my palm, melting into a spot of water. Before I could even withdraw my hand though, another snowflake landed on it... Then another and another! When the fifth snowflake landed on my skin, the blizzard struck us with its full force.

The icy wind cut through our cloaks and tunics as though we stood there naked. I gasped for breath, as the wind rudely stole it away. The snow whirled and swirled before my eyes, completely destroying my sense of direction. Determined to be brave, I grasped Oliver's hand tightly and began to shuffle through the accumulating snow. We hadn't gone far, when at last I threw up my hands in frustration. It was no use, for to continue walking would mean our deaths... yet to stay still meant death as well. I could slowly feel the small amount of courage I had built up, freezing with the terrain around us.

Oliver turned towards me, his eyes narrowed from the wind. "We're stuck aren't we?" His black hair was encrusted with icy white snow, even underneath his oversized hood.

The tears that were attempting to fall down my face were thwarted by the cold and froze in the corners of my eyes. "I don't know which way to go!" I despaired, touching my lips, which I guessed must be turning blue.

Oliver seemed unsure of what to say, so instead he threw down the heavy sack which had been burdening his back. "We haven't really gone through everything Captain Wyston packed for us," he told me. "Maybe there's something we can use for shelter..." His voice trailed off in a fit of coughing.

I didn't really see much point in going through the supplies, but I had to do something. Reluctantly, I withdrew my bare hands from beneath my cloak where I had been keeping them warm under my armpits. The rope, which bound the supply bag, was frozen with crystallized snow, so when I finally got it open, I had to stop and warm my hands once again before continuing. Not really expecting to find much, I was surprised when my hand brushed against a sturdy bundle of rather thick material. "Oliver, I think I've found something!" I exclaimed, as I fought to loosen the object.

"I knew there had to be something!" Oliver chattered. "What is it?"

It was astonishing! A tent! We had a tent in our possession and never even knew about it! By the Power above! "Oliver!" I cried. "It's a tent! We're saved!" Or at least bought some time... so that our deaths would be even more drawn out and agonizing. No, I tried to be positive, this had to be our salvation. "Oh Captain Wyston," I whispered, "wherever you are now, thank you... and I hope you are well."

"What was that?" Oliver leaned in towards me. His face was pale and drawn... he needed... we both needed... to get out of the wind and ice.

"Oh nothing," I replied, rubbing the ice from my eyelashes. "Let's get this thing set up."

It was no easy task to pitch a tent in a blizzard, for the wind would catch hold of the material and flap it violently into the air. It snapped Oliver across the cheek, leaving a bright red triangular mark, but he simply gritted his teeth and continued to help in any way possible. I was also having problems of my own, for my eyelashes continued to gather ice, making them nearly impossible to keep open. On top of that, my hands were completely numb with cold, causing me to fumble with the ties and stakes.

When all was in place, the tent was very sad looking indeed and seemed as though it might blow away at any second. I hadn't any energy left to straighten the lopsided shelter, nor the spirit to try, so wearily, Oliver and I crawled into the darkness. We had no light, nor any means to make a fire. The best we could do for warmth was huddle together and hope the storm let up soon.

The minutes ticked by and neither of us could muster up the effort to speak. By now I was so cold that I had actually begun to feel warm and rather...sleepy. A dull throbbing pain had started in my temples and a painful knot had formed in my stomach. I had heard once that you should never go to sleep when you are cold, for you may never wake up, but the sensation was a difficult one to fight.

"I know this is a bad t... time," Oliver stuttered, "but do you have a... anything t... to eat?"

Hardly aware of what I was doing, I peeled open the supply sack and withdrew a loaf of frozen bread. Finding that I couldn't break it with my hands, I slammed it hard against a rock. "H... here." I handed half to

Oliver, who accepted it with shivering hands. "Gnaw on it," I instructed, looking distastefully at my own half of the bread. Finding I had no appetite, I set it on the ground beside me.

"I... it's too bad we can't m... make a f... fire," Oliver declared sadly. I could scarcely see his outline in the darkness of the tent.

"At least we're out of the wind," I found myself yawning.

Oliver seemed to be nodding slowly. I supposed that the darkness of the tent didn't both him at all. "I guess we should be thankful for that," he tapped the frozen bread on the supporting tent pole, "and this well preserved food."

I couldn't even acknowledge his joke, for I was too sleepy and cold. The darkness was everywhere... outside the tent and inside, for night was upon us. Our poorly constructed tent shook so violently that I feared it might blow away and leave us to freeze... not as though we weren't freezing already. The wind howled and shrieked like a million voices crying out in pain and agony. Never before had I ever felt so small and alone as I did now, sitting in the cold dark tent, atop a lonely mountain. My inner light, which had been sparked, was now merely a dim ember. How could I continue to believe, when everything was so hopeless?

CHAPTER TWENTY-EIGHT

A Fair Wind

YOU AGAIN!" I cried out to the Shadow looming above my head. It had to be Ralston Radburn, there was no longer any doubt in my mind of this fact.

"At long last I shall be rid of you child!" Ralston laughed in malicious delight.

I felt so weak, so tired... I just wanted to lay down behind the jagged rocks and sleep. Ah to finally rest, the one thing I desired more than anything else. I was in pain and alone, so why fight it?

"That's it child! Give in to it and give up to me!" Ralston the Shadow was thoroughly enjoying my suffering.

So why wasn't I obeying him? I wanted to give in and enter the eternal slumber, but something was stopping me. There was a heavy weight upon my head, yet no matter how hard I tried, I could neither see, nor touch the object. Also there was something I had to do... for everyone...and for myself.

I jerked awake suddenly from my fitful slumber and all at once felt extremely grateful to be alive. I had fallen asleep, despite the dangers of doing so in the cold. Oliver and I were leaning with our backs to one another... a most uncomfortable position to be sleeping in. As soon as I began to move and stretch, he awoke with a start.

"We fell asleep!" Oliver cried in a cracked voice.

I rubbed my face wearily and mumbled, "But we're alive."

"In a manner of speaking," Oliver yawned. "Hey I don't hear the wind howling anymore. The blizzard must be over."

I listened and heard nothing but silence. "You're right." I gave a tiny smile, but it didn't last long. "I'm still not certain how far I led us off the path. Finding our way back could be interesting."

"I'm sure we're not too far off track," Oliver told me amiably, as he groped for the supply sack. He appeared to be in an excellent mood, considering the horrible night we had just passed. Either that or he was a master at hiding his true emotions. Not a word had been spoken of Carrie for a very long time, but every so often I had seen him clutching a blue Forget-Me-Not.

Tucking my hands deep inside my cloak, I puffed into the icy air. "It's still cold," I pointed out.

"I could have told you that," Oliver laughed and produced a frozen loaf of cornbread. "I'm starving! Are you hungry?" He broke the bread over his knee and handed me half. "Enjoy!" he chuckled and began to gnaw away at his piece.

"Thanks," I muttered, staring through the dim light at the unappetizing looking object. What I would give for a real warm meal! Sausage, pancakes, milk, eggs! I sighed and flipped open the tent flap. "I'll be back," I told Oliver before exiting, frozen bread in hand.

Outside the sky was dim, despite the fact that it was now morning. An icy wind whipped my long hair around and chilled me all over. The deep penetrating dampness still clung in the air, giving me a slight headache. The road we had been traveling on was nowhere to be seen and I curled my fists in frustration. A blanket of hard packed snow covered everything, including our tracks from the night before. I didn't know where we came from, not to mention where we were going!

With an angry cry of anguish, I kicked at the snow with all my might, sending a shower of powder flying everywhere. "It's not fair!" I tried to keep my voice low, so that Oliver wouldn't hear me, but nevertheless, it came out as a yell. Tilting my head skyward, I stared at the dim heavens that would not turn blue, no matter how high the sun rose. "I tried! I did my best and failed! I'm sorry but what more can I do! All I wanted to know was a little bit about my past and look where it got me!"

Pent up emotions were released and I fell to my knees. I was ashamed by my behaviour but angry at the circumstances surrounding my life. "Why?" I whispered. "Why does it have to be me?" I lowered my head and wept bitterly.

Just then, the cold wind disappeared and was replaced by a calm, warm breeze. It blew by my face in a strange manner that seemed to be urging me to turn around. It was the oddest feeling... I spun about quickly, expecting to see something miraculous, but instead saw nothing but a cold, windswept mountain range. It looked exactly the same as every other direction; cold, dull and completely desolate.

Putting an icy hand to my forehead, I stood up slowly. "It's finally happened, I've gone crazy," I muttered, feeling a strange presence in the air.

Yet, the warm wind persisted in its swirling around me in a rather insistent fashion. It almost felt as though hands... were gently pushing on my back. They were not menacing, but incredibly soft and familiar.

"What's going on?" I asked the mysterious air, which gave no answer and instead continued to urge me forward. Without thinking, I allowed the breeze to steer me onward, hardly realizing what I was doing, until I found myself at the very edge of a cliff. The breeze stopped suddenly at this point, as though afraid I would topple over the edge. To be honest, I was so entranced, that had the breeze wished it, I would have stepped over voluntarily, but this, apparently, was not the intention.

Peering over the edge, I saw a narrow snow covered valley... nothing really all that significant or spectacular. A river, seemingly frozen in time, flowed through the center of the valley, but there was no evidence of a settlement. However I had to admit that there was something... unsettling about the place, but I couldn't quite decide just what. The breeze had died down, as though it were waiting for me to do something. I turned around and was about to back up when the breeze returned suddenly. Firm hands twisted my body around to face the valley once more and held me in this position.

I should have been terribly frightened, but all I felt was annoyance. "What?" I questioned the air. "What do you want me to do?" I threw my hands up in exasperation. Something was obviously desired of me, but as to what that was, I was oblivious. I waited for the surge of warm air to come by again, but it didn't return. The firm grip on my arms faded into nothingness and I briefly wondered if I had imagined the entire episode.

Hesitantly, I backed away from the cliff and this time, nothing restrained me. Satisfied, I turned my back on the snowy valley and began to walk towards the tent. As much as I tried to put the breeze out of my mind, it kept returning with extreme urgency. It had been trying to tell me something, but what? It was too late to ask questions, for already the air had grown cold and empty once again. The invisible hands were gone... along with their non-existent touch. I realized with a start, that it had been reassuring somehow. "A breeze, reassuring?" Uncertainly I stopped my trek and returned to the cliff. Finding a large protruding rock, I heaved myself up onto it and sat down to think.

"Devona is out there somewhere," I whispered, feeling very tiny against the vast mountain range, "and maybe I don't fear being lost, so much as I fear actually reaching the destination. What am I going to do once we get to Devona? Where am I going to go first?" I gulped. "And what am I going to see?" My mind went back to the tormented images from Ms Craddock's mirror, locked away in the hidden room at the orphanage. Absently I wondered what I still had left from Ms Craddock's hidden room... I had my shoes, the map, the gold coins, my satchel...My thoughts began to wander off track as I recalled past events. Ms Craddock's hidden room, Io's cloak hiding Emma's identity, the hidden Shadow in my dream, the Temple of Wisdom, invisible until it wished to be seen.

"So many things have been kept hidden from my view," I sighed. "It's funny how things can exist and be very real, but you simply are unable to see them." Bringing my knees to my chest, I hugged them tightly and continued with my musings, while recalling the frozen piece of bread in my hand. "So many times people won't believe in things, simply because they cannot see them with their eyes. They miss out on a completely new level of the world! The unseen is just as real as the seen... I suppose it just requires one to look with their heart and have faith."

Taking a bite of the frozen bread in my hand, I stared out at the hidden valley, whose true nature was concealed by snow. Suddenly I stopped, mid-chew and nearly fell off the boulder. Throwing back my head I laughed.

"Of course! It's been staring me in the face all along! What a silly obtuse child I have proved myself to be!" The hidden valley! That was what the breeze had been trying to tell me! Captain Wyston's tune! The Hidden Valley of the Fairies! No wonder we were lost! We hadn't used the magical tune!

"Talking to yourself again Alice?" asked Oliver, as he crawled out of the tent and clumsily began to disassemble it. "You want this taken down?"

I turned to Oliver in elation. "Yes, take it down at once, for we shall soon be in Devona!"

"So you found the road?" Oliver asked, stumbling over a supporting rope. With a goofy smile on his handsome face, he brushed the snow from his cloak.

"No, not exactly," I told him and instead of explaining, stood up upon the boulder and began to sing the hauntingly familiar tune, exactly as Captain Wyston had taught it to us on the good ship Nova. Although I had never actually sung the tune before, I knew it so well that I could have done it in my sleep. I felt as though I had known the song all of my life and had heard it a thousand times before.

As I continued, with my voice rising and falling, the strangest events began to occur. The dense impenetrable clouds overhead started to part and a single beam of life giving sunshine shone down into the snow covered valley. The spot where it touched the ground turned green and lush immediately! The beam began to move across the landscape and paint an entirely new scene. Not only did the snow disappear and grass, trees and flowers appear, but the air grew warm and fragrant. The sound of running water filled my ears as trickling streams appeared, crisscrossing their way through the valley. As the last note of the tune fell from my lips, I stood in silence, completely awestruck. Oliver, who was now at my side, could see nothing, but he sensed the change in the air.

"It's the valley of fairies, isn't it?" Oliver asked, as he reached up and I took his hand, using it to dismount from the boulder.

"Yes Oliver," I assured him. "It was right here all this time and I didn't even realize it. I guess this just goes to show that when a solution doesn't seem obvious, perhaps you'd be wise to look harder... and in a different way."

"The unseen," Oliver laughed merrily. "Everything is packed and ready to go... I hope you ate your cornbread."

I laughed and held up the half eaten loaf. "It's thawing!"

With considerably lighter hearts, we descended into the lush, warm valley. As we entered, the cold world we had previously been in, disappeared, as we became surrounded by a utopia... complete with a crystal clear blue sky. How long had it been since I'd seen the sky so pure? Ralston's reign of terror obviously had no effect on this realm.

The sounds of birds chirping and the stream babbling, filled the air and mingled with the soft scents of fresh flowers after a spring rain. Everything seemed so new, so untouched... it was like paradise. The landscape had a little bit of everything; a meadow, a forest, a glade... A hard packed pebble path, wound its way through the trees and over a rather large hill on the other side of the valley. Devona presumably, was on the other side of that hill.

"This sure is a lot easier than yesterday's traveling!" Oliver commented with a cheery air.

"Definitely," I agreed as we briskly made our way down the trail, "and the scenery is so beautiful! I wish you could see it Oliver. The best part of all are the glowing fairies darting about! They come in every colour of the rainbow!" The valley was aptly named, for the colourful fairy folk were everywhere... as numerous as insects, but as evasive as a rainbow itself. I was beside myself with wonder.

"Wouldn't it be wonderful to meet one?" asked Oliver. I recalled something Keenan had said... that fairies would play a major role in Oliver's life.

"Oh yes," I nodded, "but they are so quick and I think they're shy too. One minute they're there, the next, they're not."

Oliver changed the subject abruptly. "It doesn't feel as though Ralston has any control over this place."

I gazed around at the gorgeous and peaceful valley. "Perhaps Ralston isn't as strong as we thought," I suggested hopefully.

Oliver chortled. "I don't know about that. I think he'll be quite the adversary. In fact, he's already proved that point."

"Well," I straightened up, "when we get Prince Edric on the throne, he'll know what to do. He'll fix everything!" I declared boldly.

"You really think so?" Oliver asked, with a strange hint of doubt in his voice.

"Of course!" I exclaimed. "That's what we came all this way for. Nissim wouldn't instruct us to do something that wouldn't work!"

"I know, I know," Oliver agreed. "I'm just saying that maybe we shouldn't put all of our hopes on him."

"What else can we do?" I asked, suddenly nervous, recalling the suggestion in my dream that *I* would have to confront Ralston.

Oliver stared blankly ahead, with a vexed look on his face. "I don't know Alice. I don't know."

CHAPTER TWENTY-NINE

An Unexpected Encounter

A TRICKLE OF SWEAT rolled down the side of my face and wound its way around my neck. Absently I wiped it off and removed my heavy cloak. "I don't think my body will ever get used to all these temperature changes," I commented, rolling my cloak up into a tight bundle. "We nearly freeze to death one day and melt the next. It can't be healthy for a person. It's just so hot," I breathed, casting a sideways glance towards Oliver, whose black hair was damp with perspiration as well.

"No arguments there," Oliver chuckled tiredly, as he ran a hand over his face.

"Not to worry though," I squinted into the distance, "because we're almost through the valley. The trail leads up a hill and I suppose that means we'll be in Devona."

"You mean we've walked that far already?" Oliver exclaimed in surprise.

"It's not that big of a valley," I told him. "Although it contains so much... so many different landscapes... it's all condensed. Sort of like a miniature world." At the present, we were leaving behind the grassy meadow terrain, with its brightly coloured flowers and entering into a cool forest. The shade was most welcomed. The trees seemed suspended in time, during their most fruitful season. Everything was in perfect balance and coexisted in harmony.

It was then that a high pitched noise, similar to the tinkling of bells, rang out through the dense wood. That delightful sound was followed by a deeper noise, like the rumbling of an earthquake. It was not pleasant at all. Oliver's head jerked up and I knew he had heard it too.

"What was that?" he asked, as the sounds began to repeat themselves.

"I don't know," I whispered, dropping my voice considerably, "but it sounds like it's coming from over there."

"Over where?" he repeated blindly.

Without answering his question, I pulled Oliver down low and began to drag him off the road and into the shady trees. "Stay low," I whispered to him, as we concealed ourselves behind a shrub. I cautiously peered over the low growing bush and had to clap a hand over my mouth to keep from crying out. Quickly dropping into a squat back behind the protective shrub, I told Oliver, "There's a little fairy over there, but she's trapped in a cage by a... a..." I trailed off and scratched my chin.

"A what?" whispered Oliver hoarsely, with a note of impatience.

"Well, I don't really know," I confessed softly. "It was really big and ugly..."

"That could describe any number of creatures." Oliver looked unimpressed.

"It sort of looks like a creature that up until now I've only read about in stories." I paused and then voiced my hypothesis. "It looks to be a troll of some sort." I waited for Oliver to laugh, but his expression remained serious.

"That could very well be what it is. So what is he doing to the fairy?" Oliver wondered, holding his walking stick tightly.

"Hold on, I'll look," I replied and peeked around the bush once again, just as the tinkling sound pealed out. Holding the leaves away from my face, I surveyed the rather startling scene. There was the terrified fairy with a bright yellow glow, being held prisoner inside of a brown twig cage. Anyone could have easily smashed out of such a cell, but the fairy's tiny hands could do nothing but grip the bars. "I always thought fairies had magic," I mused quietly. The fairy was too tiny and too far away from me to make out much more of her. Yet without having a good view of her, I could tell she was panicked and with good cause.

Standing a short distance away from the cage, was a plump looking green skinned troll, who was covered in brown splotches, similar to freckles, only much larger. He was completely bald and clad only in a scraggly brown tunic with breeches, which were in desperate need of a patch job. The troll's feet were enormous and protected by tightly laced leather boots... the left boot had a hole in the end, from which the troll's fat green toe protruded. Using lumbering movements, he turned around with a tiny twig gripped between his fat fingers. His mouth opened and he let loose a growling laugh, as he proceeded to prod at the fairy, using the twig.

"Hello there little one," he greeted the fairy in a mock friendly voice. "Enjoying your new quarters?"

I couldn't see what the fairy was doing, but she retorted with a burst of tinkling sounds. Turning my head back to Oliver I whispered, "He's teasing her with a stick!"

"We must do something!" Oliver hissed back in a most convincing tone. "He must have some purpose with her and I don't think it's a good one!"

I gulped and turned my attention back to the scene that was unfolding. We really did have to stop the troll before he did anything drastic... but I was unfamiliar with the traits of trolls. Did they have powers? I didn't think so, but one could never be sure in a place like this. Just then, the troll, obviously agitated by the fairy's remarks, ripped the cage door off and violently grabbed the tiny fairy in his oversized fist. There was a hungry gleam in his red eyes, as he opened his slobbering mouth. He was going to eat her!

There was no time to formulate a plan! What we needed was immediate action! "Watch out Oliver," I warned, as I ripped the bow off my back. I didn't want to kill the troll... just scare him or even distract him, so that the yellow fairy could escape. Stealthily... in fact, more stealthily than I was aware I could be under pressure, I aimed for the troll's fat legs. Praying that things wouldn't work out as they had with the panther, I let my arrow fly.

The arrow whizzed straight past the troll's leg, all but grazing the knee a little... perhaps only ripping the fabric of his breeches. I bit my lip in anger at the terrible shot, for now *we* were in danger! The troll gave a sharp grunt and without letting go of the fairy, headed in our direction.

"Ummm... Oliver," I grabbed his hand, "we could be in for some trouble." I tried to make it sound insignificant.

"Let me guess, you missed?" he asked, scrambling to his feet, just as the troll ripped through the shrub we were hiding behind.

There was no time to answer, for the troll now stood towering before us, only a few footsteps away. His eyes glowed red with anger and annoyance. "Who are you?" he demanded in a loud voice. The fairy in his hand had stopped struggling and was eyeing us with curiosity.

I was at a loss for words and wondered why I had decided to get involved in the first place. If only I had learned to mind my own business, we would be far down the road already.

Placing a hand on his ample hip, the troll repeated, "I said, who are you? And why are you in the sacred fairy valley? You don't look like any fairy I've ever seen... I'd say you were an Alexandrian fairy, but you don't have any wings! In which case," he narrowed his gaze suspiciously, "you must be humans."

I swallowed and asked hesitantly, "And what if we are?"

"I don't like humans!" The troll took a large step forward. "I've been around for eight hundred years and in that time, all humans have ever done is fight and betray one another. They're good for nothing!" After a moment's pause he added, "They're not even good for eating!"

The troll obviously had neither fear nor respect for humans, which was going to act as a disadvantage for us. I had already decided since we had come this far, we might as well save the pretty little fairy. How, was the big question. Boldly I stepped sideways slightly, so as not to be directly in front of the troll and announced, "I am Alice and I was personally selected by the all powerful wizard Nissim, to restore the heir, Prince Edric to the throne." I hoped that by mentioning Nissim's name, the troll would quake. Without giving him a chance to comment, I went on, "And this is Oliver Renwick, my traveling companion and bodyguard. He has fought in many battles and is well trained in combat, so don't get him angry!" I tried to make my voice sound stern, convincing and loud. Behind me, Oliver made a sort of choking sound and I felt him grip the back of my arm tightly.

"What are you doing?" he muttered in my ear with a nervous voice.

"Instilling fear and awe," I whispered back, before addressing the troll once more. "We are passing through this valley in order to reach the city of Devona, where we will find the prince and overthrow Ralston Radburn."

At this, the troll stared blankly for a moment, then his lip began to twitch. Before I knew what was happening, he had his head back in full-blown laughter. "You…" he gripped his bouncing stomach, "are going to free Algernon? A helpless little girl? Ha ha!"

I bristled at this unexpected ridicule. His insults were more offending simply because they were coming from such scum. I was about to say something, when Oliver placed his hand on my shoulder and gave it a quick squeeze.

"Let him laugh," Oliver whispered. "It's much better than roaring."

"But just listen to him! He's laughing at me!" I retorted angrily.

"Just ignore him," Oliver advised. "After all, he is just a troll. Let it go," he soothed.

I folded my arms across my chest and faced the creature with a pout. He giggled for a few minutes more and wiped a tear of laughter from his splotched face. "And this is your bodyguard?" He indicated towards Oliver. "Some protector! Haven't you noticed that he's blind? Please don't hurt me oh mighty warrior!" the troll mocked, pretending to be frightened of Oliver.

Upon hearing this, I felt Oliver's body flinch, but he said nothing. What *could* he say? He was really blind after all and had never actually fought in any real battles. I shook my head angrily nevertheless, feeling my fear lessen at the sight of this menacing creature laughing. Taking a deep breath, I pointed an accusing finger at the troll's fat green nose. "I demand that you release that fairy at once or I'll… I'll…" I could have kicked myself for not thinking the sentence all the way through before speaking. Somehow I didn't come off as very threatening, but the troll's laughter ceased abruptly.

Pushing my pointing finger aside, he growled, "Or you'll what little girl? You're about as much a threat to me as an ant! And do you know what I do to ants? I squish them!" He made a slapping motion in the air.

"If I want to eat a fairy, I will! And," he took another step forward so that he was nearly touching me, "if you don't get out of my sight right now, I'll forgo the rule of not eating humans and make you dessert!" He fairly screamed this threat out. He then lifted the glittering fairy before his opened jaws once again.

It was at this moment that Oliver decided to act. He stepped forward and free of my grip. "Troll, or whatever you are," he declared in loud voice, "what is your name? Even the vilest of creatures have a name!"

With a start, the troll sneered and then seeing Oliver's hard face, looked slightly surprised. "Olav," he replied gruffly, not loosening his grip on the fairy.

Oliver nodded in a satisfied manner. "All right then Olav, I have a business proposition for you."

"I don't do business with outsiders," Olav answered hastily... though his face revealed a tiny amount intrigue.

"Ah, but this is why the proposition is so advantageous for you." Oliver winked. "As outsiders, we have in our possession, strange and foreign materials which you may find beneficial." Oliver gave a sly smile.

Olav scratched his cheek slowly and gave Oliver a sideways glance. "What do you have in mind?"

"A trade," Oliver answered mysteriously. "We can give you some very magical herbs and mushrooms from the infamous Forgotten Forest, in the northern wilds of Algernon. Even *you* must know that is very far beyond your borders, Olav. Perhaps they could be of some value to you?"

I have no need of magic," Olav told Oliver in a matter-of-fact voice.

Oliver did not falter at all and instead replied calmly, "Of course not, but they may add a little spice to your food. Something exotic... Your friends would be very amazed."

Olav seemed to be thinking only of ways to contradict Oliver in his proposition. "I have no friends to impress." He looked pleased.

Still Oliver was not flustered. "Well perhaps you will, once they see what amazing items you have in your possession. Think of the popularity it could win you. It's a once in a lifetime opportunity. No one in the valley but you are being included in the offer."

Olav seemed to be thinking deeply. "The Forgotten Forest, eh? Exotic spices? Magic? Friends? Popularity? Hmmm... ." He raised a bushy eyebrow. "And just what do you want in return?"

Oliver was about to make his move, I could sense it. "Oh, nothing much... A trifle really, compared to what you're getting in return." He paused and then put forth his request. "I just want that little yellow fairy in your hand to go free. That and that alone will be sufficient payment for these rare goods."

Olav protectively hugged the tiny creature to his body and exclaimed, "Oh no, not this fairy! I've been after this one all morning! She's proved to be most troublesome! Besides," Olav added with despair, "she's my lunch!"

I meanwhile, decided to make myself useful, so I unpacked the multi-coloured mushrooms and dried herbs. I recalled that one of these mushrooms once saved my life and wondered briefly if it was smart to be giving them away. It was too late to turn back now though. I presented the fragrant items in a small leather pouch. Upon opening the drawstrings, an enticing aroma swirled out and hung sweetly in the air.

Olav inhaled deeply with a snort. "They do smell powerful... and I could use some new flavourings in my afternoon tea..."

I held back a snicker, which appeared involuntarily. Somehow, I couldn't imagine this unruly creature sipping afternoon tea! What would he have with it? Buns? Cakes? Biscuits? I covered my trembling mouth tightly and pretended to be coughing. Neither Oliver nor Olav seemed to notice my amusement... but I think the glimmering fairy did.

"Come on," coaxed Oliver, "wouldn't you much rather have these rare items, rather than a common fairy?" At these words, the fairy made an annoyed sound. Apparently she didn't like Oliver's choice of words... namely, 'common'. "You'll never get another chance like this one!" Oliver added in a final bid to seal the deal.

Olav sighed heavily, his huge chest rising and falling slowly. At last he relented and released the fairy into the air. "Fine, fine. Give me the goods and you can have the cursed fairy!" In accordance with our agreement, I handed the pouch over to Olav, who threw his newly obtained treasures onto the grass behind him. There was a strange grin on his face... almost an evil one. "It's been a pleasure doing business with you..." He trailed off and looked up. The yellow fairy was still hovering in the air, watching the curious scene before her with great interest. Then with moves that were surprisingly quick for a creature of his size, Olav shot out his long arm and snatched the fairy out of the air.

"Hey!" I snapped, feeling the bitter taste of betrayal in my mouth. "We made a deal! What are you doing?"

"You outsiders know nothing about making deals with trolls! We *never* keep our word about anything!" He began to laugh, yet this time it wasn't a humorous laugh, but rather a malicious one.

I was absolutely livid! How could we have allowed Olav to make such fools of us! I should have known that he would double cross us! It had all been too easy! I was on the verge of doing something rash, when Oliver decided to take matters into his own hands.

Oliver edged his way in front of me and seemed to be pushing me back… out of the way. I glanced down and just barely saw his walking stick, concealed inside of his cloak, which he had not taken off earlier, despite the heat and my nagging. Then before I knew what was happening, Oliver was rushing forward and had the end of his jewelled stick sunk into the folds of Olav's stomach. As the troll instinctively went to grab at the stick, he let go of the delicate fairy, who had been struggling to breath in his iron grip.

Wasting no time and using actions that hardly felt like my own, I drew my bow and fired four arrows at Olav, one after the other. It seemed to be the same force that had guided my hands when the panther had pinned Oliver and Gimra back in the Sterling Hills. I might not be able to shoot when I wanted to, but when the time was right, the skills just appeared. All four of my arrows caught the edges of Olav's tunic; two on each side. Oliver had backed him into a rather wide tree and my arrows, fired at precisely the right moment, pinned the frothing green troll securely to the trunk.

Within moments I was at Oliver's side, pulling him back to the main road. "Come on Oliver! I don't want to be around when he gets free!"

Oliver's face was flushed with excitement, but he complied without complaint. "Yeah, he won't be too happy!"

"Curse you!" Olav roared as he stood struggling against the arrows. "I hope Ralston gives it to you!"

"Enjoy your afternoon tea!" I called back over my shoulder, as we disappeared from his sight.

Oliver and I ran a great deal, wishing to put as much distance as possible between ourselves and Olav, though in retrospect, he wasn't a real threat. The pretty yellow fairy had flown off quickly after Olav had been pinned to the tree. She hadn't even thanked us… All I caught was a fleeting glimpse of yellow sparkles, as she disappeared into the trees. Oliver didn't even get that. Oh well, she was probably so frightened and I couldn't really blame her, but I would have liked to see how she looked up close. Her bright glow obscured her facial features, but I was certain that she was very beautiful. At any rate, we had more important things to be thinking about.

The beautiful landscape around us was rapidly growing dim and fading away, as the road became steeper and rockier. We had begun the final ascent into Devona. It was a sad occurrence when the blue sky turned a sickly grey and the sun was suddenly snuffed out. Familiar menacing clouds whooshed in overhead, like angry attacking birds of prey.

The soft green grass, rustling trees and fresh scents, were all but a pleasant dream and fading memory. Dull barren rock, appeared on either side of us and there was a hot, smothering fog setting in. The air smelled stale and rotten, with a twinge of something else I couldn't identify. The entire atmosphere made me feel sick to my stomach.

As we approached the top of the hill, I turned to Oliver and stated in a clear voice, "This is it Oliver. All of our suffering has brought us to here. Welcome to the city of…" I waited until we cleared the hill before finishing, "Devona." The words would hardly leave my lips, as I gazed down into the valley below. As my eyes focused on the long awaited city, I could not withhold my gasp of pure terror. "No, this can't be," I whispered. "No one said it would be like *this*." But it was and it was worse than anything Oliver or I could have possibly imagined.

CHAPTER THIRTY

City of Misery

MY JAW DROPPED OPEN and wave after wave of fear washed over me, as I stared at the city I had been dreaming of for so long. So many people had warned me... tried to prepare me for this moment, but I had never taken their tales seriously. Somehow, I had always hoped that they were wrong... that Devona wasn't as bad as they claimed it to be. Now I knew... it was much worse.

I could feel the tears rolling down my cheeks, as I gazed at the ruined city that once was greatness itself, or so I'd been told. The protective city wall was nothing more than a crumbled pile of stones, surrounding the mass of destroyed buildings. Tall towers, that had no doubt been beautiful at one time, were now twisted and covered in a mat of thorny brambles. Thousands of quaint houses, which I guessed must have been a striking white colour, were now streaked with black soot and long ago abandoned. There was a cobblestone path that wound its way from where Oliver and I stood, through where the main gates had been and into the city. The road was so badly broken apart that no cart, no matter how sturdy, could possibly traverse it. Huge stones were missing from the path, but the majority of the road was crushed into dust, as though something terribly heavy had been rolled across it.

An ominous wind that came in hot puffs, surged up with a gust every now and then. I noticed strange lights flashing in the clouds overhead, but for some reason, I didn't think it was lightning. Nissim was nearby... up there, in the flashing sky. He was fighting the demons of the netherworld and if the Witch was correct, he was losing. If Nissim lost and we weren't fast enough, the veil between worlds would be broken and evil would pour into this world... not that we didn't have enough all ready. I hugged my arms in terror... It was all too much. I felt an overwhelming sense of loneliness, desolation and a pressing sadness.

"It's pretty bad, isn't it?" asked Oliver suddenly. His words were really more of a comment than a question. I jumped, for momentarily, I had forgotten that he was even there.

"Yeah," I replied. My voice came out as a whisper and my tears burned like fire on my cheeks. Words echoed through my head... words without a speaker, from long ago... 'A crushed dream, a crushed city, a crushed home.'

"Don't bother describing it to me," Oliver stated. "I can feel what it looks like and what it *should* look like," he added quietly.

I kicked at the parched dry earth, sending up a cloud of powder fine dust. "What has *he* done to this place? He has destroyed everything..." Trees still stood, but they had no leaves and were completely dried out... dead, but unable to fall. Bits of dry grass stood in clumps, but were blackened and like the trees, very dead, yet not gone. Now why was that? "This is the work of true evil..." I breathed.

Oliver opened his mouth to answer, but just then, the sound of bells could be heard behind us. I whipped around and found myself face to face with the glittering yellow fairy we had rescued from the troll, Olav.

"By the Power!" I exclaimed. "What are you doing here?"

"Who?" Oliver asked curiously, unable to see the yellow light we were bathed in.

"The fairy we saved," I replied, unable to take my eyes off of the exquisite creature. Even though she was so close, I still couldn't make out her features, for she was glowing more fiercely than ever.

"My name is Sparks. There's no need for your introductions... I was there when you introduced yourself to Olav," she tinkled out cheerfully and dimmed her light to a non-blinding glow. She spoke with far too much enthusiasm for the gloomy atmosphere around us. I could literally feel the evil stir, as though it recognized her goodness as a threat. With a flutter, she hovered before my face and gently touched my tears. "You're crying," she commented with concern and using a tiny leaf, began to mop up my face.

Now I could see her features very clearly. Sparks was a pretty little girl... Had she been human, I would have pegged her at Oliver's age, slightly younger than myself. Of course, her apparent age meant nothing, for I suspected that fairies had a very different aging process.

Sparks had lovely long golden hair that waved gently around her hips. A tiny garland of pink flowers sat perched like a halo on top of her head. Her eyes were a very striking green shade... a variation of the hue I had never seen before. It was like the green of fresh grass, a tree in full leaf and a deep pool all at once. She wore a petite yellow fairy dress that seemed to shimmer every time she moved, like sunlight reflecting off of water. Her miniature feet were bare and she had a paper thin set of butterfly wings protruding elegantly from her back. They too, were golden in colour, but more along the lines of real gold, for they glittered and seemed to give off a sort of golden dust when she moved.

"So why are you here Sparks?" I inquired curiously, for the Hidden Valley had long since disappeared behind us. "We set you free... You should be safe at home."

Her pretty face scrunched up and she twirled a little summersault. "Oh but I can't! You saved my life! I owe you a life debt! It's deemed so by the Power himself." She looked very adamant.

"There's no need for payment," Oliver assured her kindly, with a wave of his hand, "so you needn't worry."

I nodded in swift agreement and took Oliver's arm. "It was a pleasure to meet you Sparks, but we really must be on our way. Time is of the essence." I trembled as we began to descend the hill, following the hazardous remnants of the road.

Sparks immediately raced after us crying, "You can't go into Devona! No one comes out of there alive!"

"We have no choice," I called back, keeping my gaze focused ahead. If I stopped now, I might be tempted to turn back, so I had to keep moving forward... never backward.

Relentlessly Sparks pursued us, chiming and tinkling like hundreds of tiny bells. "Well then, let me come with you!" she pleaded. "I won't be any trouble, really!"

I sighed inwardly. It *would* be rather comforting to have the happy little fairy with us, but I couldn't in good conscience, allow her to walk straight into death, which might very well be what we were doing. "Listen Sparks," I tried to keep my voice from cracking, "we're on a very dangerous quest. There's no reason for you to put yourself in danger by getting involved. It's not your battle." As we neared the city, I jumped at the sounds of screaming and moans of agony.

"Oh but I love danger and adventure," Sparks exclaimed with glee. "Besides, I come here all the time to spy. I could be your... um... guide!" With that, she flew over to Oliver and perched herself on his shoulder.

"I guess she's here to stay," Oliver chuckled and turned his head to the little fairy. "You can come along, not as a servant with a life debt, but as our friend."

"Thanks!" Sparks giggled happily and planted a tiny kiss on Oliver's cheek. She then added mysteriously, "Besides, I know magic!"

My face lit up and it seemed that some of the darkness melted away, though perhaps it was simply because a tiny bit of hope had entered my heart. "Okay Sparks," I smiled, "you're in. But you must be very careful," I warned. "I wouldn't forgive myself if something happened to you." Then a new thought struck me. I turned to the fairy and asked the question that had been nagging at my mind for some time. "Sparks, if you know magic, how come you didn't use it to get away from Olav?"

Sparks pursed her lips tightly. "For some reason, fairy magic doesn't work against trolls. That's just the way its always been. That's why trolls are such a threat to the fairy race. We can protect ourselves against nearly everything but slobbering trolls!" She shuddered at the thought. "I've been lucky though," she told us, "for in my 50 years of life, I've only been caught twice."

"You're 50 years old?" Oliver asked in disbelief.

"It's not that old really," Sparks conceded. "It's about the equivalent of 15 human years."

So I had been quite close in my estimate of her age. I couldn't help but ask yet another question of the fairy. "So will your magic be strong enough to work here?" I indicated to the demon haunted city before us.

Sparks looked troubled. "Well, my magic isn't strong enough to take on a demon, but it works extremely well on humans." She flew off of Oliver's shoulder and hovered before his face. "In fact, allow me to demonstrate my powers!" Before I could say a word, she was blowing some of her golden powder into Oliver's blue eyes. Even from where I was standing I could smell it; a spring breeze. Oliver crinkled his face and after sucking in a few quick breaths, gave a giant sneeze, all but blowing Sparks away.

When Oliver opened his eyes, he released my arm quickly and stopped dead in his tracks. For a moment he didn't speak, but just stared wide eyed ahead. "Alice!" he screamed suddenly.

I grabbed both of Oliver's hands in terror and exclaimed to Sparks, "What have you done to him?"

Oliver began to shake all over and jumped up and down, as though convulsing. "I can see!" he cried in exultation.

I released his hands and stared at him in disbelief. There was something about his eyes that was different... clearer perhaps. The only word I could muster in my shock was, "What?"

"My eyesight," he stammered, "it's back! I can't believe it!"

I turned to the fairy who was hovering nearby and glowing with pride. "Sparks, how did you do that?" I questioned in awe. Our joy seemed to be agitating the surroundings.

"It's a simple spell I learned in first grade fairy school... My powers mostly have to do with healing, so it was relatively simple," she explained almost shyly.

"No one has ever given me a better gift... besides my mother who gave me life," Oliver declared as he took in the world before us.

"You're definitely staying with us," I told Sparks who glowed pink with a blush.

We were still making our way towards the city, albeit slowly, when I realized that Oliver had not said one word more. In fact, he had grown silent and almost... brooding.

When he finally spoke, his tone had lost all joviality and was deeply pained. "This is impossible," he murmured under his breath, still clutching his walking stick, which he refused to set aside. "The city is all wrong."

It seemed an odd way of putting it, but I simply agreed, "It is in poor shape. I don't know how we're ever going to fix it."

"I knew Ralston was evil... but how could anyone reduce such a great city to this pile of refuse?" A look of anger passed over Oliver's handsome face.

Sparks, who had resumed her seat on his shoulder, piped up. "What exactly is this quest of yours?"

"Originally to find Prince Edric," I sighed. So why did it seem as though we would be doing so much more than that?

"So if that was the original plan, what is it now?" Sparks inquired, as she crossed her slender legs.

"See, that's where things start to get a little grey," I explained. "We're just kind of going with the flow, I guess. We only planned to get here and now that we've made it, I don't really know what to do," I admitted.

"Well, don't worry too much about it," Sparks consoled me cheerfully. "Everything will turn out in the end."

"I sure hope so." I shivered, recalling Keenan's predictions for my future.

We crossed a small wooden bridge, which surprisingly, was still intact. Beneath it ran a stream of foul smelling black water... a former mountain stream. It was disgusting to think anyone could live in such a mess. The boards creaked as we walked over them, but luckily they did not sway, for this was not a swinging bridge. I tried not to notice the grey bones, which protruded from the mud in the stream bank... a sharp reminder of the war that had taken place only 13 years earlier.

I hung back only momentarily, before passing through the remnants of the city's gate and into Devona itself. I had been unprepared for the evil that suddenly surrounded us. It wasn't anything physical or visible... It was a sensation, a feeling. The evil was like a vice, squeezing away life and spirit. I felt as though someone had taken a heavy wool blanket and thrown it over my head.

"This place," Oliver whispered, "it's worse than the Land of the Undead."

Screams were louder now and I gasped, for lost spirits seemed to be wandering the streets at will! Translucent beings misted about the wreckage, but took no notice of us. I couldn't bear to look upon their faces, for they were so contorted with agony... the last grimace before death.

"It appears to be growing darker," Oliver noted, seemingly eager to be the first one to point out such a visual observation.

I jumped as a spirit aimlessly wandered straight through me. I felt nothing but a terrible chill and depressing sadness. Why had these spirits not moved on? If they were dead, why did they not leave this dreadful world behind? Only one answer came to mind; Ralston.

"Night is nearly upon us," Sparks told us. "We must hurry and find a place to stay for the night, as it is much too dangerous to be on these streets after dark." Her glow was our only light on the darkening streets, but even that seemed to be considerably dimmer than it had been in the valley.

The street which we were currently on, was lined on both sides with wide, crumbling, three story buildings. Most doors were boarded over and windows with tattered curtains waved in the breeze. For a fleeting moment, I thought I saw people inside of the houses peeping out, but in an instant, they were gone. More trapped spirits? Or real live people? Surely not everyone was dead. Somewhere in the distance, a door was banging open and shut in the wind.

"Where do you propose we stay?" Oliver addressed Sparks, who had unwittingly become our expert on the city. An eerie green mist had begun to settle in, bathing everything in an unhealthy glow.

"There's an inn, just a little farther down this main street," Sparks explained. "It's not much, but it's better than being out here when night falls."

"So there are still some survivors," I concluded, as the mist tightened around my ankle. Brutally I shook it off.

"There are many survivors," Sparks told me shaking her head, causing the flower garland to slip slightly, "but they quite wisely stay hidden."

"I hope there's food at the inn, because I'm starving." Oliver rubbed his gurgling stomach.

"Don't fret my dark haired friend." Sparks patted his head with her tiny hand. "They have food." She turned uncertainly to me and seemed to be considering something. "You may wish to hide those golden pendants you're wearing Alice. One look at those and the innkeepers would suspect something strange and the strange, understandably, frightens them."

"Would they hurt us?" I wondered, nervously tucking the pendants into my tunic.

"I wish I could give you a straight answer." Sparks shrugged. "Who knows? They live in so much fear as it is…" She trailed off and fluttered ahead, stopping in front of an old battered building, not unlike the others we had seen with spirits floating inside. A ripped red and white striped awning fluttered ominously above the door… The sign above was so worn that I could no longer read the writing, nor make out the picture. Rats scuffled about the sides of the building, gnawing on scraps of what I guessed to be food, though it neither looked nor smelled like it. I felt my nightmare slowly becoming a reality and I wished desperately that we'd never come.

Oliver was standing behind me with a look of disgust on his face. "It's unreal," he murmured. "The King would turn in his grave if he could see his fair city now."

I cleared my throat and took a deep breath. I had as of yet made no move to open the door. "Go on," Sparks urged looking nervously behind us. "It's much safer inside, trust me."

"Always forward," I murmured and with trembling hands, grasped the grimy door handle.

CHAPTER THIRTY-ONE

The Night Guard

A s WE ENTERED the inn, we were greeted by a blast of hot, stale air. The smell of unwashed bodies and grease hung heavily about the room. A swift inspection revealed three round wooden tables, placed randomly around the dining area... or was it a tavern? Two unmatched and tipsy looking chairs, were carelessly sitting beside each table. The far wall of the inn was lined with benches and tables, which seemed to offer a bit more privacy. There was an unlit fireplace near a swinging door, which presumably led to the kitchen, for there were a number of strong smells being emitted from that direction. A steep set of narrow stairs were located directly to our right... I craned my neck upwards. I could see nothing, save a dark corridor at the top.

"That must be where the rooms are," I mused to myself.

There were four other people in the room besides ourselves and none of them looked particularly friendly. Two were filthy looking men, who were drinking and talking in snarls at the farthest table to our left. The one man slammed his hand hard onto the table, causing the little candle on top to quiver. The other gave him an angry curse and waved his hands about menacingly in the air. They were both obviously very drunk. A pale woman in her mid-twenties, sat with a grubby looking child in a secluded corner. She was trying in vain to wipe the little boy's runny nose, but he was successfully evading her, by crawling under the table. Seeing the child reminded me sharply of baby Julia at Xenos Ranch. Like Julia, this child had been born into a world of evil. He had never seen just how beautiful life could be and that thought sickened me. I wished that there was something I could do... but even if there were, would I have the courage to do it? That was really the big question. It was fine to think about what I *wanted* to do to Ralston, but doing it was a different issue.

Presently, a stern looking woman wearing a tattered red dress with a cream coloured apron, bustled out of the kitchen to speak with us. There were large bags underneath her eyes and she looked weary with fatigue, but nevertheless presented a severe countenance... enough to rival even Ms Craddock in the old days.

Brushing her black hair aside, the woman asked suspiciously, "What do you want?"

It seemed an odd question to ask a traveler stopping in an inn. The answer to me at least, would have seemed obvious. "We would like a place to stay for the night and perhaps something to eat," I requested timidly.

The woman eyed us carefully, as if unsure whether or not we were trustworthy. "I've never seen you two around before." She cocked her head to the side, awaiting our explanation.

Oliver piped up quickly and I noticed that Sparks had concealed herself in his shirt, for I could see a faint glow beneath the cloth, which Oliver was trying to cover up with his hand. "Well you see ma'am," Oliver turned on his charm, "my sister and I are from the other side of Devona. Our home collapsed and we wandered until we came upon this fine establishment. We have coin to pay…"

The woman's face immediately softened. As to whether it was from our story, or from the mention of money, I didn't know. "Yes," she agreed, "buildings, even the sturdiest ones, tend to collapse nowadays." She shook her head in disgust. "Luckily you two weren't in it when it fell. Come now and sit down. It's well you got off the streets when you did. Dark moves in so quickly now… even faster than usual. Something's stirring up at the castle, I can feel it in my bones."

We were ushered to a bench near the woman and her child. The seats creaked as we sat down, but at least we were far away from the intoxicated men, who were now yelling angrily at one another. Our hostess turned around in a flurry and yelled, "Keep it quiet you two or I'll toss you to the Guard!" The men quieted their voices immediately and continued their argument in hoarse whispers. I had wanted to ask who exactly the 'Guard' was, but the woman would no doubt get suspicious that we weren't from the city. She turned back to us and forced a smile.

"Don't mind those two warts over there. They've had bit too much ale. Just relax. You're safe in Mary Buxabee's inn. I'll go fetch you something to renew your strength." With that, she hurried back to the kitchen, with small, quick steps.

As soon as the woman left, I gave a sigh of relief. Sparks wiggled free of Oliver's shirt and poked her head out. "Air!" she tinkled.

"Stay hidden Sparks," I warned her, "and try not to speak… Your voice is rather different from a human's." She stuck out her tongue playfully, but knew full well that my warning had cause. I turned my attention back to Oliver. "So I'm your sister now, am I?"

He grinned mischievously. "Hey, Captain Wyston said that we had similar features… similar enough to be related. I mean, look at this nose." He pointed to his face. "Doesn't it look like yours?"

I cocked my head to the side and laughed, "You're funny Oliver."

"No seriously," he pressed. "Look, doesn't it have the same shape as yours?"

"It's a nose Oliver," I giggled, picking at a splinter of wood on the table top.

"He's right you know," Sparks spoke up, then clapped her tiny hands over her mouth.

Finally I looked at Oliver's nose... It *did* sort of have a familiar shape, but that didn't mean anything. I changed the subject abruptly. "So where should we search first for Edric?"

Oliver looked thoughtful as he pulled Sparks out of his shirt and dropped her in a pouch on his belt. "Well, I don't really know. If I were a prince, where would I go?"

"The castle?" Sparks tinkled from inside the pouch. Oliver deftly pulled the flap down over her head.

Oliver then leaned back and put his hands behind his head. "She could be on to something Alice."

"The castle?" I repeated. "But why would he go there? Ralston has been searching for him! That would be walking straight into a trap!"

"I know, I know," Oliver conceded, "but that would be the very place he would be drawn to... at least I think so. Edric is connected to the castle, as that was his home. Sure he was only a child when he left it, but still, home has a powerful way of drawing its people back again."

I looked unconvinced. "You really think so? That means Edric could be dead and in which case, we're in a lot of trouble."

"But Nissim seems to think that Edric still lives!" Oliver pointed out, as he toyed with a grimy looking candleholder. "Maybe he's being held prisoner or something... or even pretending to be a servant, waiting for his chance to strike back!"

"And they say *I* have a powerful imagination." I gave a frustrated laugh.

Oliver crossed his arms stubbornly. "Okay, laugh all you want, but that's what I think. Edric is the true heir to the throne of Algernon, a destiny not easily changed."

"But easily forgotten," I pointed out. "Edric was one year old when the attack came. I don't think he would recall himself being the son of a king."

"But what if someone told him?" Oliver suddenly leaned forward on the table. "Someone from the castle, got him out of the castle. Therefore someone knew that he was the prince. How old would Edric be now... 13?"

"14," I corrected. "It's been 13 years and he was one."

"So, he could quite plausibly be waiting to claim his destiny," Oliver finished in a triumphant voice.

"You do realize we'd be walking straight into Ralston's clutches, don't you?" I chewed absently on a piece of my hair. "He knows we're coming... He's waiting."

"And I say we just go for it Alice! Face the vile man head on! For too long we've cowered in fear from his cronies! I say it's time we head to the top! We'll take out evil right from its source! What do you think?"

I felt a strange fear welling up inside of me... the likes of which I hadn't ever felt so strongly before. To think we would be facing Ralston himself at last. I feared him... terribly. He was an evil man, it was true, but I feared and hated him for an entirely different reason, though I couldn't pinpoint exactly what it was.

"I don't know Oliver," I began uncertainly. "This seems awfully sudden."

"If we don't do it now, we may never do it at all Alice," Oliver pressed. "You were sent to do a job, so finish it now!" His tone was not angry, nor harsh... but very poignant. He grabbed my hand tightly across the table. "Think of how far we've come... clear across the kingdom! Think of the trials we've endured! Think of all we have lost! It's time to end this now, before it's too late."

I gritted my teeth together. He was right and I knew it. I guess there comes a time when we must finally face our fears. I couldn't avoid it any longer, though I wished desperately that I could. I gazed up into Oliver's determined eyes. He had been so strong throughout the journey. "Okay Oliver," I nodded, "tomorrow we shall go to the castle."

Just then the hostess, Mary Buxabee, reappeared from the kitchen with two steaming bowls of soup and two mugs of what smelled like a ginger drink.

"Here you go." She gave a tight smile as she set the dishes before us. "I'll go prepare a room upstairs for you." She nodded and using her quick gait, walked swiftly up the groaning staircase.

I sipped the ginger drink slowly. It was weak tasting, but quite refreshing after having drunk from water flasks for so long. The soup itself smelled rather odd and I had no idea what was in it, for the floating chunks revealed nothing. However I was too hungry to question anymore. Oliver in the meantime, had already polished off all of his soup and was slugging down the last bit of ginger drink.

"A bit strange tasting, but nevertheless satisfying," he commented and stretched his arms.

I shook my head slowly at his eating habits. How could anyone eat that fast and not get sick? I plugged my nose and proceeded to eat the food before me. It didn't taste too bad and I found that I actually could eat it without pinching my nose.

"Do you think Sparks is hungry?" I asked Oliver, pausing with my spoon in midair.

"She's asleep." Oliver grinned widely and then gazed around the room. "These people," he sighed, "they haven't a bit of hope left. How can anyone live like that?"

"I don't suppose they have a choice," I replied. "Judging by the amount of ghosts and spirits around this city, death is just as bad as life. There is no escaping the suffering. There's no way out..." I trailed off, realizing that we were now just as trapped as the rest of the city. I didn't know how I knew, but there was no way to leave the city. Once you were in, you stayed in.

Mary Buxabee reappeared from upstairs. "Your room is ready now, if you're all finished. It's ten o'clock and I'll be putting the candles out momentarily."

I looked around and suddenly realized that the rest of the room's occupants had already turned in and the room was now deserted. "Thank you," I replied standing up. "We are ready to go upstairs."

"It's the second room on the right," Mary Buxabee instructed. "It overlooks the main street, so remember to keep your windows shut and tightly bolted. Draw your curtains and avoid walking or looking out of the window when *they* come by. I'm sure you're already aware of those precautions, but I always like to remind my tenants. Goodnight to you both." With that, Mary Buxabee hurried off to the kitchen with our dirty dishes in hand. I noted that the front door to the inn was tightly barred.

As we crept up the dark staircase, Oliver whispered in my ear, "Who did she mean by *they*?"

I shuddered inwardly. "I don't know, but I didn't like the sound of it one bit."

*   *   *

About four hours later, I awoke to the thunderous sound of horse's hooves. There was obviously a great disturbance in the street below our window. This must be what Mary Buxabee had been talking about. I slid off the bottom bunk where I had been sleeping and strode silently over to the window, which we had locked according to instructions. Recalling the rest of Mary Buxabee's advice, I just pulled the curtain back enough to see into the darkened street. What I saw, froze my blood and turned my soul. I stood absolutely still, even though my knees were like jelly and my head light as a feather in the wind.

It was unlike anything I could have imagined. There on the cobblestone streets were several skeleton horses, complete with skeleton riders mounted on their backs. The riders wore bits and pieces of old dented armour, covered in rusty splotches. They each held a round shield and a large silver sword with a golden hilt. The horses were adorned with various pieces of horse armour and a saddle, though all were in poor condition.

The skeleton riders appeared to be searching or rather patrolling the streets, with their deep, glowing eye sockets. It was then that I noticed out of the corner of my eye, one of the men who had been eating at the inn earlier on… the one who had slammed the table. He was sneaking about in an abandoned building, directly across the street from where we were.

At that moment, one of the skeletons jerked his head up. He had spotted the man! I wanted to yell at him to run, but it was too late! The skeleton rider gave a shrill whistle and his companions surrounded the building, drawn swords glinting metallically.

Whether it was out of fear or madness, I could not say, but the trapped man suddenly dashed out onto the street cursing. Perhaps he was still drunk. Two skeleton riders approached him from either side. I quickly released the curtain and turned my gaze back into our dark room. I covered my face, as my breath came in ragged gasps. A moment later, I heard a blood curdling scream and a ghostly light flashed through the thick curtain, casting shadows on the wall. Another spirit had been trapped.

Confused and horrified, I crawled back into my uncomfortable bed. The top bunk creaked as Oliver sat up, awakened by the screams and my muffled sobs. Sparks, who had been sleeping on the bedpost, fluttered down to see me.

"I'm sorry you had to witness that Alice," Sparks apologized. "I should have warned you. Ralston's Night Guard is an everyday thing for the citizens of Devona. There now, don't cry." She looked sympathetically at me.

"What do you mean… Night Guard?" I asked, as I drew my knees up to my chest in fear. I couldn't stop shaking.

Sparks seated herself on my bed and looked pensive. "Well, it all goes back to Ralston's original siege on the castle, 13 years ago. He had his minions from the Land of the Undead," Sparks was cut off by a little gasp from Oliver, who had no doubt been reminded of our near death experience in that realm. Sparks looked annoyed, but continued on in her sweet voice, "As I was saying, Ralston had his minions cast a spell over King Alfred's castle and all of its occupants, so that he could have slaves. I have heard that Ralston took some of the castle's bravest, strongest guards and turned them into those evil, skeleton guards. Collectively, they are called the Night Guard. He uses them to enforce the curfew, which is in place over Devona. Anyone caught in the streets after dark, suffers dearly at the hand of the Guard. The most diabolical part of it is that you don't really die when they catch you." Sparks was out of breath. "Your spirit stays trapped here in Devona, doomed to roam the streets for as long as Ralston is in power." She shook her head sadly.

"This information would have been a lot more helpful earlier," Oliver mused.

I considered everything for a moment, tears drying tightly on my face. "So if Ralston and his minions are destroyed, will all of those spirits be free to move on?"

Sparks shook her head. "No, they would be returned to their bodies and allowed to continue on with their life. Ralston's magic is very powerful."

I looked up at Oliver, who was hanging his head from the top bunk. "We have to help these people," I told him softly and added with resolve, "which is why we head for the castle at first light."

Dalton Castle

WE STAYED IN BED for only a few hours more, although I couldn't really fall asleep. I kept seeing the drunken man running out onto the street where the skeleton guards were waiting. It was horrible... the scream of despair... worse than the scream of terror. I managed to doze off and on, but was relieved when Sparks hovered in front of my face and tapped my nose gently.

"It's time to go," she whispered. Her voice was like the chiming of morning bells, even though it didn't seem like morning, for there was hardly any light outside. As if reading my thoughts, Sparks continued, "There is an ominous feeling in the air this morning. The sun won't even show his face today."

I sat on the edge of the bed for a moment and wondered if I would ever live to see another morning again... with or without a sunrise. I felt as though I were going to see my executioner and perhaps that was exactly what I was doing.

*   *   *

Downstairs we met with Mary Buxabee in the dining hall again. She appeared exactly as she had the night before, although her apron seemed slightly cleaner. "Will you be coming back tonight?" she asked us, as we paid her the last of our golden coins. Now we were out of money, so if we wanted to return, that would no longer be feasible.

I shook my head slowly. "No, we shan't be returning, but thank you so much for your hospitality."

Taking the money happily, Mary Buxabee unbarred the door for us. "You take care now young ones," she warned. "There's something different about the air today. I don't like it one bit. Mary Buxabee knows these things," she informed us. "Steer clear of Dalton Castle, for that's where trouble starts." With a brief wave, we were out on the streets once again and the door to the inn was closed tightly.

The air *did* feel different from yesterday. It was heavier, with the smell of something rotten in it. It was an effort to draw a single breath without gagging. Sparks emerged from Oliver's belt pouch and gave a little cough. "Yuck!" she exclaimed. "I've never smelled it this bad before!"

"Mary Buxabee warned us to stay away from Dalton Castle... that must be where Ralston is living," I mused, as a scream echoed in a side street. I had almost started to get used to the cries of pain and ghostly figures floating around aimlessly. They certainly didn't take any notice of us, or really anything else for that matter.

"Dalton Castle…" Oliver repeated thoughtfully. "That is where we must go."

Inside my head I asked, 'Must we?', but didn't allow myself to speak the thought out loud. Instead, I asked in as calm a voice as I could muster, "Do you know the way Sparks?"

She nodded her shimmering head assuredly and declared, "Yes, follow me! I've been there lots of times before!" With a flutter of her translucent wings, Sparks led us down various streets and through many crumbling squares.

I decided that Devona must have been a gorgeous city in its day, with massive fountains and artistic statues adorning every corner. There were just so many abandoned buildings and shops, that I finally began to grasp the magnitude of the atrocities committed. Devona was an enormous city that must have had an incredible population. Where those people were now, I couldn't say, for we only saw five humans along the refuse cluttered streets; two young men and a young woman with two small children. They were all filthy and so thin you could see their bones jutting out from underneath their ragged clothes. It was sickening to look at, especially the children. Had Prince Edric grown up on these very streets? If so, what kind of condition was he in now?

"We're nearly there," Sparks announced, as we rounded another corner and found ourselves on an extremely wide street, which could have fit nearly five large carriages across. "This is called the 'Royal Way'," Sparks told us with a broad sweep of her graceful arms. "All processions and celebrations are… were… held on this very street. It used to be a very beautiful place, with flowers and bright colours everywhere!" Her eyes lit up with fond remembrances.

"Well it doesn't look as though anything wonderful has happened here in a while," Oliver remarked, as he kicked a scrap of cloth out of his way.

"That's for sure," I agreed, while scanning the quiet, empty buildings, which towered along the edges of the street. Such stores there must have been… such prosperity.

"I know it looks bad," Sparks admitted, "but maybe one day you'll see it restored!" She tried to sound optimistic and then pointed straight ahead. "Look at the end of the street! Isn't it enough to send a shiver up your spine?"

At the very end of the Royal Way, lay the infamous Dalton Castle… now the lair of Ralston Radburn. I imagined that it must have once been a beautiful castle, with elegant ivory towers and bright flags flying in the wind. It was the true home of a fairy prince, although no fairy princes had ever lived in Dalton Castle to my knowledge. I shook my head violently. Now wasn't the time to let my imagination come back to life, for there was nothing romantic, nor majestic, about Dalton Castle now. It was really nothing more than a mass of sharp jutting towers, built with fire blackened stones. Thorny brambles covered the sides of the towers, as well as the tall outside wall around the castle.

As we made out way closer to the ruined royal home, I saw that it was surrounded by a moat full of rancid water. "What a stench!" I plugged my nose in disgust and waved my hand in the air.

"Poisoned," Sparks sighed sadly. "Everything Ralston touches turns to poison, so I'm not surprised." Then suddenly she announced, "Dalton Castle literally means, 'located in the valley city'." She looked extremely proud of this knowledge, even though it was revealed at so strange a time.

"Well it's aptly named," Oliver humoured her with a smile. "But how are we going to get into the castle of the valley city?"

We now stood before the dwelling, which loomed forebodingly over us, similar to the Shadow in my dream. There was a drawbridge to cross over the acrid moat, but unfortunately it was drawn up and I wasn't certain if I was willing to risk another way in... especially if it meant crossing the water in a particularly dangerous manner. Give me a good strong bridge any day.

We were not left to ponder long, for with a sudden squeal, the drawbridge began to lower, rusty chains clinking methodically. The bridge hit the ground with a dull thud and sent a cloud of powdery dust flying into the air. With a choke I took a step back, blinded by fear.

"Make ready for company," Oliver hissed through clenched teeth. He had gone rather white, but seemed determined not to show his fear. This was it.

With a chiming shriek, Sparks dove into the pouch on Oliver's belt and drew the flap over her head. I wished that I were small enough to hide in that manner, but instead I was left out in the open, to face whoever came out of the castle. Would Ralston himself greet us? It seemed unlikely... He would probably send out his guards, or worse still, the Witch.

I held my breath as a figure approached us from out of the dust that had been stirred up. He must have worn metal boots, for I could hear a distinct, 'clink clink' across the wooden drawbridge. On account of the dust, that just wouldn't settle, I didn't see our greeter until he was directly in front of me. How he bypassed Oliver was a mystery, for Oliver had been standing slightly ahead of me. I gulped... Perhaps the figure had been sent out to fetch me specifically! The Shadow was waiting! I could literally feel his hot breath upon me!

I looked up into the skinless face of a rotting skeleton guard. There was a great chip missing out of his cheekbone, as though a sword had sliced it off. He was however, slightly different from the Night Guard, in that he wasn't as... ruthless looking. Still, I quaked and began to cry. "Are you Alice?" His voice came out as a moan of pain.

So he *was* sent to fetch me! Then for the first time, I realized that my pendants were hanging on my chest in full view. They clanged together, as if deliberately betraying their presence.

"You have the pendants my master wants." The skeleton reached out to touch them and then drew his dead hand back quickly. "You must be the Alice Lord Ralston has been waiting for." I was still speechless and quite paralyzed with the fear of being brought before my worst nightmare. A light headed panic had begun to take over my system.

As I quaked, the guard turned his attention at last to Oliver, who had been standing nearby, watching the scene with tensed muscles. "And you must be the peasant boy who has been protecting her. My master mentioned you before too... but mostly with disinterest." The guard seemed to be considering something. "Still, I should think he would like both of you brought in. Come along then." He was suddenly brandishing a sword, covered in rust spots. "Don't make me use force please. It's useless to try and escape...I know." The guard seemed tormented.

Oliver was quickly at my side, ushering me in front of the guard, who was clucking away to himself about how he would be rewarded. "Just stay calm Alice," Oliver told me gently. "It's going to be fine."

I almost believed his assurances, since they were so laced with his patented brand of charm that could make anyone believe that the sky was indeed purple, rather than blue. However as the blast of rotten air hit me when we entered the courtyard, Oliver's assurances disappeared. Every part of the castle... down to the very last corner was permeated with evil. When one thinks of evil as something abstract, they are fooling themselves, for evil has a smell, a look and a taste, as tangible and real as any physical entity imaginable.

Though the courtyard was void of material objects, there was no shortage of skeleton servants, labouring away at tasks appointed to them by their master. There were even skeleton dogs, cats, chickens and pigs wandering around in a very lost manner. The poor creatures probably had no idea what had happened to them. A hen pecked at something on the ground, only to have it fall out through her ribcage. What had Ralston done to everyone? It was too horrible to put into words... especially the children. There were skeleton children, meandering around with heavy pots in their hands. So many bones... I began to wonder if Ralston himself were fleshless.

As we mounted a steep set of stairs, I felt as though someone were choking me. I could almost feel invisible hands around my neck actually squeezing... It was totally unlike the gentle caressing wind, which had led me to the Hidden Valley of the Fairies. I pawed at my neck and quickened my pace. "Oh Oliver!" I cried in anguish, but he wasn't listening, for he was fighting off his own demons, who were clutching at his throat.

"Into this hallway," our skeleton guard directed, using his sword to point the way.

The hall was lit with hundreds of candles, mounted along the damp walls. Skeleton guards stood underneath each candle and watched us through glowing eyes as we passed by. I held my hands tightly together, in a vain attempt to warm them, for they had become like blocks of ice.

Then all at once, I was hit with the oddest sensation. "This place seems so familiar," I murmured to Oliver, as we rounded another corner, "like something from a dream."

"Don't Alice," Oliver told me sternly. "You'll only confuse yourself. Stay focused on the present. We're going to need to think hard to get out of this situation."

However try as I might, I couldn't shake the strange feeling that had come over me. The entire castle seemed to be calling out from the past. Each room and hallway we entered... and we passed through a great many... gave me the sensation that I had been there before. I could almost see images of laughing and smiling people dressed in elegant attire. There was happiness all around in my visions and no skeletons and suffering. I shook my head harshly. What was wrong with me?

Oliver must have noticed that I was not myself, for he leaned over and whispered softly in my ear with a great deal of concern, "Are you okay? You've suddenly gone a shade whiter than you already were."

"I... I'm fine," I replied in a stammering voice. No, I was not fine. All these strange feelings...

Oliver gave me an unconvinced look and told me, "If you feel like you're going to faint or something, let me know. I'm here for you okay?"

"Stop!" the skeleton guard bellowed in front of a huge door. I jumped in spite of myself. "You will wait in this room, until I arrange things with Lord Ralston."

Two nearby guards pushed open the doors with a loud squeak. With a shove that was far from gentle, Oliver and I stumbled into the dusty, cobweb decorated room. The doors were left open and two guards were posted to keep an eye on us, as the first guard tapped down the hallway. The sound of him fading away seemed familiar... a noise echoing down a corridor...

"Our plan is not going very well, is it?" Oliver sighed and kicked absently at the dirty floor. His foot scuffed away some of the grime, to reveal bright blue tiles. "Hey, I'll bet this place was cheerful at one time," he noted and strode over to the window seat. He sat down with a sigh. "Maybe this was a bad idea Alice... Alice?"

I was only half listening to him, for my mind was being absorbed by an enormous portrait hanging on one of the walls. The sheer size alone of the painting was enough to inspire awe, as it took up nearly the entire wall. However it was not the size that interested me... It was a portrait of what looked to be the royal family of Algernon. The sides of the painting were tattered and torn, but the colours remained as vibrant as ever.

Suddenly one of the guards at the door spoke up. "That's the royal family," he stated in an almost sad way. "The King and Queen both got their throats slit by... by... my m... master. The Princesses were thrown into a river and drown, while the little Prince was burned at the stake, or so I've been told." For an instant the guard looked pained, as though he had broken out of a trance. He then made a noise like a tortured sob, as some powerful force yanked him back into a silent, solemn state.

I blinked in wonderment. The guards were prisoners too... Then I thought of what he had just said. Prince Edric could not be dead! The guard must have been wrongly informed! If Edric had been burned, Nissim would have known! It simply wasn't possible! I focused my burning eyes back on the portrait that seemed to cry out for attention.

The figures in the portrait looked exactly as they had when Ms Craddock had conjured them in her magic mirror. King Alfred stood proudly on the left, with a hint of an amused smile playing across his lips. His deep brown hair had a regal golden crown upon it, with sapphires mounted on each point. The shade of those blue jewels gave his eyes a sort of shining quality... not unlike lightning. There was no doubt in my mind that he had been a strong man and not only in the physical sense. To be sure, there was muscle strength in his thick arms and broad shoulders, but there was something else too. Perhaps it was a sort of stubbornness I sensed behind his groomed beard and squared jaw. Still, there was more to this king than the velvet robes he wore or any aspect of his appearance. I could not doubt the goodness of King Alfred. He was a man who loved his people dearly... and was utterly devoted to his family. Somehow I just knew this, simply by looking upon his portrait. Maybe it was the way in which his eyes seemed to be straying sideways towards his beautiful queen.

Rose-Mary. The very name gave me goosebumps. It was different to see her in this portrait, for she was even more striking when she wasn't crying. I recalled with a shiver, the tears on her face when I had first seen her in the mirror. Once, I had guessed that her eyes would sparkle if she was happy and somehow the talented artist had captured just that. There was a very lively aura about this petite, slim queen... perhaps even some defiance. Her ebony hair hung loosely down her back, which was something that even *I* knew was not well accepted in ladies, especially ladies of status. Ladies were supposed to braid their hair and twist it up... then preferably cover it with layered veils. Luckily I had never reached the age where I was required to do such a thing, for I enjoyed letting my own hair fly freely in the wind. Apparently Queen Rose-Mary enjoyed this as well. She did look elegant in this portrait, for there was a shimmering diamond tiara perched just above her brow... quite unlike the circlet I had seen her sporting in the mirror. The queen's large dark eyes stared intently out at me and her small mouth was drawn in a gentle smile. I knew that she would be a perfectly wonderful mother, the kind who would hold you when you fell, or touch your forehead when you were sick... and reassure you in the darkest of nights. Yet like her husband, there was more to her than met the eye. Rose-Mary was strong and ever defiant, perhaps even more so than the King. In her arms, she held a baby.

The baby had jet hair, just like his mother's. Little Prince Edric... He couldn't have been very old when the portrait was painted, for he was nothing more than a bundle in his mother's arms. The Queen held the heir tightly, as if frightened someone were going to rip him from her very arms.

Standing in front of the King and Queen were four little girls, all attired in matching golden gowns. One would have mistaken them for quadruplets, if it weren't for their varying sizes, for their hair was all brown and their eyes all blue... No wait, the smallest girl had eyes like her mother. The tallest daughter stood primly in front of King Alfred, her one hand clasped tightly in his. No doubt about it, she was daddy's favourite. The girl hardly gave any smile at all, for instead she was attempting to look grown up and solemn, though it didn't fit well with such a small child. Her brown hair was pulled up slightly and fastened with a yellow bow.

Beside the solemn child, stood a shorter girl with an irrepressible smile and vivacious looking face. She was not looking at the portrait painter and instead her eyes were focused on something off to the side. In fact, it seemed to me that she was leaning forward slightly, as though she could hardly keep still. An identical bow to the first sister, was starting to slide out of this girl's slightly mussed hair.

Yet an even smaller girl with brown hair and a yellow bow, stood beside the excited one. This child however, was paler and frailer, yet had the potential to be a great beauty I guessed. She stood quite straight and despite the fact that it was only a painting... she seemed to be standing quite still. There was a strange look in her eyes, as though she were seeing beyond the painter... seeing something else, but I had no idea what.

The smallest child was pushing herself back into the Queen's skirts. She too looked as though she wanted to be elsewhere, much like the second daughter, but at the same time, she seemed to be very dependant on the protection of her mother. I noticed that one of her tiny fists was full of her mother's dress... a natural instinct for any little girl. I stared particularly hard at the royal couple's fourth daughter. She seemed terribly familiar. There was something about her eyes and the angle of her face. She seemed to be saying, 'I am more than what I seem'.

Oliver touched my shoulder gently. "It's time to go Alice," he told me softly.

I jumped and blinked at him as I tried to collect my thoughts. "Oliver? Is that you?"

"Are you okay?" He pulled me slowly towards the doors, where the original skeleton guard was waiting impatiently.

"Move it!" the guard roared. "Lord Ralston doesn't have all day! He'll be in a bad temper if you keep him waiting."

"Keep your bones together!" Oliver retorted angrily.

As we exited the room with the portrait, I turned to Oliver and said in a dreamy voice, "That was the nursery."

He gave me a strange look. "Really? How could you tell?"

"I don't know," I replied back. "I just know that it was."

The guard stopped us before two enormous heavily jewelled doors. "My master awaits you in the throne room."

There was no time for me to prepare myself for what was to come, as the guard wasted no time in flinging open the large doors and ushering us forward, none too gently.

"Announcing Alice of Algernon!" the guard bellowed in a hoarse voice, then added, "and the boy Oliver."

CHAPTER THIRTY-THREE

Ralston Radburn

ESPITE EVERYTHING, I felt rather important being announced... I had never been announced before in my life. Alice of Algernon... It did have a rather nice ring to it. Oliver however, looked quite disgusted by his announcement, though it had seemed to be more of a reference to acknowledge his presence. However my feelings of importance died quickly, as we continued on into the chamber.

In my heart, I knew that this was the very throne room where King Alfred and Queen Rose-Mary had died. Perhaps they thought themselves safe, barricaded in this stronghold, but they had been very wrong. Ralston had fought his way here, killed the royal couple and assumed the throne. The room itself was twisted to fit his evil presence and considerably changed from the way it had been before his reign... and yet, there were aspects of it that hadn't changed at all. But how did I know all of this?

The structure of the room was unchanged, but that could hardly be altered without tearing down the entire castle. The ceiling was vaulted and decorated with arches that stretched so high up that I could not see where it ended. It seemed to me that there should have been angelic frescos painted above, but all I could see was darkness. The windows were the same... placed evenly all around the entire room, giving a perfect view of the miserable city of Devona. I noted that from this vantage point, one had a perfect view of all those approaching the castle. A weaved black carpet stretched from the door, all the way through the enormously empty room and ended near the base of the dais, atop which sat a throne. From this distance, I couldn't see who was seated upon the royal throne, but I knew instinctively that it was Ralston, for I could sense his presence... He was the Shadow.

"Be brave Alice," Oliver told me encouragingly, as we made the final approach. I could feel that he was trembling, which didn't give me any courage whatsoever.

Standing at the base of the dais, I kept my head lowered, for I did *not* want to look up, as my fear was just too great. I had felt this presence before, though not just in my dreams and that was what terrified me the most. Yes, I had felt Ralston in my nightmares, but I had also been in or at least near, his true presence once before.

"Come forward young Alice," croaked Ralston, putting a strange emphasis on my name. "I have been waiting for you," he hissed, "waiting a very long time indeed." Then in an annoyed tone he ordered, "Look at me!"

It was as though a hand reached out underneath my chin and jerked my head upward. There he was, seated upon a cushion of purple velvet on a high back throne. The armrests and legs of the royal chair were studded with a collage of precious stones; amethyst, diamond, sapphire, topaz, pearl, garnet, ruby and emerald. It wasn't Ralston's own throne that he ruled from… it was King Alfred's! Anger surged through my veins, causing a sudden defiance to enter my weary body. How dare he!

I didn't want to look at Ralston himself, but my eyes were involuntarily drawn towards him. His features were presently hidden, for he wore a flowing robe, darker than the darkest of nights. He had his hood drawn, which cast a shadow across his face, much as it had been with Io. Then without so much as a word, Ralston reached up with pale, bony fingers and pulled his hood down abruptly. I gasped loudly and quickly averted my gaze. Oliver too was horrified and made a sound in his throat somewhere between a choke and a scream.

However it was too late, for I had seen only too well what Ralston looked like. It was an experience I definitely could have done without, but now, the image was seared into my mind for all eternity. Ralston was as bald as a baby, but that was were any other similarities to a baby ended. The crown of his hairless head was covered in tiny white lumps and crisscrossed with fat blue veins. His entire pale complexion pretty much resembled his head, though his face was deeply pitted and scarred in addition to the lumps and veins. He had no nose to speak of… or at least the part that protruded anyway, for there were two holes in the center of his face, through which to breath. Ralston's mouth was a maliciously twisted thin black line that neither smiled nor frowned.

But perhaps Ralston's most terrible aspect, were his eyes, which were over sized and sunken deep within his skull. They glowed brightly, revealing red pupils, surrounded by a sickening yellow. There was no white to speak of in his eyes… only a blackish green colour where the white should have been. Ralston had no eyebrows, but he did have the strangest, not to mention longest, dark eyelashes that I had ever seen. They looked like tiny black snakes that waved when he blinked. He was not a skeleton as I had once suspected… No, he was much worse.

His terrible eyes were staring straight into me… burning through my body. I felt naked and exposed before the creature who sat upon the dead King's throne. "I did not say you could look away!" he barked, as something grabbed my hair and forcefully yanked my head upright once again. "That's better," Ralston approved, as he sat up straighter.

I realized suddenly that we weren't alone in the room with Ralston. There were strange movements in the darkness off to the sides… witches! I sucked in a sharp breath. Legions and legions of witches! We were surrounded!

"Let me take a good look at you." Ralston nodded his head. He wasn't really a very large man I noticed. His height was only perhaps equal to Emma's and there didn't appear to be much bulk to his body. A sack of bones really…

"My," Ralston clacked his clawed nails on the armrest of Alfred's throne, "how you've grown over the years. Such a beautiful young girl… *lady* you've become. Your hair… it reminds me so much of that fool…" Ralston mused. "And those eyes… the way you stare at me so defiantly! It's her all over again!" he bellowed, though I couldn't make out if he were angry. Ralston seemed a master at concealing his emotions.

My mouth twitched slightly. Was I really staring defiantly at him? I was so frightened inside, but as to what was showing on the outside, I was oblivious. Finding strength in this, I asked, "What are you talking about? I've never met you before in my life, so why do you speak as though we've met?"

Ralston's bumpy forehead crinkled… in mild amusement or wonder? "Nissim has done quite an excellent job at erasing your memory I must admit. But no matter, it shall soon be jolted."

"Nissim?" I breathed in astonishment. "I… I don't know what you're talking about," I replied stubbornly, giving no indication that I knew who Nissim was.

"If there's one thing I cannot tolerate," Ralston began with a rising voice, "it's a liar! However since you've come to surrender to me, I'll put this little bit of insolence behind us."

"Surrender?" I nearly exclaimed, in spite of myself. "We've come to do no such thing!"

Ralston seemed to ignore my outburst. "Wasn't there more members to your little party before? I could have sworn there were more," he pressed, knowing full well the sudden heart wrenching pain he had caused in me. Then snapping his fingers as though coming to a revelation, he taunted, "Oh that's right, they're dead! And all on account of you little Alice. It must be terrible to have so much blood on your hands."

Feeling something wet upon my fingers, I looked down and let loose a scream, for there was bright red blood all over my hands. "NO!" I yelled and closed my eyes tightly. Oliver was immediately at my side.

"Alice, what's wrong!" he exclaimed, shaking my shoulders.

"The blood Oliver!" I sobbed, holding up my hands. "Look!"

"Alice," he told me firmly, "there's nothing on your hands."

I opened my eyes and stared down in disbelief… for my hands were perfectly clean. Ralston had been playing with my mind and I was furious! "The only person with blood on their hands is you!" I screamed and pointed an accusing finger towards Ralston, who sat stiffly above us.

"Perhaps we both do," Ralston suggested simply. "Maybe you and I are more similar than you think."

"You're wrong!" I shook my head swiftly. "I am *nothing* like you! Nothing!"

At this, Ralston stood slowly and took a few steps towards the edge of the dais. "So how does it feel to be within these walls again? Do you enjoy seeing what has become of your father's great estate? Does it look any different to you?" Ralston eyed me carefully.

I could literally feel my heart dropping into my stomach. "My f… father's estate? What are you talking about? This is King Alfred's home," I whispered.

"Wrong!" Ralston bellowed. "This is *my* home, not Alfred's! How stupid you are child! Are you unable to draw a conclusion from all of this? Really, I had such high expectations of you!"

"I… I honestly don't know what you're talking about!" I stammered, but inside I could feel a barrier breaking down.

"I have worked long and hard to expand my empire and I shall expand it more." Ralston gritted his black teeth together. "Only one thing still stands in my way." He nodded to a witch, who began to pull curtains off of single headshot portraits, which were mounted on the walls between the windows. Ralston gave me a triumphant look. "King Alfred, deceased." The next curtain fell down. "Queen Rose-Mary, deceased." Four curtains came down all at once. "Prince Edric, deceased. Princess Emma, deceased. Princess Clara, deceased and Princess Lily, deceased." One portrait was left covered. With a nod, a witch unveiled it; it was the youngest of King Alfred's daughters. "And last but not least, little clingy Princess Alice, alive and quite well," Ralston sneered evilly.

My hands flew to my cheeks. "No," I breathed, "this can't be."

Oliver gave me a strange look and asked, "Alice, is this true?"

I shook my head uncertainly. "I don't know. I don't know about anything anymore!"

Oliver took a deep breath. "What does your heart say?"

I looked up, with tears in my eyes. Somehow, though I could not remember the details, I knew that what Ralston had said was true. "Yes," I admitted at last. "What he says is correct. I am… Princess Alice of Algernon." Inwardly I nodded to myself. Yes, I had been called this before by many people.

Oliver took a step away from me. "Did you know all along?" he questioned in a shaky, half accusing voice.

"No... even now, I don't remember anything," I murmured and covered my face with my hands. I felt a sudden deep and sorrowful emptiness in my heart... a dagger for everyone I had lost.

"You seem distraught your Grace," Ralston seethed, a strange dark glow appeared around him. "It's really too bad that you won't be around long enough to enjoy your newly recalled title. It means nothing now, for a new dynasty has been established. The Light Dynasty is over!"

I shot him a look... one I *knew* was full of defiance. "I am the Princess!"

"You have no power," Ralston told me forcefully. "Your entire family is dead and you are completely alone! There is nothing you can do!"

"Monster!" I screamed and took a step forward, only to find myself being restrained by two skeleton guards.

"Funny," mused Ralston, undisturbed by my threat, "that's exactly what your mother called me when I attacked the throne room, 13 years ago. Yes, I recall that victory so well. Your father never really had a chance, for he was a weak, peaceful king... with no ambition at all and few soldiers. Quite the pushover really," Ralston chuckled to himself, though it sounded more like he was gasping for breath. He held up his hand. "Three guards and that was it. Three guards were protecting the King and Queen. It was nothing to break through! I was very angry though as I recall, for the Queen had sent her little brats away. It just made more work for me." Ralston looked annoyed. "If it weren't for that meddling wizard Nissim, I would have finished everything that very day, but he took the Princesses and concealed them from me! Still, my guards got the little boy in the hallway and had him killed."

I struggled in the ruthless grip of the guards. "You lie! Edric is still alive and will reign over Algernon one day! You can't win!"

Ralston looked slightly disturbed and then regained his cool mannerism. "Silly little princess. Didn't you know? I have already won! Guards, relieve her Grace of those golden pendants! You have finally reached the end." He glared at me with his horrible, hateful embers.

As the two guards who had been restraining me, loosened their grip in order to remove my pendants, Oliver sprang into action. He raced towards me at full speed and kicked one of the guards to the ground, sending bones and armour flying in every direction. Not wasting a moment, I turned on the other stunned guard and gave his bony skull an enormous push, causing it to snap from his neck and roll onto the ground.

Oliver entwined his fingers through mine. "Come on Alice! We have to get out of here!"

It was a long shot to escape Ralston's well guarded throne room, but we had to try something. I was determined not to let Ralston get us without a fight... He may have taken my family without one, but he wouldn't take me. It was indeed quite a hopeless attempt, for we hadn't even reached the door when a guard brought down a lance painfully across both of our backs, pinning us to the floor. We were uninjured, but I feared we had tried Ralston's patience for the last time. A particularly large skeleton hauled Oliver up to his feet with one arm and me with his other.

Ralston was shaking his head in disappointed manner. "Tsk, tsk, children! You forgot to ask my permission to leave! I'm terribly insulted!" These last words were bellowed in a voice that shook the castle to its foundations. Ralston extended his long fingers and a thin beam of dark light shone out from them. The magic coiled itself like a rope around us and held our unwilling bodies fast. Ralston curled his fingers towards his palm and began to drag us towards him, as though we were mere puppets on a string. Giving a sharp jerk, he brought both Oliver and I to our knees and forced us to bow before him.

In a slightly more controlled voice, Ralston commented, "For royalty, I really must question your manners young Alice. The actions of your poor uneducated friend here are understandable," he glanced at Oliver in a disapproving fashion, "but when someone of your stature breaks an age old code, I'm simply shocked."

"You'll find there's more to me than meets the eye," I spat back, as I lifted my head slightly from the floor where it was being held.

"Do you know what I see when I look at you?" Ralston asked me with a sneer. "I see a little girl who clings to others because she lacks confidence in herself. You," he pointed a finger at me, "have time and time again proved yourself to be nothing more than a coward! A girl who cries at the slightest disruption and screams when she spies a shadow! I have been watching you closely Princess and testing you in many ways. You failed little one!" Ralston fairly laughed. "You failed! At least each of your sisters had a talent or skill, but not you! You were just following everyone else, while whining and complaining! All you desired was to be done with your pathetic little quest! You never cared about the kingdom or its people!" Ralston licked his dark lips with his greasy tongue. "You desired most of all to simply run away and wash your hands of it! Am I not correct?"

I stared in horror at this malicious, unrelenting killer. What he said... was it true? Did I really not care about anyone but myself? A small light deep inside of me answered my call. It cried out quite clearly, 'No!' But Ralston's words... when he said them, they sounded so true, so convincing.

"I am offering you the chance to be done with it all Alice!" Ralston almost sounded civil. "Just give the pendants to me and you can leave unharmed. Go back to the Forgotten Forest and live out the rest of your days. I shall never bother you again. Such an offer is most generous and unlike me. I *take* what I want! I don't bargain, but for a princess as lovely as yourself, I am willing to make this small exception."

Hand over the pendants and be done with all of the horror? It seemed awfully tantalizing... and yet, I truly didn't want to. Inside, I found that I couldn't... I wouldn't and I didn't *want* to take the easy road out. I actually wanted to do something, to accomplish something. Ralston thought he had my desires pegged and a short time ago I would have agreed with him, but now... everything was different. I *wanted* to make a difference, if even a small one, or die trying.

I glared up at Ralston and narrowed my dark eyes stealthily. "No," I told him with resolve. "You will never get these pendants from me! You'll have to kill me first!"

"I'm growing impatient." Ralston massaged his temples. "Guards, I'll ask just one more time and see if you can get it right... Relieve the Princess of those pendants!" he roared.

This time, there was nothing Oliver could do, for he was pinned tightly by Ralston's magical rope. Ralston raised me to a kneeling position and a guard reached out his fleshless hand towards my golden prize. Gimra died protecting the pendants and it was all for nothing! I struggled, but to no avail. Then just as the guard's fingers touched the gold, it glowed and sparked, sending a powerful shock wave in front of me. All skeleton guards in the vicinity crumbled to the ground in a lifeless heap. Ralston, who had been in the midst of the shockwave, stood unharmed, but unamused.

Ralston lost his calm and threw his hands angrily into the air. Thunder and lightning could suddenly be heard outside as Ralston raged. "That Nissim! He's always getting in my way! He must have placed a spell of protection on the pendants! He's always finding some way to delay my victory!" Ralston clenched his fists in fury and I noted the black spittle that had begun to dribble down his chin. His composure was gone and I was able to see him for the monster he truly was. With another great scream, Ralston took a breath and gritted his teeth. "Well, no matter, for I know how to break the spell. It may take three or four days, but I have time." He glared at me with his wretched eyes. "Though the pendants cannot be removed from your neck while you still live little Alice, they most certainly can be after you have died a 'natural death'... in this case starvation." Ralston released us from his magical bindings. "Take her to the dungeon to rot!"

A guard uncertainly stepped forward... it was the one we had met on the drawbridge, with a piece missing from his cheekbone. "But what of the boy master?"

Ralston waved his hand in disinterest, as he seated himself once again upon King Alfred's throne. "Throw him in as well."

"No!" I screamed, as we were roughly dragged down a flight of sharp stairs and thrown onto a cold stone floor. The iron door was slammed loudly behind us and I heard an echoing click. We were trapped.

Oliver stood up slowly and brushed his tunic off before extending a hand to me. "So what now?"

I shook my head in disbelief. "Nissim will do something, he just has to!" I sounded like I was pleading and perhaps I was. Then something in the darkened corner of the cell caught my attention. We weren't alone!

"Who's there?" I called uncertainly, grabbing Oliver's arm nervously.

There was another rustling of hay and a tall skinny, but handsome boy stepped forward. He stood under a small sliver of light that shone from a barred window and into the cell. His blue eyes glowed intensely and his hair was as black as the Witch's Raven.

Oliver held me back with an arm and stepped forward boldly. He stood face to face with the boy, who was about his exact height... maybe slightly shorter. "Who are you?" Oliver inquired suspiciously.

The boy bowed slightly and stated in a loud clear voice, "His royal highness, Prince Edric, heir to the throne of Algernon, at your service."

CHAPTER THIRTY-FOUR

One Last Chance

"**P**RINCE EDRIC!" Oliver and I both exclaimed at the same time. "The one and only," Edric declared with an almost haughty air of dignity.

He looked just as I had imagined Edric was supposed to... I mean, he had the midnight black hair and intense blue eyes, which was a known fact about the Prince. This boy even appeared to be the correct age... 14. So why was I hesitant? We had located the heir... my only brother! Perhaps it was because so many people had declared Edric dead, that I had begun to half believe it. With a dry mouth I whispered, "Ralston said he had you murdered outside the nursery. A guard said you were burned..."

Edric threw back his head and laughed, revealing pearly white teeth. "There are a great many things Ralston does not know about me!" He gestured to a small tunnel dug into the side of the prison wall that was partially concealed by hay. "Like this for instance."

"A way out!" I cried joyously and clapped my hands together.

Oliver crossed his arms suspiciously. "So if you had a way out of this place, why are you still here?" There was no mistaking the acrid tone in Oliver's voice.

Edric shrugged quickly. "Where would I go? Hmm? What would I do? Most likely I'd end up as a spirit roaming the streets. The Night Guard is relentless in their pursuit of victims. If I died, where would the kingdom be?"

"Exactly where it is now," Oliver retorted sharply. "You don't seem to be doing much for the kingdom, besides hiding out in a dungeon. By the way, how did you get here?" Oliver eyed Edric's well groomed appearance with a sharp eye.

Edric gave Oliver an icy glare. "Do you forget? I am the Prince of Algernon! There are guards who remained loyal to me, despite Ralston's enchantments. They locked me in here for my own protection!"

"They must take real good care of you," Oliver commented, glaring at Edric's navy and crimson velvet tunic, with golden embroidery.

"Of course they do!" Edric shot back with anger in his voice. "I am royalty and don't you forget it peasant!"

"Peasant! Why you little—" Oliver exclaimed, but I cut him off.

"Oliver," I began, trying to sooth his wounded pride, "give Edric a little credit. He's been through some very traumatic times."

"But what I don't understand, is that if Edric's locked up here willingly, why has he built an escape tunnel? And who raised him all this time? He was one, when the siege took place! You can't just throw baby into a dungeon and reassure him with the title 'prince'. It just doesn't work that way!" Oliver snapped, his passionate eyes full of electric blue fire.

"I'm certain that there is a logical explanation for everything, Oliver," I told him with a hint of uncertainty in my voice. There *were* some rather large gaps and unconnected points to Edric's story.

Edric in the meantime, placed his hands on his hips. "Oliver? So that's your name, peasant boy? Such a dreadfully *common* name... Oliver. Definitely not of royal status... No one with a title would ever have such a boring name as *Oliver*."

Oliver shook with the anger he was trying so desperately to contain. He couldn't very well hit the person we had come all this way looking for... even if he was slightly arrogant. With a beet red face, the best Oliver could do was splutter some inaudible words.

Edric's gaze swung over to me now and he smiled strangely. "You, on the other hand, certainly must have royal blood in your veins. Those eyes, the hair, the facial features...they all shout authority!"

"A... authority?" I repeated in a confused manner.

Edric nodded firmly and took my hand, gently pulling me away from Oliver. "Who are you? Tell me your name?" His words were more of a demand than a request.

"I'm Alice," I told him quite simply, to which he raised a questioning eyebrow.

"That is it? Alice?" Edric seemed incredulous.

Somehow my name did seem quite plain and dull when I said it. Edric had obviously been expecting something more. With the desire to please, I repeated my introduction, "I am Princess Alice of Algernon, fourth daughter to the late King Alfred."

Edric's face lit up with joy... a different sort of joy than Oliver's. His blue eyes had luster, but they seemed to lack a certain something, just as his dark hair had attitude, but not the roguish carelessness of Oliver's locks. "Could it be?" he cried. "My sister! My dear sister Princess Alice!"

I nodded enthusiastically, glad to finally be recognized. "Yes, it's me!"

Edric embraced me tightly and I returned it wholeheartedly. It was strange hugging my brother though... Perhaps it was because we had been separated for so long. I had expected to find genuine warmth and love, but all I felt was a cold emptiness as Edric held me in his arms. I tried to crush these suspicious thoughts, as this was truly a joyous occasion. "Ah, my little sister!" Edric beamed.

I stiffened slightly and tried to pull away. "I'm actually older than you *little* brother," I pointed out, wondering if he had made a joke and if I should be laughing.

He released me abruptly and stared deeply into my eyes. "Of course you are," Edric laughed, "of course."

"Hey," Oliver interrupted grabbing my arm and pulling me back towards himself possessively, "this is really touching and all, but what about Ralston? He's still running the kingdom! We must stop him before the dark gate opens! Nissim needs our help!"

"But we've done what we came to do," I stated, as Oliver put distance between the heir and ourselves. "We've found Edric, now all we have to do is reveal him."

"Correction, that's *Prince Edric*, if you please," Edric stated pointedly.

Ignoring Edric, Oliver addressed my comment. "I'm afraid it won't be quite as easy as that Alice. But don't worry, because I think I might have a plan," Oliver began, but Edric interrupted him.

"There is but one way to defeat Ralston once and for all... and put me on the throne, my rightful place I might add," Edric announced in a loud and important voice.

My eyes went wide as I gazed at Edric's firm features. It was difficult to imagine him being that tiny dark haired boy in my dreams. "How?" I asked in wonderment.

Edric paused as if he were inspecting his immaculately clean fingernails. "It involves going to the Temple of Courage," he told me absently.

A chill ran up my spine and I found myself involuntarily take a step back across a pile of rotten straw. The Temple of Courage was practically my tomb! That place, of all places, I did not want to be anywhere near! It was however, Oliver who spoke up on my behalf.

"Are you crazy!" Oliver accused. "Alice can't go there!"

Edric gave an annoyed sigh. "And just why not, peasant boy?"

Oliver held his hands out in pleading fashion, as a pained look held his face in agony. "Because she'll die, that's why! All of your other sisters died in Virtue Temples! This is the last temple and Alice is the last sister. So you see, we cannot under any circumstances bring her there!"

Facing Oliver in a very firm manner, Edric was unmoved. "Algernon is dying peasant boy. Sacrifices must be made to achieve victory. No victory was ever achieved in any alternate fashion. If it takes Alice's death to save my kingdom, then so be it. My sister is a very noble girl, so I'm certain she will step forward without any fear." Edric raised an eyebrow towards me.

I stood in shock. How could my own brother speak about me as though I were absolutely nothing to him! Did he honestly expect me to die willingly? The only words my mouth could utter were, "I... I..." before my voice failed me completely.

"Alice is not a sacrifice for goodness sakes Edric!" Oliver exploded angrily.

"Call me Prince Edric, or your highness or your majesty," Edric requested quickly.

"I'll call you whatever I please!" Oliver shot back in fury. "You speak of Alice, your own flesh and blood, as though she's not even a person! She's your sister for the Power's sake! Why would you even consider putting her in danger?"

Edric's fist came up and then he forced it to his side once again. He locked his blazing eyes with Oliver's. "I am a king!" he cried. "I am a ruler! You... you are a nothing! Do not seek to advise me with your foolishness!"

"You are no king! You are a prince right now and with an attitude like yours, I don't know if I want you as my king!" Oliver was absolutely livid. "You disgrace King Alfred's good name! Alice is my friend, in fact, she's like a sister to me. She's more of a sister to me than she is to you!"

"Of all the selfish things I've ever heard..." Edric paced across the cell.

"Selfish?" Oliver pointed to himself in shock. "Me? I'd take a good look in a mirror if I were you. Get one of your loyal guards to bring you one the next time they come for your laundry!"

Edric walked right up to Oliver and stood only a breath from his face. The two raven haired boys stood stubbornly opposite each other. "I will do what's best for my kingdom," Edric breathed, "even if it means losing my sister!"

"You are unreal," Oliver seethed back, "absolutely unreal."

I sighed and bowed my head as their angry exchange continued. Edric was distant, arrogant and determined... while Oliver was passionate, devoted and in my eyes, really quite noble. Still, Edric was my brother... we were of the same blood. However I silently vowed that Oliver would always remain more of a brother to me than that royal brat ever would. At least Oliver respected me. I scratched my head in frustration. What were we to do? We could sit in the dungeon while Ralston became all powerful... but if we went to the Temple of Courage, Edric seemed to think that we'd at least have a chance. Hmmm...one last chance to set things right. Suddenly I found myself shouting out, "Enough! We've come too far and lost too much to give up now. If the Temple is where our hope lies, then that is where we shall go!"

"But Alice," Oliver tried to plead with me.

"You heard *my* sister commoner." Edric gave Oliver a triumphant look and turned his nose up in the air. "Don't argue with nobility."

"Edric, *that* was uncalled for," I told him sharply. "Oliver is very dear to me and if I'm at all dear to you, I want you to show him some respect."

Edric ignored my comment and continued on, "Now listen, while I tell you exactly why we are going to the Temple of Courage. Inside the Temple, there is a sacred room that only members of the royal family can enter... or guardians of the Temple. On both accounts that excludes you peasant." Edric gave Oliver a disdainful look.

With a tight face, Oliver muttered quietly, "Brat."

Clearing his throat gruffly, Edric continued. "To enter the Temple Alice, you must use all four of those pendants around your neck."

I glanced down... The pendants had fallen behind my tunic and were cold against my skin. How did Edric know they were there?

"Inside of that room, is Algernon's greatest weapon... one that has only been used in my kingdom's darkest hours. This weapon," Edric looked smug, "doesn't come in any form one might expect a weapon to... It is actually a royal crown... The Crown in fact. King Alfred was not wearing it when Ralston attacked him and as a result..." Edric shrugged.

"So it's still in that room you think?" I wondered, as the light outside our cell window dimmed further.

"I don't *think*, I know," Edric snapped at me. "The Crown can only be used by a member of a royal family... any royal family," Edric added. "This means that if Ralston were to get a hold of it, he too could use it, for he has Denzelian royal blood in his veins." Turning to Oliver, Edric sneered, "*You* couldn't use the Crown boy, since you are such a mongrel."

"That does it," Oliver growled through clenched teeth. He stood up and stormed to a corner of the cell to brood.

Edric seemed cruelly pleased by Oliver's reaction. Now his sole focus was on me and truthfully, I felt rather uncomfortable. "The Crown grants great power to the royal who wears it. With it, there is a good chance Ralston can be defeated."

"A good chance... ?" I repeated. Somehow the way he spoke these words wasn't very encouraging.

Oliver now spun around in the corner, his face flushed as red as his tunic. Purposefully he marched back to Edric and asked in an accusing voice, "So you expect Alice to wear this Crown and destroy Ralston?" For emphasis, Oliver pointed a finger directly in Edric's face.

Calmly, Edric pushed Oliver's finger out of the way and replied smoothly, "Of course not commoner! I expect Alice to fetch the Crown and return it to *me*, the rightful heir. No offence sister, but you're just a *girl* and we all know that girls aren't capable of ruling a kingdom, much less destroying a demon!"

"I'm a young *lady*," I told Edric tightly. I certainly didn't feel like a child anymore.

"You are such a creep," Oliver declared standing up straight. "Alice has done more in her lifetime than you ever have or ever will! She has grown and learned so much already in her fight to save Algernon! She has come a very long way and I don't just mean by traveling! Her entire personae has expanded... and I think she knows it." Oliver cast a soft smile in my direction. "So how dare you say such things to her!"

Oliver's words stirred me. Had I really grown in the course of our journey? To me, everything was just one big blur of events... with me being frightened the entire time... but perhaps... just perhaps... courage had nothing to do with not being frightened.

The two boys were about to engage in another war of words, when I spoke up, "Listen, we won't accomplish anything by fighting. If Ralston is to be destroyed, then we must work together... Sure we don't all see things in quite the same light... but we all have something in common and that is our hatred for Ralston."

"Did you get all of that boy?" Edric asked Oliver.

"She was talking to both of us," Oliver retorted back.

Edric was absolutely impossible! As far as social skills went, he was as poor as the most destitute peasant on the streets. Nothing I said even seemed to phase him. Even now, he acted as though I hadn't even spoken.

"Well," Edric clapped his hands together, "shall we be off?" And without waiting for an answer, he began to crawl into the damp smelling tunnel in the side of the wall.

Oliver and I turned to look at each other. "What a delightful fellow," Oliver commented sarcastically. "He'll make a great king." The disgust was evident on his handsome face.

"I know, I know," I agreed breathlessly. "He's not what I expected either, but he is the heir... the one Nissim ordered us to find and Nissim knows best."

"I'm honestly beginning to wonder about that," Oliver mused with his old grin creeping back now that Edric was gone.

It gave me such a sudden, light-hearted feeling, that I gave him a playful slap, but only ended up hitting the pouch on his belt, causing an angry Sparks to come flying out in a frenzy.

"Hey what's the big idea, shaking a girl when she's sleeping?" Sparks accused angrily.

"Sorry Sparks," I giggled, basking in her refreshing yellow glow that was reminiscent of sunshine. "I can't believe you slept through all of that. When the going gets tough, the tough go to sleep," I teased her.

Sparks stuck out her tongue. "For your information, I wasn't sleeping... I was just resting my eyes."

"Like that's any better," I chuckled, then got down on my hands and knees to enter the tiny tunnel. It reminded me sharply of climbing the tunnels in the Land of the Undead.

"Where are we going?" Sparks yawned loudly.

"To the Temple of Courage with Prince Edric," I called back, as I stuck my head into the tunnel. It smelled mouldy and wet.

"You mean with that nerd who couldn't keep his mouth shut?" Sparks asked, as she peered into the tiny shaft we would have to crawl through.

"The one and only," Oliver mimicked with a swagger.

"I didn't like the sounds of him," Sparks stated seriously. "And I do not like the idea of going to the Temple. Nothing good can come of going there."

"We don't have a choice," I told her and with a deep breath, plunged forward into the escape route. I tried desperately to put down any uneasy feelings I was having, but something was afoot... Something big was going to happen... and soon.

The tunnel dropped down onto a side road outside of the castle and beyond the moat. Somehow, Edric had led us to freedom. For being locked up his entire life, Edric certainly knew his way around, as he flew through the thick brush behind Dalton Castle and onto a wide but abandoned road. Not once did he stop to decide which way to go... Edric definitely *knew* where he was going. I thought it odd that he remembered so much of our past, when I couldn't recall anything solid, besides my name. After all, Edric could barely even talk at the time of Ralston's takeover. Someone had to have raised him, but even then, just how much could a child remember from when they were but one year old? For that matter, was it even possible for me to remember *anything* from when I was two? Perhaps Emma could have recalled something, for she had been five... but Edric and I seemed a long shot at best.

Sparks fluttered around Edric in an attempt to better understand his character. "Are you really the Prince?" she asked in her lovely high pitched voice.

"Yes," he muttered impatiently and increased his pace.

"You must have had a really tough time growing up," she attempted to sympathize.

"Indeed." Edric flung his arms out at Sparks and surprisingly enough made contact with her. She flew through the air like a stunned insect.

"Keep that little firefly away from me!" he ordered, unrepentant from having struck out.

Oliver nimbly reached out and caught Sparks as she careened head over heels in midair. She lay dazed in his palms, but in no time sat up angrily. Our fairy friend didn't speak for a while and instead sat sulking in Oliver's care, trying to straighten out her mussed golden hair.

"You really could have hurt her!" I exclaimed at Edric. There was no attempt on my part to hide any anxiety.

"Quiet, sister! We're almost there!" Edric skimmed over my exclamation, as he seemed so fond of doing.

"No I will not be quiet!" I pressed. "Sparks is a fairy and you hurt her! I demand you apologize at once! Edric! Edric are you listening to me?"

He stopped suddenly and hunched his shoulders. With his index finger he beckoned me over to his side. Obligingly, I breathed a sigh of relief... He was finally going to swallow his pride and give a decent apology.

"Yes Edric? What is it?" I forced a cheerful smile at my brother.

"Alice... sister... you must understand that when I tell you to be quiet..." he gave me a stinging slap across the face and went on calmly, "I mean, be quiet. Now let's carry on." With that, Edric started up his quick pace once again, without even a second glance at me.

I stood dumbfounded on the road amongst the withered trees. Gingerly I felt my burning cheek and realized that my eyes were burning too with hot furious tears. Oliver rushed over with Sparks who blew soothing fairy dust into my face, substantially lowing the pain.

Oliver linked his arm with mine and began to lead me along the road... We were far behind Edric. "Alice..." Oliver began, but seemed unsure of how to continue. What was there to say? My brother was... was... I didn't even know what he was.

Without words, we all decided that there was nothing to do but follow Edric to the Temple of Courage. Once there, we would decide exactly what course of action to take and whether or not it would even involve the heir.

The Temple of Courage was not all that far away from the castle and probably could be seen from one of the taller towers. It looked just the same as all of the other temples, which was disappointing, since I had been expecting something unique and special.

I didn't particularly want to speak to Edric again, but we really had no choice and if Oliver were to speak, a time wasting fight would no doubt ensue. Trying to hide how betrayed and disappointed I was in Edric, I asked the simplest question I could think of, "So how do we get in? Surely we don't have to dive down to that underwater door?"

"Fairies don't swim," Sparks declared firmly, still sticking close to Oliver.

"After you your highness," Oliver told Edric with a mock bow. "Let me be the first to send you on your way."

"Really boy, if anyone were going to get wet, it would be you." A strange smile curled his lips. "But fortunately for you, that won't be necessary. Watch what the heir to the throne can do." With a flourish, Edric revealed a small lute from a fold in his velvet clothing and after wiggling his shoulders, began to play a haunting tune. The instrument's sounds rose and fell, from high to low... almost as though it were calling out to someone.

Then a strange event began to occur. Light beams as bright as the sun and lightning combined, started shooting up inside the pool of water. Waves began to slosh, creating white foam that gathered along the pool's edge. A rumbling noise started out low and grew louder, as though something were pushing its way through solid rock. The ground began to shake and rumble, until it finally split open, sending beams of light everywhere. A great explosion sent Oliver and I flying across the ground, while lighting up the entire valley.

Mysteriously uninjured, I stared up at the majestic sight before me. No longer was there just a simple circle of pillars and pool of water with a pyramid roof. In its place was an enormously breathtaking temple... a real temple, for it was a building fit for a king. Structurally designed with curious statues, fountains, stain glass windows, peaks and columns, the Temple was truly a marvel. *This* was what I thought of when someone said the words Virtue Temple. There was a large beautiful courtyard in front of the stairs leading into the temple, with a magnificent garden that seemed as though it had been growing for eons. Evil had taken control of the Temple, but because it had been so good to begin with, its physical beauty had been left untouched... a reminder that things are not always what they seem... lovely on the outside, poison on the inside. Still, the beauty of the Temple of Courage radiated throughout Devona and I secretly hoped that it would put hope into the hearts of the people.

"Behold, the final Temple!" Prince Edric declared with blazing eyes. For a moment he had looked like someone else... but it must have been a mere trick of the light.

As I continued to take in the magnificent holy place, I knew in my heart that this was where the fate of Algernon would be decided. Here, this very night, we would either rise in triumph or fall into eternal darkness.

CHAPTER THIRTY-FIVE

The Crown

"*I*T REALLY IS A BEAUTIFUL PLACE," Oliver admitted, craning his neck to see the towering arches of the Temple.

"It certainly is," I agreed. "You'd almost never know it was controlled by evil."

Sparks fluttered obtrusively in front of my face and declared importantly, "When King Alfred was in charge, all of the Temples in Algernon were above the ground like this. Although ordinary people couldn't actually enter the Temples themselves, they could pray in the courtyards and leave offerings to the Power." Spark's lower lip dropped as she continued, "When Ralston seized power, he was bent on entering the insides of the Temples and creating fortresses. Your wizard friend Nissim, so I've heard, is the one who used his magic to seal them underground. It was in this way, that at least some of the Temples' goodness was preserved."

"Really? That is very interesting Sparks." I patted her head appreciatively.

"Will someone shut that firefly up!" Edric demanded as he stamped his foot into the ground, much like a small child. "We don't have all night! If the peasant boy wants to stand around talking to a bug, then let him, but we have work to do Alice!"

Oliver rolled his eyes and I held my tongue. There was really no use arguing with Edric, since he never listened anyway. Sparks was jabbering out some fairy curses and no doubt planned to give Edric a zap, when Oliver stuffed her into his belt pouch. It certainly wouldn't do to take a shot at the heir. The heir... why did I avoid calling Edric my brother? The very thought made me cringe, that was why. As though sensing my thoughts against him, Edric roughly seized my arm and began to drag me into the courtyard. I hardly noticed the fragrant smelling blooms or peaceful trickling fountain, for my arm was being painfully bruised by Edric.

"Hey, you're hurting me!" I attempted to wrest my arm free, but Edric only increased his powerful grip. There was more strength in his skinny frame than I had realized.

We reached an enormous flight of white marble stairs, which led to two crystal doors. Edric swaggered up the steps as though he were already the King of Algernon. Gritting my teeth, I decided that when all of this was over, I would live as far away from Edric as possible. Maybe I'd stay with Sparks in the Hidden Valley of Fairies, or with Oliver out on the Plains. I blushed and realized that Carrie would probably have a rather large role to play in Oliver's future. Maybe living with Sparks was the best idea... anything to keep me away from the monstrosity of a monarch.

Edric stopped when we reached the top of the steps and stood before the glittering crystal doors... which had no handles. Then I recognized the circle with four rectangular indentations. In the center of the circle was a handprint that seemed to be an impression of an actually hand... pressed into the crystal circle somehow.

"Hurry up Alice," Edric ordered. "Put the pendants into the slots! Come on now!"

I was uncomfortable with the idea of removing the pendants from my neck, but I really had no choice, for that was the only way to open the door. Recalling the procedure from long ago, I slid each pendant into a slot and heard them click into place. Then I gently laid my hand into the print, finding with surprise, that it was a perfect match. With a bright blue burst of light, the rim of the circle spun around my hand, until it finally snapped and the doors swung open soundlessly. Before anyone could react, I had the pendants ripped from their slots and back around my neck. I wasn't taking any chances.

"You could have left the pendants in," Edric told me in an almost mocking manner. He seemed to be leaning away from the slightly ajar crystal doors.

"I rather prefer them around my neck," I told him, as I folded my arms and touched the cool feeling doors. There was a strong energy flowing inside of the Temple... I could feel its pulse, as though it were alive.

"Very well, have it your way." Edric waved into the air. "Now get in the Temple and fetch me the Crown!" he ordered and pointed the way. "There's a little side room somewhere inside. You shouldn't have any problem finding it. I shall be anxiously awaiting your return right here."

"Why won't you go inside?" Oliver wondered, taking a step towards Edric. In this outside light, I noticed once again just how remarkably similar they looked. "You're royalty, so why don't you enter your sacred place?"

"I'm afraid the stale temple air is not good for my delicate health," Edric tossed his head back, "and we wouldn't want anything ill to befall me."

"You've spent your entire life in a dungeon!" Oliver spat back hotly. "And let me assure you, the air in there was very *stale*."

Edric put his hand in front of Oliver's face so that he was no longer staring him in the eyes. "Don't rile yourself peasant boy. When we no longer require your services, you can go back to living in your slum. Don't think I won't send you back right now! I keep you around merely as a courtesy to my sister, since she seems so fond of you, though I can't imagine why. You were born into this world a lowly commoner and so shall you die a lowly common, so quit trying to be something you're obviously not!" Edric swung around and declared, "Hurry up Alice! And don't fool around!"

I started to move forward and then all at once reached back and catching Oliver's tunic sleeve, pulled him beyond the crystal doors, before slamming them sharply in Edric's astonished face. Oliver was in a panic.

"Alice! What are you doing? I can't be in here! I'm just a peasant!" He covered his head with his arms and ducked. "A lightning bolt or something is going to strike me down!"

"Oliver!" I grabbed his shoulders to steady him. "Look, nothing is going to happen to you. I'm royalty and I give you permission to be in here, so relax." Taking his hand, I led him further into the Temple and strangely enough, nothing hindered his progress.

The interior of the Temple of Courage was mostly just empty space. The floor was crafted of black and white swirled marble tiles, which our footsteps echoed loudly off of. The high vaulted ceiling was covered in paintings of cherubs, gazing down from the bright blue heavens. Their round little faces didn't seem very joyous though... in fact, they appeared quite worried and concerned... but it was just a painting. The stain glass windows on the sides would have cast lovely colours onto the floor, had there been any sunlight to shine through them. At the present, they were merely dull patterns.

I spied a glass door on my right, but realized that it led out onto a vine covered balcony. That was not where we needed to be... so we continued to enter further into the empty Temple. Alabaster columns, similar to the ones that had surrounded the pool, lined us on both sides. I felt small and insignificant amongst the magnificence of the Temple, until I reminded myself that a temple is only as good as the people who take care of it. This building, for all of its wonder, was an empty shell without good people inside to breath life into it.

Sparks poked her head out of Oliver's pouch. "Hey, we're inside the Temple!" Her chiming voice reverberated off the walls. "Where's the jerk?" she asked with a sarcastic smile.

"He's waiting outside," I explained. "The stale air in here might make him sick." I couldn't help but giggle a little at the absurdity of it all, for it didn't smell stale at all inside the Temple. In fact, the air was cool and refreshingly sweet.

"That was just his excuse to make Alice do all the work," Oliver told Sparks with a wink.

I stopped suddenly, causing Oliver to bump into my back. "There's a door between those two pillars!" I pointed. In a second, we were standing before a tall, narrow doorway with a familiar symbol carved into it. I stared for a second at the heart with a crown above it and the crossed sword and quill. It was the same as my seal ring from Isadora. It was the royal crest! Somehow, Isadora had known who I was all along! I read the motto below the crest out loud, "Oc Jykpea Yh Focohla." The door swung open without me even having to lay a hand upon it.

"What did those words mean?" Oliver scratched his head as he followed me through the narrow door and into the next room.

It was the ever knowledgeable Sparks, who answered his inquiry. "It means, silly boy, 'All Virtues In Balance'."

"How appropriate," Oliver mused bending down to pull up his leather boots.

"Didn't Edric say this was a *small* side room?" I commented wryly, while taking in the cathedral like surroundings.

Oliver straightened out and placed his hands on his hips. "Just goes to show what old Edric knows. We risk our lives and he will get all the credit."

"It looks like a place of worship," I declared hesitantly, unable to think of any other description for the pew lined room. The hundreds of pews were arranged in rows, but in a circular fashion surrounding an alter, which stood in the very center of the room. A tiny round window, directly above the alter, cast a dim ray of light down onto a blue and silver tasselled pillow... and placed delicately upon the firm pillow, was the Crown!

It glowed with a golden light far more brilliant than the precious metal used to make it. Light wasn't simply reflected off of this object... *light was emitted from it.* Although the jewels mounted on the Crown consisted mostly of sapphires and amethysts, there was also a rainbow of other stones outlined the rim, while diamonds glittered between them. The overall effect was a rippling ocean of twinkling stars.

"It's the Crown," I whispered in awe, feeling goose bumps rise all over my body.

"The key to saving Algernon," Oliver added, in an equally low whisper.

I wasn't quite sure why we were speaking so low... It just seemed the appropriate thing to do in this situation. Besides, it *was* kind of like a worship hall and Ms Craddock had always instructed us to whisper in such places, if we had to speak at all.

"Well," I licked my lips nervously and wiped my sweating palms on my tattered overtunic, "I guess I'd better take it... Edric is waiting. I don't want him to get impatient with us."

"He was impatient before we started," Oliver pointed out, to which Sparks started giggling profusely.

I began my trek between the pews and towards the blazing Crown. Oliver followed close behind me, with an eager Sparks watching from his pouch. The Crown... It seemed to be calling out to me like an old, old, friend. 'Welcome back,' it seemed to whisper inside my head. 'It's been a long time, a terribly long time.' I could hear the words quite plainly in my mind, but what did it all mean?

"It's almost hypnotizing," Oliver breathed, as we reached the alter and stood awkwardly staring at the royal accessory.

"Yes," I agreed, "it does seem to possess some sort of power." I gulped and wiped a stray lock of brown hair from my eyes, before reaching out to grasp the Crown, which had not been touched in 13 years. Suddenly I pulled my arms back, just before I made contact with the Crown. Uncertainly, I curled my fingers into my damp palms.

"Go on," Oliver urged, "don't be afraid." I stared at him with wide eyes and he smiled at me encouragingly.

Blowing out the breath I had been holding in, I swiftly reached out and clasped the cold Crown between my equally cold hands. This simple action caused a sudden and rather unexpected surge of tears to well up into my eyes. Before I knew it, I was trying desperately to remember my poor unfortunate family. Without much thought, I closed my eyelids and all at once was bombarded with visions from my first strange dream... which I realized now, was a memory.

I saw the blue tiled floor once again, shiny and completely dust free. The nursery was shaking with the earth moving vibrations from outside, sending all of the delightful pictures on the wall to the ground with a crash. The smoke drifted thickly in through an open window, burning my nostrils and I realized that no longer was I a bystander watching the scene unfold... I was one of the four little Princess experiencing the horror! I clutched at my little dress in terror as I screamed out, "Mommy! Daddy!"

Another impact, more violent than before, almost sent me to the ground, but a hand steadied me... Emma. All three of my sisters stood beside me; Emma, Clara and Lily. Their gorgeous little eyes were filled with fear too, not to mention tears. Emma reached down and gave me a little hug. "Don't be scared," she comforted me with a tiny kiss on the forehead... She was only five years old. A rough hit from the side, knocked all four of us down, despite Emma's efforts.

"The heir! The heir!" came a voice in hysterics.

Then a little voice cried out, "Lis! Lis!" It was my brother, Edric, who was standing beside the window seat, covering his delicate ears. Then as I had observed myself do so many times before, I broke free of my sisters and rushed to Edric's side, enveloping him in a hug. "Don't be scared." I spoke the same words of comfort that had been spoken to me only minutes before.

"No leave!" baby Edric wailed in my arms and I held onto him with all of my might, with the hope that I could change what I knew would happen. My hopes were all in vain, for just as expected, the plump nurse with the wild eyes appeared and swept Edric away. "Lis! Lis!" he screamed as the nurse bore him away, leaving us alone.

I turned to face my sisters, but realized that they had disappeared! That wasn't supposed to happen, I recalled. Then I heard the pitter patter of barefeet in the hallway and in toddled Prince Edric, free of the nurse's clutches. I didn't care how it was possible, for my joy was too much. I held out my arms and cried, "Come to Lis!"

Edric wiped his pudgy face and unsteadily began to make his way over to where I stood, when suddenly another child appeared out of nowhere and kicked Edric hard in the stomach. With a scream, he doubled over in pain. I gasped, for the brutal child looked exactly like Edric! Two Edrics! How could this be?

There was a brilliant flash of light and Nissim was standing beside the injured baby Edric. "It isn't true." Nissim shook his head at me, as he helped my Edric to his feet and held him tightly. Nissim's gaze then strayed over to the other Edric, who was stood indignantly in the middle of the room. In one swift movement, Nissim was at my side, handing me the injured Prince. "Beware Prince Edric! Beware! Things aren't always as they seem!"

I opened my eyes and realized that I was still leaning over the alter, with my hands clasped tightly around the Crown. Trying to slow my breathing, I gently picked up the weapon and turned around to face Oliver and Sparks. They appeared calm... No one had seen what I had seen. It had just been a dream... When I was awake? No, it had been a warning from Nissim! 'Beware Prince Edric,' he had said. Yet he had handed Edric to me in the dream, so why should I be wary of him? And how could there be two Edrics?

"Well, are you ready to go back out and face the future King?" Oliver asked me, while running a hand through his hair.

"I don't suppose we really have any choice in the matter," I commented in a sad voice.

"Alice, what's wrong?" Sparks was resting her chin in her hands on the edge of the pouch.

"I was just thinking about something Nissim said," I told my friends as we exited the Crown's room. "He told me to beware of Edric. Now isn't that funny? Beware of my own brother?"

284 *Candace N. Coonan*

"When did Nissim say that?" Oliver wondered, just as the door to the Crown's room slammed shut on its own.

"Just now," I revealed, fingering the glittering jewels that reflected my image in them. "I... I had a vision, but it didn't make any sense."

"Are you sure it wasn't just fear and fatigue induced? That can happen sometimes," Sparks told me in her most official sounding voice. She loved sharing her knowledge.

"Perhaps," I admitted. We had come to the crystal doors once again. Edric was waiting for us just beyond them and I did *not* want to see him. Still, there was no use in prolonging the agony. Abruptly, I heaved open the heavy doors and found Edric waiting right where we had left him, tapping his foot impatiently. As we came out into the oppressive air once again, Edric rushed towards me with an angry glare in his eyes.

"What took you so long?" he demanded, then softened his expression when he spied the Crown in my hands. "You got it!" His breath quickened. "Give it to me now Alice! I command you!"

Nissim's words still rang loudly in my ears. "Edric, are you sure that you know how to use this thing? I mean, won't it drain your body's energy too much?" I asked cautiously. Not only were Nissim's words now running through my mind, but it seemed that the Crown itself were shouting, 'No!'

Edric shot me an icy glare of impatience. "Are you questioning me? Just hand it over! I don't require your advice or assistance!"

The same defiance I had felt earlier with Ralston returned. "I just want to make sure you won't blow up or something!" I shot back, holding the Crown closer than ever.

Oliver, perceiving that I was stalling for time put in, "She's just looking out for you Edric, though I don't know why anyone would."

"All right! All right!" Edric sighed. "But don't worry, because the full force of the energy doesn't come through the user. There needs to be someone through which the energy is channelled and focused. This offsets the full brunt of the magic and thus the user can survive."

As I paused to consider this, my grip on the Crown slackened and during this brief moment, Edric snatched it from my hands. It was suddenly as though I had hit my head, for the world swayed in circles. My body went cold like ice and I felt terribly sick. As I wavered, Oliver caught me in the air and when I looked into his face I realized with a start, that he didn't look so well either. Above us, thunder cracked and lightning gave the sky an eerie glow. I had a sudden, brief vision of Nissim tumbling down into a deep dark hole and into the depths of the earth.

A tormented voice echoed through the air, "They're free! Evil is free!

I tried! All depends on you!" There was no mistaking that tone. It was Nissim.

"Edric," I whispered weakly, finally able to stand on my feet once again, "who will be channelling the energy for you?"

He gave me a warped grin that was so evil it sent a chill up my spine. There was something wrong with his eyes... They weren't blue anymore and his hair... it wasn't silky. "No one will be channelling for me!" he laughed. "You see, I'm not a member of the royal family and therefore the Crown's power is of little use to me." He backed down the Temple stairs slowly. "However even though I cannot use the Crown, I know someone who can... someone who's been lusting after it for a long time now."

My throat constricted and I could barely utter the word, "Who?" Oliver gripped my arm tightly and Sparks began to shiver in fear. We all knew who he was talking about.

"Don't you know little Princess?" Edric mocked. "Not so smart after all! I'm speaking of course of my master!"

My blood turned to ice as Ralston appeared in the air behind Edric, who rapidly dissolved into the Witch.

CHAPTER THIRTY-SIX

Oliver's Destiny

"N o," I WHISPERED in disbelief, as I stumbled backwards against the crystal doors. "This can't be happening!"

Oliver's body tensed, the veins in his arms protruding as his anger grew. "I knew it!" he breathed with conviction. "I sensed there was something wrong with that impostor the minute we met him!"

So Oliver was correct in his assumptions right from the start. A lot of good that did us now! Why hadn't we trusted our intuition? Why had we blindly done the Witch's bidding? Deception. Plain and simple deception. We had been sent to find Prince Edric and well… it was nice to believe that we had succeeded in that endeavour.

Ralston's tight black mouth, which had before betrayed no emotion, was now curled into a hideous smile. He clasped his hands together in a pleased fashion. "Well done my faithful servant. You have truly redeemed yourself for failing to bring me the pendants and stop these meddlers before."

"My life is but to serve you oh master," the Witch cackled in her hoarse voice. She held the Crown up triumphantly and laughed.

Ralston meanwhile clapped his bony hands together in a mocking fashion. "I must say bravo to you Princess Alice. You obeyed instructions very well, with relatively little questions. I guess I really should be thanking you for handing over Algernon, because, quite frankly without you, none of this would have been possible. You would have made a fine witch," Ralston told me as his sickly white head glowed in the darkness. The deep pits and scars across his face, cast strange shadows over his cheek bones, but his eyes burned brighter than ever.

I stood upon the steps of the Temple completely aghast by what I had done and by what Ralston had said. Although I wished to scream a thousand harsh words, I remained utterly speechless. Everything wanted to come out at once and the result was that nothing came out at all. I continued to lean against the powerful Temple doors, somehow feeling safe and protected by the Temple's aura, even though Ralston controlled it. A thought crossed my confused mind at that moment… If Ralston truly controlled the Temples, then why had he not done anything to this one? Why did it feel so pure and untouched? Perhaps the Temple of Courage was protected somehow… Perhaps evil magic had *not* corrupted it as it had

286

the other three. Heart, Strength, Wisdom... Lily, Clara, Emma. All three Temples and all three sisters had fallen, but maybe Courage still stood because I still breathed. The exception to the pattern! I took strength in this thought.

Now halfway down the Temple stairs, the Witch was performing something of a jig, probably to celebrate what she considered a great victory on her part. She caught my hateful gaze and turned about wickedly. "Oh I'm your long lost brother Prince Edric!" she mocked in 'Edric's' voice. "Oh sister, I've missed you so!" She spat onto the stairs, which immediately began to sizzle. "You can forget it!" She waved her hand violently in the air. "Edric is dead and forgotten, which is what you will soon be! No one will remember you or anything you've done! It's all been in vain child! Everything! And what's more, no one shall mourn your passing!"

My fingernails dug into the crystal doors as I leaned against them more heavily. Breathing hard, I stared down at my feet and blinked away the hot tears. This was the end? Had it all been in vain? We hadn't found the heir or defeated Ralston... Now there wasn't even a way to since the Witch had the Crown. It was true that if I died right here, I would be forgotten. Oliver was really the only one who would remember me... but he would die too. But in vain? We had tried and lost... but we hadn't quit. Somehow, that aspect was vitally important. We hadn't quit.

"No!" I screamed finding my voice. "It hasn't been in vain! I've met too many wonderful people that I wouldn't have otherwise! That makes it all worth it!"

With a scornful gaze, the Witch was about to make a remark when suddenly, Oliver rushed past me and down the stairs. Wildly, he lunged for the Witch, arms outstretched and yelling as loud as he could. In the moment he was airborne, Sparks flew out of Oliver's pocket and rushed up to me in a fright.

The Witch, who had been so caught up in talking to me, was taken completely off guard. Oliver hit the Witch in her chest and held on tightly to her black robes, as they both toppled painfully down the remainder of the Temple stairs. They didn't even stop immediately when they reached the courtyard, for they rolled several lengths more, before Oliver broke free of her grasp with a groan. When he turned around, I gasped. He had the Crown!

"He has it!" Sparks turned a gleeful flip in the air, her bright wings beating happily.

I wanted to rejoice too, but the Witch wasn't about to let her prize go so easily. In no time, she had staggered to her feet, black blood oozing out of her forehead. "You wretched boy!" she shrieked and shot what looked to be a lightning bolt towards him.

"Look out Oliver!" I cried and ran forward to the edge of the stairs, forgetting about the comforting crystal doors.

Oliver hadn't needed my frightened warning, for he had been ready for some sort of retaliation. With amazing speed and coordination, Oliver dodged the attack with a swift roll to the side. Then without wasting another second, Oliver placed the Crown securely upon his brow, without hesitation. I started, for suddenly he looked so regal, with his ebony hair under the gold of the Crown and his blue eyes sparkling with the gems. His eyes reminded me of someone... so did his hair. There was a sudden lump in my throat and I thought myself to be choking. Then I realized that I was crying. A magnificent thought had struck me, but before I could say or do anything, Oliver was already using the Crown to power up a deadly attack. He suddenly glowed yellow with energy, brighter than even Sparks in her full light.

Running part way down the stairs with Sparks hanging in my hair, I screamed, "Don't Oliver! You can't support the full force of the Crown's energy by yourself! There needs to be a channeller!" Oliver was not listening to my desperate pleas, for his face was full of stubborn determination. I turned to Sparks who had a horrified look on her tender face. The slight pink in her cheeks had faded into a sickly white. "Oh Sparks!" I cried. "Isn't there anything we can do?"

A crystal teardrop fell from her eye and landed on the steps of the Temple. Her tear truly was a crystal, for it bounced on the step with a soft 'ping'. "I can't touch him now that he's in the middle of a power up," Sparks revealed sadly, "and my magic's not nearly strong enough to bring him out of the trance he's in. He *does* need a channeller though. This magic is very strong."

The Witch knew that she was in trouble, as there was very real terror written all over her features. She was standing only a few footsteps away from Oliver and she seemed unable to move. The Crown's awesome power had to have been holding on to her. Of Ralston Radburn, there was no sign. No doubt he had gone into hiding at the first sign of trouble. I trembled as Oliver began to grow brighter. He might succeed in destroying one of Ralston's witches... but he would be sacrificing himself in the process.

I covered my face with my hands and wept. "Oliver's doomed then," I wailed, unable to stop thinking about the revelation that had shot through my head.

Sparks was scratching her chin pensively. "Not exactly," she whispered with hope in her voice. "There may yet be a way to save him." Her hopefulness was fading into solemnity. "You'd never be able to see him again Alice... but he'd live. Are you... willing to accept that?"

I gulped and sniffled. All my crying had done was give me a stuffy nose. I gasped for air between words. "Yes Sparks," I said breathlessly. "Do what you must. Please save him." Never seeing Oliver again would be next to unbearable, but I couldn't just let him die when there was a way to save him! It would be just like he was dead... except that I would know that somewhere he was alive... and perhaps even happy. There was no time to consider the repercussions now, for soon it would be too late.

Sparks gave me a light kiss on the nose for comfort. She was terribly fond of Oliver too. "I will use my fairy magic to open a portal to another fairy realm... It is called Alexandria. A fairy queen by the same name rules the land. I have heard that she is very kind and sympathetic towards humans. She would see that no harm befall Oliver... but he would be trapped there forever."

"Forever is an awfully long time," I admitted slowly and then told Sparks quickly, before my tears took over, "Do whatever it takes. But you promise me that he will be safe."

"Oh yes," Sparks assured me. "Queen Alexandria is a noble and just. I've never met her, but I've heard great things." I gave Sparks the nod to proceed. "I'll allow Oliver to take a shot at the Witch, but just before his energy is used up, I will open the portal. He will be close to death in this realm, but once out of it, he will live. I'm sorry," she touched a strand of my hair, "but it's the best I can do."

"That's all anyone can hope for," I told her with a sniffle. "Thank you." I *was* truly grateful.

With a hopeful wink of reassurance, Sparks dimmed her light and inconspicuously flew up in the air and began to weave her spell. Something similar to a spider's web began to appear in the air directly above Oliver's head... It was the portal that would take him away from Algernon forever. I swallowed a sob and began to hiccup.

I tiptoed down a few more steps, just as Oliver's attack began to heighten to epic proportions. As if suddenly aware of my presence, he craned his neck towards me, all the while growing in brilliance, which caused the Witch to shudder and wail.

"I'm sorry Alice," he called out, "but I have to do this! I understand now what Emma was talking about! This is my destiny and it is unavoidable! Our destinies tread along the same path for a long time, but they must finally diverge! Please forgive me!" he pleaded, tears in his own eyes... the same eyes that had greeted me one sunny morning in the Forgotten Forest when I had awoken in a strange little house. Oliver... the happy young boy with a famous grin and unforgettable charm. The boy who had been raised by the wizard Arvad and whose lust for adventure was rivalled only by my dear sister Clara. My dear Oliver, who had stayed with me until the very end.

At last, Oliver released the energy he had been gathering up and blasted it at the Witch. It hit her dead on, melting withered skin and bone alike. Her screams could be heard across Algernon and struck fear into the hearts of the wicked. Evil fled in all directions and high in the air, I saw the other witches fleeing from Dalton Castle. The relentless Witch had been destroyed... Her collection of hair locks would never be completed, for she had failed to get mine.

It was at this moment that Ralston decided to make his reappearance. He manifested himself where the Witch had been and glared at Oliver from beneath his snake-like eyelashes. "You are a first class fool boy," Ralston sneered.

Ignoring Ralston's taunts, Oliver only addressed me. "I'll wear him down for you," he told me. He was going to take a shot a Ralston himself! In my mind, I urged Sparks to send Oliver away before it was too late. However Oliver's power was not yet at its peak and I sensed that was what Sparks was waiting for. Oliver's face was scrunched together as he stored more and more energy. "Oh Oliver," I whispered softly.

"When I am spent, you must use the Crown!" Oliver called out to me in a tormented voice. I noticed his knees starting to wobble and his aloft arms begin to shake. "I am too weak to defeat Ralston! I'm not supposed to defeat him... you are! You were the one all along!"

I could no longer hold it in. I ran down the remaining steps, all the while screaming, "Prince Edric! Prince Edric! My little *brother*!"

Oliver sent a beam of light towards Ralston with a grunt. Ralston flew back, stunned, but quite uninjured. Sparks began to lower her shimmering web over Oliver.

"It hasn't been in vain Alice!" Oliver declared bravely. "Trying is never in vain, even if you fail!"

"You were Edric all along," I choked. "How could I have been so stupid! Oh Oliver, I can't fight alone!" I chose to ignore the fact that I was still referring to 'Edric' as 'Oliver'.

"But you're not alone! Remember what Emma said! You are never ever alone, even when it seems like everyone is gone!" Oliver was stuttering and showing signs of great fatigue.

"There's so much I want to say to you!" I came near the webbing that now completely enclosed my brother.

"I will always be with you, no matter what happens! Know that I will fight along side you to the very end! I promise you that sister!" he grunted and fell to one knee. "You were the strongest one the whole time... Nissim knew that." I couldn't bear to see Oliver suffer so… I wanted to reach out towards him, but I was barred by several kinds of magic.

"Alice, I'm running out of time," Sparks called from up above.

I kneeled down beside the magic encased Oliver. He gazed back at me in a determined manner. His body was weak, but his will was strong. He would live. "The suffering must end," he whispered, as his body began to fade away. "I… everyone believes in you… except yourself."

"Wait!" I cried, as he faded into translucence. "How do I use the Crown? What must I do?"

Oliver could only gasp a response. "The power comes from within… The Crown is a facilitator of your own inner light. You must look inside yourself dear sister! It is only there that you will find the power to conquer this evil and it is there, that you shall find yourself. You have all the virtues you need to succeed, for I have seen them! Do not lose hope yet sweet Alice! The darkest hour *is* just before dawn! The hour of despair is nearly upon us… dawn is just below the mountains…"

With that, there was a tremendous clap of thunder and Ralston broke free of Oliver's energy. Sparks released her hold on the webbing and Oliver… Edric, disappeared without a trace. With the departure of Algernon's heir, a cold hard rain began to fall, mingling with my hot tears.

I heard a funny sound as the rain fell upon my head… It was metallic. Quickly I felt the top of my head and realized with a start, that the Crown was now perched upon my brow! "Oliver! Edric! Brother!" I screamed into the dark with panicked anguish. I could see Ralston approaching through the air in the night. He had been slightly weakened, but definitely far from beaten. I backed up through the courtyard and bumped into a large onyx fountain. I was beginning to feel as I had in my nightmares when I faced the Shadow. My downfall had been predicted here… Ralston continued his approach looking quite smug. Obviously he thought it was all over… Perhaps he had reason to be smug.

"How could you!" I yelled at the demon. "My father, my mother, my sisters, my brother… my cat! What more do you want!"

Ralston threw back his deformed head and emitted a wailing laugh. "Only you little one. Only you. And have you I shall… your eternal soul that is!"

In a dreamlike state, I adjusted the Crown upon my head, feeling the unbidden bitter tears still running down my cheeks. I needed someone to help me channel the energy or all was lost. Sparks was too weak to transport me to another realm… I would die if I failed. But who was left to help me? I was alone…

Just then, I felt a brush of wings against my wet ear. It was faithful little Sparks! "I will channel the energy for you," she announced bravely, placing a fist over her stout fairy heart.

"Are you sure you can handle it?" I asked her.

"Of course!" she laughed courageously. "Ralston can't be allowed to create more pain and suffering! Besides, he isn't all powerful... He failed to detect Prince Edric when he was standing right before him! Let's do this together!"

"Together," I whispered, nodding firmly. "I'll let you know when I need the energy transferred," I instructed, clenching my fists. "Stand by and wait for my signal."

I then closed my eyes and tried to concentrate, despite the fact that I wasn't certain just what I was supposed to be concentrating on. No sooner had I closed my eyes, then Sparks began to squeal and the ground beneath me began to crumble and heave up. I opened my eyes with fright. Ralston!

"You are proving to be a most annoying monarch!" Ralston spat out, his cloak flying frantically about in the wind. I could barely keep my eyes open, as the rain now pelted down like little knives. There wasn't time to think, for suddenly I was thrown into the air by a great blast of dark energy, emitted from Ralston. I hadn't even seen it coming. My screams of terror and Spark's tinkling were lost in the great darkness that now engulfed everything. I could hear Ralston's maniacal laughter in the midst of it all.

Keenan's prophecy was coming true. This was the end! The gates of evil were now open wide and pouring their corrupted contents into our world.

The Power Within

I LANDED PAINFULLY on the sharp rocky ground, which had once been the Temple of Courage's beautiful courtyard. Everything around me was warped and twisted by the darkness and suffocating fear in the air. Ralston was tightening his fist over all of Algernon... People everywhere were feeling his power.

The evil in the air was increasing by the second, as darkness continued to pour out of the dark gates. Nissim must have lost his valiant battle in the netherworld. 13 years of trying and all for nothing... Oh Nissim, how I've failed you! The minions of evil from the Fallen's world, would help Ralston to take over Algernon once and for all. Was there nothing I could do? If I defeated Ralston quickly, maybe the damage wouldn't be too great... but how was I going to manage that?

Then in a panic, I felt the top of my head. To my relief, the Crown still sat firmly upon it, as though it had taken root in my skull. I stood up and moaned in pain, for my ankle was badly twisted. I supported myself against a pillar of stone and sighed. My body felt numb from fear and though I wanted to run, there was no place *to* run. Besides, the darkness was so great that I could scarcely see anything... Wait, where was Sparks? My heart began to race as I groped about frantically in search of my fairy companion. Had Ralston disposed of her? Feebly I took a few steps forward and wobbled unsteadily.

"Just great," I muttered. "What a time for my ankle to give out." Squinting into the blackness before me, I called out desperately, "Sparks? Are you out there? Answer me please!" I hobbled around, clutching my arms tightly. "Don't leave me alone," I whispered mostly to myself. I hadn't realized just what a comfort Sparks had been until she was gone. Now I truly was alone.

Suddenly I heard a faint tinkling noise to my right. I swung my head around immediately and wiped the cold sweat from my brow. "Sparks is that you?" I asked the silence. Another round of tinkling replied to my inquiry, but nowhere did I see her familiar yellow glow. Maybe she was hurt and needed my help! I turned and starting limping in the direction of the noise. "Hang on Sparks! I'm coming!" I called, forgetting that I myself was in danger as well. After hobbling a great distance, my legs gave out with weariness and I collapsed, completely out of breath. A sudden uneasiness stole over me and I realized too late, what a mistake it had been to go blundering around in the dark.

There was a tremendous 'thump' behind me and my entire body shuddered. Tremors shook the ground, causing loose pebbles to vibrate. Uncertainly I turned around, only to find an enormous version of Ralston looming under the eerily glowing sky. He was over a hundred times his original size and looked more disgusting than ever.

"Tinkle tinkle Alice!" he laughed, imitating the noise I had been following. It was a trap! I had walked straight into his clutches! With a maliciously crooked mouth, Ralston raised his enlarged foot and attempted to bring it down upon me.

I just managed to break out of my trance-like state of fear and throw myself out of the way. My elbow struck a sharp stone and began to bleed profusely. Tears sprung into my eyes, as I gritted my teeth against the pain. I had to try using the Crown again! It was my only chance! But where was Sparks? I needed her for the energy transferral or I wouldn't be able to hold on long enough to defeat Ralston! I had to buy myself some time, but what could one weak, pathetic little girl do? Then I realized that I was beginning to believe the horrible things Ralston and the Witch had said to me. I shook my head angrily. I wouldn't fall into their trap!

I lifted myself to one knee and reached onto my back for my trusty bow. Aiming an arrow at Ralston's enormous figure, I let go with a 'twang'. I fired another and another and another, until there were no more arrows left in my quiver. I stood up and stared mutely at the monstrosity before me and felt my bow drop onto the hard ground and break in two. My small wooden arrows had bounced cleanly off of Ralston's flowing black cloak and landed harmlessly on the ground all around him.

Doing the only thing I could think of, I turned and fled, holding in screams of pain as I put pressure on my ankle. Then my foot struck something hard and I fell forward... It was the stairs to the Temple! If only I could get to the crystal doors... I could go inside and be safe. Despite what had happened to the courtyard, the Temple of Courage still stood proudly atop its little hill. I began to scramble up the steps, crawling like a little baby.

Ralston laughed thunderously behind me and the icy rain which had slackened, started up again. "You are such a naïve princess!" he called out. "Atop your puny head is the most powerful weapon in the world and you shoot wooden arrows at me! Pathetic!" Ralston sounded very confident that his victory was at hand. I almost agreed with him. "Tell you what child," Ralston's voice was sly, "I'll make you another offer, even though you denied me before, which was very foolish. Hand over the Crown and I shall let you go."

I never halted my ascent, even as I yelled back, indignantly, "Never! You are nothing but a liar and a murderer! You *want* to kill me! You lust to kill me! You've waited a long time to kill me! For you, it will be the achievement of a lifelong obsession!" My foot slipped on the wet stairs, but I pushed on. "I am living proof of your failure! You will never truly rule Algernon until I am dead! So long as there's still a breath in my body, you are a failure!" These words spilled out of my cold lips before I could even comprehend what sort of a reaction they would bring about.

Ralston fairly tore the earth itself apart with his anger. I had been absolutely right, but he would never admit it. "No Princess," Ralston seethed, as he held his long arms up towards the sky, "*you* are the failure. Algernon is mine, whether you live or not." He shook his arms skywards. "Come forth dark forces! Your master is calling!"

I collapsed at the top of the Temple stairs and pressed my wet cheek against the cold marble landing. The crystal doors glowed in front of me like an old friend. I drew myself up against them and stared at Ralston who had his horrid eyes closed and was muttering some sort of incantation. He was bringing forth his minions. I had to stop him, before it was too late! Sparks or no Sparks, I would use the Crown. Pressing my back against the powerful Temple doors, I closed my eyes and attempted to concentrate.

Inner power, inner power… where was it? Surely I had some sort of inner power, but where? A sick feeling clutched at my stomach… What if I didn't have inner power? My thoughts were interrupted by hundreds of painful teeth tearing into my flesh. My eyes snapped open and I let loose a scream. Little wrinkled brown lizards with leather spiked wings, were biting, tearing and scratching my clothes and skin. One turned his head towards me and let loose a gut wrenching hiss, before sinking his teeth into my wrist. I wanted to fight back, but found myself to be paralysed. There must have been some sort of poison in their teeth that was killing me with every bite. It was much more powerful than when I had broken the poison bottle, for I could feel my throat constricting from the venom inflicted by these creatures from the netherworld.

"It's over child! I have won at last!" Ralston cried from above, his black lashes waving wildly. "That is the fearsome poison of the Roa Lizards you feel coursing through your veins! It won't be long now! I shall have the Crown and all of Fadreama!"

I let my head fall back against the crystal doors heavily. I was now so weak that I could hardly draw in a breath… My face… I could feel it turning red and blue… Keenan was right in his prophecy. He saw the

Shadow and the end… It is written in the stars he had said. Destiny is inescapable… Now who had told me that? It was hard to think clearly. I had failed… and in doing so, I had fulfilled my destiny. It wasn't even a noble one as my sisters had experienced. It was terribly disappointing to find I wasn't as important as I'd hoped to be.

"Alice!" a sharp voice chimed by my ear. A bright yellow light appeared before my face, sending glitter flying in all directions. It was the real Sparks, not some concoction of Ralston's. "Alice!" she called again and blew something in my face. It had no smell and I could hardly feel it upon my skin. I was beyond her magic. "You have to use the Crown!" she told me. "It's not too late!" There was very real fear in her eyes. "Don't underestimate the power within!" She desperately touched my forehead… I was unable to speak or move to acknowledge her. At least the lizards had disappeared.

"We are in our darkest hour!" Sparks tinkled fearfully. "Now is the time for dawn to break! Just like Oliver said before, the darkest hour is just before dawn! Please Alice, don't let go! Don't let him win! Fight! For everything you've suffered, fight!" The crystal tears were flowing down her delicate features. "Together we'll beat him! I'll transfer the power when I see the time is right. Can you hear me Alice?" She stared intently into my eyes. "Use the Crown now!"

I felt my eyes drop closed and suddenly all the pain I had been in disappeared. It was a very strange sensation indeed, for I felt calm, serene and light as a feather. I was floating and drifting like a cloud in the sky. Was I really dead this time? No, I wasn't done… I had to fight! I *would* fight Ralston… and even if I didn't win, I wouldn't let it be so easy for him. At that moment, my feet hit something hard and I realized that I was firmly planted on the ground. I couldn't see where I was, for everything was dark.

Then my world went blindingly bright and images started to flash in rapid fire motion. I saw Ms Craddock in her younger days, with her dark hair and sparkling amber eyes. Eve Craddock, who had undertaken a great burden to save her family. She had sacrificed her youth to keep the Princesses of Algernon safe. Before we left, she had said, 'I have faith' and 'never lose hope.' Ms Craddock was with her family now, for she had completed the difficult task. Her image disappeared into the air and I briefly saw the orphanage and Oliver's abandoned hut.

I saw the Deans' and their new wagon, all freshly painted and clean smelling. Petra and its frightened citizens flashed by with slamming doors and bolting locks. Then Xenos ranch appeared before me, with our beautiful ponies… Moondancer, Nightflame, Lady and Storm. There was Matilda Sanderson, with her bright red hair, holding baby Julia, who was gurgling happily. Dear Isadora sat in her rocking chair, with bright and alert eyes. The Forgotten Forest blinked and was gone. Only for a fraction of a second, did I see Charon's blue hair fly by.

The little dwarf man Keenan waved to me from his house by the hill, while sleek white Gimra curled herself protectively around his ankles. I remembered him saying, 'Perhaps your destiny can be altered' and 'You have great abilities Alice, if only you have the courage to use them.' Then Keenan was gone and I saw Carrie with her golden hair flowing in the plains. There was a pleading look in her eyes, as I recalled what she had told me on the last day I saw her, 'Even when everything else has been plunged into darkness, your own light will guide you. If only you believe, then you shall never be alone.'

With Carrie gone, the Harpy we had faced, swooped down towards me, but disappeared before its glinting talons struck. I looked up and found myself in Jadestone once again, with an angry mob in close pursuit. This scene changed abruptly to Captain Wyston's eccentric cabin aboard Nova. First Mate Barlow stood nearby, his giant arms folded peacefully. Wyston was sitting in his worn armchair, repeating the very words he had said to me before, 'You are much more powerful than you think' and 'You may end up playing a very unexpected role.'

I seemed to race through the Sterling Hills, stopping twice and only for a second... One time to see the black panther I had killed and the other time was to see Io standing atop a cliff, cloak fluttering mysteriously. Next an image of the mudslide appeared and of Oliver and I crossing the ancient bridge. Images were coming faster now... as if gaining momentum. The snowstorm came, as did Olav, Sparks and the Hidden Valley of the Fairies.

Then came Devona... but not as I'd seen it with Oliver. It was not a city of misery but rather, a city of glory. The outer wall was not crumbling, but instead was high and sturdy, with guards posted in lookout towers. The sky above was a clear blue and the air was fresh and sweet. The even cobblestone path led over a sparkling brook and into the gleaming city of Devona. The buildings fairly shone, they were so white and the brightly coloured awnings dabbled colour into the atmosphere. I could hear laughter and various market chatter all around... It was unbelievable. Then suddenly, I was on the magnificent 'Royal Way' and Dalton Castle was beckoning at the end of it. The castle towers were pearly, its parapets golden and the royal crest was engraved on the outer drawbridge.

All at once, the scene about me dissolved in a cloud of mist and once again I found myself in a different place. I was now inside a brightly lit castle... the throne room to be precise. Rectangular windows were evenly spaced on the walls all around, with little wooden tables covered in aro-

298 *Candace N. Coonan*

matic flowers underneath each one. Upon the dais, seated on jewelled thrones, sat King Alfred and Queen Rose-Mary.

"Good morning sunshine," my father called out to me in a hearty voice. He beckoned me over with a smile. A beam of light was shining from one of the windows and onto his golden crown.

I found myself skipping joyfully towards the dais, wearing a long blue dress, trimmed in silk. I was happy and content... without a care in the world.

"Come say hello to your baby brother," my mother offered and held up a gurgling raven haired child... Edric.

As I made my approach, three small girls... my sisters... raced out from behind the thrones, playing tag. Their laughter echoed throughout the halls and the court members standing off to the sides smiled knowingly. I stood stark still and gulped. I remembered. I remembered my family and life as a princess... a life I was so brutally denied. From my father's protective smile, to my mother's warm hugs, to my pink canopy bed. It was there in my mind all along... I had but to look.

I grew suddenly cold as I watched Lily, Clara and Emma play and though the room did not disappear, it filled with damp mist. My father stood up. "There's my little girl, though not so little anymore. A grown up lady I should say." He gave me a proud look. "You can defeat Algernon's greatest enemy, Ralston Radburn. There is no question about it. And afterwards, you can do whatever else is requested of you."

"You carry very powerful emotions daughter." My mother dazzled me. "That is where your greatest power lies. Your loves are so deep, so strong, so binding, that nothing can harm you as long as you hold true to them."

"But with those strong bonds, comes terrible pain." Emma was suddenly standing before me. "You love deeply, but you hurt deeply. I know it seems a difficult burden to bear, but it is what makes you... you."

Clara stepped up beside Emma. "None of us are the same... You can't compare yourself to anyone else. Instead of trying to measure up to others, just focus on being the best *you* can be. That's all anyone can do in this short journey called life."

"You will find peace when you can accept and love yourself... strengths and weaknesses alike," Lily offered, as she took her place beside Clara.

And though Oliver was not there in the same form that my sisters were, I could feel his smile, breaking through all barriers that separated us.

"You have the heart to triumph." Lily bowed her head.

"And the strength," added Clara, lowering her own head.

"Don't forget, the wisdom and courage to complete what you have started," Emma finished, before looking downward.

Then one by one, I watched as each member of my family met their destinies. It was painful, but I did not try to reach out. I let them go. I let them rest. As everything became entombed with mist, Nissim called out through it, "We are all with you on this one your Grace. Let's put Ralston in his place!"

Everything faded and when I opened my heavy eyelids, I found myself back in dark Devona. However now, I wasn't lying on the steps of the temple. No, now, I was floating high in the air, surrounded by a tremendous circle of shimmering white light. Out of the corner of my eye, I could see Sparks floating faithfully beside me, her tiny eyes squelched tightly shut. A beam of light was going from me to her and back into my outstretched hands.

A few paces from me, shrunken to normal size, Ralston stood shooting a beam of dark energy. The beam was as thick and noxious as his very soul... if he still had one.

I was not yet shooting my light towards Ralston... rather I was dodging his attacks in the air. No mystical forces were going to control my actions for me... That was something I had to do on my own. Consciously, I allowed myself and Sparks to float back down to the crystal doors on the steps of the Temple. My feet made contact with the solidness and I braced myself against the door.

"No more running, nor more hiding," I whispered out loud. "I've always avoided my fears... or complained that I was tired or hungry. No more," I shook my head, "no more... like Carrie, I've no more tears to cry."

With a great effort, I stepped away from the Temple doors and stood on the very edge of the stairs, still facing Ralston, who narrowed his eyes at me. Did I detect some fear?

"You can't do it!" he screamed at me.

"I can!" I shouted back, encouraging the light to grow.

"You will fall!" His eyelashes grew longer as though trying to escape.

"I will stand right here and when day breaks, this is where I shall still be standing! They say my destiny is to fail... Then I defy destiny! I shall change destiny!" My words seemed amplified, although I spoke in whispers.

"You won't!" Ralston shot another beam towards me, which bounced dangerously close to my head, but instead reflected off of the crystal doors.

"I will," I replied defiantly, "and you know why? Because I believe! I believe in the peaceful life my parents wanted! I believe in the bonds I share with my family that extend beyond death! I believe in the goodness that still resides deep in the hearts of all people! I believe in this land that so much was sacrificed for!" Now it was my turn to narrow my eyes. "But most of all, I believe in myself! My inner light! It may be small now, but it burns bright and with time and experience, it will grow!"

I released the light from my hands, which was fairly burning me. "Destroy me then!" Ralston screamed. "Kill me!"

"NO!" I yelled as I focused the beam from my hands. "I am not like you! I do not lust for blood or death. I do not seek to kill anyone... even you!" I smiled and stared intently for the first time, directly into the depths of his hideous eyes.

He scowled at me... just as defiantly as I had towards him. "Then evil shall triumph!" Ralston seethed.

I released the full force of the energy I had built up. I let all of the light leave my hands and head towards him. With my last ounce of strength, I retorted, "But it shall not conquer!"

Ralston let loose an agonized shriek and an enormous explosion blinded me. I was thrown backwards with tremendous force and gently slipped into unconsciousness.

CHAPTER THIRTY-EIGHT

Dawn

I AWOKE GRADUALLY to the tinkling of bells and a gentle hand on my forehead. "Sparks?" I murmured and opened my heavy lids. It took my eyes a moment to adjust, for everything was a blur of colours. When the world finally came back into focus, I gave a little start at the white bearded face staring down at me. The kind eyes shimmered with happiness when they saw me wake. "Nissim?" I breathed.

A look of enormous relief swept over his kindly old features that actually seemed to have become slightly younger than the last time I had laid eyes on him. "Ah, so you have returned to the land of the living at last Princess." Nissim gave me a gentle smile and patted my forehead. "I was beginning to wonder if you had decided to stay with your family..."

"But I said you would never do that to us!" a sweet bell-like voice piped up.

I sat up quickly and exclaimed joyously, "Sparks! You're safe!" She floated before me, looking prettier then ever in all her glowing glory.

"I was just going to say that," Nissim told Sparks with a slightly annoyed tone. "I knew Alice wouldn't take such a route. Her destiny is far higher than even a noble death."

"I thought my destiny was to die at the hands of Ralston." I was becoming confused and my head was swirling with thoughts and emotions.

Nissim threw back his head and gave a thunderous laugh. "Oh quite the contrary my dear. You were meant to *triumph* over Ralston. Although," he looked grave, "it could have gone either way. Just because something is your destiny, it doesn't mean that is how it will be. We all have choices to make... We can choose to follow, or to take a stand and lead. You my dear, did exactly as I had hoped you would. I am very proud of you." Nissim was fairly beaming.

Rubbing the back of my neck, I gave a great yawn. "So Ralston is gone then? The gates of evil are closed? Algernon is finally free?"

"Whoa!" Nissim held up his hands. "Slow down, slow down. One question at a time." He rocked back on his heels, for he was squatting by my side. "Ralston is banished. You saw to that. He is trapped within the Land of the Undead. The dark gates are closed and evil is locked out for the time being." Nissim held out his hand to me in a gesture to stand up. "So, Algernon is indeed very free."

I feared falling over from my injuries as Nissim helped me to my feet, but I soon discovered that my ankle no longer hurt and that the rest of my cuts had disappeared. A slight weight upon my brow, reminded me that the Crown was still perched on my head. The Crown's magic, in combination with Sparks and her healing abilities, must have put me on the mend.

As I gazed around at the scene before me, I was at a loss for words. I was still at the top of the Temple of Courage's steps, which had gone unscathed by Ralston's attacks. Even the crystal doors still shimmered brilliantly behind me, their energy pulsing and coursing throughout the stone. The courtyard... it had been restored to its former beauty. All of the jagged cliffs Ralston had shot out of the ground were gone and all around was soft green forest. I could hear birds chirping from within the foliage and a soft breeze rustled the fresh leaves.

I clasped my hands together in awe and grabbed Nissim's heavy robes in ecstasy. "Oh Nissim! Everything's restored!"

He stroked his beard thoughtfully. "Weeelll... not quite. Things under Ralston's enchantment are certainly restored to goodness, such as the Virtue Temples and Dalton Castle. The skeleton guards and court at the castle are human again... as are the spirits of Devona. Everyone who Ralston put a spell on, had their lives held in suspension, so they are exactly as they were before the siege 13 years ago." Nissim looked sad for a moment. "There will be a lot of rebuilding to do though... but in time, Algernon will prosper once again."

"Oh Alice look!" Sparks pulled gently at my hair, in an attempt to turn my gaze eastward. The heavens above were incredibly clear and tinted a blush pink. The last stars of night were fading away, as the sun began to rise over the mountaintops.

"Dawn," I breathed in awe, feeling my body tingle with happiness.

Nissim leaned on his tall staff and looked pleased. "Yes, the first dawn Devona has seen in a long time. The sun will cleanse the land and purify any remnants of Ralston's reign. Then the moon will cool everything in its silver light and the cycle of life will have begun again...just as things should be."

A tiny inkling of fear crept over my soul, as the awe began to wear off and anxiety of the future set in. "Do you think Ralston will ever come back?" I asked Nissim in a tight voice.

He laid a hand upon my shoulder and stared off into the distance. "Prophesying the future is a tricky task, my dear Alice. One can predict all they like and be really quite wrong... Even *I* am prone to mistakes every millennia or so." He winked at me. "Take each day one at a time.

The past is gone and the future will be here soon enough. Work on improving the present. Ralston is back with his master for now."

I knew that I wouldn't get any more specific of an answer out of Nissim, even if he did know what the future held. So I tried to discover answers to a new question... a question that had been weighing heavily on my mind. The question that in some ways, had started everything. "Nissim?"

"Yes your Grace?"

"What happened on the night of the siege?" Nissim of Quinn was truly the only person who could answer the inquiry that had been posed to Ms Eve Craddock around 20 days ago.

"Meaning you and your sisters, or your brother?" Nissim's eyes twinkled.

"Both." I shook my head voraciously and Sparks made herself comfortable on my shoulder.

Nissim took a deep breath and straightened his tasselled rope belt. "I was once the advisor to King Alfred, as I had been to his father before him and his before that. I have been the advisor to the rulers of Algernon ever since the Light Dynasty began, thousands of years ago."

I gasped, "But that would make you so old!"

"Indeed," Nissim laughed and patted my back. "Very old, but I am no ordinary man either. I'll tell you about it someday, but not today, for that is a different story. I have much to teach you... Oh, but now I'm all off track!" Nissim looked flustered and then regained his composure. "Now, I told King Alfred that darkness was coming and that we needed to take precautions to protect the kingdom. However when things have been calm since before anyone can remember, people start to make mistakes. Guards don't guard as they should and armies don't train as they should. There was a lack of security and we all paid dearly for it. Ralston attacked one morning and by noon, Algernon was under his control. King Alfred and Queen Rose-Mary were killed. The Crown was locked away in the Temple, for there had never been any use for it for some time, therefore King Alfred had no weapon."

Then Nissim's tone changed to one of pride. "This is where I came in. The children... the four Princesses and the little Prince, had been sent to the nursery. The Queen had dispatched them there by a secret passage, moments before her death. Two nurses were sent after them, one for the girls and one for the boy... I alone knew that nurses were no match for what we were up against. The Princesses' nurse didn't even make it out of the throne room before being killed. I knew there wasn't much time, so seeing as there was nothing left to do for the royal couple, I moved swiftly along with my young apprentice, Arvad, to try and overtake the witch army."

Nissim sighed. "I was delayed and by the time I reached the nursery, only the Princesses were left. Luckily Arvad managed to steal back Edric from a witch, who had murdered the nurse. I fled north with all four of you children." Nissim was nodding his head, as if to attest to this fact. "Let's just say I know a thing or two about destiny and safety, which is why the girls went one way and the boy another. Everyone's memories were erased by a little magic spell and then you were hidden... in the Forgotten Forest to be precise. I knew that there would come a time when the royal children would step out of the shadows and into the light once again, so I arranged for all of that. There's not really much left to tell." Nissim eyed me carefully.

"That's a lot of information to take in," I told him, shaking my spinning head. "So we were meant to meet up with Oliver all along... You always knew that he was Prince Edric?"

"Of course I did child! Of course!" Nissim seemed amused. "I decided that young Oliver... er... Edric, would be a lot safer if nobody knew his true identity until the time was right.

I hung my head sadly and wondered where Oliver was at this very moment. "I really miss him," I admitted, feeling a great emptiness inside. I had won and yet, I had lost so much in the process.

"I wouldn't worry too much Princess," Nissim smiled mysteriously. "You have a long life ahead of you and I don't think it will be an uneventful one. Someday, you may see Oliver again. I know things seem very mixed up right now, but trust me, in time, things work themselves out."

"I'll always be here for you Alice!" Sparks piped up. "I'm never leaving your side again!"

"Oh Sparks." I smiled down at the cheerful fairy. At least I had her with me... I hadn't known her for long, but since she had acted as my channeller, I felt a deep connection with the fairy. We had a bond, fused together by trust and desperation. It was unlike any kind of relationship one could have with another human... My ties to Sparks transcended the physical world and melded into the spiritual.

"And you always have me." Nissim nodded in a grandfatherly way. "I will stay by your side and serve you faithfully."

"What do you mean, serve me?" I asked suspiciously. Ever since I had awakened, I had sensed something in the air... something new and altered... I wasn't the same person I had been before. Although nothing had been said, I knew that Nissim had something to tell me.

Nissim made his way over to the edge of the stairs and stared off into the forest path. "Soon people will be coming," he mused. Then turning back to me, he tapped his staff on the ground and suddenly I was wearing an elegant, but simple silver dress, with blue velvet trimmings and pearls sewn into the hem. My hair was not put up, but lay straight down my back, with the slightest curls at the bottom and silver ribbons woven through it.

Sparks laughed happily and sprayed fairy dust all over me. Now my dress held a distinct fairy sparkle, as did my hair and skin. The refreshing scent of lavender drifted around me, enthralling my senses. Still I couldn't help but be bewildered.

Tapping my silver shoes on the ground, I gave Nissim a look of helplessness. "What's going on?" I knew I was a princess, but there was something strange about the way Nissim had been talking.

"Alice," Nissim firmly took my shoulders and faced me squarely, "you do realize that you're the only member of the Light Dynasty that's alive, don't you?"

"Oliver's alive!" I protested.

"Yes," Nissim admitted slowly, "he's alive, but for all practical purposes he's dead. Edric is the heir, but he is no longer with us, therefore he forfeits his claim.

"And that means?" I knew exactly what it meant, but I needed Nissim to say it.

"You must be Queen Alice of Algernon, of course." Nissim confirmed my thoughts. "It is your royal obligation... your duty."

I was beginning to wonder whether there would ever be an end to my obligations and duties. I had thought that once Ralston was defeated, I'd be able to go back to my old way of life. I knew now that it would never happen. Events had been set into motion that could not be stopped. The wheel of fate had begun to turn and it was beyond any earthly power to stop it. I had left the old Alice behind a long time ago... I was still the same person, but I was different. I had grown and matured. No, I wasn't perfect by any stretch of the imagination. I was still fanciful (that is, I still believed in my fairy prince) and I still had fears and weaknesses. However, I now had something that I hadn't possessed before... and that was confidence. I had a belief in myself... it wasn't very much just yet, but somehow I knew it would grow with experience. My very own inner light. I had finally learned to have faith and when I needed my light, it hadn't failed me.

"The people need a leader your Grace," Nissim pressed me, but I silenced him with a soft wave.

"I know Nissim," I replied softly. "I understand... well, sort of. I'm learning." I gave him a smile. "I don't know anything about being a queen, but I'll give it my best."

"And I'm going to help her!" Sparks declared, just as a crowd began to gather in the Temple courtyard, in accordance with Nissim's prediction. Right at the head of the crowd, I spotted the innkeeper, Mary Buxabee. She recognized me immediately and waved enthusiastically.

"You must make a speech." Nissim gave me a slight push forward.

I trembled at the thought. I still had much to learn. "But I don't know anything about making speeches," I hissed back.

"Just say what's in your heart," Nissim advised. "Don't try to be anything you're not, but remember, you *are* a queen."

The crowd was growing larger by the minute, as former skeleton guards raced down from the castle, along with the court and many citizens of Devona. Thousands of faces stared expectantly up at me.

Clearing my choked up throat, I addressed the crowd. "Greetings people of Algernon!" What to say now? I paused and then continued, "M... my name is Princess Alice." At this Nissim frowned slightly, but I ignored it. "I am the fourth and youngest daughter of your late King Alfred and Queen Rose-Mary. The other Princesses... Lily, Clara and Emma, have passed on. They are now the official guardians of three of the Virtue Temples... Heart, Strength and Wisdom respectively. The official heir to the throne, O... Prince Edric, is no longer in this realm. He fought valiantly against Ralston, but in order to spare his life, he was sent to the fairy realm of Alexandria." I gulped, for now I had a major request to make... at least I thought of it as a request. "I am therefore the only member of the Light Dynasty left in Algernon and... if you'll have me, I should be honoured to be your queen."

"She wears the sacred Crown!" a voice shouted out.

"And she banished Ralston!" another cried victoriously.

"Saved us all, she did!" a still louder voice exclaimed.

Then all at once, the crowd began to shout, "Hail Queen Alice! Long live the Queen of Algernon!" This shouting spread throughout the city... and I dared to think even the kingdom. Voices from as far away as the Forgotten Forest echoed throughout the land. Still the people wanted me to say something, for the expectancy in their gazes was undeniable.

As I prepared myself to speak, the sun cleared the mountains and shone warmly down onto my face, greeting me like an old friend. There were tears in my eyes, but they weren't tears of fear, but rather joy at the new life I had been handed. It wouldn't be easy, but nothing in life ever is. "My good people," I declared, "just as a new day begins in Algernon, a new life begins for all. A new Age of Light is beginning! Much has been sacrificed for this, but together, we shall rise again! Filled with hearts of strength, wisdom and courage, together, united as one, we will rebuild our kingdom and create a bright and prosperous future for all!"

A great cheer went up at the conclusion of this speech and spread throughout the land once again. I wiped my profusely sweating palms on my nice new dress and gave Nissim a shaky grin. He nodded with a smile, obviously very pleased with my performance. Sparks still sat respectably on my shoulder, waving her tiny fairy arms at the crowd, enjoying the attention.

Nissim then took my arm and began to lead me down the Temple stairs. As soon as we reached the bottom, the guards parted the crowd and escorted me down the pine scented trail and back out into the open air.

"You did well your Grace," Nissim told me, his beard swaying as we walked.

"Thank you." I blushed. "I was frightened, but I still did it."

"That is excellent. You are well on your way," Nissim agreed. "But still, learning is a lifelong process. I have much to teach you."

"And I have much to learn." I laughed, feeling happy for the first time in a long time. I could almost feel my inner light growing with every step forward I took. We rounded the last corner and stood for a brief moment. To my left was the road I had taken to Devona... To my right was the castle, gleaming with dew. The choice was always there, as far as destiny was concerned. You could either go left or right, forwards or backwards, the decision lay in the individual.

Putting on a brave smile, I threw my shoulders back and held my head high. Then, with the sun rising swiftly in the morning sky, I turned towards Dalton Castle and headed home.

Appendices
to
The Darkest Hour

The Creation of Io

The horse's hooves thudded dully on the grass covered ground, as Emma rode swiftly northward. This was in direct contrast to the previous day's ride, which had been decidedly southward. Why had this 18 year old lady changed directions so suddenly and where was she going? More importantly, what would she do when she got there?

Emma's long dark hair flowed behind her in the wind, fluttering and dancing like a flag mounted high atop a castle tower. Her gentle features were contorted painfully, as tears flowed from her oceanic blue eyes, leaving trails in the black soot, which concealed her fair complexion. She held her body rigidly in the saddle, as if to prevent any involuntary movement.

"I mustn't look back... I mustn't look back," Emma muttered to herself through tight lips. She blinked rapidly as another flood of tears momentarily blurred her vision. Holding firmly to her horse, Lady, Emma kept her gaze fixed stubbornly northward. Her tattered and fire blackened dress whipped sharply in the wind.

Anyone observing Emma's flight would truly believe that she was leaving... abandoning the quest and her own sister. This of course, was Emma's intent. It all had to be convincing and realistic, no matter how much it hurt. Deep within her heart, Emma knew that one look back, however brief, would destroy her plan before it even began. The sight of her youngest sister Alice, standing heart broken among the waving prairie grass, would cause Emma to turn around and go back to comfort her. Even young Oliver, who had been lying in a deep sleep upon the uneven ground, would draw her back. Oliver was injured... that much Emma knew. As to the severity and nature of the injury, she was uncertain, but there was no doubt about it, something had happened to Oliver.

Emma shut her heart to the possible consequences of what she was doing. She was a comforter and a healer by nature. To turn her back on herself was a very difficult thing to do. Though she was only 18 and had no children of her own, the maternal instinct was strong in her blood, as it had been with her mother, though she had never even known her. What Emma was doing went against every fiber in her body and it was ripping her apart inside. She was... no, she *had* broken her little sister's heart.

Emma squeezed her eyes tightly shut, but could not block out the image of Alice's anguished face. There had been shock and disbelief there... but mostly fear. Yes, there had been a great deal of fear in Alice's dark eyes. She would be panicking now... looking for a way out.

And yet within the darkness, Emma had seen a glimmer of hope... a

312 *Candace N. Coonan*

small spark of light that had the power to banish darkness. Alice had refused to follow her and that was reassuring. Emma had presented her with the choice, hoping for this result and though it pained her, it was also a very promising sign. Alice would press on with the quest to find Prince Edric and she, Emma, would assist her in secret.

It had been prophesized that Emma would have a series of difficult decisions to make. Leaving Alice was only the first of many and Emma knew this. At first she hadn't believed in the prophecies of Keenan the dwarf man, for she knew that the future was a very precarious thing. Predicting it was dangerous business, but then the prophesy made to her other sister, Clara, had come true. A fire in a storm... Emma shivered. These were the words spoken to lively, adventurous Clara.

Emma fought back the bitter tears with all of her strength. If only she had listened! If only she had the power to see like Lily! Then Clara might not have died in the Temple of Strength, the night before. Alas, Emma had not heeded the warnings and instead pushed the others onward in the quest. Destiny had something in store for everyone, but whether or not that could be predicted... well, for Alice's sake, Emma prayed to the Power, that this was not the case. Doom had been foreseen for her youngest sister. Still, Emma had to believe there was hope, for only now had she truly begun to see.

Out of the pain and sorrows endured along the quest to the capital city Devona, a pattern had begun to emerge. Emma had wisdom buried deep inside her soul and because of this, she had finally become aware of the pattern. All of the pieces were beginning to fall into place. Emma had then formulated a plan within mere seconds, from which there would be no turning back.

It was in principle, really quite simple and Emma chided herself for not discovering it sooner. The kingdom of Algernon had four Virtue Temples, located in various regions and landscapes. Nissim, the wizard, had chosen four people, specifically, Emma and her sisters, to find the heir to the throne and thus challenge the usurping demon ruler, Ralston Radburn. So, four Temples, four maidens... equipped with four mysterious golden pendants. Emma never would have seen the connection, if it weren't for the deaths of two of her sisters.

Sweet, quiet Lily had been taken at the first magical point... the Heart Temple. Then, Clara had fallen at the Temple of Strength. There were now two temples left and two sisters. It was at this point that Emma saw the pattern... their company would press on until each had perished at a temple. It was similar to some sort of warped game, but Emma had caught on after only two rounds. Now she refused to play, at least not by the rules anyway. The stars were stacked against them, but Emma was determined to change that, even if it consumed her very identity.

Hardening her heart and stifling her emotions, Emma had feigned anger and defeat. She had yelled at her little sister and then left her alone with the injured boy Oliver. Where he fit in all of this, Emma did not know, but she maintained that he should have stayed in the Forgotten Forest. At any rate, Emma had left, which was the hardest decision she had ever made in her life. Still, had she remained with the group, they all would have died and the quest would have failed. Of this, she was certain.

No, instead she would leave and protect Alice and Oliver in secret. Emma sold herself to the mysterious and unseen. She planned to vanish with the winds, become one with the shadows and set with the sun when the time came. She would accomplish all of this in her mortal form, fragile, yet determined. What Emma did not realize, was that this was the passion and determination handed down to her from her mother, Queen Rose-Mary. Such action was in tune with the former Queen's attitude.

Emma reasoned that Ralston and the Witch would forget about her if she left... in fact, she was counting on that reaction. She would then be free to do what she must. Despite all of this determination though, Emma was hurting... badly. Things could never be the same again and Emma knew it. She hadn't even allowed herself to hug Alice goodbye. Would she ever see her again?

Emma knew that Alice was now out of her line of sight, but still, she did not turn around to look. The temptation to ride back was still far too great. Emma loosened her grip at last on Lady's reigns and, drawing herself up high in the saddle, drew a steadying breath.

"I need to transform myself," Emma mused out loud. "I require a new unrecognizable image... not to mention skills. So many skills... and little time to acquire them in." Emma sighed uncertainly; it was not an easy task she had placed before herself. Though she did not want to, Emma knew that there was only one place... one person, whom she could turn to for assistance. He would be expecting her.

*   *   *

At the closing of the day, Emma at last spied the odd little shape that was Keenan's house. She feared returning to him, but he was the only one with the power to help her. Emma rode Lady to the door and noticed pale candlelight flickering through the drawn curtains.

"I can't turn back now," she whispered and dismounted Lady, tying her to a post conveniently planted near a watering trough. Surely that hadn't been there during her last visit.

Emma's feet made scarcely a sound as she strode up to Keenan's door and knocked gently. As she awaited a response, she wondered where Alice and Oliver were. She prayed that wherever they had gone, they were safe.

A faint voice from within the house called out, "Come in Emma. The door is unbarred."

Emma opened the door quickly and entered, all the while keeping her eyes upon the ground. "I have returned Keenan," she whispered. At last she looked up and found Keenan eyeing her gently from his willow rocking chair near the hearth. Emma stared at him resolutely. "You know why I have returned. I dare say you knew I would. I place myself in your hands to make of me what you will."

Keenan gave a small smile. "You are truly brave Emma. I wasn't certain that you would actually make the decision to come back. I didn't think you trusted me very much." He twisted a few whiskers on his grey beard. "I am pleased that you are here though. With your help, perhaps Alice's fate can be changed." Keenan beckoned Emma over to a wooden chair, similar to his own, but without the rockers. There had been no chairs when Emma had come with the others.

"You must forgive my tears Master Keenan," Emma told him ashamedly as she delicately seated herself opposite the dwarf. "This has been a terribly trying day. I just want to know that my sister is safe."

"Well now, that is easy enough to do." Keenan seemed to have lost the forgetful and simple air that he had demonstrated before. Now, he had the focus of a wizard and the aura of a great master. He indicated towards the fire. "The flames will show you all you need to know. Just look deeply into them and focus your mind on what you wish to see."

Wiping her eyes, Emma turned her gaze into the inferno within the hearth. At first, all she saw was the orange and yellow flames curling and flickering as though fighting one another. Then slowly, images began to emerge... shadows at first, but quite suddenly they developed into clear pictures. Emma saw a bright white house with sweetheart roses climbing all over one side. This image suddenly changed to the interior of a house, decorated everywhere with flowers. It looked like a kitchen... there was a table... and three people sitting around it eating.

"It's Alice and Oliver!" Emma breathed a sigh of relief. "There's another girl, but I don't know who she is... Her hair is like the sun." She furrowed her brow suddenly in confusion. "What is that across Oliver's eyes? A bandage?" Emma's hand flew to her face in understanding. "He must have burned his eyes in the fire! Poor boy!"

"Listen for voices," Keenan probed. "Discover what they are saying. It may help us."

Emma pursed her lips together tightly and strained her ears. The crackling noises within the fire seemed to be changing pitch... softening and become more like voices. The girl with golden hair was speaking. "Here you go Oliver," she said, "I cut up the meat too... here's a fork. Can you manage?"

"Yes Carrie, thank you so much. You're very helpful," Oliver told her with a smile.

"Oliver can't see if you blush," Alice suddenly spoke up in an amused tone, to which the girl called Carrie, looked uncomfortable.

Emma mused out loud, forgetting she was supposed to be listening, "That other girl is called Carrie and she seems to really like Oliver... Alice doesn't understand. And Oliver... Oliver must be blinded... How horrible!"

"If you speak, you shall lose your focus," Keenan observed and it was true, for Emma lost not only the voices, but the picture as well. Dejected, she looked up. "Don't feel too bad," Keenan soothed. "You learned what you needed to know. Your sister and the boy are safe for now."

"Is my part over in this tale?" Emma looked sad as she reseated herself before the fire. "I haven't been gone long and yet I feel as though I'm a lifetime away from those I love."

Keenan reached out and gently patted Emma's hand. "I saw more in the flames than I told you before." He looked slightly guilty. "Your role is definitely not over Emma. You must help Alice and Oliver... They will need you. Are you willing to do what you must to help them?"

Emma nodded vigorously. There were no longer tears in her eyes, as Alice was safe for the moment and now Emma must put her plan into action. "I will do whatever you say Master Keenan. You are no ordinary dwarf."

"True." Keenan smiled slightly. "Once, long ago, I dwelt in Jadestone near the mighty Jade River." His voice lowered. "There are few who know this... perhaps none living who do; I was a member of a secret society of sorts. We were known as the Vanishing Lights... though hardly any actually knew us by this name. To ordinary folk, we were merely strange, cloaked strangers who appeared and disappeared with the night." Keenan looked pleased with the memory. "There were many of us in the order and it required strict training under a Master. Unfortunately, by the time I had attainted Master status, we were all nearly killed off."

"By Ralston?" Emma suggested.

Keenan shook his head. "No, it was before Ralston came to power. A rival order from Denzel, called the Black Daggers, all but destroyed us. My own Master... his name was Liam of the Ellwood... he was killed by a Black Dagger. So many lives were lost... The society eventually splintered and crumbled. I am all that is left and soon I shall be gone as well."

Emma clenched her fists together tightly and jumped up, all but knocking her chair over. She was swiftly on her knees before Keenan, head bowed obediently. "Please Keenan," she begged. "Please! You must teach me to be a Vanishing Light! Help me learn! I will do anything if it saves Alice from the fate you prophesied!"

Keenan crinkled his wizened face up into a pained grin. "That," he helped Emma to her feet, "is exactly what I wanted to hear. I never had an apprentice before, but I shall be glad of one now. But," he stood up quickly and made his way over to a wooden trunk, partially hidden within the shadows of a corner, "it shall not be easy. The training is difficult… not just physically, but mentally also."

Emma followed Keenan with quiet footsteps. Her mind was made up; she must become a Vanishing Light. Her destiny was unfolding and it was much greater than she could have ever imagined.

Keenan opened the ancient trunk, disturbing the thick dust as he did so. From within the vessel, he withdrew two dark coloured cloaks. "When you wear this cloak, you will cease to be Emma," Keenan explained, "just as I shall cease to be Keenan… I am cloaked as we speak. We will be Vanishing Lights, with no earthly name. Our presence will come and go as the winds and we shall be beyond all mortal things, save death. Are you still willing?" Keenan handed Emma the cloak.

With trembling hands, Emma deftly pinned the garment about her neck. Her stomach turned and she felt her heart tighten, but she answered firmly, "Yes, Master." She would not leave her sister to a horrible death. No, she would become what she must… she would do what was required, forsaking all else. This was what it meant to be a leader. She noticed that Keenan had donned his own cloak, which made him seem taller and younger. It was strange… as though he was really someone else and that 'Keenan' was merely a guise.

"Come." Keenan reached out his hand and Emma placed hers into it. She started, for the hand was not that of the decrepit dwarf, but firm and strong, like that of a young man. Emma could not seen Keenan's face, for he had pulled the hood down until he was bathed in shadows. Slowly, he waved a smooth hand through the air in a circle and with a strange gust of air, a green portal appeared. "We must go into the Old World," Keenan explained, "for that is the proper place for a Vanishing Light to train."

"The Old World?" Emma repeated, more intrigued than frightened now.

Keenan nodded vigorously… Yes, he was now taller… even more so than Emma. "It is the past. Back to the time before Denzel was evil, when all the world was still young. We shall go to the years when the Vanishing Lights were founded, as all trainees do." Keenan seemed strangely pleased. "The year will be 230. This is when King Edgar established Devona." He paused. "You tremble my Lady. There is no need to be frightened. Though we will spend many years training in the past, no time will pass in the present. When all is complete, we shall return to this very moment and you will go forth to complete your destiny and I mine."

"I am not frightened," Emma replied and squeezed his hand. "Let us go now, I have much to learn."

With that, Keenan and Emma stepped into the green light and vanished completely from the world. Some distance away in Verity, Alice glanced up at the evening sky as she walked quietly in the night with Carrie. The stars twinkled and blinked overhead, but a particularly bright one caught her eye as flickered violently, before vanishing altogether.

Forest Lore: Nissim's Plan

Nissim was exhausted. After all, he was 3675 years old, which, though not unheard of for his native race, was nevertheless an accomplishment. Long lives were a natural characteristic of his people. Why, Nissim's own father was still alive and well, though impossibly old. Unfortunately the same could not be said for his mother, who had not been of the same race as his father and thus had passed into the Spirit Realm long ago. Still, after everything Nissim had lived through during the course of his long life, it was a wonder he found the strength to rise in the morning.

Mission after mission, age after age... Nissim had faced many. Now he was presented with quite possibly the greatest challenge of all. So much depended upon his choices and though he had great wisdom, there was always some measure of uncertainty in all that he did. Would he choose right? Would all go as planned? Even a wizard could not go back in time... though he had heard that the secret group known as the Vanishing Lights could do so for training purposes. Alas, he was not a Vanishing Light, nor had he any desire to be... they demanded too much from a person. He required complete freedom to perform his work and the Lights called for strict allegiance. Nissim would not allow himself to be bound by petty laws that might interfere with his purposes.

Nissim was not cruel by any means. He simply knew that sacrifices sometimes had to be made and that even the right choice often had negative repercussions. He hadn't lived this long without learning that much. Even magic was a dangerous thing, for to use it, one must give back and the giving almost always came directly from the taker. Fortunately for Nissim, he was trained so that he knew the balance and could thus survive while using powerful enchantments. Now, he was planning to weave a very elaborate and sustained spell, the likes of which he had not used in this age. Someone would have to suffer though, for he would not be around to support the magic. Nissim bowed his head in agony... he did not like to draw mortals into his plans, but now he had no choice.

Devona was lost to the demons that he had foreseen long ago. If only the King had heeded his warnings! Algernon had the weakest army in Fadreama and the most need for protection! Even the remote northern kingdoms had great armies to protect their people! Algernon had experienced too much peace and the rulers had become complacent. How anyone could be complacent living beside Denzel, was beyond Nissim's reckoning. Algernon required a ruler who knew of Denzel's power first hand and feared the Dark Coast enough to be vigilant. The Alexandrian Fairies had excellent forces, but Nissim was wary against setting a foreigner on the throne. Most other nobles in Algernon, though loyal, were fools better suited to lounging than ruling. No, the throne must go to one of the children.

"Ah, the poor babes of Queen Rose-Mary," Nissim spoke these words aloud.

Arvad, Nissim's apprentice, lifted his head from the tree upon which he was leaning. "What about the children Master? They are asleep in the wagon." Arvad's long dark locks revealed that his age was nowhere near Nissim's but more around that of a 23 year old. He was still young and very much a mortal human. Nissim disliked apprentices in general. He hadn't the patience for them, but Arvad was an obligation. His mother had been a dear friend and upon her death, the boy had found himself alone in the world at the tender age of 10. So it was that Nissim had taken the boy in for fostering, hoping to make him into something of a wizard. Even as the responsibility had been thrust upon him, Nissim did regard Arvad as a son. Yet his aims to make the man a wizard, were rapidly dissolving.

"It's nothing Arvad." Nissim waved his wooden staff. "Let them sleep, but we must move on. The sun shall be rising soon and our time grows short. The children must be hidden and I must return to Devona. I fear much evil has transpired after our escape, but we cannot think of that now."

Arvad nodded obediently and scrambled off to the wagon, his skinny features making him look rather awkward. Nissim raised himself off the dusty ground and gazed thoughtfully about the forest. This was the perfect place to hide someone, for the growth was thick and unsuited for travel.

The plan was basic enough. Nissim would leave the young Prince under Arvad's care and the four Princesses with a female guardian. Their memories would be erased using a mild charm and they would grow up unaware of their past... at least until the appointed time arrived. Nissim would make certain of that.

Stiff from sleeping on the hard ground, Nissim hobbled sorely over to the front seat of the wagon. Arvad extended a friendly hand down towards the wizard. "Let me help you Master."

Hoisting himself up with Arvad's hand, Nissim clapped his apprentice on the back. "Thank you my boy. You are a great help to an old man."

Arvad looked startled for a second, his tanned features blanching. "You're not old Master! Your kind ages differently, that's all! If I were of your people, I would be a better apprentice to you." Arvad stared off into the dense forest with a troubled look and he gripped the horse's reins tightly.

Nissim gently patted Arvad's arm in a moment of tenderness from his harsh mission. "Never speak of such things my boy. One does not need blood for the ties of kinship, nor to be a great wizard. You are my son Arvad, don't ever forget that."

Arvad's face lit up and he said no more, for he sensed that Nissim wished to leave the subject be. There were of course, more important matters at hand.

*   *   *

As Arvad brought the wagon into a small clearing with a broken down thatched hut, Nissim held up his hand. "Hold Arvad. This is the spot. We must be swift, so quickly lad, take the baby Edric."

Handing the reins over to Nissim, Arvad scrambled into the back of the wagon where the royal children lay in an enchanted sleep. Gently he picked up the one year old prince who was heir to the kingdom. A shock of black hair fell over the boy's closed eyes, not unlike Arvad's. They were similar enough in appearance to proclaim kinship, which was part of Nissim's plan. Arvad was to foster Edric under the ruse of being the boy's uncle. This was the extent of Arvad's knowledge: raise the boy and teach him some of the wizard's craft. All else would take care of itself, Nissim had said. Arvad unloaded some supplies as well, then stood obediently beside the wagon, awaiting Nissim's parting words.

Nissim gave Arvad a kind smile. "Take good care of the Prince now. Raise him properly, as I raised you." Nissim's features grew serious. "Do not call him Edric though... his name will be Oliver Renwick. Let him believe he is a peasant, for this will keep him safe. I will return if I can, but matters may be pressing and if so, a visit will not be possible." Nissim looked around. "The forest will shield you both from harm... it has an essence all its own. Pay it homage and you will be well cared for. Now I must be off. Take care my son." Nissim turned his head quickly and gave the reins a whip, sending the horses off into a swift trot. He could not let Arvad see his pain. Nissim was a wizard and as such, was trained to control his emotions, yet they raged inside. Nissim knew he would never see Arvad alive again.

It took most of Nissim's strength to regain his composure, yet he did so quickly. The first portion of his plan had been set into action and now he must complete it. Nissim glanced into the back of the wagon at the four sleeping Princesses. He crinkled his brow at the youngest child, Princess Alice. This tiny girl was special and would be the key to Algernon's future. Nissim knew only too well that the heir, Edric, would never rule the kingdom. This immense task would fall upon little Alice, but it would not be easy for her. The child's life would be full of danger... but that could not be helped. It was her destiny.

"We have met before little Alice," Nissim whispered quietly, "long ago..." He trailed off and then continued, "I must find the one who is fated to foster these children. She is not far away."

*　　*　　*

Eve Craddock, a willowy girl of 19, with black hair like silk and eyes of shining amber, heard the rattle of a wagon coming through the forest, long before she saw it. A strange chill crept over her body and her hand clutched involuntarily at her heart. "There is a strange feeling in the air," she whispered in terror. "It is the sound of my fate."

Eve stood rigidly amongst the berry bushes, where she had been gathering fruit for her family. They were not doing very well as a result of the trouble in Devona. With the borders closed, her merchant father, found work to be scarce... and there were eight children to feed. Normally the forest would provide... but there was something wrong... something evil had changed the forest's aura. There were strange creatures that had never existed before and people from the local village of Petra often went missing. It seemed that they were fighting a losing battle.

Eve made a tight fist and said defiantly, "If there is anything I can do to save my family, I swear by all that I believe in that it shall be done."

"I am glad to hear you say that Ms Craddock," Nissim said in a kindly voice, referring to Eve with a title she had never heard before.

With a start, Eve turned around and found herself faced with the white bearded wizard, dressed in a dusty brown traveling cloak. His wooden staff lay deftly across his lap and his face was strangely calm. He had found his headmistress and was thoroughly pleased.

"W... who are you?" asked Eve in a soft, almost musical voice.

Nissim gave a curt bow and smile. "Fear not Eve, for I mean you no harm. My name is Nissim of Quinn and I am a wizard."

Eve's face remained unchanged, though her heart was about to burst from her chest. "And just what does a wizard want with me?" She fought to keep her voice steady.

Again, Nissim gave a smile that revealed nothing of his intentions. He had put Arvad behind him and was once again the master he had trained to be. "I have sought you out to make an offer of great importance."

Eve finally gave way to fear and stepped back. Wizards were virtually never seen in the Forgotten Forest and when they did appear, only trouble followed. "I wish to make no deal with a wizard. They bring evil and trouble!" Eve declared, feeling all of the hot anger from Ralston's takeover, aim itself squarely at the old man. "Leave me in peace and seek some other mortal to do your bidding!"

Nissim shook his head slowly. "I am sorry Eve, but you are the only woman in Algernon who will do. I have come far to seek you out. I require a noble, trustworthy young lady to run a girls' orphanage. There now, does that sound so bad? In return for this service, I shall ensure that your family never wants for anything... and I understand that they are doing poorly."

With a sigh, Eve dropped her hands to her sides. How could she argue with that proposition? How tempting and simple it sounded! And he had called her noble! Yet, there had to be a catch... "It cannot be so easy as that," she commented lightly, but took a few steps forward, thus closing the distance between herself and the wagon.

Nissim regarded the girl carefully. Indeed she would be perfect for the job, yet it was such a shame, for her life would be ruined in the process. Such decisions made Nissim angry, for there were no alternatives... no, there were, but they were not pleasant. This was Eve's role, whether anyone desired it or not. From the back of the wagon, one of the children stirred... the sleep spell was wearing off. It had been nearly three months, so Nissim was not surprised, but he would have to work quickly.

"Lady, I will not repeat my proposition. Simply state whether or not you will accept it," Nissim told her firmly.

Eve felt another chill creep across her body, but the prospect of helping her family seemed so inviting. She could still hear echoes of her youngest sister Violet, crying with a fever the night before.

"Things will not improve for a long time Eve," Nissim told her quietly. "They will get much worse before they get better, but you can help the process. You know of what I speak. The nightmares that have plagued you are true. Ralston's wrath and ambitions are boundless. He has taken Devona and has his sights set on Jadestone. His minions will soon reach the plains and then the forest. Charon's wall will not hold them off. I built that wall myself, but its magic is meant to ward off mortal invaders, not demons." Nissim's features looked haggard and grim. "My duty is to face this chaos head on. And I shall go to it, though it may prove to be my undoing at last. So just as I shall do my duty, will you do yours?"

Eve nodded slowly and naively went to Nissim's side. "You speak of dreams... how could you know? A wizard has such powers I suppose. I would not want to be you though... You face much peril..." Eve paused for a moment before continuing. "I'll do it then, for my family and as the duty bestowed upon me by the Power. Where is the orphanage?"

"Behind you in the clearing," Nissim replied.

"What? There is no clear..." Eve trailed off, for the berry bushes were gone and in their place was an impressive looking manor, surrounded by tall, sturdy oaks. It seemed to Eve like a fortress. It was at this point that Eve realized the strength of Nissim's magic. "How is this possible?" she asked in a breathless voice.

"You made it possible," Nissim replied not looking at her. He could not bear to see her face when the truth was revealed.

"Me?" Eve looked astounded. "But I have no magic!"

"Yes, but you have a life force," Nissim pointed out. "Your life will maintain this world and protect all who dwell within the clearing from harm."

Now Eve felt her stomach turn. "But what does it all mean? If my life force goes into maintaining this place, what will become of me?"

"You will grow old Eve... much faster than normal," Nissim told her, his voice was gentle but factual. Inside he grieved for the girl, but this had all been foreseen long ago.

For a moment Eve was silent and when at last she spoke, her voice was emotionless. "Then so be it... if this helps my family." There were tears glistening in her young eyes, but also determination. In a shaky voice she asked, "But tell me Nissim, why is all of this necessary? Surely there is a reason?"

"Indeed there is Eve and a very good one at that. Look in my wagon."

Lifting herself upon her tiptoes, Eve peered in at the four girls who lay peacefully upon delicate satin pillows. "Who are they?" she asked in wonderment.

"The Princesses of Algernon and our hope for the future," Nissim replied and scratched his beard. "As you know, the King and Queen are dead. I must return to Devona to try and prevent Ralston from doing irreparable damage... In my absence you are to raise these girls to womanhood. Teach them to be strong and self-sufficient. They will need many skills for their future mission."

"A mission?" Eve wondered, as she reached in and picked up the smallest child. Gently she brushed a lock of brown hair from the girl's round baby face.

"That one's job shall be the hardest of all," Nissim nodded to Alice, who slept in Eve's arms. "You hold our future Queen."

Eve gasped and her eyes went wide. "How do you know all this?"

"I am a wizard my dear, I have been trained for ages to recognize such things. All you need do is trust me. Now, come inside the manor, we have much to talk about."

*   *   *

When the sun had disappeared for the night and the moon hung like a sickle in the star speckled sky, a lone figure riding a horse, rode swiftly away from the circular clearing. Nissim was gone... off to Devona, to spend over a decade in battle and torment. Though he left Eve Craddock in an unfortunate predicament, he rode towards much worse suffering. Still, this was Nissim, the only remaining wizard of the ancient Three left in Algernon. He had faced the enemy before and he would do so again. In troubling times all must do their part. Arvad and Eve would perform their tasks, as Nissim would his. Then when the time was right, the next generation would step forward. Out of the darkness Nissim believed one star would outshine the rest and peace would once again reign in Algernon... at least for a time.

With a click of his tongue, he urged his horse forward and disappeared into the dense trees.

TALES FROM FADREAMA

Continue your adventure with Book 2 in the series.

Alice is the Queen of Algernon and Nissim is once again the Royal Advisor. All has been peaceful for years, but a change in the air suggests something is afoot. And what of Oliver, lost in the fairy realm of Alexandria? Has he moved on with his life and forgotten about the Flower of Verity? The journey continues in:

Where Shadows Linger

Coming soon!

About the Author

Born in Alberta, Canada, Candace Naomi Coonan has been writing for as long as she can remember. What began as a simple hobby, soon turned into a lifelong passion.

Candace began her writing career with poetry and short stories, but quickly realized that she had much longer tales to tell. Novel writing allowed Candace the freedom to create complex plots, characters and worlds. Though she still writes poetry and short stories, they more often than not relate to one of her novels.

To contact Candace, email:

Fadreama@hotmail.com

http://geocities.com/candace_coonan

ISBN 141201277-5